More Critical Praise for Joe Meno

for *Office Girl*

- Named "Best New Novel by a Chicagoan" and "Best Book for the Disillusioned Artist in All of Us" by the *Chicago Reader*
- Selected by the *Believer*'s readers as a favorite fiction work of 2012
- One of *DailyCandy*'s Best Books of 2012
- A *Kirkus* Best Fiction Book of 2012

"An off-kilter office romance doubles as an art movement in Joe Meno's novel. The novel reads as a parody of self-obsessed art-school types . . . and as a tribute to their devil-may-care spirit. Meno impressively captures post-adolescent female angst and insecurity. Fresh and funny, the images also encapsulate the mortification, confusion, and excitement that define so many 20-something existences." —*New York Times Book Review*

"Wonderful storytelling panache . . . Mr. Meno excels at capturing the way that budding love can make two people feel brave and freshly alive to their surroundings . . . The story of the relationship has a sweet simplicity." —*Wall Street Journal*

"Meno has constructed a snowflake-delicate inquiry into alienation and longing. Illustrated with drawings and photographs and shaped by tender empathy, buoyant imagination, and bittersweet wit, this wistful, provocative, off-kilter love story affirms the bonds forged by art and story." —*Booklist* (starred review)

"The talented Chicago-based Meno has composed a gorgeous little indie romance, circa 1999 . . . When things Get Weird as things do when we're young, Meno is refreshingly honest in portraying lowest lows and not just the innocent highs. A sweetheart of a novel, complete with a hazy ending." —*Kirkus Reviews* (starred review)

"Along with PBRs, flannels, and thick-framed glasses, this Millennial *Franny and Zooey* is an instant hipster staple. —*Marie Claire*

"Odile and Jack are two characters in search of authentic emotion . . . their *pas de deux* is somehow dynamic. Meno's plain style seems appropriate for these characters and their occasions, and the low-key drawings and amateur photographs that punctuate the narrative lend a home-video feel to this story of slacker bohemia, the temp jobs, odd jobs, and hand jobs." —*Chicago Tribune*

for *The Great Perhaps*

- Winner of the 2009 Great Lakes Book Award
- A *New York Times Book Review* Editors' Choice
- A Booktrust Best Book of the Year

"Meno is thinking hard about why the world is the way it is and about where hope for change might reasonably lie. For most of the last decade, a lot of prominent fiction writers interested in establishing their realist bona fides, the relevance of their work to the way we live now, seemed to feel they had no choice but to incorporate 9/11. But Meno dares to consign it, and our response to it, to a larger historical and spiritual context, and even to suggest that there is nothing new under the sun. A few years ago that might have seemed heretical, but traditionally such farsightedness is part of a novelist's job."

—*New York Times Book Review*

"Laugh-out-loud funny but frequently sad, Joe Meno's new novel runs the gamut of emotions and techniques as it depicts a Chicago family in turmoil . . . They achieve no earth-shattering insights, and neither does the author; he simply reminds us with wit and compassion that the human condition is 'both astonishing and quite ordinary.'"

—*Chicago Tribune*

"This postmodern portrait of an eccentric family delivers equal parts humor and heartbreak, raising questions about love, identity, and faith."   —*San Francisco Chronicle*

"Tender, funny, spooky, and gripping, Meno's novel encompasses a subtle yet devastating critique of war; sensitively traces the ripple effect of a dark legacy of nebulousness, guilt, and fear; and evokes both heartache and wonder."   —*Booklist* (starred review)

"The text contains more elements of magical realism than Meno's previous work, yet even the human-shaped cloud that Madeline chases for weeks somehow seems real thanks to the note-perfect dialog and narrative. Highly recommended for all public and academic libraries."

—*Library Journal* (starred review)

"Meno's writing seems to have hit a new gear . . . The overall effect is one of mature mastery of form and a deepened compassion for his characters."   —*Poets & Writers*

for *Demons in the Spring*

- Finalist for the 2009 Story Prize
- A *Kirkus Reviews* Best Book of 2008
- A *Time Out Chicago* Best Book of 2008

"An inspired collection of twenty stories, brilliant in its command of tone and narrative perspective ... Creativity and empathy mark the collection ... Illustrations enhance the already vivid storytelling."
—*Kirkus Reviews* (starred review)

"Spanning worlds, generations, cultures, and environments, each of Meno's short stories in this stellar collection explores depression, loneliness, and insanity in the world, while never quite offering a clear solution or glimmer of hope. Misery loves company, and Meno's assortment of off-center, morose characters fit seamlessly together ... Catering to all the odd men out in the world, this short story collection succeeds word to word, sentence to sentence, and cover to cover."
—*Publishers Weekly* (starred review)

"The author of *Hairstyles of the Damned* and *The Boy Detective Fails* is back with a handsome new collection, pairing twenty short stories with original artwork from illustrators like Charles Burns and Nick Butcher. Meno is at his best when he mixes raw emotional realism with tender insight."
—*Time Out New York*

for *Hairstyles of the Damned*

- A selection of the Barnes & Noble Discover Great New Writers Program

"Captures both the sweetness and sting of adolescence with unflinching honesty."
—*Entertainment Weekly*

"Joe Meno writes with the energy, honesty, and emotional impact of the best punk rock. From the opening sentence to the very last word, *Hairstyles of the Damned* held me in his grip."
—*Chicago Sun-Times*

"The most authentic young voice since J.D. Salinger's Holden Caulfield ... A darn good book."
—*Daily Southtown*

"Sensitive, well-observed, often laugh-out-loud funny ... You won't regret a moment of the journey."
—*Chicago Tribune*

"Meno gives his proverbial coming-of-age tale a punk-rock edge, as seventeen-year-old Chicagoan Brian Oswald tries to land his first girlfriend . . . Meno ably explores Brian's emotional uncertainty and his poignant youthful search for meaning . . . His gabby, heartfelt, and utterly believable take on adolescence strikes a winning chord."

—*Publishers Weekly*

"A funny, hard-rocking first-person tale of teenage angst and discovery." —*Booklist*

for *The Boy Detective Fails*

"This is postmodern fiction with a head *and* a heart, addressing such depressing issues as suicide, death, loneliness, failure, anomie, and guilt with compassion, humor, and even whimsy. Meno's best work yet; highly recommended." —*Library Journal* (starred review)

"Comedic, imaginative, empathic, atmospheric, archetypal, and surpassingly sweet, Meno's finely calibrated fantasy investigates the precincts of grief, our longing to combat chaos with reason, and the menace and magic concealed within everyday life."

—*Booklist* (starred review)

"Mood is everything here, and Meno tunes it like a master . . . a full-tilt collision of wish-fulfillment and unrequited desires that's thrilling, yet almost unbearably sad." —*Kirkus Reviews* (starred review)

"A delicate blend of whimsy and edginess. Meno packs his novel with delightful subtext." —*Entertainment Weekly*

"A radiantly creative masterpiece . . . Meno's imaginative genius spins heartache into hope within this fanciful growing-up tale that glows like no other." —*PopMatters*

"The search for truth, love, and redemption is surprising and absorbing. Swaddled in melancholy and gentle humor, it builds in power as the clues pile up." —*Publishers Weekly*

"At the bottom of this Pandora's box of mirthful absurdity, there's heartbreak and longing, eerie beauty and hope." —*Philadelphia Weekly*

"Verbally delectable." —*Chicago Tribune*

MARVEL
AND A
WONDER

MARVEL
AND A
WONDER

JOE
MENO

Published by Akashic Books
©2015 Joe Meno

Hardcover ISBN: 978-1-61775-393-0
Paperback ISBN: 978-1-61775-394-7
Library of Congress Control Number: 2015934078

Akashic Books
Twitter: @AkashicBooks
Facebook: AkashicBooks
E-mail: info@akashicbooks.com
Website: www.akashicbooks.com

To grunt and sweat under a weary life,
But that the dread of something after death,
The undiscovered country, from whose bourn
No traveller returns, puzzles the will,
And makes us rather bear those ills we have
Than fly to others that we know not of
Thus conscience does make cowards of us all.

—William Shakespeare, *Hamlet*

Over the low-lying fields, over the wide meadows, the sun—rampant, galloping westward—beating back the night. On and on across the white hills, the dun-colored hills, the hills ripening with green, rays of light striking the sun-bleached henhouse, marking faint flecks of painted wood gone a vulgar gray; the land itself shadow-quiet, blue, blurred by fog. On and on, toward its apotheosis, the sun rising higher in the sky, interrupting a faint-hued dark.

On that Sunday in July 1995, the grandfather woke early, thinking of the boy. He placed his two feet on the bare floor and stood, his limbs giving some dispute, before dressing in the near-darkness. He made his ablutions in the bathroom and then bared his teeth in the mirror. Lean-faced, tall, thinning white hair. Jim Falls, aged seventy-one.

He walked down the short hallway to find the boy was, once again, not in bed. He took in the odd odor of the boy's quarters—dirty gym socks, exotic pets, and rubber cement—but could not make out the smell of sleep. He glanced around the room in silent despair and then closed the door behind him.

He went downstairs and put on his white cattleman hat and

boots, then walked outside, half a dozen paces to the henhouse, where he found the boy, Quentin, asleep beside a pile of comic books.

The boy's Walkman was still playing, his eyeglasses folded near his face. At the boy's feet was a backpack, crammed with clothes and junk food, a map, and other odds and ends. Jim leaned over and switched the tape player off, then nudged his grandson awake with the toe of his boot. It was five thirty. The sun had been up for twelve minutes already but none of the birds had made a sound.

The boy startled, wiped a silver streak of drool from his chin, then put on the glasses. Though he was almost sixteen, he was only a fraction of that in sensibility, closer to a child in both manner and maturity. He was also a halfie, or a mulatto, or what the grandfather had sometimes been known to call a mix-breed, though that wasn't the right word either. The boy's face—rounded, olive-complected— appeared even darker in the shadows of the henhouse. Lying there, he looked like a bairn, like some strange nursling.

They found the boy's mother, Deirdre—Jim's daughter and only offspring—asleep at the wheel of her rusty foreign-model hatchback. She was passed out, with an empty vial of someone else's painkiller medication spilling out of her purse. Inside, the windshield was cov- ered with a brilliant dew. When the grandfather shook her awake, she looked up and smiled like a child, though she was thirty-seven, her eyes opaque and unnaturally lovely, these the symptoms of her ongoing dependence on pain pills and methamphetamines.

Before he could get her into the house, she vomited on their clothes. Jim nodded at his grandson for help. They carried her up the back porch, through the kitchen, and then upstairs to the bathroom, where they got her out of her soiled things. Her jeans were covered with beige-gray puke; the grandfather grabbed her under her arms while the boy pulled off her pants, her thighs as soft-looking and fleshy as they had been when she was a baby. She was not wearing underwear. Her pubis had been shaved. And above that blank space was a mottled tattoo of the Tasmanian Devil, the one from the Bugs Bunny cartoons, operating an old-fashioned push lawnmower. The sight of such a thing made Jim's privates wither. Also his daughter's flesh seemed to be covered in an extravagant amount of glitter. Why, Jim did not know. The boy tried to look away. They did not say a word to each other nor exchange a single glance, Jim and the boy, sick with compassion for a thing they could not fix nor understand. Quickly, he put a bath towel over her nakedness and together he and the boy dragged her into her bedroom. They looked down at Deirdre's doughy face and saw an unexplainable purple mark in the shape of someone's thumb forming over one of her eyelids, her face the face of absolute, unthinking selfishness and the source of both of their frustrations.

"Get yourself cleaned up and come down to breakfast," the grandfather said to her before quickly making his way from the room, the boy following at his heels.

At breakfast, the grandfather glanced from his daughter to his grandson at the kitchen table. Deirdre held her head up with one hand, poking at a plate of runny eggs. The boy ate greedily, his headphones blaring. Somewhere, once again, the grandfather felt a familiar ache. Looking from one to the other, both his daughter and grandson seemed predestined for failure. Already he had a presentiment—an unconscious belief—that the country, the world, was coming to an end. Everything in the fields outside their window seemed to be tilting, wilted over, blossoms already blown. He glanced from the window back to the table and saw Deirdre slumping over her plate.

"If you're sick, get yourself to bed," he grumbled, and then, nodding at the boy, "Let's go."

That morning the grandfather and grandson started their work by candling the chicken eggs, one by one, holding each above the milky floodlight. At the beginning of the chore there was no conversation, both of them coming awake in their still-asleep bodies, and then, tossing a yolker into the tin bucket at his feet, the grandfather said: "Go on and tell me, what kind of girls do you like?"

The question seemed to unfairly puzzle the boy. Quentin shrugged, looked away, and then sniffed his brown fingernails. He was in the middle of reenacting a moment from a video game, torturing a hen with the handle of a rake.

"I dunno," the boy said. "Any kind, I guess."

"Skinny girls?"

"No."

"Fat girls?"

"No way."

"Redheads?"

"No."

"Brunettes?"

"No sir."

"Blond girls?"

"No."

"Black girls?"

"No."

"White girls?"

"I guess."

"You like white girls?"

"I dunno. I guess so."

"Well, I'd think you'd have better luck with black girls," the grandfather said, tossing another yolker into the tin bucket.

The boy seriously considered his grandfather's words for a long time in silence, feeling that he had somehow been insulted but not knowing the exact reason why.

After an hour, the grandfather and grandson had finished candling the eggs and began counting peeps, carrying the newly hatched chicks over to the brooder, a circular pen made of corrugated cardboard, with three heat lamps hanging directly above it. The boy handed a peep to his grandfather, who studied it for a moment, and then carefully set the animal inside the pen, dipping its beak into a pan of water—getting it acquainted with the trough—and then let it run free. Already there were a few chicks piled up on top of each other in the middle of the brooder, frightened, their eyes blinking widely. With his large hand, Jim spread some of the wood shavings around, checking to be sure their food was not wet or moldy. The boy—overweight, with his soft, smooth cheeks, cheeks that had yet to know the sting of a razor, and his glasses, the round frames of which made the chubbiness of the boy's head even more exaggerated—searched out the frailest-looking peep among them and found one with an inflamed, distended stomach. He knelt down beside the unlucky creature and closely inspected it, its shape reflected in his oversize glasses.

"Sir?"

"Hmm." The grandfather turned.

"This one looks like it's got mushy chick."

Jim leaned down, poking the animal with his forefinger, and nodded. "You're right. Go on and put him in the other brooder. We don't need them other ones to get it too."

The boy nodded and carried the animal over to the small brooder, filling its trough pan with a flash of cold water. The grandfather watched the boy out of the corner of his eye, seeing his grandson making small kissy-faces at the sickly animal.

The boy was wearing a T-shirt with some black man's face emblazoned on the front. *Ice Cube*, it read beneath the man's portrait. On the back of this T-shirt, it read, *AmeriKKKa's Most Wanted*, or something equally stupid. The shirt was something the boy had picked up at the beginning of summer when he and his mother had spent a week with her new boyfriend up in Detroit. Whenever the boy happened to wear the shirt, Jim believed it made him look like a turd, an actual walking, human turd. Upon first seeing it, he decided he would pay the T-shirt no mind, as even considering the implications of such foolishness—or the cost of manufacturing an article of clothing such as that—would cause the left side of Jim's face to freeze and go dead.

The boy was now talking to the sick peep, nuzzling it against his chin.

"All right, go on and leave that one alone. We got other chores to get to yet. You can come back and visit with him when we're all done."

"If he dies, I'm never going to church again."

"What?" the grandfather asked.

"If he dies, then that's it for me and Jesus."

"Well, I guess you can worry about that later."

The boy nodded and went back to counting the other peeps. He placed his headphones back over his ears and soon the rapid thump of an angry voice howling over some sort of Africanized drum rattled from his vicinity. Kneeling there in the sawdusted coop, Jim took a hard look at the boy's face, searching for some resemblance to himself, something in the character of the boy's nose, ears, or lips— an activity that always left him with an unquestionable feeling of aggravation.

There was nothing in the boy that looked like him.

The color of his grandson's face was ashy, almost gray—as the boy was not white nor black nor whatever else anybody knew to guess. The truth of the matter was Deirdre—a sometime telemarketer and habitual liar—was not in possession of the true identity of the boy's father, though she had successfully narrowed it down to two men, or so she claimed: A black who lived in the city of Gary named Cousins, a man who was rude on the phone whenever Jim happened to answer. Or else it was a Puerto Rican whom Deirdre did not particularly like, whom she admitted to having slept with a number of times in exchange for "favors." *What kind of favors?* Jim had not allowed himself to ask.

The boy turned to ask his grandfather a question then, pushing his headphones off, his small eyebrows looking concerned, dividing his wide, round face. "Sir?"

"Hmm."

"Do you believe it's possible for a human being to talk to an animal?"

Jim smiled curtly. "We talk to the chickens all day."

"No. Not tame ones. Wild ones. Like in the movies. Like in cartoons. So they can understand you."

"I don't know if I can say I ever thought about it."

The boy nodded and then looked away. "I can do it."

"You can?"

"Yeah, I'm pretty sure I can. I can talk to animals and some trees. It's because I have developed a new way of using my ears. I can hear things most other mortals cannot."

The grandfather frowned and in that moment felt neither disappointment nor pity, only a slight grief.

"Quentin?"

"Sir?"

"Do you ever have a thought you keep to yourself?"

Quentin shrugged. "I don't know. I don't think so. Why?"

"You might want to think about trying that sometime. Keeping those sorts of things to yourself."

The boy nodded and went silent. Another few seconds passed and then the blare of the boy's headphones once again began to desecrate the air.

Deirdre did not appear at lunch. Together the grandfather and the boy ate leftovers in silence, and then, after the meal, went to separate rooms.

The boy had acquired the odd habit of sniffing glue. What he was most fond of was its unpleasant, melancholy odor. Sitting on his bed, holding his flaring nostrils over the jar of rubber cement, he would inhale deeply, the acidic fumes making his eyelids shudder; the smell reminding him of fall, of late afternoons after grade school, nearly ten years before, of paper animals snipped from brightly colored construction paper, which his mother, sitting at the kitchen table, would carefully cut out, the two of them, the boy and his mother—who nowadays went missing for weeks at a time—marching the animals past the sugar bowl, the salt shaker, his mother's half-filled ashtray, in a zigzag parade of blue elephants and yellow tigers, red zebras and green snakes, a long crocodile—with thorny-looking jaws—cut from a single black sheet. He would close the door to his bedroom and huff a jar of rubber cement every day or two. More than once he had fainted doing it—the jar falling to the floor, making a limpid puddle on the gray carpet, or worse—the boy collapsing backward onto the bed, the adhesive running all over his neck and chest. He had his video games, the exotic animals he was trying to breed— snakes, lizards, a hedgehog, kept in a dozen half-lit aquariums placed on low shelves all about the room—his infinite loneliness, and his huffing glue.

The grandfather, on the other hand, favored amateur radio and was a serious CB enthusiast. In the front parlor, there was a gray Heathkit shortwave transceiver sitting on a small wooden desk; tacked above the desk was a map of the United States, with tiny colored pins placed at odd intervals throughout the continent, marking the old man's acquaintances in places as distant as Florida and Wyoming. There was also the brand-new CB he bought every year, installed in the cab of his faded blue pickup truck. It was something he and his wife Deedee had liked to do, before she passed away three years before, the two of them driving downstate to sell a gross of eggs, killing time chatting with the truckers or lonely hearts or whoever frequented channel 17. At quiet moments during the day, after a meal or in the evening, the grandfather would sit at the tiny desk, his voice and the voices of other familiar strangers bouncing off the sun and moon and passing satellites and stars, whispering to each other into the narrow hours of night. The house was noiseless as the grandson, in the bedroom above, inhaled toxicants, staring vacantly at the abstract patterns on the ceiling, while the grandfather cleaned his radio in the room below.

Around one p.m., Deirdre appeared briefly, stealing a can of soda from the fridge. But before the grandfather could call out to her, she was gone once again to the isolation of her bedroom.

By evening, their chores had been done and their dinner eaten. In the dark, the boy wandered around outside, searching for insects to feed his reptiles. He found a pill bug and dropped it into a glass jar. He looked up and heard the sound of a cricket, then followed it into the henhouse. There, inside the brooder, the boy discovered the peep with mushy chick had died. It lay on its side in a pile of sawdust, its tiny abdomen crusted open and red. The boy called out for his grandfather, who came out, looking worried.

"What is it?" he asked, and the boy only pointed. The grandfather frowned and then cradled the creature in his palm, and after a moment made to toss it in the trash. But the boy insisted they bury it. The grandfather looked down at the animal, shook his head, and said no. The boy pleaded with his eyes until, finally, the grandfather went against his better judgment and said, "Get a shovel."

In the dark, they held an informal service, burying the animal near the roots of a birch tree the boy seemed to favor. The boy said a prayer and then covered the animal with two shovelfuls of dirt. *It was despicable*, Jim thought, looking away from the face of his grandson. It occurred to him that this, this was what was wrong with the country, the world today: it was what happened when you stopped seeing things get born, and live, and then die. It was what happened when a person, when a town, when a whole country didn't have a rudimentary understanding of how things ought to be.

After the peep's funeral, they went back into the house and sat quietly in the living room. The grandfather did not watch television. Their entertainment was the mayflies that soon appeared on the windows, crowding out the dusk. After a few minutes of that, the boy drifted upstairs to his bedroom. In a moment, Jim could hear the sound of video games, of music.

Jim frowned and then sat down at the kitchen table, put on his cheaters, and went through the bills once again. Tally after tally, sheet after sheet, they all said the same thing: they owed more than they were taking in. The factory-farm boys had muscled him out and the land was all they had left. But the utilities, the upkeep on the place, was burying them. Another year, two at the most, and they'd have to sell. And then what? Jim squinted down at the bills, trying not to imagine the future.

The phone rang at eight o'clock. He heard his daughter stumble around upstairs to answer it. Almost immediately she began to shout. He sighed and walked over to the Heathkit and switched it on, preferring the distant voices of strangers, the far-off static.

At nine p.m., the grandfather got undressed and went to bed. Remembering it was Sunday, he made a halfhearted attempt to flip through his wife's Bible but gave up after a single page. Then he laid back in the flat, wide dark and stared up at the cracks in the ceiling, imagining the shape of his wife somewhere above.

Two hours later, he awoke with a terrible urge to urinate. He did his business, patiently making water, and then passed the boy's room on the way back down the hall. The boy was once again not in his bed. The grandfather sighed, tromped down the carpeted stairs, and pulled on his muck-covered boots.

Quentin was in the chicken coop again, asleep on a plank of hay, headphones blaring, glasses folded up, open rucksack near his feet. Once more, he had only made it this far. Jim nudged the boy awake, taking a seat beside him.

"You running away?"

The boy nodded.

"Well, how come you don't get any farther?"

The boy shrugged.

"What are you running away from?"

The boy sniffed.

"Is it me?"

The boy shook his head.

"Is it your mother?"

The boy hesitated, then slowly shook his head.

"Is it the peep? The one that died?"

The boy shook his head again.

"Well then, what is it?"

After a long pause, the boy finally muttered, "Everything."

Jim let out a disgruntled snort and forced himself to clear his throat. He looked around the coop for some witness, for someone, anyone to see the boy's cupidity, his off-putting weirdness, but found there were only the chickens asleep in their roosts. He felt for the boy a familiar sadness then but did not know what to say or do.

The blue light before dawn, breaking through a sunless sky, thinning clouds, a weary moon. Blood on a willow, a barn owl devouring its prey. The world asleep. A loose beam, the creak of the back porch steps, a shattered window in a neglected corner of the house, whistling its familiar tune.

Around four a.m. the grandfather awoke to the sound of broken glass. Jim did not know if it was a Wednesday or a Thursday. He fell out of bed and crept downstairs barefoot, finding the jam jar broken on the kitchen floor. Small change had rolled everywhere. His daughter Deirdre looked up from her knees, too desperate to be ashamed. She wore some man's black bomber jacket and had the distant, unrepentant look of a criminal.

Jim switched on the light. The boy crept down the stairs behind him, wiping some sleep from his eyes. He had forgotten to put on his glasses.

"Go on back up," Jim whispered. The boy nodded and, slowly peering around his grandfather's shoulder, treaded upstairs. Jim turned back and searched his daughter's face. She seemed to sink into the floor, head falling into her hands.

His daughter's face was the town, the state, the country. With her broad forehead and big blue eyes, the feminine cheekbones and soft pink lips, it was hard not to look at her and imagine who she had been twenty, thirty years before. A girl much loved, though sometimes too much, sometimes ignored, sometimes whupped, sometimes overindulged with chocolate or sodas or candy, and then, at once, the face he was remembering was no longer the face he saw. What had been open, trustworthy, wide-eyed with all of the world's possibilities, those eyes like a newborn colt's, dark blue, the eyelashes dark and lengthy, the eyelashes being the only thing Jim felt had come from him, her hair once blond, soft and feathery as corn silk, cut in a simple schoolgirl fashion or tied up in pigtails, her skin once a bowl of pinkish cream, without mark or bruise or blemish, except a little crumb or two at the corner of her lip, the nose pert and rounded, the teeth small, delicate, always at the service of a mischievous smile, a single dimple then appearing on her left cheek, her neck long and splendid like her mother's, well, all of it had become something else. What had once been a face you looked at and saw hope in, the future in, some different world in, a face that had once been named "Best Smile" and "Best Looking" two years in a row back in high school, a face he had said made him proud of who he was, able to endure all of his failings as a father, a face that had led a Fourth of July parade, not once, not twice, but three times as a girl, and had seemed downright beatific standing among the choir each Sunday, a face which had been fawned over as lovely, as one of a kind, as special, had become masked in secrecy and disappointment and guilt.

The face kneeling before him in the near-darkness was the face of the world out there, of the plains that extended in all directions from the back steps just beyond the door, the face of the failing little town, and the failing little state, and the failing little country. It was the face of a girl who had been spoiled, spoiled by comfort, spoiled by safety, spoiled by trinkets and gewgaws and love, a face that had sat before the television and muttered, pointing with tiny white fingers again and again, "I want! I want!" half in love with whatever advertisement was on. It was the face of a girl who had once believed in God but nothing more, not school, not hard work, not work of any kind, a faith as reckless as chance itself. It was the face of a girl who as a baby cried whenever she ate mushed apples—the sweetness being too sweet—the girl demanding more, more, more, her mother unable to spoon the mashed-up fruit into her daughter's mouth quick enough. It was a face that had been told one too many times that it was pretty, only to discover that there was nothing there but the surface of the skin, the shape of the nose, the structure of the bones themselves, nothing more than the flesh, and all of it had begun to go bad, because it was made of nothing that was meant to last. All it was was flesh. There were waitresses at truck stops who were better looking, and thought much less of themselves. This face, the face of a girl who had been told she was more beautiful than she was, who at the age of twenty decided to leave home without a word, and three years later returned with the boy—already two years old—standing in her shadow, this face that brought more heartbreak than all the beauty it had possessed, this face was lurking in the dark there, eyes downturned, hiding from the glow of the shaded kitchen lamp.

Staring at his daughter, he now saw her face had gone yellow and gray. Yellow in the tone of the skin and eyelids and teeth, gray beneath the eyes and around the mouth. There were wrinkles at the corner of those eyes, the flesh like the flesh of an old chicken, pocked, bumpy, irregular. The eyes themselves had gone from blue to a bruised violet, milky, clouded over in a hazy film, the recurring expression in them of plain confusion, as if she was forever staring off into the near distance at something she did not comprehend—her past, her present, her future maybe. The forehead was perpetually furrowed, a permanent notch having formed between her eyes, the eyebrows themselves having been shaved off, their suggestion now made in sooty pencil. Her hair, once a pride to Jim, the tresses of it like something from a fairy tale, had been bleached and colored so many times that it looked like the hair of a doll that had been left in the weather, or abandoned in a musty attic, the color now being close to copper, like old wires torn from the walls of a vacant house.

"Please," she said, not looking up at him.

"Empty out your pockets," he said.

"Please."

"Go on."

She nodded and dropped a fistful of dimes and quarters to the tile.

"Now clean this up," he said, stepping past her. He went and took a seat in his armchair in the parlor, hands still shaking. When she finished, she banged open the kitchen door and disappeared. Her car made that terrible sound again—the alternator or ignition now shot—before she tore away, down the gravel road. Jim sat in the dark and worried about if and when she'd come back.

When the sun began to rise an hour later, the grandfather was still sitting in the chair. He heard the first cocks begin to crow and stood slowly. He walked over to the kitchen table, started a pot of coffee, and saw the feed store calendar with a red X marking the date. It was the boy's birthday. The grandfather stared at the X solemnly, went upstairs, got dressed, opened the boy's bedroom door and saw him snoring facedown on the pillow, then decided to let him sleep. He closed the door, trod out to the henhouse, fed the birds, and began candling the eggs. Rodrigo—a Mexican illegal who helped during the summers—was already at work. With his well-trimmed black mustache and his half-buttoned vaquero shirt, he was hunched over the pen, counting chicks.

The boy was still asleep at seven. The grandfather came indoors, buttered some toast, ate, then puttered off into the field to check on the corn. It was just past his knees now, the leaves a keen, rich green. He squatted there among the rows, poking his fingers deep into the soil, cupping some of it in his palm, taking in the pleasant corruptness of the dirt.

Next he and Rodrigo cleaned out the roosts. All the dust clouded his vision and caused him to cough. At nine a.m., he got a

little winded and came indoors to make another pot of coffee. While
it percolated, he stood at the counter and stared out the rectangular
kitchen window. The sun was poking a hole in the sky and he leaned
there, taking in its rays. Then the phone rang. The old man's heart
sank; he had every right to assume it was his daughter. He stared
at the yellow plastic device for a moment and then answered on the
third ring; it was the electric company.

"Mr. Falls, sir, I'm sorry to be the one to tell you this, but you've
got until the end of the month."

They had been telling him the same thing for the past three
months. He took a seat at the kitchen table, yellow phone cord
stretched across the room, and studied the bill before him.

"The end of the month?"

"That's right, sir, or we're going to have to switch off your
power."

"Well, I can get you some of it by then. How's five dollars?"

"Sir, your bill is for $139."

"If I had the $139, don't you think I would have sent it to you?"

There was an awkward pause. "Sir, I've just been asked to call
as a courtesy . . ."

"What about bartering? Do you ever take in trades?"

There was the awkward pause again. "Sir?"

"I can pay you in eggs," he joked.

"We take cash, check, or charge."

"No eggs?" Jim asked with a laugh. "How about hens?"

"No sir."

"Well then, we'll see what we can do. End of the month, you
say?"

"Yes sir, Mr. Falls. We here at Indiana Light and Power thank
you. Have a pleasant day."

Fifteen minutes later the telephone rang again but the grandfather decided he would not answer it. It kept ringing, making his
hands shake. Worried it might be his daughter, he broke, and then
stood to angrily grab the phone from its cradle on the wall.

"Hello?" he said.

"Hello?"

He did not recognize the voice. It was a female, someone friendly.

"Is this Mr. Falls?"

"It is."

"Mr. James Falls?"

"The same."

"Rural Route Road 20, Mount Holly, Indiana? Is that correct?"

"It is. Who'd like to know?"

"Mr. Falls, my name is Mary, I work in the office of Donadio and Sons, a law firm in Manhattan."

"Excuse me, miss, but I don't know anyone in Manhattan."

"No? Well, as I was saying—"

"Are you a collection agency? Because I just told the light and power company I'm spent. Can't squeeze blood out of a turnip. Maybe you never heard that one."

"Mr. Falls, I just wanted to call to confirm that we have the correct address."

Jim felt a flash of rage and then spoke. "I know what goes on here. I was an MP back in Korea. You work for a collection agency and you're calling to get my whatdoyoucallit? My personal information."

"Mr. Falls, like I said, I don't work for a collection agency."

"So you say. If you're going to lie to me, missy, I wish you'd have the decency to do it to my face."

"But Mr. Falls—"

"I believe we're done speaking." Jim gummed his jaws. "I believe this is where I say goodbye. I hope you have a nice day in Manhattan."

He stared out the window for a half hour after that and thought of the farm, the future. He paged through the bank book once more. There was twenty dollars and some odd cents until the end of the week when his Social Security check would arrive.

Then there was the problem of a present for the boy. It was his birthday and he ought to have a present. Jim glanced around the kitchen, hoping there might be something he could give him, but there was only Deirdre's unemptied ashtray, a stack of bills, and a catalog from Farm & Fleet. He pondered these circumstances before striding upstairs, taking a seat on the corner of the boy's bed, studying his lumpish shape. After a moment or two, Jim gave the boy a rough shake. Quentin groaned a little, pulling the blanket over his head.

"You planning on sleeping all day?" Jim asked.

"What time is it?"

"Half past ten."

The boy rubbed his face and put on his glasses, ballooning his eyes. "Why'd you let me sleep in?"

Jim did not respond. He itched the side of his nose and stared at the dust-covered drapes.

"Is my mom home?"

Jim shook his head.

The boy looked confused for a moment and then said, "Oh. She must have forgot."

"Forgot what?"

The boy looked away, an expression of painful embarrassment crossing his wide, gray face. "Today's my birthday."

Jim smiled and patted him on the shoulder. "She didn't forget."

"She didn't?"

"No. She'll be back."

"She will?"

Jim nodded, feeling every inch the liar.

They went about the rest of their chores, Jim doing his best to be patient, allowing the boy to drift from his work, ignoring him as he played and cooed with the chicks. He studied the boy's happy face, though there was nothing in it that gave him any relief.

The boy searched the house for his present, going through his mother's room, the downstairs closets, even the supply shed. In the refrigerator, he was surprised to find there was no soda, no frozen pizza, no cake.

At dinner, the grandfather piled microwave mashed potatoes onto the boy's plate. He inspected the way his grandson ate, watching the boy shovel forkfuls of potatoes into his oblong mouth. The boy noticed him watching and asked: "You're sure my mom's gonna be back?"

"She'll be back."

"She would have left me a present if she was going to be gone all day."

"She'll give it to you when she gets home."

The boy nodded slowly, unconvinced.

The grandfather saw his doubt and asked, "What kind of present were you hoping for?"

"I don't know," he said, chewing. "An Indian cobra."

"An Indian cobra?"

"I told her I wanted an Indian cobra."

"An Indian cobra? A live cobra? What are you going to do with an Indian cobra?"

"I dunno. Try to breed it."

Jim did not respond.

The boy continued to chew loudly, alternating with giant gulps of milk. "Did she leave me a cake?"

Jim shook his head. Instinctively, he piled another helping of mashed potatoes—the boy's favorite—onto Quentin's half-full plate.

"Thanks," the boy said a little sullenly.

"A cobra?" Jim asked, though it was not even a question now.

The boy nodded, looking down at his food. "It was a stupid idea."

Jim felt a surprising pang of guilt and so heaped on another helping of potatoes. He waited a moment and then said, "Come on. I want to show you something."

From a shelf in his closet, Jim retrieved a dull black metal box, placing it in the center of the linoleum kitchen table. Remembering the digits—his wife's birthday—he tumbled the numerical keys and unlocked it. The boy stared wide-eyed as Jim lifted the hinged lid. It was a pistol, a black, glossy-handled, military police corps–issued Colt .45 M1911, its harrowing sleekness dark and visible. Jim quickly fieldstripped the weapon, then reassembled it and slid ten rounds into place.

"What are we going to do?" the boy asked, but the grandfather did not answer.

Outside the two of them took turns shooting at soda pop cans in the dusk. Jim was a fair shot though the boy held the gun too loose and squinted so much it was no surprise he couldn't hit anything. They blew off three or four dozen rounds, their ears ringing, and when it got dark, they went back inside. As the grandfather slid the Colt back into its case, he looked up at the boy, who had a finger in his ear, and said, "Now you know."

"Now I know what?"

"Now you're sixteen. Now you're a man. Now you know where it's kept." He gave the boy a hardy stare but Quentin did not seem to know or understand. The boy only shrugged his shoulders and went back to fussing with his ear.

Later the boy played video games upstairs in his bedroom, his bedroom which had once been his grandmother's sewing room, and which wasn't much more than a closet. He sat on the carpeted floor in front of the rabbit-eared television playing *Doom II: Hell on Earth*. What he liked about *Doom II* was that it had both science fiction and demons, together. And the megasphere, good for 200 percent armor and health. And the Mancubus. And the Hell Knight.

On the small portable TV behind him, a tabloid-style show replayed moments from the O.J. Simpson trial. Keeping the TV on while he played made him feel like he had an audience. On screen there was a clip of the LA detective Mark Furhman faltering behind the witness stand, as an audiotape of his voice played for the court: "*People there don't want niggers in their town. People there don't want*

Mexicans in their town . . . We have no niggers where I grew up."

The boy heard the word, heard it again, and then sniffed once, pushing his glasses against his face. He had heard it so many times, the word, from his grandfather, from his mother, from the kids at school, that it no longer meant anything to him.

He finished a new level and then decided to work on his WAD. The cool thing about *Doom II* was that the designers had made their code available on a separate disc so, if you were inclined, you could try to design your own levels and characters. Instead of the space marines and the demons it could be the characters from *Batman* or *Star Wars*. So far all he had done with the program was try to make a replica of his own town, the rectangular buildings, the vacant glass windows, the central square, the statue, the birds that huddled around the benches. The biggest difference between his version and the original game was that there was no one to shoot, no demons, no Joker, no Darth Vader, as he had decided to leave the digitized town empty of higher-functioning life forms. Instead, he would walk his faceless character through the uninhabited streets, armed with all manner of extraordinary weapons, from brass knuckles to a chainsaw to a shotgun to the BFG blaster, his computerized footsteps and breath echoing in the neglected half-light. Like a deputy sheriff in a ghost town, he would patrol the streets, walking in and out of stores he had created, knowing there would be no one to trouble him. Somewhere within the dim digital town was his mother. He had built a character that looked almost exactly like her—short blond hair, narrow frame. It was his job to find her and keep her safe. But he could never find her; she was in some secret room he had forgotten how to get to. So on he searched, the pixelated gun held out before him, ready to be fired, and yet knowing there was nothing to shoot. He did not know why he did this; why he had built these replica buildings and had not created any enemies to attack, why he had hidden his own mother somewhere in the imitation town, except that marching along the computer version of those same deserted streets gave him a certain kind of loneliness he often looked forward to.

After dinner, the grandfather sat in the parlor alone and fell asleep in his armchair, the radio playing, the old man stumbling between a dream and a distant memory, unaware of which was which.

When the phone rang around ten o'clock, the grandfather woke with a start. He strode into the kitchen, pulling the phone from its cradle in a half-daze. It was Deirdre; he could tell right away from the irregular patter of her breath.

"Hello?"

"Daddy? Dad?"

He sighed without meaning to, and grasped the plastic phone hard in his hand. "Deirdre. Where are you?"

"I called to tell you I'm not coming back. I'm done with you. I'm through. I can't take it anymore."

"Deirdre." It was not a name, not even a word, just an utterance.

"I'm not coming back. You can tell him whatever you want, but I'm not coming back. I can't live in your fucked-up house with your fucked-up rules."

Jim bristled at her anger more than her language. He placed his forehead against the cool of the faded wallpaper and asked, "How much do you need?"

But she only laughed and said, "No, Daddy. This is it. These are the last words you're ever gonna hear from me."

"You told me the same thing a year ago. And the year before that."

"This time I fucking mean it. This is it."

"Deirdre."

"This is it. Goodbye, Daddy."

Then there was the sound of the line going dead.

He stood there with his forehead against the wallpaper for some time, waiting for a sound, a voice, an apology that did not, would never come. After a few moments, the phone gave off a dull, irritating buzz and Jim placed it back in its cradle.

Later he did not know why he walked straight to the field and stood there, the rows of corn spread out against his legs, brushing against his fingertips. The left corner of his lips began to twitch and then his legs gave way, and suddenly he found himself kneeling among the rows, unable to breathe. He managed to crawl a little ways and get to his feet, staggering the thirty-odd yards to the back porch steps. There he sat, holding his rigid left arm in the dark, out of breath. It was the third time something like this had happened—two months before there was another spell, then six or seven months before that. He made a little prayer then, unsure of what he was praying for or to whom. "Please," he said. "Please. Don't let me go. Don't let him find me like this." Finally his breath became regular and he was able to climb inside. He called out the boy's given name and Quentin came trotting down the stairs, alarmed; then the boy helped his grandfather to the parlor sofa. The look of worry on the boy's face, his childish expression, was frightening.

"Are you okay?" he asked. "Sir?"

Jim nodded, unsure if he could answer. They sat side by side on the sofa for some time, the mayflies jostling the windows, his heartbeat slowing down, his breath coming hard.

Twenty minutes later, the boy broke the silence. He looked over at his grandfather, who had his hands before him, folded as if in prayer, and asked, "When is she coming back?"

The grandfather put a hand on the boy's knee and slowly shook his head.

The boy nodded and sniffed, then hurried from the room.

A half hour later, when the grandfather fell into bed, it felt like death.

The white mare appeared on a Monday. Neither the grandfather nor the grandson had any idea who'd sent it. At first there was only the violent agitation of the pickup as it rattled along the unmarked road, towing behind it a fancy silver trailer, all ten wheels upsetting the air with a cloud of dust high as a steeple. The grandfather raised his hand to his eyes to try to make out the shape of the thing coming. It was a late afternoon in mid-July and the sun had just begun to falter behind the hills and tree line. The black pickup with its out-of-town plates bounced through the gate then pulled to a stop near the corner of the bleachy henhouse. Every bird on the farm, all the Silver Sussex roosters, all the Maran hens, turned to face the commotion with a prehistoric silence, waiting for the grit to begin to settle. When a man with sunglasses like a state trooper pulled himself out from behind the truck's wheel, stretching his legs from what appeared to have been a long trip, Jim asked him what it was about. The man had a clipboard and some papers which he asked Jim to sign, in triplicate, before leading him around to the back of the trailer. There he handed Jim a pink sheet of paper and pair of silver keys. The horse, sleek-looking even behind steel bars, huffed through its pink nostrils, disappearing back into the darkness.

"It's yours," the man said.

"Mine?"

"Yours."

"But . . . but what for?" Jim asked.

The man with the sunglasses shrugged, itched his nose, and said, "I just get paid to deliver it," then he put away his ink pen and began to unhook the trailer from the pickup's hitch. It seemed the trailer had also been bequeathed, though Jim still did not know from whom. The man with the sunglasses handed another pink piece of paper to Jim, stepped clear of a mud puddle, and climbed back inside the cab of the pickup.

"But there's been some kind of mistake," the grandfather said.

The man readjusted his dark sunglasses, lit a cigarette, exhaled—the smoke rising in twin, nearly invisible tendrils about his craggy face—and looked down at the clipboard and said, "This the right address?"

Jim nodded.

"You Jim Falls?"

The grandfather nodded again.

"No mistake." The man scowled and gave the ignition a start. "By the way, it's got a name. Right here," the man said, pointing to the pink page. Then the black pickup was pulling away, was driving off, then was gone. Jim walked over to the rear of the trailer. The horse was turning back and forth before him with an air of expectancy, the old man and the horse like children then, hesitant at their parents' ankles, waiting to meet. The grandfather had never been fond of horses; there had been a pair of mules his father had borrowed to plow furrows for the corn, but those days were long gone.

The hired hand, Rodrigo, had always claimed to have been raised on a horse ranch. Without so much as a word, he set down a Maran rooster, stepped up to the trailer, unlocked the bar, opened the gate, and slowly led the horse down the ramp. He whistled through his front teeth once the animal was standing there in the full sun where they could take in its shape.

"It's a racehorse, Mister Jim," Rodrigo grinned, patting its sleek flanks, then looking under, apprising its sex. "And a lady."

Jim reached out a tentative hand in the horse's direction, feeling the humid moistness of the animal's nose, placing his palm against its neck. Its ears flicked, the blue-black eye staring back, expressionless. In its stoicism, in its stony quiet, the grandfather saw what he most often loved about the land, the country, the world. It was enough to say he had not nor would never have dreamt of standing this close to a horse on this day or any other, and the unexpectedness, the absolute un-reason of the animal's arrival, is what gave the grandfather a sense of joy.

"What you going to call her, Mister Jim?" came Rodrigo's voice.

The grandfather studied the animal's shape, tried to take in its perfect, imperturbable appearance, and then, looking down at the pink paper, he said, "It says here her name's John the Baptist."

"John? For a lady?"

"Yes, John. For a lady. That's what it says."

"From the Bible?"

"I guess so."

Rodrigo shrugged, and then searched inside the trailer and found an expensive eastern saddle and bridle. He whistled once again through his front teeth and then set to tack up, the horse remaining completely still as the blanket, then saddle was fit into place, then the bridle. It huffed once, not even a snort, and became silent again.

"You ride her, Mister Jim?"

Jim stared at the ghostly creature, at its formidable stature, and shook his head with a frown. "Not in this life, buster."

Rodrigo shrugged his shoulders again, holding the leather reins in his hand, asking a serious question by raising his eyebrows slightly.

By then the boy—having heard the unfamiliar pickup rambling back down the gravel drive—walked out of the house and stared at the animal suspiciously. He stood a dozen feet away, pushing his glasses up against his face, trying to decide if this interruption was going to be worth his time. "Whose horse is that?" he asked.

"Fella said it's ours."

"Ours?"

"Mine, I guess."

"But what for?"

"He didn't say."

The horse gave a soft whinny, which would have gone unheard if it wasn't for the open air of the farm and the nearby highway—quiet at this time of day.

Rodrigo pulled lightly on the reins, turned to face Jim once again, a daring smile crossing the farmhand's face, the question having already been answered, in his mind at least, awaiting a sign, which Jim gave without begrudgement, nodding in a curt manner.

"Okay," Rodrigo said, slipping his left boot into the silver stirrup, then pulling himself up and fitting in his right. The horse took no notice of the stranger upon its back, its nostrils flaring slightly, its tail alighting back and forth, until the lean-faced man gave a short, gentle kick and the horse, as if having heard some celestial trumpet, was off, bucking and rearing in a flash of dust and dirt, clearing the low wire chicken fence, wreaking havoc in the dry-looking field of corn. Before the man on its back could whisper, "Whoa, whoa, whoa," the animal seemed to have made one full pass of the entire property, galloping breakneck alongside the culvert, its hide speckled with sunlight.

"Good God," was all the grandfather could get out.

It was clear from the first that the horse had been bred as a racer; standing fifteen hands high, it was lean-muscled with long legs, the hindquarters a rig of fibrous muscle. Four years old, it looked as spry as a filly.

By the time Rodrigo had slowed the animal down to a canter, then a trot, then was heeling the horse before them, the farmhand's face had lost none of its expression. There was a wide smile frozen below his black mustache, creeping from one ear to the other, his dark eyes runny with tears.

The boy hung behind the fence apprehensively, excited by the creature's presence, but too frightened to get closer.

Jim, on the other hand, felt a weakness well up in him. He carefully strode over to the animal, slowly raising his hand to the side of its broad neck, and then he began to pat it, in ever-widening circles, the horse breathing huskily, its blue-black eye momentarily lidded by the longest eyelashes Jim had ever seen on an animal. It felt like the horse was the answer to something. He had an ache just then, not in his joints nor his stomach nor his liver, and remembered the place where he had been struck one afternoon when catching sight of the back of his wife Deedee's knees as she stood on a chair and reached to retrieve a box from the top shelf of the school supply closet where she was teaching. He put his hand over his chest now, wondering if this is what it was like to get hit by lightning.

"Do we get to keep it?" the boy asked.

"I don't know," Jim said.

The horse turned before them and snorted. Jim gave an easy smile.

"But where's it gonna live?"

"We'll see."

The boy held out a hand and patted the horse's flank.

Later it was decided they would drive to the nearby hamlet of Mount Holly the following morning and make an appointment to see Jim Northfield, the former lawyer and judge.

Approaching the silver trailer the next day, both the grandfather and the boy tried to catch a glimpse of the animal asleep inside. But it was already awake, poking its great pink nostrils through the metal slats. The boy held out his hand and felt its breath—humid, so much like a human's. It was a marvel. The grandfather watched the boy and pondered what they had done to deserve such a thing.

Once they had finished their morning chores, they led the horse out of the trailer and mucked the urine-soaked dirt and straw, making sure the trough was filled with cold, clean water. The grandfather held the animal by its fancy silver bridle while the boy raked out the rounded lumps of manure with the flat edge of a shovel, piling them into a wheelbarrow. Then they dumped the remaining bag of feed in a bucket and placed it near its feet. As the horse ate, the boy gently touched its neck, trying to read its thoughts. "Hello, hello, hello," the boy whispered. "I am your friend."

The boy and his grandfather made their way to town. From behind the dashboard of the blue pickup, the nearby fields looked fearsome, zigzagging with bayonets of rippling corn. The boy had his head-

phones on, and was nodding along to the persistent rhyming annoy-
ance of rap music; Quentin listened to his Walkman even when riding in the truck, because, as he had said a number of times before, he
did not care for his grandfather's "shitkicker" music. The music Jim
preferred was old country—Jimmie Rodgers being his favorite—a
habit he had picked up in Korea, listening to the Armed Forces Radio while he was stationed as an MP, the deejay then being like the
voice of God, playing songs that put into words the faraway feelings
of his young, wrong heart, though now there was no radio station
within fifty or sixty miles that broadcast anything like that. Everything on the radio around here was oldies or new country or Christian secular music, none of which Jim could stand.

Interstate 65. Interstate 69. Interstate 64. Interstate 70. Interstate
74. Interstate 80. Interstate 90. Interstate 94. Route 6. Route 20.
Route 24. Route 27. Route 30. Route 31. Route 33. Route 35. Route
36. Route 40. Route 41. Route 50. Route 52. Route 136. Route 150.
Route 224. Route 231. Route 421. Hope. Laurel. La Fontaine. Mar-
kle. Churubusco. Kokomo. Hamlet. Peru. Macy. North Liberty.
Santa Claus. English. Tell City. Bellwood. Russiaville. Mulberry.
Zionsville. Brownsburg. New Whiteland.

   Or the sign saying, *Mount Holly*, the pale-blue pickup driving
on through the afternoon into the full brightness of day.

Over the past two decades, Mount Holly had become a ghost town.
The town square was surrounded by a failing copper fence that had
begun to go blue and was guarded by an iron statue of a soldier from
the Forty-Fifth Regiment of Indiana Volunteers, a cavalry unit com-
prised of locals who proved their valor during the Civil War at the
grisly Battle of Antietam. The memorial to the town's fallen soldiers
was a bleak depiction of a lone volunteer heeding the call to arms, his
steel rifle slung in a weak position over one shoulder, his untrimmed
mustache and beard a favorite nesting spot for the town's wrens. In
this ignominy—the birds roosting beneath his neck—it appeared as

if the soldier had truly accepted his ruin. The square was usually vacant except for the gray and purple birds, a small flock of them crowding the only bench, the birdsong of this particular species the exact melody a grieving Civil War vet might find himself singing. The stores on the square observed a similar air of mourning, their windows dim, shaded with unwashed blinds, the shops empty of life; there was a café where three customers had been murdered nearly a decade before—the speckles of blood and chalk-lines encircling the bodies becoming irreducible, forever marking the meager restaurant with the lurid drama of a dime-store pulp novel; a failing hardware outfit whose owner had become a born-again Christian—the store's tools, supplies, and other merchandise now replaced with handmade crucifixes, all whittled childlike; an unmarked department store whose sign out front—announcing the name of a local chain—had been taken down and never replaced; a shop that only sold greeting cards, some coated with thick dust; a corner saloon whose windows had been painted over in blackish film—the blurred phantom shapes of loners and old-timers drinking away their troubles adding to the town's sense of vague gloominess; and, last of all, a farm supply and feed store whose street-facing wall leaned precariously west, tilting farther and farther out of shape each year, the store no longer a rectangle but a kind of trapezoid. All of these stores' facades looked ghostly, a picture-postcard town that had seen better days fifty years before, the glassy windows desolate, unmarred save for the reflection of the pale-blue pickup truck that was pulling into a parking spot alongside the boarded-up café.

Jim Northfield was a gray-haired gentleman with bushy eyebrows who no longer practiced law but who was kind enough to look over the receipts and bill declaring the transfer of property. They sat before the judge in his tiny second-floor office, the air of which smelled like a public library, wooden bookshelves filled with ancient half-opened law volumes.

"Well, what have you got yourself into?" Jim Northfield asked, glancing down at the documents. "I didn't know you owned any horses."

"I don't," the grandfather said, rocking on his heels. "Which is why we've come to see you."

"Hmmm," the old judge proclaimed, "don't pin your hopes on me. I lost the last three cases I had. It's the reason I became a judge." He eyed the wide-faced boy and then nodded at the glass jar of moth-eaten lollipops on the corner of his desk. "Help yourself."

The boy made a motion forward but caught his grandfather's eye. He lowered his hand to his side and said, "I'm not supposed to eat sweets."

Jim Northfield looked over his glasses. "Never mind him," he said, nodding toward the grandfather. "Here, go on, now," and the boy smiled, an awkward smile, reaching forward. Jim Northfield opened the jar and the boy took out a yellow one. Then he slipped the boy a tattered-looking business card. "If you ever need a good lawyer . . ."

The grandfather rolled his eyes. The boy carefully took the old business card as Jim Northfield apologized. "Old habits. Now tell me: how did this horse show up?"

The grandfather sighed and beat his cattleman hat against his leg. "We were counting chicks yesterday when this truck pulled in, towing a trailer. The man asked me my name and address and then handed me the keys. Then he gave me that," he said, pointing to the pink carbon-copy sheet.

"Hmmm," Jim Northfield said. The grandfather tapped his fingers against his knee, growing impatient. "It's all here: horse, trailer, saddle, bridle. There's your name and your address. And that's all correct?"

The grandfather nodded.

"Hmmmmmmm."

The grandfather cleared his throat as Jim Northfield pawed through a few law books on his desk, and then reread the transfer of property. Smiling, he leaned back in the warped brown leather chair. "As far as I'm concerned, that animal is yours."

"Ours?"

"That is, unless someone brings forward a suit."

"A suit?"

"Claiming it's theirs. But you got the transfer of property and, better than that, the horse itself. You know the old saying, possession's nine-tenths of the law."

"So," the grandfather asked, "that's it?"

"For now. Let me get the phone number of the delivery company. See if I can give these folks a call and get some information on where it came from."

"I'd appreciate it."

Jim Northfield copied down the address and phone number of the delivery company back east, then reclined in his chair again. "Confidentially—if it was me, I hope I'd have the good sense to keep my mouth shut, count my blessings, and try not to court trouble."

"That's exactly what we aim to do," the grandfather said.

The two old men shook hands and then, reaching for the glass jar, squinting at the grandfather with a taunting smile, the judge offered the boy another lollipop.

Outside, they shuffled along the near-deserted street. At the corner they ran into Lucy Hale, Burt Hale's widow. She was parked in front of the feed store and was struggling to get a bale of hay into the back of her rundown station wagon. The grandfather quickly ran up and grabbed one end of the bale, and helped shove it inside. She turned to him and smiled, pushing back a loose strand of dark-blond hair that had fallen across her eyes. He had not seen her nor talked to her since they had buried Burt, more than two years before.

"Hello there, Jim."

"Lucy."

Lucy Hale was a bona fide beauty; soft, dark-blond curls of hair, a narrow neck, a wide chest and waist covered by a white blouse, her thighs looking plump in a tight-fitting pair of jeans, the sunlight doing wonders for her dark eyes, the eyes themselves strengthened by her laugh lines, face like a television star—broad, irrepressible, fifteen years his junior.

"Thanks for the help."

"Don't mention it. What happened to Burt's pickup?"

"I never learned how to drive stick."

"Deedee was the same way. How are you?"

"I've been better. I lost two farmhands this month. Seem to think I'm ready to fold."

Jim frowned and asked, "Are you?"

"I'm doing what I can. I don't want to let Burt down."

Jim smiled, leaning against the rear of the station wagon. "There's nothing you could do to let him down. You've kept it going for two years, with all that land. That's more than most people'd be able to do."

"I can hear the whispers whenever I go into the grocery store. They're all waiting for me to sell."

"Never mind those people. You ever need a hand, you give me a call. Burt had plenty of friends. Plenty of people would be glad to help you out."

"I couldn't put you out like that. Burt would never forgive me."

Jim nodded, touching his right ear. She was right. "Well, like I said, if you ever need anything, you just give me a ring."

"I will. Thanks, Jim."

"And don't be a stranger."

"I won't. Goodbye."

He watched her climb inside the car, realizing then that he had forgotten to return her goodbye, standing there on the curb, imagining the other words, the other ways the conversation might have ended.

On the way back home, driving past the furrowed rows of corn, the boy looked at him and grinned.

"What?" Jim asked, but the boy only kept on smirking. "What? What is it?"

"I saw you talking to that lady. Hubba-hubba."

"Very funny," Jim said, and then switched on the radio.

Dusk came in as they approached the house. They helped Rodrigo with the rest of their work: cleaning the roosts, watering the corn, giving a sickly Maran hen a dose of antibiotics. Her chicks ran scurrying from their mud-caked boots, the boy chasing them with a rake.

Later they led the horse from the trailer to watch it run. Rodrigo saddled up the horse and climbed atop with a soft grin. Together the animal and farmhand tore across the empty field toward the end of the property. The sun was just beginning to set. The grandfather stared at the animal's gray muzzle and gray eyelids and gray ears, the pale gray mane, everything else sleek and muscled and altogether colorless. When it moved, it seemed to be absent of any color at all, only a flash, like a zipper of lightning, a pulse of absolute blindness. *Whoom, whoom, whoom.* It was sort of like watching your own death, but beautiful too, something so mysterious and fulsome, something beyond any world he had imagined, that he dared not stare for long, fearing the questions he still had about life would make their answers apparent all too soon.

The grandfather had never owned a horse or had even thought to own one, as his father, like him, had only ever raised chickens and a few acres of corn, the farm passing from the father to the eldest son, and from his grandfather before that. There had been a team of scraggly-looking mules his father rented twice a year before he bought the old red Ford tractor, and even then, those mules, with their long rabbit ears and lean legs, seemed skittish, unpredictable, spastic in their quick movements. Jim, as a boy, would stand on the lowest rail of the fence and watch his father try to drive them, his father unknowledgeable in the language of equines, shouting *Haw-haw-gee-haw* over and over again, the team making irregular gullies in the westernmost corner of their narrow spread of land. He would see in their twin shapes the frustration of his father's labor, another reason for the old man to be curt at the dinner table.

His father eventually saved enough for the Ford tractor, picking up night shifts at the creamery. Just after it arrived, Jim was drafted into the war in Korea, at the ripe old age of twenty-four. It was 1948. For the next three years, Jim was in the employ of the United States Military Police Corps. He did well as an MP because he had a quiet interest in the simple order of things and also a good sense of humor, generally. His work, as judged by his commanding officers, was thought to be exemplary, providing security and working the vice squad around the army base at Pusan. After three years of service in the Military Police Corps, he rose to the rank of lieutenant.

Then it was May 1951, the month of his undoing.

As it turned out, the same year Jim had been drafted, Truman had signed Executive Order 9981, meant to integrate the military and outlaw racial mistreatment, going so far as to make racist remarks illegal. Although there were still several all-black units, like the Twenty-Fourth Infantry Regiment, it wasn't until the jailing of a black lieutenant by the name of Leon Gilbert—and his eventual trial—that the law began to be enforced. After Lieutenant Gilbert refused an order from a white officer—claiming it would lead to the unnecessary deaths of many soldiers in his unit—he was found guilty in a military court and sentenced to be hung by the neck. Protests broke out until Lieutenant Gilbert's sentence was eventually commuted. By 1951, the slow wheel of progress had begun its rusty motion forward, the American military finding itself forced to abjure its unfair history, though Jim Falls found this all out a few months too late.

Jim had been on duty, patrolling the back rooms of a well-known Pusan whorehouse, when he had come upon a black boy harassing a Korean prostitute. It was well known that the baby-faced girls of Chuncheon were the property of the white servicemen only. The josans had a name for the black soldiers who they were not allowed to fraternize with: "crumbs" or "number-ten GIs," which meant the worst, the lousiest, of those they beheld.

Jim immediately intervened, giving the colored soldier the explicit choice of removing his hand from the prostitute's leg or forever losing the use of it. The young serviceman—a rail-thin radioman fresh from the slums of Pittsburgh, who believed he was a soldier enlisted in the United States Army with all the rights and privileges therein—made a mistake by ignoring the threat. Jim set down his helmet, handed his sidearm to his junior partner, and commenced to beat the hell out of the younger man. Of course, by then Jim had tussled with a number of colored soldiers, but this fellow was the only black he fought who didn't bother to fight back. The more Jim whupped him, the more pleased the kid looked; maybe it was some new kind of colored psychology, Jim wasn't sure. He did not think the black boy would have been hurt so bad if he had only raised his hands once or twice, but he had not. The contented look on the radioman's face bothered him, but other than that Jim did not remember feeling very bad about the incident, only a queer sort of dissatisfaction. In the end, the radioman lost the use of his right eye and his commanding officer, a white bleeding heart from Los Angeles, made a formal complaint.

In the makeshift courtroom, Jim sat confidently, his hands folded before him not in prayer but surety. He watched as the acting judge, an Irish fellow with a jutting lower jaw, returned from his chambers with a hangdog look and the unfathomable guilty verdict. The sentence was more harsh than anything Jim had dared to imagine: a dishonorable discharge and a reduction in rank back down to private. It seemed that the military brass could not condone Jim Falls's personal views regarding racial miscegenation and the prostitutes who populated the sweating back rooms around Pusan. Jim stood there in the courtroom, completely befuddled, his head spinning, as the world turned away from him and the lengthy sentence was read out loud.

Arriving back in Mount Holly in August 1952, he stepped down from the Indianapolis-bound bus and breathed the dry air—familiar with its stink of henhouses, motor oil, and the fetid dust of ground-up corn. He was disheartened but not surprised to find no one waiting for him. There were no colored balloons nor a ticker-tape parade.

He lit a cigarette which had been given to him from a fellow inmate while in stir—a young grunt from Oklahoma who had been caught filching from his bunkmates and had a welt the color and size of a plum across his cheek—and thumbed a ride back to his parents' farm, leaving all sense of duty, honor, and importance behind. He was twenty-eight then. He had seen the world and the world—with its clap, its smeared-on makeup, its drooping black stockings, its desperate foreign mouth—hadn't been much. He placed his rucksack in the high rafters of the shambling barn, searched out his denim overalls and mud-caked boots, and found his father wrestling with a bawdy Silver Sussex who refused to leave her nest. The two of them commenced to count her eggs, barely speaking a word. Fifty years elapsed like that, or very nearly fifty, before Jim looked up and realized he was already much older than his own father had been the day the old man had turned to face the afternoon sunlight streaming in from the slats of the newly erected chicken coop and had fallen over dead.

Remembering himself, the grandfather glanced up at the horse now, seeing its eyes blink thoughtfully. Watching the gray eyelids shudder open and then closed, the eyelashes looking like they belonged on a doll, it was hard not to think of the things you ought to have done, the things you had been too afraid to do, or the things you'd done and wished you hadn't. It was sort of a second chance, this animal. He petted the horse's neck and tried to dream up a better life for himself, for the boy, for the both of them.

Days later, a week on, they still hadn't heard anything from back east. It looked like, for now, the horse was theirs without contention. In its own way, this was as strange a dilemma as the grandfather had faced. At night, he would lie beneath his untucked sheets, unable to sleep, trying to figure out the how, the why—quietly contemplating this odd occurrence of luck.

One morning toward the end of July, he and Rodrigo put together a tiny ramshackle stable—a lean-to made of tin and two-by-fours—and bolted it onto the side of the sheet-metal chicken coop. They led the horse inside, filled a large trough with clean water, and stood back, watching the animal take in its quarters. It gave a weak snort and then began to munch at the stand of hay, quickly ignoring them.

On their next trip into town, the boy stopped off at the public library, which had all but closed. He checked out their only book on horses, *An Encyclopedia of American Equines.*

At the kitchen table, the grandfather and grandson flipped through the encyclopedia's pages until they found the right breed—an American quarter horse. Technically, American quarter horses were not white—they were perlino, cremello, or a startlingly light shade of gray—but in both of their hearts the matter had already been decided.

In his most private thoughts, the boy dreamt of fitting the silver-stitched eastern saddle onto the horse, then the custom-made bridle, then putting his feet in the black and silver stirrups and climbing on top, and then flashing swiftly over the mud-specked earth, the animal and the boy moving so fast as to transform themselves into a steady white blur, a spark, a haze of constant colorlessness, a single thing without color.

But he was afraid, believing the animal was smarter than him. In the solitude of his imagination, he had a notion which he had not dared to share with anyone—his grandfather included—that the horse, in all its splendor, was actually the Holy Ghost; that it was God made in the flesh and spirit; that while running there, its eyes showing silver, it knew everything the boy did, it knew his own mind, it could bear witness to his most private thoughts and sins. The boy told no one of these strange intimations, only stood there against the wooden fence rails, silent, like a penitent before a cross.

One afternoon at the beginning of August, they were cleaning out the horse's stall when Rodrigo asked, "You ride her?"

The boy looked up from the shovelful of manure and shook his head. The farmhand repeated the phrase and patted the boy on the back. "You ride her. Come on."

"But I don't want to," Quentin mumbled. "I'm scared. Besides, she doesn't like me."

The grandfather shot him an impatient look and the boy sunk a little. "She's an animal. She'll like you if you tell her to like you."

"But sir . . ."

"Just give it a try," the old man said.

The boy frowned and nodded in defeat. Rodrigo slipped on the saddle and then the halter and led the horse to the makeshift paddock. He crouched over and helped the boy climb up, Quentin's gym shoes squeaking with dew against the metal rings.

"I don't like this," the boy said, trying to get his balance. "This is a bad idea."

"Give a little kick," Rodrigo said.

"I don't want to kick it."

"Just a little one."

The boy sighed and gave a small kick. The horse did not move, only knelt over, nosing at the grass.

"A little harder," Rodrigo said.

The boy obliged and this time the mare took off, jerking the reins from the farmhand's fist, trotting a sharp path along the fence line. The boy's stomach leapt from his mouth as he tried to cry for help.

"Whoa!" Rodrigo called, but the horse kept bolting forward, the boy letting out a high-pitched sound, his glasses flying from his face. "Whoa!" Rodrigo repeated. "Whoa!" until he could catch up and grab hold of the reins.

Rodrigo and the grandfather were laughing, the boy tumbling out of the saddle, cursing, finding his glasses in a bowl of mud. He wiped them off against his pants and cursed again. "Very funny, very funny, laugh it up," he muttered, and then at the horse, "We're not friends anymore. We're not friends."

"Go on," the grandfather said. "Give it another try."

"No way. She tried to kill me."

Jim watched the boy storm into the house, the kitchen screen door slamming behind him. He turned and glimpsed Rodrigo combing the mare's hindquarters, then slowly headed inside.

The boy was at the kitchen table eating cereal. He did not look up. Jim poured himself a cup of coffee, staring out the rectangular window, his back to the boy.

"When I was just about your age," he began, "or maybe just a few years older, they made me an MP and sent me over to Korea. I was stationed in a place called Chuncheon. In the north. Right by the thirty-eighth parallel. The other side of that line was all the bad guys. They sent all the roughneck American soldiers up there, the ones they didn't mind seeing shot or blown up. I was in the vice squad. That's what it was called. We were supposed to keep the other soldiers, the enlisted men, out of trouble. They'd get themselves drunk and get in a fight or go and get VD from some Korean prostitute, or else they'd steal something and then try to sell it, and it was our job to make sure none of that happened.

"The place I was stationed in, they had all kinds of superstitions. The people up there said there were demons that lived in the jungle. And sometimes you'd believe them. There were all kinds of weird lights, like tracer bullets. Strange things were always happening up there. One time, my partner Stan and me were driving in the jeep, and I had to take a leak, so we pulled over and I went off in the brush a little way, trying not to step on a mine, and there was this tree full of dead mice. They had been hung there with string, hundreds of them. Like a kind of sacrifice, I guess. I guess some of them were rats. Well, I seen them and I ran off. It was spooky. These Koreans, they had hung them up there to keep the demons of the woods happy. I was convinced it really was haunted.

"Another time, Stan and me were driving somewhere else. He outranked me, so he always drove. He said I drove like a civilian. We were driving and this Korean fella jumps out of the woods, right in front of the jeep, like he was going to kill himself. Stan swerved out of the way, and the vehicle goes off the road, into a ditch. I swear I nearly broke my neck. Stan gets out, he runs over and grabs the guy and starts shouting at him in Korean, and I ask him what it's all about. And then he tells me that the guy said he had a demon. And the only way to get rid of a demon was to scare him out. So the guy jumped in front of the jeep trying to scare off the demon but he almost got all three of us killed. Stan said later that it wasn't the first time something like that happened.

"So this one night, a soldier goes AWOL, some nineteen-year-old kid, and we searched all the regular hangouts, the dives, and we're about out of ideas when a local came up to the jeep waving his arms, saying there was a ghost in his chimney. Stan and I looked at each other and followed the old man to his house. Their houses weren't really houses, just shacks, I guess, and the old man was pointing and Stan glanced at me like I should be the one to take a peek, because I had the lower rank, and so I took out my sidearm and tried to squeeze my way through. The whole thing was about as wide as a bread box, and I poked my head inside but there was nothing but black."

"What did you see?" the boy asked.

"I didn't see anything. But I heard something, this low kind of moan, and I thought it was a demon who was going to pull me up the chimney, and I got my flashlight out and tried to see what was ahead of me as I was climbing up, but there was no room to maneuver, so I put the flashlight in my mouth and started climbing, and the chimney was all at odd angles, and I could hear the moan again, and I looked up and saw this face, but it wasn't a face, just this pale white shape peering back at me, and I screamed and the face screamed back and I tried to get my arm up to shoot, but I couldn't, so I screamed again and then I glimpsed a face, the face of some nineteen-year-old boy, the kid we had been looking for who had gone AWOL. For some reason, he thought to hide in a chimney and he got stuck and broke his leg trying to escape. Eventually we got him out, and he did his time before getting shipped back to the front line. But the thing of it was, I was scared. I thought for sure I was going to die up in that chimney."

The boy sniffled again and set down his spoon. "So?"

"So I'm telling you this because it's okay to be scared. Scared means you're smart. Scared keeps you alive. There ain't nothing you can do to avoid being scared. But being scared all the time isn't any way to live."

The boy stared into his empty bowl.

"Finish up and meet me in the coop. We got eggs to candle yet."

The boy nodded, contemplating the murky reflection in his spoon.

Later, sometime after lunch, the grandfather was cleaning the dishes in the sink when he glanced up across the field and saw Quentin feeding the horse, one hand holding the bucket of oats, the other on the animal's neck, the boy singing or talking. Jim smiled, holding the boy's dirty plate in his hands.

On the first Friday of August, Jim Northfield came for a visit. He pulled his dilapidated gray Chevy into a corner of the drive and climbed out, stepping around the mud in his Sears catalog boots, which looked like they had never been worn.

The grandfather peered up from the rusty irrigation hose and grinned. "To what do we owe the honor?" he called out, putting down the wrench before standing.

Jim Northfield smiled and made his way over. "I've got some news."

"You could have phoned. You didn't need to come all the way out here."

"I don't mind driving for good news."

"Hate to see you get your fancy boots dirty."

Jim Northfield's smile grew. "You like these?"

"Those boots look like they cost more than I make in six months."

"Well, you should have paid better attention in school."

"Ha. There wasn't any school when I was a kid," the grandfather joked.

"I know, I know. But you still walked uphill both ways."

The grandfather chuckled. "What brings you out?"

"I came to see your horse. I like to meet all my clients face to face."

The grandfather tipped his hat.

Rodrigo led it out to the squared-off pasture, holding the fancy reins in his hand. The sun fell on its coat, making it look like the mare was built of silver, like the ornament on some king's tomb. Then it began to run, its pink nostrils tightening then going wide, long legs crossing the muddy field quickly.

"What do you say?" the grandfather asked.

"She's a beaut. You time her yet?"

"Time her? What do I know about racehorses?"

"You don't have to be an expert to see that animal likes to run."

The grandfather nodded, conceding the point. "So what's this good news you brought?"

"I got ahold of someone at the delivery company; said they weren't allowed to give out the name of the folks who hired them."

"Hmm."

"Then just last weekend I was over in South Bend; met a few of the boys I went to law school with. One of them is a federal judge now. I told him about your predicament. He asked me if you had the transfer of property. I said yes. He told me he thought you were in the clear. He said if it was his client, he'd tell 'em to keep his mouth shut. Things like this happen all the time."

"But it ain't ours."

"Listen, I can keep trying to get ahold of those folks on the East Coast for you, but the thing is, that horse was sent to you, for whatever reason."

"There wasn't any reason."

"Who are we to say?"

"It was sent to us by mistake."

"Don't you read your Bible? A miracle is a miracle. You don't question that sort of thing."

The grandfather frowned and thought on that, staring across the field.

Before turning in that evening, the grandfather knocked on the boy's bedroom door to say goodnight.

The boy looked up from his video game, nodded, and, just as the grandfather was walking away, asked, "Sir?"

"Hm."

"Where do you think it came from?"

"Hm?"

"The horse. Where do you think it came from?"

The grandfather smiled. "I don't know."

The boy said goodnight, then went back to his game.

One week after that, on a Thursday around four p.m., there was a long-distance call from New York, from the office of a female lawyer asking to speak with Jim Falls. The grandfather stood in the kitchen and held the phone to his ear, then took a seat at the table, trying to steady himself.

"This is him," the grandfather said. "I've been wondering when you were going to call."

The voice on the line introduced herself as Lila Winn, saying she represented the office of the executor of the will that had awarded Jim the horse. Apparently, several parties were now challenging the executor's interpretation, which, in their opinion, had "injudiciously" reallocated a number of the deceased's holdings. The ownership of the horse as well as several other assets were being called into question.

"Is the animal still in your possession?" the distant female voice asked. "Or has it been sold?"

"No, we've been taking care of it. I told my friend this was all some sort of mistake. I'm happy you all figured it out, but we'll be mighty upset to see the horse go."

"Well, as of right now, Mr. Falls, the horse technically belongs to you. Or at least until these other countersuits are settled. Which may not be for some time."

"No? Well, how long?"

"I've known cases like this to go on for years."

"Years," Jim repeated. Then again, quieter, "Years." He held the yellow plastic receiver in the crook of his neck. "So you're telling me it's mine?"

"For now. Or at least until this other business is adjudicated. Is this the best number to reach you at?"

"Yes ma'am." And then he asked, "Do you mind saying that all again? About the horse."

"It's yours, for now," she said softly.

"For now," he repeated. "Do you think you can do me one more favor, miss?"

"If I can."

"Do you think you can tell me where it came from? Who sent it, I mean."

"I'm not able to give out that information at this time."

"No?" Jim frowned. "We'd just like to know, that's all."

"I understand. I'm just not authorized to give out that information at the moment."

"I see. Well, this certainly is interesting. I . . . I thank you for the call."

"We'll be in touch, Mr. Falls. Have a good evening."

Jim said goodbye and set the phone back on the wall, holding his hand against the cool plastic device, waiting for it to begin to ring again, to tell him it was all a joke. But it did not. He thought maybe the conversation had taken place inside some childhood dream—the fields gone purple, a girl with an apple for a face, a tea kettle that could speak. He stood there in the kitchen with his hand on the phone for a long while.

In the dark later that same night, the grandfather crept out alone to the stable and put a hand on the mare's neck. *What if?* he began to think, looking into its blue-black eyes, measuring the gentle slope of its shoulder, feeling its breath on the palm of his other hand. *What if? What if it really is ours? What if we were to race it? What if this might be the thing, the one thing that saved us?*

But soon August was more than halfway over; summer was already coming to an end. The grandfather felt an ambivalence about this, as he did with most things; though the heat would be gone and with it the reek of the henhouse—the odor altogether unignorable, unpleasant, the chalky smell of dry feed, sawdust, and molted feathers forever hanging about their clothes, their hair, their fingernails—soon Rodrigo would be heading back to Mexico and the boy to school, which meant that the grandfather would have to once again work the farm on his own. On the other hand, there was the mare and a host of other prospects, a life that had, before the horse's appearance, seemed impossible.

On a Saturday morning in the middle of August, just around ten a.m., a big shot named Bill Evens came around to appraise the animal. Bill Evens was an operator, a former state congressman, and construction contractor who owned nine or ten racehorses, which he kept on an immense spread of land about forty minutes south of town.

He drove up to the farmhouse in a brand-new Ford pickup without an introduction or invitation, his wide, bald head covered with a dented straw cowboy hat, dark prescription glasses obscuring his face. He walked right over to the small pasture they had set up and leaned against the snake-rail fence, then let out a piercing whistle.

"Look at them hinds," he said, squatting down, grinning through the fence.

Jim came out of the coop, a Delaware rooster in hand. "Howdy."

Evens turned and smiled. "She looks like a racer," he announced, grinning wider. He stood and extended a wide hand for Jim to shake. "Don't believe we've met. Name's Evens. I own the Triple A, near Bellwood."

Jim nodded and shook the stranger's hand. It was the practiced grip of a politician or businessman. Jim set the rooster down near his feet.

"You looking to sell?" Evens asked.

Jim shook his head, turning to look at the mare.

"You race her?"

"We let her run."

"Against other horses?"

Jim shook his head. "I'm not familiar with the ins and outs of your profession."

"Profession? Hell, you talk about it like it's a legitimate business. All it is is a disease. My wife got me to enroll in Gamblers Anonymous. I go to the meetings then right off to the track."

Jim frowned.

"Jim Northfield told me you got her as an inheritance. Is that right?"

Jim nodded again.

"Some inheritance. Well, I'd like to see her run. I'd like to see if she's as game as she looks."

Jim called for Rodrigo, who set down the peeps' medicine and walked over, tipping his hat.

"Mister Jim?"

"Rodrigo, Mr. Evens here wants to see the horse run. Do you mind taking her for a ride?"

Rodrigo glanced from Evens back to Jim and winked. "Sure, sure, no problem." He dashed off and then grabbed the saddle from inside the dog-hanged stable.

Ten minutes later they were off, Rodrigo riding close like a jockey, the mare tearing across the field with a headlong ferocity, coming up to the turn at the end of the oblong meadow, hooves colliding against the dirt with their daring rhythm. Then they bolted back around, Evens turning to watch the gray-white blur; he let out another wet-sounding whistle and pushed back his hat.

"You need to get her on a track. See what time she draws."

Jim nodded, unsure how to respond. Evens took note of the other man's suspicion and grinned. "Here's what I tell you I'm going to do. I'd like to set up a race, your horse against one of mine. I'll give you three-to-one odds. To be honest, I'd just like to see what she can do."

Jim gave the man an uneasy stare. There was $112 in his checking account until the first of the month. He itched his nose and considered the bet. Evens offered another big-operator smile. "So what do you say?"

"I'll take your bet," Jim muttered. "I'll put up two hundred. But I want five-to-one."

They shook on it, deciding the race would be the following afternoon. "My wife goes to church all day," Bill said.

Jim nodded softly and then they both turned back to stare at the animal, their eyes wincing in the sunlight.

As soon as it was dawn that Sunday morning, Jim went out alone to feed the horse and watch it run, not bothering to tack up, letting the animal hurl itself this way and that without a rider, loose, momentary, its eyes gleaming as it tore along the fence. The grandfather snuck a Fuji apple from his coat pocket and, pulling out his utility knife, split it into a pair of uneven halves. A bleary wetness filled the air, from the metallic tang of the blade and the sweetness of the fruit. The grandfather held one half of the apple in his hand while placing the other half along the irregular plane of the fence rail to be gobbled up as the animal fled past.

Sometime later the boy joined him at the fence line. The horse jetted before them. The grandfather again had a feeling that their lives were about to change.

That afternoon they looked in on the corn; the grandfather pulling a green ear free, checking to be sure it was clean of worms. Together he and the boy squatted in the rows, the wind whispering through the leaves, the silks brushing up against one another like some forgotten music. "Here," he said, handing the ear to the boy. "What do you see?"

The boy looked at the green ear and shrugged. "Some corn."

"Any bugs?"

The boy dug his fingernails into the kernels. "No."

"You sure?"

The boy squinted again. "Pretty sure."

The grandfather nodded, satisfied, and said, "Good." The rows swayed over their heads like the echoes of a distant church. In all honesty, it was as close as the grandfather liked to get to any kind of service. He listened to the cornrows for a moment longer and then said: "Shhh. Do you hear that?"

"Hear what?" the boy asked.

"Just listen."

The boy sniffled and tilted his ear toward the sky. "What am I listening for?"

"Shhh."

The boy tilted his head again, eyes squinting in concentration. There again was the pleasant murmur. The grandfather smiled, then hearing it, the boy did too.

Rodrigo soon arrived from town, having hitchhiked the few miles over. They were not used to seeing him on a Sunday and noticed his black hair had been slicked back with soap, his vaquero shirt buttoned all the way up. Together the three of them led the horse into the trailer. The boy kept the animal calm by talking quietly to it. What he was whispering neither the grandfather nor Rodrigo was sure. But it was placid clomping inside the trailer, and even when the door was locked shut, it still didn't utter a neigh. Then they drove over to Evens's spread, on the back forty of which he had built a racetrack, complete with aluminum stands. Evens, in his straw hat, waved the blue pickup over, then helped lead the mare out himself.

"If you want a jockey, I'd be happy to loan you one of mine," he grinned. "Free of charge, of course. Your fella, he looks a little long is all."

Jim glanced over at Rodrigo, who quietly nodded.

The race took place on Evens's racetrack with Evens's horse and two of his jockeys. Jim thought that he had made a mistake somewhere. The other horse was a black, long-necked gelding, which took careful, high, prancing steps. It was ridden by a jockey in blue. Jim's mare was being ridden by a stubby man in an orange helmet. Evens patted the orange-helmed jockey on his rear and pretended to whisper, "Just because I'm your boss doesn't mean you shouldn't give it your all," smacking the flanks of the mare with the same easy motion. The white horse whinnied, charging at Evens until the jockey reined her in. Then another farmhand fitted the mare with purple blinders. The horse kicked a little so the grandfather gently touched its nose, placing the palm of his hand against its muzzle. Then he and the boy and Rodrigo followed Evens to the aluminum stands and stood behind the metal railing. There were eight or nine onlookers—some neighbors, retired layabouts, all friends of Evens. He greeted each cordially and offered the grandfather a cigar, which Jim accepted but did not light. The two horses came down the track, their jockeys piloting them into their stalls. One of Evens's farmhands closed the gates and backed away from the course.

Then there was a loud ringing bell and the green gates flung open.

Jim watched the animal and the jockey take off, a bolt of white horseflesh followed by a cloud of dust, a spray of dirt. The horse bounded across the track in a phantasmagoric blur, all steady whiteness and steam, its coat shiny, hurling itself like a muscled locomotive. The report of the mare's hooves against the dry earth rang out like thunder, *whoom, whoom, whoom,* the hooves hitting the dirt with their specific, tremendous explosivity, the sound of horses running unlike any other sound in the world, a sound suggesting tireless movement, joy, an escape from the past, from the present, from the uncertainty of the future. Seeing the mare go, the grandfather imagined the sound of its hooves against the clotted dirt was his own heart racing to meet its end. He felt something well up inside his chest and forgot what it was, the word for it. Then he turned and glanced at the boy and saw the same expression on his rounded gray face. *What if?* the grandfather began to think again, turning to watch his animal pull three lengths ahead, then four. The horse and rider flew past the finish line, coming in at twenty-one seconds on the nose. Evens looked at Jim, bug-eyed, wet cigar sloping from his mouth. Jim refused to give him the satisfaction of being surprised. As the dust settled, Evens opened his wallet and snorted. They collected on five-to-one odds, returning to the blue pickup with a billfold padded roundly with cash.

In bed later that Sunday night, Jim flipped through his wife's Bible. He stopped on a page near the middle and read:

When the daughter of Herodias herself came in and danced, she pleased Herod and those sitting with him. The king said to the young lady, "Ask me whatever you want, and I will give it to you." He swore to her, "Whatever you shall ask of me, I will give you, up to half of my kingdom." She went out, and said to her mother, "What shall I ask?" She said, "The head of John the Baptizer." She came in immediately with haste to the king, and asked, "I want you to give me right now the head of John the Baptizer on a platter." The king was exceedingly sorry, but for the sake of his oaths, and of his dinner guests, he didn't wish to refuse her. Immediately the king sent out a soldier of his guard, and commanded to bring John's head, and he went and beheaded him in the prison, and brought his head on a platter, and gave it to the young lady; and the young lady gave it to her mother.

Before the sun had made its way over the tree line on that last Saturday of August, they mucked the horse's quarters, fed it, and curried it as best as they knew how. The grandfather broke a carrot in half and handed one part to the animal, who gobbled it down. The other part he handed to the boy.

"Watch this," the boy said. Quentin took a bite and then leaned over, holding the carrot in his mouth, laughing as the horse carefully took it from his teeth.

The grandfather smiled and said, "It's good to see you two are friends again."

"We are," the boy said. "We'll be friends, even after our deaths."

The grandfather shook his head, unsure what the words actually meant, though for some reason he was pleased.

Next they counted out the peeps—checking their beaks, their fluffy stomachs, their reptilian feet—for any sign of infection. The boy squatted beside his grandfather, petting the head of a round chick, letting it nip at his finger. Then he looked up.

"Sir?"

"Hm."

"Nothing." The boy glanced back down at the peeps.

"Go on," the grandfather said.

"Did you . . ." But the boy paused again.

"Go on."

"Did ever you hear from my mom?"

Jim frowned, unable to hide his disappointment. "Not yet."

"Do you think she's coming back?"

Jim itched his nose and gave a short nod. "Like as not. But she's got a lot to figure out first."

"Did she tell you where she's staying?"

The grandfather stood up, setting the peep back into the brooder, and shook his head. "I bet she's with friends though. I'm sure she's all right. How come you're asking?"

"I dunno," the boy said, scratching at a scab on his arm. "I guess I'd like to call her."

Jim gave a slow smile. "Of course you would. It's nice, a boy thinking of his mother like that."

"I'd like to tell her about the horse. I think it would make her happy."

"Sure it would," Jim said.

"I'd like to tell her."

Jim tilted his hat a little and put a hand on the boy's head, feeling the coarse, fine hair, and mussed it gently. "Anything is possible," the grandfather said.

The boy rode with his grandfather into town to get supplies that Saturday. As they drove, the grandfather glanced over from the rubberized steering wheel and asked the kind of question he always seemed to propose during these sorts of trips. "What would you do with a million dollars?"

The boy answered without thinking: "I'd try to breed a rattlesnake with a water moccasin. Or a cobra."

Jim smiled. "Breed a what? You'd spend all your money on that?"

"I'd sell their offspring and then I'd be even richer."

The grandfather nodded, though with an undisguised air of doubt.

On his lap in the passenger seat, the boy held a small shoe box with holes in the top, which had been jabbed with the rounded edge of a butter knife. There was a sound, an indefinable, nearly indescribable movement, a kind of gentle scraping, coming from inside the box. The boy turned and faced his grandfather with a curious expression.

"Sir?"

"Hm."

"Are we gonna race her again?" he asked. "The horse, I mean."

"Hope to."

"You think she'll win?"

"It'd be nice," he said, turning back to face the road.

They parked the pickup in its usual spot near the closed-down café. Opening the driver's-side door before the street of similar-looking, redbrick, two-story buildings, Jim pulled his cattleman hat down to shade his eyes and said, "All right, I'll meet you back here around five o'clock. Mind you're not late. We still have some other work to do when we get back."

"We're not gonna eat in town?"

"No sir. I got to get home and give them hens their medicine."

"Okay."

"I'll see you in a couple hours."

"Okay."

Quentin heaved his backpack over his shoulder, took hold of the small shoe box, and walked off. A rusted-out Camaro with a Confederate flag license-plate holder rattled past. The boy took notice of the faded plastic stars and bars and inwardly felt aggrieved, though no actual sign showed on his face. He was used to it by now. He walked on. In a strip mall around the corner was the exotic pet store, located right between a Chinese takeout place and a you-wash-it laundry.

The sign above the pet shop was fading white—a painting of a lizard above the words, *Exotic Reptiles*, all spelled out in blue, though Mr. Peel, the store's owner, had been smart enough to branch out into other kinds of pets—a few odd mammals like chinchillas, all types of snakes and lizards, some of which were legal, some of which weren't, and a tortoise which the store claimed was more than a hundred years old.

The boy stopped by the store whenever he could; he had an interest in getting rich, specifically through the illegal and sometimes forcible breeding of a random selection of exotic pets. He considered himself a regular amateur herpetologist, though no one in the boy's life but the pet store owner Mr. Peel or Gilby—the distracted, ill-kept, twenty-two-year-old pet store clerk—had any sense of what that particular word meant. The boy had said it once, by accident, as a means of introduction, to a group of girls at a church picnic a few years before, and had spent the rest of the day off in the woods alone, itching mosquito bites on his arm, watching various strangers squint at him and laugh. He thought of that now, that embarrassing moment, two or three years removed, and muttered, "A herpetologist is someone who studies reptiles," to the empty town, to the sound of the abandoned buildings staring back.

A little bell rang as Quentin entered the pet store; he walked up to the counter where the clerk, Gilby, was busy inspecting a nudie magazine. The periodical was open to a two-page spread and featured a pair of Asian girls, bound up with silken white ropes. There was no freckle or flaw on the flesh of either one of them, which gave them a phantomed look.

"What you got today?" Gilby asked without having to look up.

"Pinkies."

"How many?"

"Three dozen."

"You want cash or trade?"

"Cash."

Gilby nodded, still staring down at the slick magazine pages, walked over to the cash register, rang the transaction up, hit the sale button, and stood back as the drawer whirred open. He got three dollars from the till and placed them in Quentin's hand, eyes still on the entwined women.

"I don't usually go for Asian girls, but these two . . ." Gilby confided. "I only wish there was a war over there so I'd be inclined to go visit."

"I guess," the boy said, looking away, then glancing up at Gilby's face. "What happened to your eye?"

Gilby sniffed, his long nose twitching, as he placed two fingers below his left eye. It was swollen black and purple, and some of the white of the eye was pink with burst blood vessels. The rest of his face looked equally disheveled; his narrow upper lip was marked with what appeared to be a cold sore of some kind; his pointy chin and sallow cheeks looked like they had not been shaved in days. "Somebody I know doesn't understand the meaning of a joke."

"Who was that?"

"No one," he sighed, and then, "My brother."

"Walt?"

"Walt? Shit. Walt's still in high school. And he ain't brave enough anyway. No, my older brother, the cocksucker, he's back in town."

"Who's that?"

"Edward. Everybody calls him Cocksucker. He's the oldest."

"You got an older brother?"

"Yeah. He just got back yesterday."

"Where was he?"

"I don't know. Jail. In California. Then he was in Chicago for a while."

"How long was he gone for?"

"I don't know. Three or four years, I guess."

"I didn't even know you had an older brother."

"He comes and goes. My mother don't let him stay too long. He usually gets himself thrown out after a week or two."

"And he's the one who gave you the black eye?"

Gilby glanced back down at the two girls forced together, their pale bodies crashing upon each other like some kind of mysterious sea foam. "He don't look like he's tough, but he's mean. You think he's got a sense of humor but then you find out he don't. I always end up saying something I wish I hadn't. And then I get one of these." He tapped his two fingers below the eye again. "It's a goddamn shame because we used to have fun when we were kids. Now he takes himself too seriously. Which is a problem if you don't happen to think he's kingshit of everything."

Quentin nodded then, though he did not know why.

"Hey," Gilby said, remembering something. "We're trying to get rid of that old reticulated python back there. He's an albino . . . Nobody wants an albino. They all want the tiger kind now. You got any interest in it?"

Quentin shrugged his shoulders and took a few steps down the aisle toward the glass tank. The python was fearsome-looking, long—almost a dozen feet, and curled up on itself in round, lazy loops. Its skin was a creamy white, with pale yellow and gray markings, its arrow-shaped head a yellow brighter than any kind of tropical flower.

"We tried to feed him a live rat but he wouldn't touch it. We had to take the rat out because we were afraid it would scratch him up. I wanted to leave it in there and take bets but Mr. Peel said the snake wasn't worth anything to us dead."

Quentin tapped the glass. "He looks bored. You ever take him out at all?"

"Nope. He tried to bite me last time I did that. He's got an attitude problem. He thinks he's better than everyone else." Gilby tapped the glass once, then again, the snake flicking its tongue in response. "But he ain't. He's the wrong color and so he ain't shit."

Quentin squinted a little. "What's this?" he asked, staring at another glass tank. "When these come in?"

"Those are Chinese water dragons. They came in a couple days ago. They're like iguanas pretty much. Except they like living in the water. Supposed to change their water every day because they shit in it and then try to drink it."

"They're terrific."

"They're all right."

"You got a pair?" the boy asked.

"Yeah. Why?"

"I dunno."

"You thinking of breeding them?"

Quentin nodded, pressing his hand up against the glass. "How much are they going for?"

"For the pair is thirty."

"Thirty?"

"It's an investment. You going to make money off them. As soon as you get some young ones, you can sell 'em back to Mr. Peel. The folks we bought them from said you can play this one cassette tape with Chinese music and then they'll start breeding like crazy. You get the pair and I'm sure Mr. Peel will throw in that cassette tape too. Easy money."

Quentin nodded once more, tapping the glass carefully with his fingertip, making as if he was touching the ridged neck and bumpy skin of the creature on the other side. "I'm gonna buy them. As soon as I save up enough. How long have they been here for?"

"A couple days. But Bobby Dare supposed to come in next weekend. He's going to a trade show in Ohio and he usually cleans us out."

Quentin tapped against the aquarium glass again and turned, glancing down at his watch. "I got to go. I'll be back Monday. Or Tuesday. Don't sell them until then if you can."

Gilby nodded, once more returning to his spot behind the small glass counter. He stared down at the unfolded magazine. The boy gave the glass door a shove and stepped back outside into the distant glare of the sun.

* * *

Cocksucker was back in town. Mount Holly. There he was. On the
go. A shadow in Mount Holly's town square, the only shadow. It
crossed over the birds on the bench. An omen, a bad cloud, scaring them all off. Flap-flap-flap. The dusty feathers, in summer, bird
snow, made him cough. Lungs like asbestos, hack-hack-hack. He
made his way past the feed store, trying not to have a coughing fit.
Inside the feed store, civilians gathered around the counter, talking
irrigation and drainage. Hayseeds in overalls. Mud on their boots.
Not for him. Stopping at the corner now. Spitting at the side of the
mailbox, taking his time to get the phlegm up, making a regular
show of it. What came up was translucent and a little yellow, tinged
with some pinkish blood. It was the consequence of smoking ge-
neric, unfiltered cigarettes and also doing a few lines of crystal cut
with inferior cleaning products. He coughed and spat again. This
one landed directly above the majestic outline of the blue post office
eagle. Why an eagle? Who do you think you are? America. America.
You ain't nothing anymore. And he strode on, his boots rattling as he
walked. His mother had chased him out of the house this morning,
so he had not bothered to fasten the buckles. He tripped once, then
again, before leaning over and hitching them. He looked up, out of
breath.

Two boys, school-age, were playing with their yo-yos on the
corner, sitting on the curb. Red-yellow, red-yellow, the yo-yo rearing up and down, the other silver-flecked like a comet, both of them
spiral-like, spinning scientifically beside their knees. The sight of it
made him dizzy. And then angry. He made a grab for one, yanking
it from the boy's hand. Boo. The kid screamed like a girl, the yo-yo
rolling down the curb toward the sewer grate, lying faceup beside
a soda pop bottle. The other kid dropped his, the two of them running off together. Two shadows disappearing down an alleyway. The
sound of rubber soles on hot pavement.

On he strolled. The Band-Aid on his nose falling off. He
stopped in front of the Bide-A-While and found the door to the saloon locked. He made a disappointed sound in his throat, and then

coughed again. He squinted inside, the glass window coated with a black film that only reflected his unwashed face. His jawline was coated in blackheads and stubble. He looked like a charity case in need of a haircut. The hair was dark hanging over his ears. He tried the door again. Locked. He blinked up into the sun. Hot for August. Too hot. He turned to squint at the clock tower in the center of the square. One of its faces read 1:30, the other 2:15. The sign on the door read 4 p.m. Either way, it was still too early so he fumbled for the pack of smokes rolled up in his sleeve, lit one, then ambled back down the street. A semi pulling a trailer full of dairy cows crawled past. A song was blaring from its cab, *I know it's only rock 'n' roll but I like it* . . . He whistled along, traveling westward now.

On down the sloping street, he stopped before the parking lot where as a boy he'd always run whenever he had stolen something. There. He might have curled up right there in between those rows of parked cars, the smell of motor oil and gasoline and his own fear as distinct a memory as the taste of the powdery, brittle bubble gum that came with each pack of baseball cards he slipped inside his coat. The gum not at all enjoyable but something which you put in your mouth simply because it was there. It being part of the practice of opening a pack of cards which had been carefully pocketed. The ones he stole always came out to be doubles of players he had already. Carlton Fisk. Dwight Gooding. Reggie Jackson. Even at a young age he learned that crime was something you did simply for its own fun. Because when you stole something, it usually wasn't worth the trouble you spent.

When he crossed the street again, back to the saloon a half hour later, he found it was still locked. So. He had a serious coughing fit just then, his chest feeling like it was on fire once more. Until he could bring up the phlegm which looked to contain little pieces of his lungs. He fumbled for another cigarette and again noticed how the tips of his fingers were swelled up. Much too round, like the digits of a cartoon character. A boy he had been fucking back in San Diego, Derek, another ex-con, had said he had Mickey Mouse hands.

The boy's sister was an RN and took one look at them and declared, "You got something wrong with your circulation. You oughta make that cigarette your last," and he had tried for a week or so, even going out to buy the nicotine patch. But it didn't last, and neither did the boy. Derek had been the only one he had ever met who did not say no to anything he asked for in bed. But he had given the boy a black eye and the boy pulled a can of mace on him. Then that was the end of that. So.

When he stopped coughing, he stood on the corner. Watched the traffic go by for a while, then headed back to where his own red pickup truck was parked. He fooled around with the driver's-side mirror, which was just about ready to fall off. Hung there with banding wire. Would not stay in place, no matter what. Lit another cigarette, searched underneath the bench seat. Found the pistol, a .45 Chief's Special. He slipped it into the waistband at the back of his pants. Found the pair of black gloves. The black ski mask in the truck's glove compartment. Shoved the mask and gloves under his left arm, and glanced around to be sure he wasn't being watched. Coughing once more, he struggled to catch his breath. It took a few minutes before he was breathing right again. He searched in his pockets and found some Nembutals. Took two. Then he popped some caffeine pills. Four of those, their shape odd against his tongue. Looking around again to make sure he had not been seen, he stomped off in the direction of the drugstore at the shady end of the street. Okay. Now don't forget to breathe.

By three p.m. the grandfather had finished his business at the feed store, slinging the sacks of oats and a few bales of hay into the back of the pickup, holding his shoulder where it was now sore. He did not ask the clerks at the feed store for help with the hay, as he had never needed it before. So he leaned his left arm against the door of the pickup, the metal panel having been warmed by the sun, and soon the throb and ache slowly faded. He groaned with a little relief, closing his eyes, the joint and muscle once again settling into place.

A shadow fell across his tightened eyelids and so he quickly opened them.

"That arm still bothering you?"

It was Doc Milborne, with his round face, gray beard, and craggy mouth. He had to be ninety if he was a day, still practicing, his blue eyes like carnival glass behind a pair of narrow specs.

"No, doc. Shoulder's just a little stiff is all."

"Why don't you make an appointment to come by the office sometime next week? We'll take another look at it."

"Much obliged," Jim said, tipping the white cattleman's hat. "I'll call when I have the time."

"You either make the time or the time'll be taken from you."

"You go to all those years of medical school just to learn sayings like that?"

"No. I went for the chance to meet girls. And I still haven't found the right one yet." His eyes seemed to fog over with a distant memory before he said, "Now don't be mulish. You give the office a call. I expect to see you sometime this week." Then the good doctor stiffly marched off.

Stepping around the corner, the grandfather walked up the stairwell and found Jim Northfield's office empty. He trucked back down to the street and discovered the saloon had not yet opened, and so he decided to pay a visit to the Masonic lodge. The door to the lodge—a pair of offices on the second floor of a two-story building, directly above a vacant optometrist's shop—was slightly ajar.

"So much for secrecy," Jim mumbled, slipping off his white hat. The walls of the lodge were now bare; the outlines where Egyptian-motif banners had recently hung were all that remained of the baroque decor. Everything had been packed into boxes, which stood piled in a corner. The three senior officers, all old-timers, Jim Northfield, Jim Dooley, and Jim Wall, were sitting around a table, tipping a fifth of bourbon. At the center of the table was a framed photograph of Burt Hale, the lodge's longtime treasurer. The officers all muttered their salutations to Jim, conducted their secret handshakes, and managed to find a fourth chair somewhere among the debris. Jim took the seat, swallowed down the shot of whiskey that was quickly placed before him, and felt his left eye begin to water.

"So what's all this?" he asked, looking around.

"We come to say goodbye," Jim Dooley said. "So to speak." Jim Dooley's forehead was shiny with sweat. Before he had retired, he had been both a soybean farmer and a schoolteacher. "We were expecting you last week with everyone else."

"What was last week?" he asked.

"We're closing it down," Jim Wall, the former groceryman, announced, pouring himself another shot. "Everything must go."

"There ain't enough names in the roster," Jim Northfield explained, his bushy eyebrows adding a comical counterpoint to his dignified lawyerly expression. "We don't have any new members. And the old ones we have," and here he surveyed the room, not gazing at anyone particular, though slowing before the grandfather, "they either don't show up to the meetings or they haven't paid their dues."

Jim Falls went a little red in the face.

"Northfield's right," Jim Dooley added. "We was meant to be a civic organization. But what's a civic organization without a town?"

"First we lost the manufacturing plant . . ." Jim Wall started.

"Then we lost the knife factory . . ."

"And after that, the hospital . . ."

"And the creamery . . ." The men's voices began to blur together.

"Now that it's all gone, nobody growing up here has got a reason to stay." This was Jim Dooley again. "That café has been closed for almost ten years now."

"God bless Ruthie, that poor girl. I can still see the way that blood was circling her head on the floor. Looked like a halo."

"God bless."

"And if they ever find the villain . . ."

"God knowing they will . . ."

"If they ever find him."

"Which they will."

"The problem is we ain't got nothing left to point to. To hang our hats on, so to speak," Jim Dooley said. He was getting maudlin now, his wrinkled forehead creased with regret. "All the kids, they get bused over to school in Dwyer. You got to drive an hour south for a job. We can't even get the chain restaurants interested."

"Those folks at Hardee's wouldn't even take our call," Jim Wall confided, his wide face tightening.

"All we got left is that statue in the square. And a few family farms. And that don't make a town," Jim Northfield said, pouring another shot.

"It's happening all over," Jim Dooley said. "Every part of the country. All those jobs, factories, going overseas. And we let it happen. We got no one to blame but ourselves."

"America," one of the men muttered.

"Here's to a good run," Jim Northfield toasted, holding up his shot glass. "When it's all over, all said and done, we can at least say we had some times up in here. It saved my marriage and kept me from murdering my boy."

"That boy is a lawyer now, if you don't happen to know," Jim Dooley whispered.

The four downed their shots in silence, one of them coughing, one of them rolling his eyes, one of them humming, one of them groaning.

"Before we say goodbye, let's all drink one more to Burt," Jim Dooley suggested, nodding at the rectangular framed photograph.

"Old Burt Hale."

"Old Burt."

"That fella was lucky. He didn't have to live long enough to see this place shut its doors."

"It was only a few months ago."

"It was two years, last June."

"Why, I'll be."

"Oh, you will be, all right. Sooner or later, all of us will." Jim

Northfield was quicker with the bottle this time, spilling the amber liquid a little, his hands liver-spotted, white-haired, and rusty with rheumatism. "To Burt Hale. A better, more even-tempered fellow I've never met."

"Here here."

"And a wife as good-looking as an ice-cream sundae," Jim Wall added.

"Without the nuts."

The men chuckled at that one. Jim Northfield's hand trembled, holding the shot glass aloft, pleased at his own joke.

"Here here!" someone else exclaimed.

"One of the best treasurers we ever had," Jim Dooley remembered. "One of the few who didn't rob us blind. We bought new books for the library with what he saved."

"And got the coffee shop built at the old hospital."

"A man who could quote from the autobiography of Benjamin Franklin."

"And knew nearly everybody in town."

"With a wife as good-looking as a peach pie," Jim Wall said.

"Without the nuts."

This time no one but Jim Northfield smiled.

"And a better sheep farmer this state has never seen."

"Burt Hale."

"Old Burt."

"Old Burt Hale," Jim Northfield repeated.

They held the glass cylinders before their lips, each of them closing his eyes, remembering better days.

"Here's to swimming with bowlegged women," Jim Falls mumbled, speaking finally, and then quickly downed the shot.

A red stop sign. A green lamppost. A rounded water tower, dulled from powder blue to white. A faded town, fading, harried with dusty light, midafternoon.

Gilby was teasing the albino python when Mr. Peel came in. There was definitely something wrong with it, because it still would not eat. The pinkie—its small, nude body—lay curled up beside the snake's angular head, breathing heavily. "He won't eat," Gilby called over his shoulder. "It's been a week already."

"You might have to kill it for him and see if he goes for it then," Mr. Peel responded, moving behind the cash register. He was wearing a white T-shirt, so old and washed so many times as to appear nearly see-through, and green canvas shorts. His black-rimmed glasses caught the light coming in from outside and made it look like he had no eyes. Gilby, kneeling there on the dirty tile floor, wondered what Mr. Peel was doing here so early on a Saturday afternoon. Saturdays he usually didn't come in until five, when the store closed. "How's it been today, Gil?"

"Pretty slow. We sold a couple newts and that was about it.

Some lady called to say she was looking for a caiman but I told her we don't got any. I told her I'd talk to you and said she could call back later if she wanted."

"I'll have to call that redneck from Florida, I guess. He's the only one I know still dumb enough to sell 'em."

Gilby carried the pinkie over to the counter, reached beside the cash register, and found a long, plastic-handled flathead screwdriver. He placed the small pink mouse on the counter, holding it there with two fingers, and raised the handle of the screwdriver above the tiny creature's head, measuring out the blow.

Mr. Peel looked over his black-rimmed glasses. "Gilby, don't do that here. The counter's made of glass, son. Use your head."

"Right. Sorry." Gilby carried the squirming animal over to the floor in front of the python's cage. He held the shivering mouse in place with his two fingers, then lifted the screwdriver's handle once more, measuring out the proper distance and force.

"Gilby, don't do it on the floor there. What did I build that feeding table for?"

"Right." Gilby stood, walking a few short paces over to the feeding table—an unsquare construction of wood and metal that leaned precariously to the left, slapped with a tacky coat of black housepaint—Mr. Peel's ingenious solution to the problem of where to store and prepare all the reptile's medicine and food.

The mouse, being relocated a third time, let out a tiny squeak as Gilby inched his fingertips over its narrow body, pressing it against the tabletop. Once more, Gilby raised the screwdriver's handle, squinting so as to better approximate the distance and torque, imagining it was his older brother he had pinned to the tabletop in the mouse's place. Before he could follow through with this fantasy, delivering the deadly blow, Mr. Peel called out, "Gilby, why are we thirty dollars short?"

The screwdriver handle hung suspended in the air, only an inch or two from the trembling mouse. Gilby sniffed, closing his eyes for a second, wondering if he had miscounted or if by chance had borrowed more from the register than he should've. "Huh?"

Mr. Peel finished counting through the bills a third time. "We're thirty-four dollars short, Gil. You pay any bills today?"

"That black boy came in with pinkies."

"How many?"

Gilby closed his eyes and tried to figure it quick, but under duress, all he could come up with was the truth. "Two dozen. No, three."

"That still leaves thirty-one dollars that's missing."

"I don't know."

Flustered, Mr. Peel counted through the bills and coins a fourth time. The final bill he laid down on top of the rest with an exhausted air, staring down at the short pile of cash, lowering his head, as if steeling himself for something.

"Gilby."

"Yeah?"

"This is the third or fourth time this has happened this month. Now, did anyone else come in to sell anything?"

"Nope. No, a wait a minute . . ." He scratched his unshaved chin, tugging at the hair growing along there. "No."

"And no one else came in with a bill? What about Paul? From the town council? Or the guy from the woodchip place? Was he in here?"

Gilby bit his lips, figuring it might be better to try to be creative with some outrageous lie. An imaginary bill that had come due. Some unfamiliar pet food salesman. A suspicious character lurking near the cash register while he had been busy feeding the animals.

"Gilby?"

"Huh?"

"Was there anyone else in here today?"

The sore spot beneath his eye began to throb, from Mr. Peel and his whited-out glasses. "No. Nobody else was in. There was a guy and his daughter, they bought the newts. And the black kid selling pinkies. That was it."

Mr. Peel peered back down at the stack of bills on the glass counter. He lifted the black-rimmed glasses from his face, pinched the space in between his eyes, groaned, then replaced the frames, turning his eyeless stare back in Gilby's direction.

"Gilby?"

"Yes?"

"Do you see we have a problem here?"

Gilby wondered if maybe this was a trick question. Did Mr. Peel think he was an idiot? "I guess."

"You guess?"

"I guess."

"Gilby, how long have you been working for me?"

"Three years."

"That's right, three years. And how I am supposed to keep trusting you with the store if I come in and find the count off?"

"I don't know."

"You don't know? Well, neither do I. Can you give me one good reason I shouldn't fire you right now and call Sheriff Burke and ask him to come down and search you for my thirty dollars?"

"No."

"No?"

"No. Except I didn't take it."

Mr. Peel pulled the glasses from his face. "Gilby, I don't want to have to fire you. I like you. I do. But Jesus. Do you want to be fired?"

"No."

"No?"

"No."

"Do you think I'm stupid? Is that it? Do you think I'm too dumb to notice?"

"No. I don't think you're stupid at all."

"Well, I appreciate it, Gilby. I do."

"No problem."

And here, for a brief second, hearing the young man's reply, Mr. Peel couldn't help but smile. "The way I figure it, you've stolen about five hundred dollars from me over the last three years. And we got enough troubles trying to keep the place open as it is. I mean, I can't have somebody in here that I can't trust. I can't. I mean, that's like . . . that's like stealing from my kids, you know? Jeez. I don't know. I mean, I don't want to, Gilby, but I guess I'm gonna have to fire you."

Gilby stood, his face now red with embarrassment and anger. "I didn't steal anything from you, Mr. Peel."

"I wish that was true, Gilby."

The younger man nodded, found his baseball cap beside the register, fitted it over his head, and walked slowly out, glancing behind him to see if Mr. Peel was on the phone with the police. He wasn't. He was staring down at the mismatched pile of currency, and then, shaking his head, he began counting it once again.

Edward came up to the pharmacy counter. His teeth were itching; they felt like they were made of fur. Something was all wrong with the light in this place. It was too much. It was actually a plot to make everyone feel sick. Vis-à-vis supply and demand. Vis-à-vis sick people. Meaning more profits for the drug companies. Or something like that. There was more to this thought but he could not get himself worked up about it. Because right now. Right now. Right now. He was doing something. What? His veins felt like they had calcified. The pharmacist, a stiff with a lab coat and glasses, asked him what he could do for him. What a question. Where to begin. How about a million dollars? Would that make anyone happy anymore? No. How about an operation? The one where you remove my heart? So I am just dick and guts. Because that is all I want anymore. Is there a pill back there that has the same effects? I would like to be an animal. All I want is to roam in the woods. Civilization has become too intelligent. What do you prescribe for that? Then he remembered the .45 at the back of his pants. Ah, yes. But he was sure he was being videotaped right now. There was a camera right above the counter. "Tell me where, good sir, where your pseudoephedrine products are, and be quick about it, as I am in a bit of a hurry."

"Aisle twelve, cold and cough."

"Thank you, my good man, thank you, a thousand thank yous."

He moved like a plastic skeleton, at odd angles to the ceiling and floor, searching for aisle twelve. Things in this place smelled different. Like they had been experimented with. It was the phosphates. Or the plastics. The hormones. Nothing looked or tasted the way he remembered it. It was a part of the problem of everything. Nothing rotted anymore. The torment of nature had finally been escaped. It was the chemicals that had done it, the same ones flashing in his brain. He found himself staring at a freezer full of beverages, wondering what it would be like to be an Eskimo. My good man. Aisle twelve. He was feeling better now. The lights did that too. That was how all these stores were making record profits. It was called halcyon. You couldn't smell it or taste it except in the negative. Soda pop tasted too good because of it. All the fast food was full of it. And then again, it was okay to feel good. He was back home and his mother had not turned him out. Not yet anyway. And already he had plans. A plan. Before the California biker-gang cartels made their move into the Midwest and crystal meth was as big as it was back on the West Coast, he needed to set himself up in distribution. And production. He could corner the market. If he could get together enough cash to mix the first batch. And if his timing was right. Which was why aisle twelve. There were half a dozen boxes of different cold medicines with pseudoephedrine, and he decided he would take them all. Cradling the cardboard boxes against his chest, he limped up to the counter, his nose running once again. He set the boxes down on the black conveyer belt and the clerk—an old woman with hair like cotton candy—looked up at him, and he just nodded and said, "And this too," placing a pack of gum on top.

He was out the door, plastic bags in hand, staring down into a small creek before he remembered the mask and the pistol stuffed into the back of his pants. He shouted, bearing his fangs. It was one mistake after another with him. It was like his head was on someone else's body. Angrily, he shoved the bags of Sudafed into the cab of his truck and wondered where in town he might find some blue iodine. His plan was to use the red, white, and blue method for cooking up his first batch. He had the red—phosphorous, which he had brought back with him from California—the white—the ephedrine which he had just bought—but not the blue, the iodine. He had closely watched the homo he had been sleeping with and his nurse sister who had decided to turn their garage into a meth lab. There was something he was supposed to do with lithium batteries but he could no longer remember. His head was throbbing. His eyes were making a weird noise; he could feel them vibrating like electric bug lamps. A terrible violence was now coursing through his veins. He felt that unless he saw something injured, he would not be able to breathe again. He snatched the pistol and mask from the back of his pants and limped off toward the adult bookstore, which was situated behind an abandoned creamery. All at once he was frightened by the sound of his own teeth.

In glossy letters, the billboard reads: *Private Pleasures. Lion's Den. Dancers Show Club. Brad's Brass Flamingo. Brad's Gold Show Club. Wild Cherry Show Club. The Torch. Silk 'N' Lace Gentleman's Show. Alaskan Pipeline. PT's Show Club. Night Moves. Pair-A-Dice. Pandora's. Kitty Kat Lounge. Satin Lady. Shangri-La. Shangri-La East. Shangri-La West. After Hours. Danzers. Black Cherri. Bleu Diamond Show Club. Body Heat. Busybody Lounge. Chances Are. Chances R. Class Act. V.I.P. Show Club. Club Zeus. Club Rio. Club Centerfold. Club Paradise. CT Adult Store. Déjà Vu Love Boutique. Déjà Vu Showgirls. Industrial Strip. Dream Club. Twice as Nice. Exotic She Lounge. Red Garter. Filly's. Rising Sun. Stimmelators. Strippers. Sunset Strip. Jokers Wild. Glo Worm Lounge. Suzie-Q's. Hideaway. Lucky Lady. Our Doll's House. Stardust. Hoosier Girls Showclub. Harem House. White Diamonds. Poor John's. Lollipops. Peaches. ShowGirls. Visual Enjoyments. Hots.* A face, a shoulder, a rampart of blond hair, of red hair, of hair as black as the evening, the suggestion of cleavage, or no suggestion at all, an unflattering shot of some girl's surgically enhanced décolletage, the mascaraed eyes staring out lonely-like from the flat plane of the billboard unto the side of a gas station, unto a cow pasture, unto a field of corn.

On the way to the blue pickup, Jim found his legs had become unsteady. He leaned against a parking meter, watching the sun as it sunk behind the rectangular facade of the deserted post office. He made wayward steps from the Masonic temple, his knees buckling some, as he strolled from one parking meter to the next. When he glanced up he saw a station wagon pull up in front of the realty office across the street. A good-looking woman climbed out, shoved the door shut, then glanced at the reflection of herself in the passenger-side window. The woman dabbed at some lipstick at the corner of her lips and stepped lightly into the realty office, Jim's eyes escorting her the entire way.

It was Lucy Hale.

Jim blinked once, then again, disbelieving his luck. He groaned, pulling himself to his feet, fixing his hat atop his balding head, checking to be sure his breath was okay and his shirt was still buttoned right, then slowly made his way toward the end of the block, staring through the glassy windows of the realty office, watching as Lucy shook hands with Eugene Tibbs, a greasy-looking real estate agent. Eugene placed his free hand on Lucy's shoulder, grinning like a wolf, walking her over to his desk, where the two of them took a seat. The agent placed a few papers before Lucy to sign, which she did, pausing for a moment; then, nodding discreetly to herself, she put the pen to the page, signed, and stood up quickly, offering her small hand to the real estate agent again before turning back toward the office door, rushing out, one hand already reaching up to her dark eyes, the other fumbling for something in her purse. She was unlocking the rusty car door now, climbing inside, slamming it shut, holding both hands up to her eyes, her mouth drawing closed, her chin rising and falling slightly. Leaning there against the signpost on the corner, Jim hesitated, seeing the tears running down her face; then, seeing the stoplight had changed in his favor, he crossed, moving in a rickety fashion down the gray pavement, slowing up beside the station wagon, knocking gently on the driver's-side window twice.

When she looked up, Lucy Hale did not appear to be anything other than stunning, even with the tears and mascara streaked along her cheeks. There was something about this woman that made you wish for courage or ignorance—either one, or both. Lucy smiled, dabbing at the corner of her eyes with a balled-up tissue, and rolled down the window.

"Wouldn't it be my luck to have to run into you today," she said, stuffing the tissue into her shoulder bag. "Here I am, not even dressed and carrying on like an absolute idiot."

"Lucy," Jim muttered, for the word seemed to sum up all he felt at that moment, a kind of tenderness, a shared sense of the widower's and widow's grief, and an out-and-out roused-up pleasure in seeing the shape of her crying face.

"Of course you of all people would have to catch me crying like this."

"I was passing down the street and saw your car there."

She edged a finger along her eye again, catching a final, solemn tear, and then she exhaled deeply, her sizable chest heaving slightly. "Well, Jim, I finally did it. I finally did it."

"Did what?"

"I put it up for sale. I didn't know what else to do. I talked to the lawyer, I talked to my brother, I even talked to my dad. And they all told me the same thing: if you can't run it, there's no sense in hanging on to it."

Jim pulled the brim of his hat down to block some sun that had begun to make the wrinkles near his eyes ache.

"So I finally decided to do it. It's been two years, and I've tried. God knows I have. I feel like such a traitor, Jim. I do. He worked so hard for everything we had, and he tried to make that place a palace. But I don't know the first thing about raising sheep, and try as I might, it just doesn't come natural to me. I'm fifty-three years old, Jim. I am. No matter what anybody tries to tell you. I never married that man when I was fourteen. I was young but not that young. And here I am, fifty-three, having to start all over again. I don't know the first thing about sheep. I tried to learn but I'm just too old, I guess."

"I don't know anybody in town that would ever use that word to describe you. There are some folks I know who don't even think you've turned forty."

"Well, that's because they only see me in town. I've got a face, Jim, the kind you put on. It takes all kinds of makeup and smiling when you don't feel like smiling. When I'm at home, I'm a mess. Who am I kidding? I'm a mess now. I've been one since Burt died on me."

"I'm sure some of us, Jim Wall or Jim Dooley, we could lend you a hand. If you were still interested in running the place."

"I appreciate that, Jim, I do. You fellas, all of you, Jim Dooley and the Walls, all of you have been awful kind to me. But I just can't keep it up anymore. To be honest, I never much cared for sheep. When they cry, it sounds like a child crying. They're just too ghoulish to have to hear every night when you're trying to get to sleep."

"Well, you did your best. And nobody can fault you for that."

"I know one person who could."

"Who?"

"Burt."

"He wouldn't fault you. I'm sure he wouldn't."

"You didn't know how he built that place, Jim. Out of nothing. Absolutely nothing. My father gave him a pair of sheep as a dowry. He had an acre maybe and worked it all the way up to what we got now. He'd be up in the morning before me and wouldn't get to bed until after I was already asleep. He loved it, Jim, that place. He loved it the way you love another person. It's our family, that place."

Jim nodded, knowing there was nothing more to be said. He glanced down at her hands, saw them busy fumbling for another balled-up tissue.

"The funny part is he's the only person I'd like to get advice from on all this. I keep thinking if I could only get him to look at these papers for me . . ."

"I'd be more than happy, if you wanted a second pair of eyes on anything."

"I wouldn't dare bother you, Jim. You been too nice already."

"Just being neighborly. Burt woulda done the same in my place."

"Well, what's done is done, isn't that right?"

"I guess it is."

Jim saw that she was smiling again, her pearly teeth tucked behind a pair of lips that looked softer than anything ought to be.

"Who knows? Maybe no one will buy it," she said, her voice brightening.

"Who knows?"

"I guess I oughta be celebrating. Though I don't feel much like it."

"You should."

"Hey, I just got an idea," she said, her eyes meeting his. "How do you feel about having a drink with me?"

Outside the sunshine was being uncooperative. Everywhere Gilby turned, he had to squint, his eyes sore from it, his neck beading over with sweat. The reflection of himself in the glass windows gave him a definite guilty feeling. He looked like a crook, his longish hair scraggly in the back, his chin unshaven, a hood, a lawbreaker exactly like his older brother. Who knows? Maybe Mr. Peel with his Sunday school bifocals was right. Pulling the brim of his baseball hat down over his eyes, Gilby decided the only thing left to do now was to head over to the Bide-A-While and see if he couldn't use the money he had borrowed today to win big off the video poker machine. He turned the corner, finding Main Street deserted, with the saloon in sight at the end of the block.

At first they tried parking behind the Baptist church, but a cleaning lady gave them the evil eye. Lucy Hale blushed a little, pulling the station wagon out of the parking lot and turning down another alley. "I got a half-pint of blackberry schnapps in the glove compartment," she said. "Unless that's too low-class for you."

"Not at all," Jim stammered.

The station wagon pulled down a narrow side street off Main, flying over the brick-paved road, then they idled before what remained of the CutCorp Knife Corporation, a tan-colored manufacturing plant that seemed to blot out all the angles of the sun with its rectangular shape. Lucy put the car in park, switched off the engine, and unlatched the glove compartment, retrieving the stout-looking bottle of schnapps. She offered him the first sip, which he refused on principle. "Ladies first," he smiled.

She unscrewed the plastic cap, pressed the glass against her soft lips, drinking deeply, a single thread of purple liquid looking glossy on her chin. She grinned when she was done and handed the bottle over to Jim who, overcome by the sweetness of it, only took a small sip. He could feel the waxy traces of her lipstick against the bottle's ridge, the glass still warm from her mouth, and a pang of nervous disappointment at immediately knowing what would—in a million years—never happen. He coughed a little as the sweetness bit against his tongue, his eyes tearing up, him smiling as he passed the bottle back.

"Too sweet for you?" she asked, and he nodded, wiping the corner of his eyes. They both turned and looked at the boarded-up plant hulking before them, the many broken and missing windows gaping there like the missing teeth of a corpse.

"We had money in this place," Lucy whispered. "Not a lot. But some. They're over in India now. We sold everything we had in it before they went over. We could have pulled in a fortune but Burt had made his mind up."

"My Deirdre worked a summer there. When she was done with high school. I used to drive her here, every day, six in the morning. She was a different girl then."

"It was all different."

"It was."

"When I was little, there was a pond out here we used to swim in. Now there's just this. It makes you feel like you been robbed, don't it?"

"I guess so," he said.

"That's the feeling I can't live with. Right after Burt . . . it's like I've been stolen from. You know what I mean? It's like I was asleep and woke up to find someone stole an arm or leg from me. And where do you go looking for an arm or leg? Nowhere."

Lucy took another sip from the bottle and offered it again to Jim, who raised his hand, kindly refusing.

"Do you know anything about coyotes?" Lucy asked.

"Some. Not much."

"They're coming inside my fence now. Derrick, he's that high school boy who still works a couple days a week, he said they took two lambs. Dragged them right out into the woods."

"They aren't too hard to get rid of. All you need is to tighten your fences, find out where they're coming in, and set a few traps. We can come by and do that for you whenever you like."

She turned to him, her dark eyes staring him right in the face, her left hand moving up to touch the crags of his cheek, the other still holding the bottle. It felt like Jim's heart had maybe stumbled off the edge of a cliff. There in the shadows of that failed business concern, in the widow's passenger seat, he felt like he was going to faint, the heat of the sun through the car's windshield making his forehead sweat, his lips sticky from the blackberry schnapps, his left shoulder and hand not numb but tingly as it was the appendage closest to Lucy, her face, her chest.

"Well, I guess we oughta head on . . ." was all Jim got out before he felt her mouth against his. She was fast, this one, her lipstick smearing upon his lips, her teeth clinking gently against his own, her hands quickly finding his. She was leaning over, setting the glass bottle between the two seats, beside the parking brake. She was acting bold, unbuttoning her rayon blouse, and Jim, his hands feeling like they had grown ten sizes, fumbled for her breasts, finding only the hard wire of her brassiere. Everywhere he turned, her mouth was already there, and then she was sliding her left hand, the palm and fingers unfairly soft, down the front of Jim's jeans. He felt his breath go, like the wind had been knocked from him, wondering what he was supposed to do next, but in that moment, Jim—the silent, lean-faced chicken farmer, the former MP and frequenter of a few Pusan whorehouses—found his ability to attain an erection, like his optimism, like his once wavy hair, was gone, gone, gone. There was nothing to be done about it, no matter how quickly she kissed him or where. Below his waist there was just a dull ache, the feel of her fingernails tracing an arc around his uncooperative privates. When—after a few more minutes of smiling, then laughing, then her face growing a little sour—she saw that what she was tangling with was more of a medical impossibility than simply the shyness of a man unaccustomed to someone else's touch, she slipped her hand back out from beneath his waistband and placed her palm flat against his chest.

"It's been a problem," he muttered.

"Are you sure? I don't mind . . ."

"No ma'am. I should have warned you."

"We could . . ."

"No, I better get on. The boy will be waiting for me and I got a horse back home that needs to be fed and a couple chickens too, I guess."

"Are you sure?"

"Yes ma'am."

She nodded, buttoned up her blouse, and turned to stare out at the factory's broken shadows. He had hurt her feelings somehow, not meaning to, but he had hurt her deeply, he knew that now, and wished he had had the sense or the guts to never have climbed into her car.

"How is that horse of yours?" Lucy asked, giving the key in the ignition a quick turn. "It's a quarter horse, isn't it?"

"Yes ma'am. She's fine. Raced against one of Bill Evens's two weeks ago and won."

"Bill Evens? He's awful smooth. You better keep an eye out for fellas like him."

"I got faith in our little mare."

"She sounds like a sleeper. I grew up riding horses, you know."

"I didn't."

"You ever ride her?"

"No ma'am. One of my farmhand does. She's too fast for someone who don't know how. To be honest, the idea of climbing on top of it makes me a little sick to my stomach. We set out there and watch her run, though. That's enough for me."

"That's a shame," she said flatly. "She being a racehorse with no other horses around. They're pack animals, you know. They do much better in pairs or a herd."

"Well, we try not to let her get lonely. I've been thinking of maybe getting a goat for her. Keep her company."

"Well, I won't keep you," she whispered, pulling up beside the curb on Main.

"About them coyotes, ma'am? Would you still like us to come out your way?"

"I don't know. You all have done enough for me already. Jim Dooley was just out there the other day fixing my septic tank."

"Well, I believe I got a few traps laying around. It wouldn't be any trouble. You name the day."

"I hate to burden you."

"How's tomorrow afternoon?" Jim asked.

"Tomorrow afternoon it is," she said with a little smile.

Jim opened the car door and climbed out, then turned and leaned in through the open window. "Ma'am?"

"Yes, Jim?"

"About that other thing?"

"What other thing?"

Jim stared at her, her dark eyes now shaded by a pair of sunglasses. Somehow, without him even noticing, she had touched up her lipstick. He looked away quick, understanding it had all been a mistake and nothing she wanted to mention or hear talked about again.

"We'll see you tomorrow, ma'am."

The station wagon pulled away, rattling as it went, its muffler sparking along the pavement. Jim looked across the street and noticed that the screen door of the Bide-A-While had been propped open. He glanced down at his watch and saw it was already past four o'clock. He straightened the white cattleman hat, made sure his shirt was buttoned, and then moseyed across the street, his constitution upended, his whole body in fierce need of a stiff drink.

The arcade at the truck stop a few blocks from the town square was the only place that had both *Galaga* and *Centipede*. They were old-school. They were the real deal, from when video games were about the future. The future when people would just be brains. Everything now seemed like it was being made for the jocks at school. They were all about guns or cars. Because outer space was for little kids.

And nerds. The boy, Quentin, had no problem admitting he felt like both. He stared down at the overly simple, blockish shapes, smiling, seeing that none of his top scores had been beaten on either machine. There were a couple of truckers, he had seen them playing before, who were pretty serious about *Galaga*. They were a lot older than him but remembered the game from when it had first come out. It didn't matter, because these two machines were his, his high-score nickname *QQQ* glowing brightly at the top of each of their electronic registers. The boy turned and shoved his crumpled-up dollars into the change machine. Three dollars would give him twelve games, which he had more than enough time to play. He turned his headphones up as loud as they would go, the bass causing the Walkman's small speakers to vibrate, Biggie shouting, *"Catch me if you can like the gingerbread man / You better have your gat in hand,"* the white spaceship darting back and forth along the bottom edge of the arcade screen, the angular insects making their march forward. Two truckers, both of them with greasy-looking ball caps atop their heads, one with a reddish beard, the other leaner, stepped over from the tiny diner to watch.

"I seen this kid play before," the tall one said. "He can play the hell out of this game."

They stood over the boy's shoulder as he jerked the joystick back and forth, tapping the *fire* button feverishly. One line of insects after another disintegrated in tiny puffs of smoke. There were the red and yellow honeybees, the red and pink butterflies, the greenish-looking mantises. When a boss Galaga swooped onto the screen, trying to capture his ship, the boy quickly dodged its blue-green waves, hiding in the corner until it was safe.

"Dang," the one with the red beard muttered. "This boy is like Rain Man."

"He is."

The boy smiled, tapping the *fire* button again and again, the reflection of his two admirers making brief, ghostly shapes along the surface of the screen. When he had finished his first game, only using three quarters to get to the thirty-second level, finally biting it on the challenge screen, he turned and nodded at the two men standing nearby.

"I can put your names under the high score if you want me to," the boy said. "I'll do it for thirty dollars."

"What?" The two truckers looked at each other, completely confused, then smiled back at him.

"I'll sell you my high score. For thirty dollars. I can put your name there instead."

The one with the red beard laughed, the other shrugged his shoulders, and both said that they were not much interested in having their names recorded as the best players at *Galaga*. Quentin pushed his glasses up against his face, then went back to his game, dropping another quarter, capturing the top three high-score positions entirely for himself, entering *QQQ* each time, glancing over his shoulder to see if maybe the two truckers had changed their minds. But they hadn't.

When he saw it was almost quarter to four, he purposefully crashed his spaceship three times, killing himself and ending the game. And then, like a gunslinger, he strode away from the tiny truckstop arcade out into the shallow, vanishing sunlight. Though his headphones were still blasting Biggie's rhymes, he was almost certain that the two men were standing behind him, watching him go, talking to each other, wondering what his real name was.

What the grandfather tended to drink when he came to town was beer. Two beers, in bottles, always Miller Lite. He had rarely failed to order the same thing, every Saturday, for the last thirteen or fourteen years, ever since the boy and his mother had appeared one day, squatting on the front steps, a single suitcase and a paper sack full of clothes at their feet, both of them looking dirty and scared. Since then, he had made it point to drive into town at least once a week, whether for supplies or simple escape.

But today he asked for a shot of Crown Royal. Gordon the barkeep smiled, staring down at the already uncapped bottle of beer in surprise. Gordon was a leather-faced old-timer with a patch of closely cropped white hair, cut exactly the same way it had been in the navy nearly fifty years before. His arms and hands were covered in age spots and brown moles. A blotchy tattoo of an eagle perched on an anchor was fading to a blue smudge along his right forearm.

"Whiskey? But I already popped the top on this one for you."

Jim sighed, wiping the sweat on the back of his neck with a white handkerchief. Somehow the handkerchief smelled like her, like magnolia, and something else, syrup or sugar water, he wasn't sure what.

"A man's got the right to change his mind once in a while," the grandfather said.

"You don't want the beer then?"

"I'll take the shot of rye like I said."

"Well, you don't go changing something like that, just like the weather. You sure you don't want this one?"

"Gordon."

"Jim."

"Do you got a shot of whiskey back there or not?"

"I do, but I'm wondering if I might be a little too superstitious to serve it to you."

"They serve drinks at the VFW still?" Jim asked, picking up his hat.

"Not until after six. So I guess you're stuck with me until then."

"Are you going to serve me or not?"

"I haven't decided yet. Is everything all right out your way?"

"It's fine."

"Well, if I wake up tomorrow and the moon's where the sun's supposed to be, I'll know why."

"Fine, fine, just pour me my drink."

Gordon turned, sought out the bottle, poured a generous amount into a filmy shot glass, and then slid it suspiciously across the counter to Jim. "We got peanuts too," he muttered.

"I don't care for peanuts. You know that as well as anybody."

"Well, I'll tell you, seeing you drinking hard liquor, I don't know what I know anymore. I'm wondering if I'm having one of them, whatdoyacallit, out-of-body experiences."

"It's not likely."

"You got a reason to be drinking hard liquor? Is it an anniversary or something? Maybe I shouldn't be joking." He squinted at the grandfather and then spoke in a tender voice: "Is today the day you lost Deedee?"

Jim heard the name out loud and a nerve as raw as winter sprung in the corner of his eye like he'd been stung by something. He stared at the amber liquid before him, closed his eyes, then flung it back. It burned all the way down, turning to heat near his chest, landing at the bottom of his stomach.

"Nope. Just wanted a change of pace is all."

"Well, you're entitled to that. As much as anyone, I guess. How is everybody out your way? Your grandson heading back to school?"

"Supposed to go back in a week. All he does now is sit up in his room listening to his music and playing the video games. It's a chore to get him to raise a hand to help, but he does. I don't know what kind of future a boy like that is gonna have. I'm thinking he oughta consider joining up. The army, I mean."

"These army boys today, they don't got to worry about nothing. They get sent to Germany, Japan. They got nobody shooting at them, nobody looking to do them any harm. We got rid of all the bad guys and now these soldiers just sit around playing pretend."

"He ain't got the meanness for it. He cries to see a peep get sick."

"You don't say."

"He takes after his mother in that way. His grandmother Deedee too. She would sob if a sparrow fell."

"Well, they ain't like us anyway. The world's a different place now, that's for sure."

"That it is."

"You want that beer now?"

Jim looked down at the empty shot glass and shook his head. "I'll take another one of these if that don't send you into a spin."

Gordon smirked, surprised once again, and slid the glass into his palm. "You drinking to remember or drinking to forget?"

The cigarette smoke from the rest of the bar seemed to curl about Jim's head, the cloud of it reflected in the mirror behind the rows of glass bottles in the half-light of the bar. He did not answer, just gazed down at a cut on his left thumb and noticed that the jukebox was playing a song he used to know by George Jones and Tammy Wynette. They sang raucously, *"Our Bach and Tchaikovsky is Haggard and Husky . . ."*

Gordon poured a second shot and slid the stubby glass across the counter. "I said, you drinking to remember or drinking to forget?" Gordon repeated, proud of his own cleverness, which, in this particular atmosphere, was not a feature he could always show off.

"Neither one, I guess."

"You just in a drinking mood then?"

"I guess."

"You mind me asking how's that daughter of yours?"

Jim considered the question and the liquid before him, like a glassful of honey, its surface serene and still. "You'd have to go over to Gary if you want an answer to that one," he muttered, tossing back the shot.

"She's over there now, huh? You think she'll come back for her boy and bring him to live in Gary with her?"

Jim, feeling the tremendous warmth extending all the way up from his belly, just shook his head, his thumb resting on the rim of the empty shot glass.

"Well, you're a right-kind fella in my book for taking him in. A fella of your age, expected to look after some young person whose own mother don't have the time. You're a better man than me. My girls bring their kids around, and after a half hour I've had my fill. You say you thinking about getting him to join the military?"

"It's a thought."

"Sounds like a losing battle," Gordon said. "Either way, you still be worried about him."

Jim nodded, once again in silence, not wishing to engage Gordon on the subject any longer.

"You want that beer now?"

"All right."

Gordon dug into the cooler under the counter and found the bottle that had already been uncapped. He set it before Jim with a grand gesture, even going so far as to slide a paper napkin underneath it.

"So how's that horse of yours?"

"Fine."

"*Fine,*" Gordon said, mocking Jim's curt answer. "Someone gives you a racehorse and all you say is fine? Is that all?"

"We haven't had much of a chance to run her. Busy with the chickens like always."

"Heard she beat one of Bill Evens's a few weeks ago."

Jim grinned. "She did."

"Bill Evens, that's mighty rich company."

"So they say."

"You plan on racing her again?"

"If the right situation came up. Sure."

"Right situation, huh." Gordon gave a quizzical look. "You never found out who sent it, did you?"

"Some lawyers back east. It's part of some settlement. That's all we ever heard."

"Well, I sure do like your luck. I do. Nobody ever dropped off a racehorse at my place."

"You don't ever know. You're still young."

"That I am," Gordon said, grinning ear to ear. "I appreciate you noticing."

"Couldn't help it. Wouldn't nobody but a young person talk a fella's ear off while he's trying to drink."

"How do you like that? I always thought you come in here for the conversation."

"I come in here to be alone," Jim said, smiling now, though speaking the truth. "But someone always ends up hassling me with a pile of questions."

"Well, there's an empty table over there," Gordon said, his feelings obviously hurt. "You can be my guest."

Jim lifted the beer from the counter and stepped over toward the empty table. As it turned out, the whole place was empty except for an ornery-looking couple muttering threats to each other over their watered-down mixed drinks and a boy, not older than twenty-one, twenty-two at most, playing the digital poker machine. The kid seemed to study Jim's face for a moment, then glanced back down at the game.

Jim paused at the jukebox, pulled a dollar from his wallet, slid it into the machine, and commenced to search for the Tammy Wynette song that had just been playing. Gordon strolled toward the end of the bar and called out, "A fella gets himself an expensive racehorse and then walks around putting on airs," to no one in particular. "It's a shame is what it is. An honest-to-God shame."

Jim found the Tammy Wynette song, which was named "(We're Not) The Jet Set," and punched in the number, B-31, then again, then a third time, the jukebox lighting up brightly. He turned, ignoring Gordon standing there, and took a seat at the table, nodding a hello to the kid playing computer poker. The kid, from beneath the bill of his dirty hat, nodded back, his eyes narrow and uncertain.

"You sure you don't want us to order some caviar?" Gordon called out, mopping the bar's counter with a dirty blue rag. "I'm sure they got some down at the A&P."

"The beer's fine, Gordon," replied quietly. The song started up again, and he tapped his boot along it.

"You would think a fella coming in here for the last ten, fifteen years would be kind enough not to rub his glad tidings in your face," Gordon cackled to the empty seats before him. "But then you'd be wrong. Some people, they come into wealth and they change."

Jim took a tug from the glass bottle of beer and checked his watch, already tired of being hassled. Besides, it was near five o'clock, or at least it was close enough for him to forfeit the songs on the jukebox and the nearly full beer. He stood, pushed in the chair, and made his way up to the bar, wallet in hand.

"How much do I owe you?"

"Who, you? Mr. Moneybags over here? Daddy Warbucks?"

"Yeah. Daddy Warbucks."

"How about a thousand dollars and we'll call it even?"

Jim sighed, staring down into his wallet. "Gordon, what do I owe you? I got to meet the kid."

"One-fifty for the beer. Two each for the shots. That makes about one thousand by my figuring."

Jim fumbled for a fiver, then a single, set them down on the bar without further comment, and turned toward the door, Gordon's laughter echoing all the way back into the streaming daylight.

Afternoon giving way to a purple dusk. The town a wasteland, a desert. Three spent dandelions, their rounded white blooms bowed beneath the arcing sun, growing from between the upset pavement. The red, white, and blue debris of a bottle rocket blown up against the rusty metal gutter.

On the way toward Main, the boy pondered what else he could do to scrounge up the thirty dollars he needed to purchase the pair of waterborne lizards. Other than robbing a bank or the donut-and-pie shop—the only place in town where anyone still ate—he couldn't think of anything. He walked along the sidewalk, his snowman-shaped shadow stretching before him and to the left, the headphones whistling with Biggie's rage, "*Nigga, you ain't got to explain shit / I've been robbin' motherfuckers since the slave ships.*"

He mouthed the words along to the music, the sentences themselves feeling hesitant and small. Then something flew at him from the corner of his eye. In a moment he felt a clod of dirt hit him on the side of the face. He glanced over his shoulder at a shabby-looking A-frame house, the spot where the dirt had been launched. There were two small boys, shirtless, wearing rubber Halloween masks. One was a Devil, the other a Dracula. The Devil had a second handful of dirt at his side; Dracula was holding a pair of nunchakus in a threatening manner. They were maybe eight or nine years old, both of them wearing blue jean cutoff shorts, their skinny white chests bare.

"Hey, O.J.," the one in the Dracula mask called out.

The one in the Devil mask hit him on the shoulder with the patch of earth but Quentin only shook his head.

"O.J.!" the boy wearing the Dracula mask shouted, his red mouth armed with gigantic white fangs. "What you doing here, O.J.?"

"My name's not O.J.," the boy finally said.

"But you're black. You're a nigger."

"I'm not a nigger. I'm not black."

"What? You're not black?"

Quentin looked away for a moment, a red splotch of embarrassment spreading across his shiny face. "I'm not black."

"What are you then?"

"I'm Italian."

"What?"

"Forget it," Quentin said.

"The police gonna get you," the boy with the Dracula mask declared, leaning against the white fence. "I'm gonna tell them you're black, and then they gonna get you."

"I don't give a shit." And then borrowing a line from Biggie, "I kill cops for target practice."

Both young boys looked at him, stunned.

Quentin started walking again and then paused when he saw the boys' mother step out quietly onto the front porch. "Randal, who was that?" she asked, folding her arms across her chest. Quentin did not turn back to glare at her, only shuffled on like an outlaw in his own mind, the steady thump of the bass and drums marking his unstoppable forward momentum.

* * *

Gilby stole inside the adult bookstore, Private Pleasures, the glass door banging behind him, a faint buzz ringing out, the sound of which had once been something like a bell but was now a sort of electronic gasp. *Leg Show. Barely Legal. Creamers. On Golden Blond. Dirty Lancing. Jurassic Pork. ET, the Extra Testicle,* the box covers and magazines all agonizingly slick, glowing in a Plasticine haze. Freddy Saps was behind the counter, a giant of a man with large bifocal glasses. He was sipping from a Big Gulp and watching the Detroit Tigers on a small black-and-white television set. He nodded silently at Gilby, taking a long draw from the bendable red straw.

"My brother been in here?"

Freddy nodded again, arching his eyebrows and tilting his head in the direction of one of the private booths. Gilby glanced over, feeling a little conspicuous, a nettle of red bumps rising along his neck. Whistling, he approached the two doors at the rear of the store, marked with the gold-plated numbers *1* and *2*. He peeked over his shoulder once more, scratching at his itchy neck, and then, with some hesitation, knocked on the first door. There was no answer. He knocked again, heard what seemed to be a handful of quarters fall to the floor, the sound of a pair of pants being jerked up, a belt buckle being tightened, followed by two quick steps before the door swung open. His brother's face was splotchy and red, the way it looked when he was embarrassed or mad about something. It looked like his nose was running too.

"What the fuck do you want?"

"I got something."

"You got something, huh? You got a dick in yer ass is what you got."

"No, I got something, man."

"I oughta blacken your other eye."

"Go ahead then."

The older brother sniffed, his nostrils flaring large for a moment, as he inspected the bruise he had made on his younger brother's face. The sound of a porno flick still running on the close-circuit television echoed in the background. Some person unleashed a low, deep-throated moan, the kind someone undergoing a major operation without the luxury of anesthetic might let out.

"You're a runt is what you are," the older brother decided, sniffing again.

"What I got to say is important."

"I bet."

Gilby glanced around once more. "It's money."

"What money?"

"Money."

"What kind of money?"

"A couple thousand. Maybe ten. Got to be."

The older brother squinted, his nostrils still flaring, glanced up at the front counter, at the empty aisles and glossy covers, and seeing that they were alone, he led his brother into the private booth. Originally, the booth must have been a bathroom, as there was the mounting for a sink and the remnants of cut pipes. A small color television was bolted to the wall, in front of a rough-looking vinyl chair. In the corner was a garbage bin, a box of tissues sitting above it on a narrow shelf. There was his brother's jacket and a pair of black gloves lying beside the chair. What his brother was doing with black leather gloves Gilby did not know. He took everything in, and just then noticed that the flick his brother had been watching featured an enormous black man with a preposterously large dick. He had on a white cowboy hat and was, with his penis, aiming at a target of some kind.

"What are you watching?" Gilby asked, amused, but his older brother was not having it.

"Mind your own business. Now what the fuck do you want?"

"I was in the bar down the street—Mr. Peel came in and sent me home early."

"Make your point or leave me to my considerations."

MARVEL AND A WONDER

109

"I'm getting to it." Gilby glanced up and saw two women tied to a tree, naked. The cowboy, outfitted with a holster and chaps, found them and immediately began to take charge of their happiness. "So I went to the Bide-A-While because it was early and there was nobody but the old-timers inside. I was playing that poker game and then I overheard Gordon behind the bar talking to this guy, this old one, and they start chatting about this old fella's horse, how it's a racer, but the old guy ain't got the time to run it. Someone he didn't even know gave him the horse, and it's a racehorse just sitting out there all by itself, and there's nobody out there but the old guy and his grandson, this half-nigger kid that comes into the store all the time, and I don't know, all of a sudden, I thought of you, I guess."

"Yeah, what about me?"

"How it might interest you and all."

"How the fuck would you know what interests me?"

"I don't. I just was . . . I was just . . ."

"What?"

"I was just thinking is all."

"Thinking, huh."

"Yeah."

"Say what's on your mind."

"I was just thinking . . . we could take it. I heard they got a fancy trailer out there. All you'd need to do was lead it to the trailer, hook it up to your truck, and drive off."

"What the fuck do you know about it?"

"What do you mean?"

"All you know about that kind of thing is what I told you or what you seen on TV."

"That ain't true."

"Really."

"I've done all kinds of stuff."

"You're soft, Gilby. You run when you get scared. You're candy."

"You don't know about me."

"I don't?"

"No, you don't."

"I know you don't open your eyes when you fight. I know you ain't hard enough to go through something like stealing a horse without crying to Mom."

"Fine. Forget it. And fuck you."

"Fuck you too, candy-ass."

"You're the candy-ass."

"Really?"

"Really. You fuck men."

"Say that again so I can stab you."

The older brother reached over and got his hand on his younger brother's throat. Gilby gagged and sputtered.

"You ain't nothing but a child in this world," the older brother said. "You're all talk. You say you're gonna cook meth for me. You're a hot-air balloon, Gilby. That's how you always been."

"I don't care what you say," Gilby muttered. "I heard you crying the other night. You ain't as hard as you act."

"What you heard was the prayers of a lost soul coming to grips with the failure of the American dream."

"What?"

"If you ever cracked a book you'd know what the fuck I was talking about."

"You think just 'cause they made you get a GED, you're some kind of professor. I don't think you know half of them words you throw around."

"That's the plague of ignorance you're describing."

"I'm leaving," the little brother announced. "You got too weird. California made you somebody else."

The older brother's face went soft then. There was something in his eyes, an unsteadiness in the pupils, that showed just how frightened he really was. "I think you're right. I think maybe I got bit by something out there."

The younger brother smiled uncertainly, the grin hiding behind his unshaven face.

"What kind of horse is it?" the older brother asked, turning serious.

"I don't know. Some kind of racehorse. Thoroughbred or something."

"And there ain't no one on that farm but the boy and the old man?"

"No. They out there all alone, off Route 20. They might as well be on the moon."

"You know the way out to their place?"

"Yep. I been out by there a couple times. It's on the way to the lake."

"Okay, little brother," the older brother said, smiling. "Show me."

Jim stood on the corner, feeling as if he were at sea. Now he was tipsy. He found the boy waiting near a pair of train tracks that hadn't seen a working locomotive in six or seven years; his grandson had his headphones on and was nodding along to the music, the boy's shadow lengthening before him in the afternoon's dim light. The town's buildings stretched away from the sun in brief shadows, dividing the street into several parallelograms of lusty darkness.

When they climbed into the cab of the pickup, the grandfather wondered if he ought to ask the boy to drive home but he was feeling a little steadier, so he inserted the key on the red plastic Indiana-shaped key chain into the ignition without trouble. He started it up and listened to the eight cylinders hum. The fact that the pistons' capacity was judged in horsepower—*horse power*—made him smile. He thought he ought to tell his grandson this, and other things—like how at that very moment he'd decided that the white mare would one day be the boy's, not just part of a meager inheritance to be divided equally with his often-absent mother, but the boy's alone, as there was nothing else—not the land nor even the chickens themselves— that would provide much in the way of a future life worth living. He wanted to tell the boy how the horse would have to do, as it was the only thing of value the old man had to offer, and how the two of them standing there, watching the animal run in the morning or at night, was the closest he had been in a long time to not feeling like a failure. Because he was certain the boy's mother would try to sell the place as soon as he was in the ground, and spend whatever paltry sum she was able to get for the land and equipment on the useless entanglements of her various maladies, which would be only the latest in her lifelong adventure of mistakes, and he wanted the boy to keep the horse if he could; and if he couldn't, then it would be all right to sell it too, if that was what the boy wanted, though again, the grandfather hoped the boy would not. He hoped the boy would hang on to the horse for as long as he could.

All these things flashed through Jim's mind as he listened to the blue pickup driving through the approaching dark. He even opened his mouth to tell the boy some of these plans, his lower jaw unclamping itself to reveal the still-startling white teeth, but then, thinking on it a little longer, he chose to let the fading colors of dusk—pearl-blue and pink and red—fill the empty cabin air with their own kind of conversation.

The sign along the right side of the road exclaims: *Phantom Fireworks. Shelton Fireworks, Home of the $3 Artillery Shell. Pilot Fireworks. USA Fireworks. Holiday Fireworks. Mr. Fireworks. Wild Bill's Fireworks. Patriotic Fireworks. Fireworks City. Boomtown Fireworks. Woodpecker's Mulch & Landscaping & Fireworks. Indy Fireworks. Uncle Sam's Fireworks. American Fireworks. Dizzy Dean's Fireworks. Victory Fireworks. Sky King Fireworks. Dirt Cheap Fireworks. TNT Fireworks. Fireworks Depot. PYRO VALU Fireworks. Fat City Fireworks,* the flat white billboard bedecked with a red firecracker, an exclamation point, a cartoon explosion.

By the time they arrived back home, it was dark. He parked the pickup at an angle and climbed out. The grandfather and the boy did not go inside the darkened farmhouse. Instead, they led the horse out of the lean-to and tied it to the snake-rail fence. There they combed it and brushed the small brown burrs from its white legs. Quietly the grandfather set a hand upon its gray muzzle, staring at it. It was sort of like gazing up at the sky, or down a well, or arriving at church before anyone else had got there; you could not help but contemplate the steady, profound beauty of this animal, standing only a few feet away on the other side of the fence, to consider its flawlessness and shape.

Once it had been curried, they turned it loose, watching the horse's long legs and smooth, rounded hindquarters spring and return, spring and return, in a staggering kind of symmetry, appearing utterly mechanical. The grandfather grinned, watching it go. The boy smiled in return, then glanced back as the horse drove past again.

After a half hour, after the sun had fully departed, they led the mare back inside its stall, replaced the bolt-through slot, and drifted toward the house. They ate their TV dinners at the kitchen table, occupied by their own thoughts, lapsing into a silence that lasted the duration of the evening.

Inside the red pickup that Saturday night, the two brothers drove west toward the highway. Then they slowly braked and turned down the long rural drive, the dust rising high, clearly visible even at this time of night, one a.m. About half a mile farther, they switched the headlamps off, the two brothers silent within the darkness of the cab. The truck began to slow along the fence line, and pulled to a stop along a culvert. One body climbed out, then the other, one slow and shiftless, the other rife with agitation. Someone had a pair of binoculars. They passed them, one to the other then back again, and listened. There, right beside the dilapidated metallic chicken coop, was the silver trailer. The tumbledown stable. The squared-off pasture. The two shapes stood there for a moment longer, staring, no words being spoken. One body followed the other back into the cab. The truck pulled around, driving off, its headlights snapping awake. The night air contained clouds of mayflies even though it was nearly September.

At dawn the horse was quiet within its stable, the morning light streaming through its mismatched slats. For a moment the animal looked golden, its mouth nuzzling the open palm of the grandfather's hand. A sugar cube disappeared from his wet fingers. "Hello, old girl," he said, leading her out. He filled up the water trough and raked out the manure, then petted its muzzle, feeling the animal's breath against his warm palm. Then he led the animal over to the paddock and watched it make abstract patterns beneath an advancing sun.

By seven a.m., Jim had made a second pot of coffee and considered the work they had to get done—clearing the western field, counting and candling the eggs, feeding the birds. He walked across the kitchen and poured himself another cup. The boy had now woken up and was standing in the doorway, in a black T-shirt and blue pajama bottoms, looking troubled.

The boy hung his head low and announced, "I require thirty dollars." The words hung in the air like a cloud of gnats, buzzing with a certain irritation all about Jim's ears.

"Thirty dollars? What for?" the grandfather asked, but there was only a stony silence as the boy apparently did not care to answer. This morning he had on a black T-shirt that said *Slayer*, with skulls and knives and other ridiculous illustrations on the front—chains and sobbing angels and pentagrams—drawings that would probably qualify as satanic, though Jim was confident that his grandson lacked both the know-how and temerity to participate in witchcraft.

"I require thirty dollars," the boy said again, still not looking Jim in the eye.

"Is that a fact?" the grandfather muttered. He took another sip from the chipped coffee mug and turned to face the uninterrupted light coming in through the kitchen windows. The fields outside were flush with a magnificent glow.

The boy groaned then, ruining his grandfather's enjoyment of the moment; Jim shook his head and turned back to face the boy still standing there in the doorway. "Son, I want you to answer a question for me before I answer yours. What is my name?"

"Sir?"

"What is my name, son?"

"Jim."

"First and last."

"Jim Falls."

"Jim Falls. That's right. Not Jim Rockefeller, not Jim Wool-worth, not Jim Ford, or any other. So what does that mean to you?"

"You're not gonna loan me the money."

"No sir. What kind of fool would I be to loan you money with-out even knowing what it's for? I'd be a sorry case, just like you, without a cent to my name. And I don't care to have that in common with you. Now, unless you want to tell me what it's for . . ."

"I don't want to have to tell you what it's for."

"Well, of course, I can appreciate that. You're a man with your own needs. What I suggest is you head over to the bank in town. You remember you got a checking account we started a few years ago? Go in there and ask them if maybe they might be interested in giving you a loan for something you don't want to talk about. I got a sneaking suspicion that Bob Blair or one of his clerks is gonna ask you the same thing I just did. And if that idea don't suit you, well, you can do what I've always had to do. Which is to go out and get a job and earn a dollar and spend it any way you see fit."

"Okay, okay. Jeesh. It's for a water dragon."

"A what?"

"A water dragon."

"Water dragon."

"It's an animal. From China."

"You sit there and you tell me you want thirty dollars for a dragon from China? What kind of imbecile do you think I am?"

"It's a lizard. It's like . . . a reptile. It's no big deal."

"It's a lizard? Why is it thirty dollars then?"

"It's like an iguana, but it's rare. It spends most of its time in the water."

"You want thirty dollars for a lizard that lives in water?"

"Yes. No. It's called a water dragon. They got them for sale at the pet store."

"Well, I would have guessed as much."

"It's thirty dollars for a pair. A male and female. Gilby there said he can get me a deal."

"Oh, Gilby can, can he? Why a pair? You don't even have enough for one, how do you expect to get two?"

"To breed. All it takes is a cage and a recording of some Chinese music, Gilby says. He said he could loan me a cassette tape."

"To breed? And where exactly are you gonna do this breeding?"

"Upstairs. In my room. Or out in the coop. It's an easy way to make money. Gilby said if I breed them I can sell the babies back to him."

"Oh, Gilby did, did he? Well, I tell you one thing: I wouldn't have those things out there in my coop. No sir. I got enough troubles out there without having to worry about whatever disease those creatures might be carrying. All the way from China, who knows what sickness they might have with them."

"Are you going to let me have the thirty dollars or not?" the boy asked again.

The grandfather did not answer at first, only stood, reaching for the white cattleman hat. He fitted it over the dull gray remains of his hair and said, "Thirty dollars of work will get you thirty dollars in pay."

Thereafter, the grandfather and grandson ran through their list of chores. They began the day clearing the scrub and weeds from the westernmost field. Jim looked at the boy's small, bare hands and asked, "Where are your gloves, son?"

"I don't need them."

"You don't need them? There's lots of weeds and brambles out here."

"Nah, I'm good."

The boy had on his headphones as usual, the clamor of which Jim could hear from ten feet away.

"Did you lose them somewhere?" the grandfather asked.

"No. I just don't need them."

"Well, do you want to borrow mine?"

"No sir, I don't need any gloves. I'm training myself to withstand all sorts of human pain." What this meant Jim did not care to know.

They continued on with that section of field, which, a week ago, when the weather had turned bad—hot, humid, then rainy, the kind of weather that often made for a late-summer tornado—Jim had been forced to abandon. He looked around for his grandson and saw him leaning over a pile of wet-looking tree limbs, which had been knocked loose from the line of nearby oaks, planted as windbreak.

"Get an armful of those branches and drag them over to the coop. We'll run them through the chipper."

The boy pulled the black headphones down over his ears once more and stumbled as he gathered the branches into his arms. Jim started up the tractor but switched it off when he heard the boy screaming. He climbed down off the machine in a hurry, rushing over to where his grandson was holding his left hand, leaping up and down.

"What is it?"

"A snake bit me. I think it was a female cottonmouth."

"A cottonmouth?"

Jim turned and eyed the pile of branches. He hiked up his jeans and kicked at the limbs with the toe of his boot. Nothing moved. He kicked again, moving the pieces of rotten wood with his foot, turning it over. There was nothing, only a few black pieces of mud-clung oak.

"It felt like a snake."

"Here," the grandfather said, handing him the gloves. The boy frowned and put them on.

Jim turned, climbed back aboard the tractor, and started it up. The small circular rearview mirror along the tractor's left side reflected the shape of the boy as he stumbled, dragging a few limbs along the muddy earth, tripping over his own feet. Jim gave the mirror a gruff shove, adjusting it so that the boy's figure was out of sight.

At lunch, after the field had been cleared, after the boy had spilled a full bag of grass seed, after he drank all of his grandfather's coffee, the boy asked, "What about my money?"

Jim smiled, piling a few burnt twigs of bacon upon a mound of scrambled eggs in the middle of the boy's plate. "What money?"

"For all the work I did."

"We still ain't finished."

"But you said—"

"I said thirty dollars of work will get you thirty dollars in pay."

"But you said—"

"We got to pay a visit to the Hale place this afternoon."

"What for?"

"Miss Hale asked for our help. She's got coyotes coming in her fence."

The boy set down a strip of bacon and sighed.

* * *

Out to Lucy Hale's at two p.m., they passed the Presbyterian church which Jim was upset to see had been defaced by graffiti. Fantastic gray circles and lines, what looked to be some manner of gigantic genitalia—near the size of a grown man—filled the redbrick facade. Jim slowed down the pickup as they came along the side of it, taking notice; he glanced over at his grandson, eyeing him hard. The boy was occupied, listening to the noise on his Walkman. The grandfather studied the boy's face, but there was no sign that he had done anything so stupid. His grandson's stupidity was of a whole different sort.

Driving on, the grandfather signaled a turn into the parking lot of the A&P; the boy switched off his Walkman and perked up.

"Where we going?"

"I'm stopping off for an errand."

"What errand?"

"I thought I might bring her some flowers."

"Flowers?"

"Yes, flowers. You ever hear of them?"

The boy began to laugh falsely, a kind of whinnying donkey laugh, smacking the dashboard with a too-wide grin. "I thought we was going over there to do chores."

"We are."

"No. You're going over there to have intercourse."

Jim glanced over at his grandson once more, then drove on, speeding past the entrance to the supermarket's parking lot, a thorny look in his eyes. What was wrong with this boy exactly? Jesus Christ. It was too much. It was enough to get you to consider the limitations of both schooling and religion.

What the grandfather thought as he drove past the slanting wooden gates of Lucy Hale's home was how sad and weepy the place looked. The white paint on the old homestead had begun flaking, the fences were a tangled mess of post and wire, and nothing anywhere—not even a tulip or hyacinth bulb, let alone a field of corn or soybean—had been planted on the hundred-fifty-acre spread. It was a shame. The place had been something when Burt Hale had been running it, one of the nicest little sheep operations anywhere in the state. Now, like almost everything else in the world, it had been left to rot.

Ignoring the flaking paint on the porch, the grandfather, with the boy standing in the shadow behind him, paid the widow a call at the front door. Lucy answered, looking slender in a pair of jeans and a green blouse. She held a cat in her arms, the animal glancing up suspiciously from the comfortable cleave of the woman's chest. Surprisingly, Lucy was all smiles and cheer. What Jim decided he liked best about this woman was both her softness—the softness in her eyes and lips—and her firmness—the firm line of her hip; the whole shape seemed put together as solid as anything he had known.

"We come to take a look at that fence," Jim told her. "And to get rid of those coyotes. I have my daughter's boy Quentin here with me."

"I know Quentin. I had him in Sunday school three years ago," Lucy said, turning a gleaming smile toward the boy. "Hello there, Quentin. You look taller every time I see you."

The boy uttered some intelligible word or sound that would have to do as a reply. He mumbled a little more and then said, slowly reaching his hand forward, "I like your cat. Does he bite?"

"No. He's just bashful is all."

The boy put his hand tentatively near the animal's face, then scratched behind its ears. The creature gave a soft purr, arching its neck against Quentin's hand.

"It looks like you made a friend," Lucy laughed. "Here. You can hold him if you like."

The boy gently took the cat in his arms, carefully rubbing it beneath the neck. "He's a good cat," the boy muttered. "We had a cat once, but then he was killed by a rooster." He handed the cat back to Lucy and stared down at his feet.

"I don't think I've ever heard of that happening before," Lucy said with bemusement.

"It definitely happened. I saw it. It was pretty awesome."

Jim shook his head and rolled his eyes at the boy. "Well, I guess we should go take a look. I was thinking we would poke around the fence line and try to find where they've been sneaking in. We'll set a few traps and see if maybe that doesn't do the trick."

"I don't know how to thank you." Lucy paused for a moment, glancing down at the cat in her arms. "Only if one of them does get caught, a coyote, would I have to go out there and kill it? Because I don't believe I could. I have Burt's gun upstairs but I don't know, if something was caught . . ."

Jim smiled at her, nodding seriously, and glanced over at the boy. "Well, we don't mind waiting around a little while to see what turns up, do we?"

The boy did not answer, only gave a grunt, then pulled his Walkman over his ears. He started heading back toward the pickup truck, karate-chopping at the air with a soundless scream.

Alone with the widow for a moment, Jim immediately grew awkward. He was like a cigar-store Indian, standing there too stiffly. He peered down at his shoes, then hers, then reset the hat upon his head and tried to look for an exit.

"Well, ma'am, I guess we oughta get to it."

"Let me get you a cup of coffee first . . . I'll put on a new pot before you get started."

"Thank you, ma'am, but we brought a thermos with us."

"Okay. Well, how about I put some supper on for you then? For when you get finished? I got a few steaks and a leg of lamb in the deep freeze. You just tell me what time you'd like to eat."

"Deirdre will be expecting us back home," the grandfather stammered, glancing away, the lie coming out slow and easy.

"I see."

"Well, we oughta get to it then. We'll come around back when we're all done. How's that sound?"

"Okay. I'll be here," Lucy said, her eyes cast down, her voice sounding a little disappointed. All of that was more than enough to get him to hurry back to the truck, his weak left leg moving faster than it had in weeks.

Together, the grandfather and boy set to work mending the fence, which, in Jim's estimation, was the real problem, even worse than the coyotes. He dragged the fence stretcher from the pickup while the boy carried the roll of wire. There were eight spans that needed to be replaced. As soon as they had set to work on the first one, Jim noticed the boy had his Walkman turned up as loud as it could go. He heard what sounded like a failing tractor's engine. He finished stapling the edge of the new wire in place and then stood staring over at the boy beside him. "What type of noise is that you're listening to? God almighty, I can see why your brains are no good."

"What?" the boy asked.

Jim just shook his head, dragging the fence stretcher toward the next slack span.

"I was thinking," the boy mumbled. "About Mrs. Hale. Maybe she should sell this place if she can't take care of it."

"Well, I'm sure she'd be obliged to take advice from a financial wizard like you. When your way to get rich is by asking me for a loan."

"I just don't know why we have to come out here."

"Because she lost her husband. And she don't know how to run this place. You think I want to be out here on a Sunday? No sir. But here we are. Because there are things you do because they're the right thing to do whether you want to do them or not. That's what the Lord calls life. I can see from your expression that you don't have the foggiest idea what I'm talking, so you can go on back to your headphones now if you like."

"I think you just want to bone her."

Jim stared at his grandson's face, then knocked the oversize headphones off the boy's ears. "If you don't got anything intelligent to say then don't say anything. And that's a rule you can think on."

The boy was quiet for a long time after that.

* * *

Edward had not slept in days. How many he did not know. Probably since he had come back. The way the moon and sun worked here, it was different, like they were on strings, like night and day were part of a pageant at a children's hospital; none of it was real. California was real. Derek was real. Even the old black-and-white movies they watched together while tweaking on homemade crystal seemed more real than the people back here. This was not even his old room. One of his half-retarded brothers had taken his room over. Now he was forced to sleep on the closed-off back porch, which smelled of turpentine and rust.

From his knapsack he pulled out a ball of tinfoil and found a few specks of meth or angel dust; he didn't know which, couldn't be sure. He licked his finger and rubbed the powder against his bloody gums, the inside of his cheeks. Everything began to burn and it made him wonder if it was maybe just bleach or cleaning powder. He looked out through the slanted blinds and saw the sky turning from violet to the color of a bruise. He scraped the remaining white powder up with his long pinky nail and snorted it with his left nostril. Then he bit nervously at the cuticle; he began to pace again. That's when it happened: the small fingernail came loose, dropping to the floor. He held out his hand, horrified, shaking his fingers, his arm trembling. He pulled on the nail of his index finger and it came loose too, with a sickening ease. He cried out and then crept up noisily to his brother's room, eyes wild with panic.

Gilby was still asleep, beatific as a young girl. His longish hair, his pockmarked face, the length of his dark eyelashes. Edward shoved him with his left hand, shaking him awake. He sat up and blinked, glancing around, asking, "What time is it?"

"Time? Who cares what fucking time it is? Look at this fucking thing. Look!"

Gilby held up the clock radio, saw that it was past nine a.m. He yawned, wiped at his eyes, as his brother pushed his hand right in his face.

"Jesus. What is it? Get your fucking hand out of my eye."

"Look," Edward whispered, face wet with tears. "Will you just fucking look? I knew it. I just fucking knew it." Edward stretched his fingers out before his brother. Two of his fingernails from his right hand—the first and the last—were gone.

"What's happening to you?" Gilby asked.

Edward let out a soft sob. "I'm changing. I'm turning into something else. Look. I got the black mark on the palm of my hand."

Gilby nodded though did not see it.

The older brother stopped crying long enough to announce, "We got to come up with a plan. I don't have much time before I do something terrible."

After they had finished the first three spans, the grandfather noticed his left arm had begun to shake. For a few seconds he felt as if he would fall over. Trembling, he leaned uncertainly against a fence post, his ears ringing. The noise was like a far-off song, something hesitant. He put his hand out for his grandson, stumbling a little against the boy's shoulder, startling him from his own reverie.

"Grandpa? You all right?" the boy asked.

The grandfather did not utter a word, fighting to catch his breath. Finally, the feeling returned to his arm, to the left side of his face, and he found that he could speak again. "I got winded is all. Too much sugar in my coffee."

"You sure?"

For a few moments the grandfather leaned against the boy. Something—some sort of ancient pact, some sort of affinity— glowed in their faces for a moment, and then, just as soon as it had appeared, it was gone.

The grandfather and grandson each took long sips of water from the green hose that had been left unwound along the side of one of the outbuildings. The water was warm at first, then got deliciously cold, the tang of the metal nozzle making it taste like it had come from a well. The grandfather watched the boy drink, the boy's face sweaty, rosy-cheeked, the boy giggling to himself, accidentally spraying his own feet. It was not that he did not love him. *No,* the grandfather thought. *No, it's only the things that make us so different. How far apart we are. That's all.*

By the time they had finished mending the fence line, the sun had disappeared, leaving a smudgy cloud of orange in the western edges of the sky. From the cab of the pickup, Jim retrieved a large paper sack. They walked along the outside of the fence and squatted down beside one of the spans they had just fixed—having found a breech in the wire marked by a half-dozen sets of coyote tracks. A few sheep, curious, yellow-eyed, came up to watch them work. Their wool smelled wet like winter. Jim made a few high-pitched noises in their direction and then knelt down, studying the problem at hand.

"What's in the bag?" the boy asked, but the grandfather didn't answer. He opened the sack and lifted out four No. 3 coil-spring traps, the jaws six inches in length. He wound the end of a short length of chain through the eye of one trap, closed the end of the chain with a rusty pair of pliers, and connected the chain to the nearest post, a few paces away. All of a sudden he got winded again and had to lean against the fence, looking over his shoulder toward his grandson. He pointed with his chin down at the muddy earth.

"Dig there," he mumbled, and the boy set a spade against the dirt and commenced to dig, his face wracked with sweat. Once a shallow hole had been made, Jim leaned over and set the trap carefully inside.

"What about the smell?" Quentin asked.

"Smell?"

"The smell of our hands. Won't they get scared off?"

"They ain't afraid of the smell. If they're coming this close to the house, and they know they gonna find a meal here, the smell of us ain't gonna spook 'em any."

Jim took a handful of twigs and leaves and camouflaged both the trap and chain before moving to the next one, a few paces on. Again, they chained the trap to a post, dug a hole, buried both the trap and chain, and then carried on, setting four traps altogether.

Past seven o'clock and the grandfather and the boy had finished the last of their work. They could hear the familiar commotion of crickets and locusts. Together the two of them marched up to the front door of the farmhouse, Jim taking off his hat to murmur his respects, once again turning down Lucy's offer for dinner, his grandson shyly saying goodnight. They climbed back into the pickup, tired, salt-faced, worn-through. The grandfather did not start the engine up right away. Instead, he sat there in silence, staring out at the field, a few stars so distant they might as well be imaginary. The grandfather leaned over and, out of habit, switched the CB on. The voices—fragile, full of static—interrupted the quiet for a moment before the grandson decided to speak.

"What are we waiting for?"

"We're waiting to see if any of them try to come in. Why? You got somewhere to be?"

"No," the boy said glumly.

"You did good today."

"What about my money?"

Jim dug out the worn leather wallet from his back pocket and searched for a ten and a twenty; his grandson had worked as hard as he knew how, and although he did not show any kind of initiative, he also did not once complain or try to disappear the way he would have a year before. Jim lifted the bills from his wallet and placed them solemnly in his grandson's hand. "This is only an advance."

"A what?"

"We got plenty left to do around the house. You want this money, you got to promise me you'll help before you go back to school."

The boy considered the proposition, staring down at the money in his hand.

"Do we have a deal or not?" the grandfather asked.

The boy nodded and folded the money into the front pocket of his shirt.

"Glad to hear it." The grandfather stared at the boy for a moment and said, "Now lean back there and get my shotgun."

The boy reached over the backseat and lifted his grandfather's gun from its mount—a Winchester Model 12—and passed it across the front seat. Jim switched off the CB, took the rifle in his hands, and checked the magazine to be sure it was loaded.

"What are we doing?" the boy asked.

"We'll go shoot off a couple slugs."

"What for?"

"So she thinks we scared them off. It'll give her peace of mind. Go on. Grab the flashlight."

"Right," the boy said with a wise-looking smile.

Jim was surprised at how happy the boy seemed to be a part of some secret. He stared at the boy's face and then said, without much of a thought, "Anything ever happens to me . . ."

At those words, the grandson's eyes went wild with doubt. "What?"

"Anything ever happens, that horse is yours. I want you to know that. I'm going to tell Jim Northfield to put it in writing."

"But . . ."

"But nothing."

"But . . ."

"We can talk about it later. I just thought you oughta know." He patted the boy on the shoulder and opened the driver's-side door. "Come on now. Let's go finish up."

Once more they trampled through the mud, back along the fence line, careful of their own traps, the air still warm in their lungs and noses. Vapor from the heat of their breath rose between them like apparitions. Jim lifted the gun into the air and fired, shooting twice. Their reports crackled in the air like a storm hovering off in the distance. They walked on a little more. As they approached the third or fourth fencepost, something gave a scream, the sound of which was like a spirit being skinned.

"What's that?" the boy asked, his eyes bright with fear.

"Don't know."

"It sounded like a banshee," the boy whispered.

"A what?"

"An avenging ghost. They walk the night in search of all sorts of evildoers."

"Well, I can rightly say I don't think it's that. Mind you don't step in a trap."

Before they made it to the middle of the fence line, Jim knew it wasn't a coyote. The pale arc of the flashlight in the boy's hand leapt back and forth as they walked, both of them wary not to get too close to the fence, the narrow chains of the traps momentarily visible and then gone again. A few dozen yards from the eastern corner of the property, they could hear it and see it clearly: it was a cat. Its soft white fur was smeared with blood, its eyes wide with panic, its neck broken mercilessly by the trap.

"Damn," Jim mumbled. "Damn, damn, damn."

It was Lucy's cat, of course, its white fur now mottled pink. The cat continued to hiss and wail for a moment while its tiny face wound itself into a horrible grimace, and then, with a soundless twitch, it seemed to give in and die. Jim did not know he could ever feel so old or bleak. He held his hat in his hands, stamping back and forth over the same patch of dirt, cursing to himself.

The boy slid off his muddy jacket and knelt down beside the dying animal, and with his small, unsteady hands, he pried open the jaws of the trap. He wrapped the animal up in his coat and held the lifeless creature against his chest. The look on the boy's face was both ghastly and serious, lit up from the far-off lights of the farmhouse. He was mumbling to it now, some kind of song, though it was no melody the grandfather recognized.

The grandfather and the boy rode silently in the blue pickup, the hour closer to midnight than eleven o'clock. Lucy Hale could not be consoled. Neither the grandfather nor the boy knew what to say—what excuse, what explanation, what promise to offer to get the pale-eyed woman to stop her crying. Finally, after her third round of sobs, they offered their condolences one more time and decided they had no choice but to give up.

Premier Arms. Don's Guns and Cast Bullets. Bradi's Guns, Plainfield Shooting Supplies. Gander Mountain. Elmore's Firearms. Popgun's Indoor Range. Lingle Guns. Bill's Guns. Uebhelhor's Bait and Gun Shop. Cosner's Gun and Knife Shop. Second Amendment Guns. 500 Guns. No permit to purchase a handgun in Indiana. No registration to purchase a handgun in Indiana. No license to purchase a handgun in Indiana. No permit to carry a rifle or shotgun. The billboards flashing past along the side of the highway like the white faces of wandering souls.

The pickup drifted to the dark farmhouse. The grandfather shut off the engine and swung the door open. As they walked indoors, the boy stopped and held out his hand. Jim glanced down and saw the two folded bills—the ten and the twenty. The boy frowned, holding out the money, Jim watching with surprise. Something about the gesture carefully moved the old man. Without a word, Jim took the bills and put them back in his wallet.

Monday morning was a whole new day. The sky was pale pink and blue, the clouds strung up in picturesque rises. It was the last week before the boy had to go back to school, which called up certain feelings of tenderness in the grandfather. He stood over the boy, glancing down at his watch, then up at the drapes, which were blocking out the rising sun, then down at his watch again. 6:01 a.m. He took in the shape of the boy's open mouth, recalling the same funny tilt when he used to come in and watch Deirdre sleep. Something in him went soft and he slowly clodded away, deciding to let the boy have his rest.

He and Rodrigo fed the horse and the birds, then counted the peeps, candled the eggs. The grandfather stood alone in the corn, the leaves as high as his shoulders now, some rising higher than that. He broke off an unripened green ear, pushing the silk and smooth leaves apart, checking to be sure the cob was free of vermin. He loosened a yellowish-gray kernel free with his thumb and placed it on his tongue, enjoying the bright, tart greenness.

At ten a.m., he roused the boy from his bed. Playfully, he dragged the blanket off, then the sheet, the boy moaning, falling onto the floor in his dingy briefs.

"For God's sake, look at you. You're almost a grown man. Get some clothes on."

The boy looked up from the floor and smiled.

Downstairs the grandfather whistled, frying up some eggs and potatoes in a pan, placing them on the boy's plate with an unfamiliar flourish.

Later they mucked out the horse's stable and combed her, giving her coat a wash with baby shampoo, softly rubbing it in the direction of the short fur.

Around noon, the telephone rang. Jim set down his sandwich and stared at the phone suspiciously, then glanced over at the boy. The boy shrugged and gave him an uncertain look. The grandfather frowned, walked over, and wiped his hands on his shirt. By the time he put the plastic earpiece to his ear, the dial tone had already begun buzzing. He put the phone back in place on the wall and stared at it awhile before sitting back down at the table. He tried to finish his sandwich but kept peering at the phone's yellow shape. The thing he did not like was that they could call at any time. At any time they could call now and tell him they wanted the animal back. It was what made life and everything so hard: the not knowing, the never knowing. He waited for the phone to ring again and when it did not, he slid his sandwich across the table to the boy.

On Monday afternoon Bill Evens pulled up in his brand-new Ford, rolling over the grandmother's flowerbed, which both the grandfather and the boy had been dutifully trying to ignore. Bill Evens climbed out laughing, slapping the straw hat over his head. From the passenger seat of the Ford, a lean-looking stranger appeared, dressed in a business shirt and tan slacks, with a face as red as a rummy's. They marched right over to the fenced-off pasture, staring at the mare, while the grandfather wiped his hands on his pants and approached tentatively.

"Afternoon," Jim said.

"Afternoon," came the reply from both men. Bill Evens turned, tilting his hat up, and said, "This here is Duane Rose. He came up from the state capital. He's got some business in Bellwood but I told him about your horse and he'd like to see her run."

Jim glanced at the other man's bright red face and extended a hand. They shook firmly, and the man turned back to study the horse.

"You raise racehorses, Mr. Rose?"

"I do. I heard this one here ran the quarter-mile in twenty-one seconds. That's awfully good."

"She likes to run," Jim said.

"I'd say. How about we set us up a race, your mare versus mine? I got a five-year-old with legs like you've never seen. We all say she's part giraffe."

"When were you looking to race?"

Duane Rose smiled slyly. "I'm in town for a couple of days. Working on that bridge over in Bellwood. How's Thursday night?"

"Thursday night. Where at?"

"How about over at Bill's place? I brought my mare up all this way. Thought we could have a few runs."

"I don't know," the grandfather said. "Thursday's awful short notice."

The stranger grinned, leaning against the fence, his face now looking pink as a baby's in the sun. "Come on. You look like a gambler. It's easy money, isn't that right, Bill? What do you say?"

They shook hands, the three of them, Jim turning to watch them climb back into the manicured Ford. He put a hand on the boy's shoulder and they walked over to the shed, the grandfather whispering, "Looks like we got ourselves another race."

Gilby did not know what he was doing. In the afternoon, he laid on the dirty sofa beside the brown-eyed girl, the baby monitor crackling with static on the end table beside them. Some police show was on the TV though no one was watching it; someone was chasing someone else in the dark.

"What's wrong with you today?" the girl asked. It was the third time she had posed the question, passing the lit joint his way. The thing he liked about this girl was how skinny she was; he liked looking at her and seeing the narrow-looking collarbone jutting out of the top of her shirt. Also, she always had weed and the house where she babysat was nice; he liked to come by in the afternoons, when the baby was taking its nap, and lay together with her on the couch. It seemed like the house was their house, the kid their kid, the two of them grown and married, all the frightening decisions, all the uncomfortable choices already made.

He took a deep hit and exhaled, the smoke jetting out through his nostrils. "Belinda," he whispered, smiling.

The girl laughed, coughing up a mouthful of smoke.

"Belinda," he repeated, enjoying the way her name sounded, like some foreign country, or the name of a castle maybe.

"What?"

"Belinda."

She laughed again. "Jesus. You are being so weird today."

He closed his eyes, laying his head down against her chest. The girl put her hand in his greasy hair, watching the TV for a moment. The monitor crackled again, the baby shifting in his sleep. Gilby kept his eyes closed and moved his mouth over the girl's collarbone, his hands going greedy. He pulled himself on top of her, lifting up the dark gray faded sweatshirt, her bra soft pink, his mouth moving over that too, his eyes still closed, his stubble tickling her chest, his mouth moving down, across the soft white plain of her belly, the invisible hairs there getting wet, the girl not laughing anymore, turning the television set up, as his mouth found the slanted harp of her hips, her kicking the blue jeans off, his mouth edging along the lines of her pink and white panties, the cop show getting louder now—a police siren followed by gunshots, then more gunshots—the girl's hand in his dark mass of hair, his eyes still closed, the girl making the short little hums, eyes glued to the TV, more gunshots, her hips rocking back and forth, him unbuckling his pants, yanking the girl's

underwear down to the end of one of her feet, finding the dampness
there between her legs and putting it in, but slow, trying to go slow,
the girl's eyes still fixed on the television set, the police sirens and
gunshots, slow, slow, slow, then too late, overcome, cumming, her
still watching TV, him shuddering, the baby monitor beeping again,
then fading, the two young people lying there half-dressed, a police
detective standing over a dead body. And then the quiet, the cop
show ending, the girl's hand still in his hair, his head on her chest,
his ear up against the collarbone, him turning to face her, the round
eyes, dark brown, with flecks of gold in them, the next television
show starting, some tabloid program about celebrities, the look on
her face pleased, content but still questioning. Him staring at her,
wondering if he would ever know what it meant to love something.
The way her mouth looked, when she was not smiling, still a kind of
smile. The two of them watching each other for a while, the television loud beside them.

"Can you keep a secret?" he finally asked.

Around seven p.m. that Monday evening, the telephone rang. Jim
set down *An Encyclopedia of American Equines*, pulled himself up
from the sofa, and slowly crossed into the kitchen. "Hello?" he answered, lifting the cheaters from his eyes.

"Mr. Falls?"

It was the female voice again, though he did not recognize it
right away.

"This is him."

"Mr. Falls, my name is Lila. I work in the offices of McNamara
and Holt. We spoke a few weeks ago."

"Of course."

"As I mentioned the last time we talked, there have been some
complications with the will in which you were named a beneficiary.
It's come to our attention that several assets may have been improp-
erly distributed, including the property that was signed over to you."

"The horse."

"Yes sir, the horse. I'm calling because there's been an interesting development. One of the countersuits was recently dropped, which means the horse is to remain in your possession."

"It is." Jim smiled, stunned, holding his hand out against the back of the kitchen chair to keep himself steady.

"I've been in touch with your lawyer, Mr. Northfield, and he suggested I give you the news myself."

"He did?"

"He did. As far as we're concerned, the matter is now settled."

"Settled. Just like that?"

"Just like that."

"It's ours."

"It's yours."

"Ours." Jim leaned forward, pressing the phone closer to his ear. "Do you mind doing me a favor then? Would you be nice enough to tell me where it came from? Who sent it, I mean."

"Now that the countersuit has been dropped, I'd be happy to. It was from an estate up in Boston. The Hollaways. Maybe you've heard of them? They're involved in a lot of manufacturing. They have a soap plant about an hour north of the city. Terrible shame. William and Florence, they were both in their eighties . . . well, there was an automobile accident and . . . apparently, you happen to share the name of a former horse trainer of theirs . . . It seems the Hollaways were great horse enthusiasts."

Jim looked out the kitchen window at the darkening sky.

"Mr. Falls, are you still there?"

"Yes ma'am."

"Are you still listening?"

"I am. It's just . . . well, is this all the honest-to-God truth? Someone made some kind of clerical error and that's how the horse showed up here?"

"It is. Apparently, a mistake was made by one of the lawyers representing the deceased's estate; as I said, I believe it was Mr. Holloway's intention to leave the animal to a man from East Hampton, another Jim Falls. The difficulty we now face is that this other Jim Falls is deceased, has been for some time. So you can see where that puts us. As I may or may not have mentioned, there have been a number of other similar mistakes, as all of this was done rather quickly in order to avoid further legal . . . entanglements among the deceased's children. Their children . . . as you can imagine with an estate that size . . . there have been some disagreements as to . . . It's already taken more than two years to reach this current settlement. To be honest, one missing horse is hardly of value compared to their other assets."

Jim stood, staring out the back kitchen window, then turned away, looking down at his feet. "Well, I guess I'd like to send it back to the family so they can sort it out."

"Mr. Falls, as I've said, mistake or not, the horse belongs to you. You've already signed for it, so, as I've said—"

"But is there someone else I can return it to? Some other relative? If it was all just a mistake, like you said, then you should be able to find who it actually belongs to."

"I can assure you, Mr. Falls, that if any error was made, it's going to be in the best interests of all those involved to remain disengaged from the ongoing legal battle over the remaining properties. Including you."

"Then I'd like to send it back to you if I can."

"Mr. Falls?"

"I wouldn't like to keep something that doesn't belong to me."

"But it does belong to you, sir."

"By accident."

"By accident or not, the papers of ownership have been legally transferred into your name."

He took a deep breath, the sound of which reverberated as static through the telephone's receiver. "Now I'm going to tell you something," Jim whispered into the phone. "I'm going to tell you a secret, if you don't mind."

"No, it's quite all right, Mr. Falls, I don't mind."

Jim breathed through his nose, feeling his tongue go soft against his teeth. "I had a wife that died a few years ago. Three years ago. All this time, I guess I thought she was the one who sent it."

The line was quiet for a few moments after that.

"I'm sorry," Jim said. "I appreciate the call. I do. It's just a lot to think about."

"I'm sure it its. I hope you have a good evening, Mr. Falls. I don't believe we'll be speaking again, so good luck," the voice said, and then there was another long pause before they both finally hung up.

Later Jim made his way to the stable and crouched down beside the animal. Staring at it eye to eye, he put a hand to its muzzle and thought he might cry.

The boy followed him out a few minutes later and asked, "What is it? What's wrong?"

Jim looked up and smiled, blinking a few times. "It's ours."

Before any daylight had shone on Tuesday, the boy had already fed the horse, squatting beside the animal as it ate, petting its long neck and whitish-silver coat. There was a gray-colored marking along its neck shaped like a handprint or a crown. The boy thought: *God the Holy Ghost, God the Holy Spirit.* He placed his palm on its side and felt the short, bristly hair and the warm flesh beneath. "Good morning, my friend," he said, careful not to speak too loud, not wanting to be heard. "Good morning."

Then they led her out of the stable and into the side pasture. Rodrigo put the fancy-stitch saddle on and drove her back and forth along the snake-rail fence, getting her ready for the upcoming race, the horse like some kind of flag, some kind of semaphore, some sign the boy could not make sense of nor decipher—appearing and disappearing before him.

Later that morning the boy was going to empty the trash into the gray bin when he got startled by a dog; it was one of the Farrells's from down the road. A big, black-flecked mutt with front legs wider than its hindquarters, it had snuck into the poultry yard and gotten hold of a hen and was now shaking it by its neck. The boy hated dogs, had feared them ever since he was a child. One of his mother's boyfriends had raised pit bulls, and one of these brutes had bitten him on the arm when he was five, leaving several pink keloid scars along his shoulder. Since then, large or small, the boy felt nervous around them. Now he saw the dog shaking the bird hard, so he deposited the bag of trash and yelled out for his grandfather. The beast quickly dropped the hen and began barking, inching closer as Quentin backed away. A few feet behind him was the snake-rail fence. He shouted again for his grandfather and Rodrigo appeared, poking his head around from the side of the henhouse, holding a rooster by its feet. He spotted the dog and turned the rooster free, then scrambled around for something with which to fend off the animal. He came back with a rake and held it before the dog. The mutt lunged forward, snapping its short jaws, and Rodrigo quickly leapt over the chicken wire.

The dog now bared its teeth, the boy letting out a high scream as he backed toward the split-rail fence. He fell, stumbling over a post, and the dog leapt forward, seeing an opening. The boy pulled himself between the long wooden slats of the fence, his gym shoe getting stuck, the dog catching hold of the sneaker and tearing at it. The boy screamed again, crawling on his hands and knees into the muddy field, the dog snarling at the fence rail, poking its muzzle through. The boy screamed once more and looked up and saw a lengthy oblong shadow; he crawled toward it in his panic, confusing it for shelter. But it was the mare, which had been left in the paddock to eat. The mare reared up, striking out with its forelegs, the dog scuttling back in fright, the horse's fearsome shadow falling upon the lesser animal like the appearance of night, the boy watching, amazed, still down on his hands and knees, the dog disappearing along the path at the east end of the property, the grandfather running around the side of the henhouse, shotgun in his hands, firing twice awkwardly into the air.

After dinner, the boy went off to the woods at the end of the far west field, crawling into a fort he had made of plywood and sticks three or four years before, when he was twelve. Buried under a piece of limestone, inside an old, weathered Lone Ranger lunch box—its paint flaking, revealing the rusty metal beneath—were all his treasures. A useless Zippo. A shark tooth his mother had brought back from a trip to San Francisco. Some girl's blue kneesock he had found in the boy's room after school. A picture torn out from an ancient nudie magazine he had discovered in the basement of an abandoned farmhouse. He glanced through the photos, the paper soft from frequent handlings, seeing a dark-eyed beauty pinning up her hair with a provocative gesture, her faded pink negligee having fallen open. Beneath the pictures from the magazine, there was a school photo of a girl two years older named Belinda Clarke. It had been neatly cut out of the boy's yearbook. In the black-and-white photo, the girl was playing the clarinet with an elegant, wistful expression. Her eyes were closed as if waiting to be kissed. There was something about her wrists, with several of her fingers held aloft, that made the boy feel weak, like he was the trilling sound the girl must have been making. Beneath that, there was a Polaroid of his mother, from when she was twenty: hair blown and sprayed back, dyed an unnatural white-blond. She looked like a model from the magazine rack at the drugstore.

He sorted through all these riches, then added a pencil sketch he had done of the horse, placing the drawing on top of the pile. In the picture the hind legs weren't quite right, and neither were its proportions, but he had captured the feeling, its personality, the horse rearing up majestically in a daunting, protective pose. He studied the drawing once more, folded it up, and forced the lunch box closed.

Quietly, the boy slid the bolt open and crept inside. He did not know if the horse was asleep. Through the opening where the slats of wood met the roof, he could see stars. It was later than he had thought. He rested his hand lightly on the horse's mane and placed his cheek against its bristly coat. The horse stirred a little, the boy setting his hand against his narrow jaw.

"Do you know the future?" he murmured. "Can you tell me what you see?"

The horse blinked its long eyelashes, nuzzling his palm.

"What happens to me? What happens to my mother? Do you know where she's at?"

The horse rubbed its nose against his hand. The boy grinned.

"What about my grandpa? Can you tell me what happens to him?"

The horse snorted gently. The boy petted the animal in ever smaller circles.

"Everything was bad before you showed up. But now you're my friend. You're my only friend. Don't try to leave. If you try to leave, I'll follow you. I will."

The boy closed his eyes and carefully placed his forehead against the animal's neck.

In the night, not quiet, the land settling itself from the day's heat, its loamy fields becoming as dark as the evening sky. It was like some ancient mirror; one meadow coal-black, the other interrupted by the age-old invention of stars.

The brothers timed the drive to the rural road on Tuesday after midnight, calculating how long it took to get to the farm, then how long it took to get from the farm to the highway for their escape. They did it on one attempt in ten minutes, another twenty-one. Each trial was wildly different depending on who was driving. Gilby, the younger, was too cautious, observing the speed limit, signaling with each and every turn. The older brother drove faster but could not be counted on to keep the red pickup in the center of the lane. After some mild bickering, it was decided the elder would drive, though Gilby thought this decision—the first of many—would be their downfall.

Around eleven a.m. on Wednesday, they were giving a hen with a respiratory infection a dose of antibiotics. The bird pecked at their gloved hands, the boy holding the chicken over the wings to stop her from flapping or trying to fly off, the grandfather taking hold of her tiny head from behind to carefully pry open her beak. Rodrigo stood grinning, believing it a better course of action to simply put the dose in the hen's water, though there was no real way to tell if she took the proper amount. The grandfather ignored the farmhand and shoved the plastic syringe deep down the bird's throat, pushing past the bulging windpipe, then squirted the solution in. The bird squawked, dropping feathers, and the grandfather took her by the legs and put her back in her own cage, afraid she might infect the others.

Just then a cloud of dust began to rise along the far dirt road. They were unsure who it was at first. Both grandfather and grandson looked up and saw the gray-blue, foreign-model hatchback zigzagging down the lane, its engine uttering a deathly rattle.

"Who is it?" the boy asked.

"Looks like your mother," Jim said.

The boy watched the hatchback slow in front of the farmhouse, awkwardly sideswiping the blue pickup. Rodrigo shaded his eyes, then shook his head. He walked off, hurrying back to the chickens.

Jim looked over at the boy. Deirdre had driven a decent-sized dent into the passenger side of the old Ford; Jim gaped at it for a moment before walking around the front of his daughter's car. The radio was blaring and she was behind the windshield, smiling or crying, Jim could not tell which. He opened the door and peered inside. Her upper lip was swollen now, and a red mark had blossomed along the left side of her face, both these insults something more recent. Grandfather and grandson, father and boy, stared at the face for a moment more before Jim finally spoke.

"Deirdre?"

She glared up at her father, the blank eyes going even blanker for a moment.

"Deirdre?"

Now she glared at him.

He saw the hatred there in her eyes and something in him went cold. "Quentin," he said.

"Sir?"

"Give me a hand."

The boy nodded. Jim grabbed her under the arms and lifted, the boy taking hold of her feet. They got her up the porch and through the kitchen and then dragged her onto the sofa in the parlor. She looked at them and smiled, reaching out a hand to the boy.

Quentin asked, "What happened to your lip?"

She placed a finger against her swollen face and frowned. "Someone busted it."

Jim was through being angry or sad or even worried. All he felt now was a peculiar kind of embarrassment on his grandson's behalf. The boy stood there observing his mother, only able to glance at her out of the corner of his eyes.

"Why did you come back?" he asked.

"Because," she said. "Because I love you. I missed you."

The boy shook his head. "Why did you come back?" he asked again, watching as his mother's expression became a false, rigid mask. She looked from him to his grandfather and then turned and started crying, burying her face in the sofa cushions.

The grandfather put a hand on the boy's shoulder. The boy wiped a few tears from his eyes and hurried off, the kitchen door banging behind him. The grandfather stood there for some time, listening to his daughter's sobs, then turned and hid in the quiet of the coop.

Before dinner, Jim came back inside and found her smoking at the kitchen table. He took off his hat and flapped it about, trying to force the cloud of cigarette smoke outside. He went over to the refrigerator and removed two small steaks, and then thinking on it, took a third.

"Are you hungry?" he asked.

"No," she said, stubbing out her cigarette.

"Maybe you'd like to cook something for your son."

"He's old enough to cook for himself," she replied, lighting another. "He's in high school. The way you treat him you'd think he was an infant."

"How much would it take?"

"What?" she said, painted-on eyebrows turning to daggers.

"How much would it take? For you to stay out of his life. For you to leave the two of us alone. For good."

She huffed. "For good?"

"For good."

"You're fucking crazy, old man," she said, and gave a sharp laugh. "Ha."

The grandfather sighed and walked over to the larder. In a metal flour jar, he found the roll of cash, bound up with a heavy-duty rubber band. He peeled off four bills, then a fifth, then carefully placed them before his daughter at the table.

Deirdre looked down and scoffed. "You're not going to buy me off with fifty bucks."

The grandfather added two hundred dollars to the pile and said, "You take this and you don't come back. You don't call. You don't even send us a letter."

She narrowed her eyes and hissed, "Are you fucking nuts? What makes you think I'm going to take your stupid fucking money?"

Jim stared at her impassively and said, "You will."

She laughed again, her knee jerking up and down. "You're fucking nuts is what you are."

"Take it."

After a long drag on her cigarette, she said, "Fuck you and your stupid fucking money," with as much venom as he had ever heard, then, placing three fingers down, slowly slid the money into the front pocket of her bomber jacket. She crushed out her cigarette and stood, one high heel slightly bent, the other unclasped. At the screen door she paused, her back to him, and said, "You never gave me love. You and Mom, you were always so fucking stingy. That's why I'm the way I am."

Jim did not look up. "No," he responded, putting a hand on the counter. "If you come back, I'll call the police." Then there was the sound of the door slamming shut, the screen vibrating in its frame. When he glanced up again, there was only sunlight—obscured by the rectangular shape of the door—and the round, distant sun.

At eight p.m., the boy came back, trotted up to his room, and locked the door. It was dark and the constant sound of the cicadas and crickets reminded Jim how long he had been gone. He heard the sound of the boy's music and video games come on, then stood and made his way upstairs. He knocked twice on the door before the boy opened it.

"I'd like to talk to you," Jim said. "Man to man."

For some reason the boy had his Walkman on, while the TV and hi-fi were both blaring. He nodded and took a seat on the bed.

Jim grimaced weakly and sat beside him. He cleared his throat once, then again, then put a hand on the boy's knee. "Your mom . . ." he said.

"Is a bitch."

"No," he said. "No. She's sick. She's gone to get some help. She won't be back for a while. I just wanted you to know where she's at."

The boy sniffled. "I hate her."

"No," the grandfather said. "You love her. We both do. This is why it hurts like it does."

The boy let out a squeal, then a sob, and the grandfather, hands upraised, feeling unsure, pulled him into an awkward embrace. After some time, he patted the boy on the back, then left him and hurried to his room, happy for the dark.

Nighttime once again; the moon one evening larger, a glowing porcelain figure, a knickknack on a cloudless mantle.

There was a gun shop on Route 9 that sold used handguns. The younger brother had no priors and, as it turned out, you didn't need a license to buy one. They drove out by the Burnham bridge, parked down in a culvert, and blew off a few rounds, broken bottles glinting faintly in the dark. It was frightening—the look on the older brother's face—as he squeezed the trigger again and again. It was like he wasn't a real person at all.

After they were back inside the dirty red pickup, after they were headed back to the highway, the younger brother asked, "So when?"

The older brother, Edward, shot him a disapproving look and held a finger to his lips.

"Fuck that," the younger brother said. "I need to know when. I got a fucking life too, you know. I can't wait around until you get your head together."

The older brother nodded, glanced back toward the road, then said it: "Tomorrow."

Dawn that morning was a cold one, the fields dewy. The sound of boots on the slick green, brown, yellow grass. The smell of coffee in an old metal thermos. The chickens noisy, their voices the primitive racket of daylight arriving. The horse silent in its stall. The sun like some mythical animal already beginning its western run.

First they candled the fertilized eggs. The good ones he handed to the boy to be put back with the hens, while the bad ones—the quitters which had stopped growing, already beginning to smell a little off—he tossed into the silver bucket at his feet.

Later that morning, they mucked the horse's quarters and fed her, then Rodrigo tacked up. He turned to the boy and asked, "You ride again?" but the boy only shook his head shyly.

"Go on," the grandfather said. "Give it another try."

"I can't."

"Why not?" the grandfather asked.

"I'm scared."

"That's no reason. I'm scared of plenty of things. I still got to do them. Go on."

"Do I have to?"

"Just try."

The boy began to inch away but Rodrigo put an arm around him and helped him up, left foot into the left stirrup, his right leg swinging awkwardly over. On top of the horse he looked less like a child. Rodrigo gently led the horse along the fence line. The farmhand made a few kissy sounds, keeping the horse calm.

"How does it feel?" Jim asked.

The boy smiled nervously.

"Let her run!" Jim shouted.

"Now we go," said Rodrigo, giving the horse a pat on its hinds. Then the animal was alive, a kind of curious machine, bounding forward, the boy doing everything he could to stay in the saddle. They were going so fast he forgot to be scared, feeling himself blinking out tears, the animal galloping beneath him, wind whipping in his eyes.

Afterward, Rodrigo helped him down. Though the boy walked stiffly, his legs and groin sore, he was still smiling ten minutes later, his grandfather patting him on the back, his breath coming hard.

"I love her," the boy said. "We are like brother and sister. I'll never let anyone ever take her away."

Jim glanced over at Rodrigo, who smiled back.

They ate lunch early, the boy spreading the bologna sandwiches with a thin layer of mayonnaise before setting the plate in front of his grandfather. As they ate, Jim stared at the boy's features once again and asked: "Did I ever tell you about the first Fourth of July I spent over in Korea?"

The boy shook his head, eating around the crust of his sandwich.

"No? Well, when I was over in Korea, I would get homesick. My mother used to send me letters, photographs sometimes, news about the farm, people in town. Once it was Fourth of July and our jeep broke down along this supply road and so we had to spend the whole evening hiding in a ditch. We had a bottle of GI gin, stuff the soldiers used to make themselves, and we sat in the jungle all night waiting for a convoy to come pick us up. It got dark and we could see the lights in the sky; I thought they were mortars at first, but my partner, Stan, he said they were fireworks. The GIs made their own. They were pretty, but it was strange to see them in some other place. The kind of houses they had over there, the kind of trees, it didn't look right. It made me feel strange, seeing those fireworks. It was the first time I felt like I belonged to anything. To a country. I couldn't see it until I was over there."

The boy chewed thoughtfully on the corner of his sandwich.

"I don't know why it is the way it is," the grandfather said.

The boy set down his sandwich, quietly contemplating the grandfather's words.

Jim went on: "You did a fine thing today. You were afraid but you got up there anyway."

The boy smiled.

"You're figuring out what it means to love something. Because when you love something, you got to be ready to give up everything." He patted the boy on the shoulder and wandered from the room.

The boy glanced out the kitchen window, seeing the shadow of the horse as it quietly grazed in its paddock, stretching out upon the ground.

On Thursday, both brothers woke up late. It looked like their mother had finally decided to go to work. So they both slept on through the morning, undisturbed, one in his bed, the same bed he had known for as long as he could remember, the other curled up fetal-like on a sofa infested with fleas, abandoned on the screened-in porch. They did not wake each other, but somehow, perhaps through telepathy, the kind of which is known to develop between siblings, twins, or participants in phenomenally disastrous events, they both tottered over to the kitchen table, a silent argument then arising over the final contents of a box of Cocoa Krispies, the younger brother, Gilby, having to settle on Honeycombs instead. Before their bowls of lukewarm cereal, they went over the plan: They would each have a gun. Or only Gilby would have a gun, as Edward had already done a stretch in the pen, and if circumstance or dumb luck intervened, and the duo happened to get pinched beforehand, etc., etc. Or they would wait until midnight, when the old man and the boy would be asleep. Or one would wear a mask and knock on the door of the house and keep the inhabitants at gunpoint while the other tended to the horse and trailer. Or they would both wear masks and tie up the old man and the boy—less of a chance of something going wrong that way. Or they would simply pull up in the truck, hook on the trailer, lead the horse inside, and drive off without having to use any guns at all.

"Don't be stupid."

"You don't be stupid."

Gilby looked down at his cereal bowl, a ribbon of yellowish sugar swirling beneath the remainder of milk. "And then what?" he asked, afraid to look his brother in the eye.

"And then we drive off."

"When?"

"Tonight. We take off. I already made a couple phone calls. I'm waiting to hear back from a friend of mine who lives outside of Lexington. We get the horse, drive it down there, drop it off, come home. Mom won't even know we're gone."

It was true. Even if Gilby didn't want to admit it, his older brother almost always had some kind of plan.

There was a faint squeaking and groaning on the stairs, the sound of their youngest brother, high school age, in his stockinged feet, clambering down the steps. The two brothers shot each other the same look, both of them glaring down at their near empty bowls of cereal, the baby-faced Walt scratching his rear before he belched and took a seat at the table.

"What are you faggots up to?" he asked, pouring himself a generous serving of Honeycombs.

They walked the mare up into the trailer. The boy made whispering sounds, keeping the animal quiet. They threw the door closed and locked the bolt into place, and as the three of them were climbing into the front seat of the pickup, the boy asked, "Do you think she'll win?"

The grandfather looked from the boy to the farmhand and shared a bashful smile. "Did you ask her?"

The boy nodded.

"Well, what she say?"

"She said she likes to win. She said she'll win every time we race her."

The grandfather smiled. "Do you believe her?"

The boy nodded.

The grandfather grinned wide, slapping the boy's leg hard, and said, "That's good enough for me."

On Thursday evening, the mare seemed to run faster than ever. There was a crowd of nearly forty onlookers gathered in the hot aluminum stands with three other horses running: Duane Rose's cobalt-colored mare, its legs splaying out like stilts; Bill Evens's black, long-necked gelding; and a buckskin stallion from over in Gypsum. After the starting gates were flung wide, the white mare pulled out two lengths ahead, then three, dust rising beneath its hooves, pink nostrils flared, the orange-helmeted jockey hanging onto the irons for dear life. She came in at 19:76, and the grandfather, the boy, and Rodrigo leapt into the air. Duane Rose dropped his cigar and almost fell from his seat.

"We got to get this horse down to Indy," Bill exclaimed.

"Indy? Heck, she should be over in Oklahoma or Kansas," Duane Rose grumbled. "You got no business running her around here. What you need is a proper trainer."

"What you need is a manager," Bill Evens corrected. "Somebody who knows the ins and outs of the business. A genuine sportsman."

The grandfather smirked. "Have you got anybody in mind?"

"I'll get you to one of the futurities. Or Los Alamitos. I'll make you and your grandson there rich."

JOE MENO

Jim smiled, but did not answer at first, tilting his hat from the setting sun. He put a hand on the boy's shoulder and said, "We'll have to see about all of that."

Later, the grandfather divvied up the winnings—$2,500—half in cash, the other half made out in a check, handing $500 to Bill Evens for his jockey and the use of the track. The rest he stuffed in his pockets, front and back, putting a hundred of it in his left boot like when he was an MP back in Korea.

On the way home, they pulled into the town of Dwyer for an ice cream. There had been a Tastee-Freez that was now a Dairy Queen, and the three of them sat in the cab of the pickup, licking the soft-serve, grinning goofily at each other. It was late, past ten as they drove back, and the lights of the highway made the grandfather squint, causing his smile to appear even larger.

Then they dropped Rodrigo in town. The grandfather put several loose bills in the migrant's hand. They drove on, the boy beside him, the radio blaring an old cowboy song by Gene Autry.

The pale-blue truck passed the large wooden fence just before eleven o'clock—turning up the final curve of the drive—the grandfather and the boy having remained silent the rest of the ride home. Jim backed the trailer into place beside the awkward-shaped stable, switched off the engine, and climbed out. The boy followed, unlocking the bolt, sliding it free, and carefully walked the mare down the ramp. The grandfather unhooked the trailer from the hitch and parked the pickup near the house. The boy dawdled near the shed, saying goodnight to the horse, and then headed inside. The boy and the grandfather grinned at each other once more, standing in the kitchen, the grandfather sorting out the remainder of the winnings on the kitchen table.

"Pick one."

"What?" the boy said.

"Pick a bill. Any one."

The boy smiled and reached out for a twenty, then seeing a hundred, picked out a Ben Franklin instead.

Both of them climbed the stairs, the boy first, then parted in the hallway with a shared nod of their heads. The grandfather fell into his bed, sleeping more soundly than he had in some time. The boy sat down in front of his video games, turning his headphones down low, dispatching all manner of foes with a renewed interest.

At half past midnight, the boy thought he heard a car door close. He flinched a little, thinking of his mother, and removed his headphones. He pulled himself up and off the floor and parted the dust-covered drapes slightly. Parked askew in front of the chicken coop was a dirt-flecked pickup, in the dark looking more purple than red.

The boy waited to see his mother fall out of the passenger-side door. Instead, when the doors opened, he saw two men, one with dark hair, one wearing a mask, the masked one walking over to the stable with a profound sense of urgency, the other, the dark-haired one, glancing back at the farmhouse again and again.

The boy flew down the hall and gave his grandfather a heavy shove, the old man coming awake with a groan.

"Sir."

"Mmh."

"Sir?"

"Huh."

"Grandpa. Somebody's outside. By the horse shed."

The grandfather sat right up, bare feet hitting the cold wood floor.

Down the stairs and peering out the kitchen door, they saw the red pickup parked beside the chicken coop, the odd shapes of the strangers moving there in the shadows of the stable like figments from their imagination. "Stay here," the grandfather said, and slowly opened the screen door. But the boy did not obey. So they stepped outside together, the grandfather switching on the front porch lights, the glow tracing the outline of some kind of motion—the shadows of shoulders, legs, hands—drowning out the features of the strangers' faces. "Stay here now," the grandfather said again, and this time the boy listened. The grandfather hurried down the back porch steps and pulled the driver's-side door of the blue pickup open in a flash, reaching behind his seat for the shotgun. He switched the safety off and came around from behind the shadow of the old blue truck, gun upraised, taking aim at the figures in the dark.

It took Jim a good moment or two before he understood what was happening: somehow they had already rigged the fancy silver horse trailer to the red pickup. Someone was leading the mare from the rickety stable, its blue-black eyes flashing in the glare from the headlights; up the silver ramp it went, right into the trailer. The grandfather held the shotgun before him, stunned for a moment, only watching; the one leading the horse was wearing a black ski mask, and a sidearm had been shoved into the back of his pants; the masked stranger now turned and saw the old man with the rifle pointed at him. The second intruder came out of the stable, dragging a sack of oats. Seeing the lights on the porch and the old man standing with his shotgun pointed before him like a divining stick, the intruder's face became a rictus of shock, the mask having been placed on the top of his head like a hat. In that moment, both the grandfather and the young interloper suffered the same odd pang of recognition, the young man pulling the mask down over his face, dropping the bag of oats at his feet, the first one shoving the trailer gate closed, locking it in place with the bolt, taking his time, just as coolly as he pleased, then turning, grabbing ahold of the pistol at the back of his pants, lifting it to take aim, the old man seeing the gesture but not believing it.

The grandson, screened behind the haze of the glowing porch lights, recognized the familiar face, the same one he saw every Saturday—scruffy, unwashed, goateed—the face quickly disappearing beneath the folds of the black fabric mask, the boy opening his mouth to shout something, the grandfather already taking aim at the older brother, then pulling the trigger, feeling the unsatisfying stillness of the weapon in his hands, the stock not thundering backward into the soft padding of his arm, thinking, *The dog . . .*

that dog. I used both shots scaring away that dog. The slower-moving one, the older brother—saw the surprise on the grandfather's face, the shotgun in his hands not firing—and raised his pistol eye-level, then fired. The sound of a single gunshot. The boy screaming. The grandfather falling, his white hat flung back. The two strangers hurrying around the side of the trailer to the idling pickup. The doors torn open, one by one, the two of them climbing inside in a rush. The red pickup speeding off, its taillights glowing bright, then fading, the silver trailer rocking a little over the bump at the foot of the drive; the boy having leapt off the porch at the sound of the shot, the grandfather's body lying in the dirt like a felled tree, all stiff-looking angles, fingers splayed open, bloodshot eyes staring up at the cloudless sky; the echo of gunfire still ringing in the night.

Out on the highway the night became a town, a fortress, a structure of fluorescent radiance, shadow upon shadow, light upon light: the billboards, the signposts, the unconvincing trees, the weeds, the abandoned cars, the startled animals, the sagging wire fences, each becoming the beams and joists from which a complete city materialized. The city was cyclopean in its dimensions: a city tremendous in its bleakness, a city staggering in its quiet. They were lost in this nameless world of night and no matter what speed they drove, what direction they headed, they still could not outdistance it, nor find its boundaries. An anxious throb of dread filled the cabin. The tires spun. The radio antenna rang back and forth along the right side of the hood. It was not the darkness now but the emptiness of the land that was so terrifying, stretching out forever in all directions beyond the limitless, unseen horizon, so that the late hour was not only the numbers flashing there on the dash but a place, as real as any town, state, country, extending in front of them; humid, stormy with the inexhaustible current of late-summer static, heat lightning splitting the black sky every few moments, then growing calm again, the taste of rain in the air but none coming. The wind through the open window was no comfort; it was warmer than they had hoped or expected, the sound of it rattling the panes of glass, winding itself along the contours of their agitated bodies, striking their screwed-up faces, one more irritation, making it impossible to keep a cigarette lit, the worry of which caused the older of the two to curse, finally rolling up the driver's-side window in a fit and a fury.

In the darkness, the hood of the truck would flash from red to black for a moment, then back again, as they passed under the highway lights, crossing beneath an overpass, heading away from some unwelcoming exit, the miles on the speedometer ticking up, the hulking, insistent shape of the trailer behind them giving them the feeling that they were being followed.

On and on, the infrequent blur of a vehicle passing in the opposite direction drew out the vague shapes of faces, hands, limbs in the skeletal figures of solitary trees, fence posts, and highway debris. Every thirty miles or so there was the expression of the younger brother, white, tightened around the mouth, appearing and reappearing, the shocked look of a plea welling up in the eyes—the plea being ignored, then rebuked by the older brother—the truck hurtling itself farther and farther away.

Indianapolis. The lights and structures of tall buildings, houses, backyards, streets, cars moving back and forth even at this late hour, going on two a.m. The faces of the people behind the windshields of the cars passing by were dark, indistinct. A billboard advertising a new movie. An ambulance screaming past. A child, curled up asleep in the backseat of a station wagon. The sound of someone else's music roaring through gigantic car speakers. Lights in the office buildings, in the houses, red taillights arcing before them. Smokestacks that even in the dark spoiled the sky with dusty smoke, signifying the unalterable presence of man. Cigarette stubs. Beer cans. The detritus of a civilization concerned only with itself. The city rising up before them, with its concrete barriers, metal railings. The shape of it suddenly like a graveyard, the lights the hallowed glow of thousands of unknowable spooks. The skyline captured in the rearview mirror. The return of darkness. Then the eerie silence. Them driving on.

The farmland having been recently harrowed. The plow marks stretching out infinitely in all directions, the upturned earth reeking of musty growth and decay, the fields sodded with manure. All of it like a ripe wound. A fistula of stalk, metal, seed, excrement, and dirt.

An apple core on the dashboard, a crumpled pack of cigarettes, a half-drunk bottle of whiskey, three plastic bottles of Coca-Cola, all purchased from a twenty-four-hour Quik-E-Mart. The songs of Hank Williams, like an accusation, echoing from the AM band, then fading.

Over the plains, leaving the farmlands of Indiana behind, the highway darting past slowly rising hillocks, thatches of woods, the flatland of the Midwest giving over to the slanted, unsteady ground of northern Kentucky. Then farther still, the road signs marking their approach toward Louisville, a smallish city, a half-dozen skyscrapers reigning over a crooked skyline, the billboards promising food and gas and somewhere to rest for a moment but the older brother shaking his head, keeping the accelerator pressed flat with the edge of his boot, the younger brother silent, watching another city pass before his eyes, then the land once again growing flat, the deciduous woods cropping all along the newly paved highway, the radio once more losing its reception, the younger brother listening to the static for a moment, the static the sound of his conscience now, his clouded mind, then switching the radio off, the noise of the truck's engine and the trailer rattling behind them the only distraction to his troubling thoughts.

The guns they had gotten rid of as soon as they were out of town, ditching them in Deer Creek, standing beside the long metal railing, the older brother wiping them down with a red oil rag from the truck, then tossing each one over, watching them vanish into the slowly moving stream.

It was past three o'clock in the a.m. now, going on four, Friday, the first of September, and the cab of the pickup had begun to stink like the cage of two animals, the sweat of their bodies, the unchanged clothes, the discarded wrappers of candy bars and empty soda pop bottles—all gave a particularly unpleasant crookedness to the air inside. The younger brother noticed it and took it to be a sign of the mistake they had made. He lifted the collar of his T-shirt up over his mouth and nose, then leaned his head against the vibrating window, once again trying to sleep.

The older brother drove on steadily, amusing himself with a toothpick.

Although Rick West preferred pussy for breakfast, this was fine, this was all right. He said as much out loud, leaning over the counter at the greasy truck stop; the runny eggs and coagulated sausage gravy and biscuits stared back up at him, looking like slop. The waitress—peroxide blond, black roots, dark eyebrows, fake beauty mark, with smudged lipstick and a man's name tattooed on the side of her neck in blue-black ink—did not seem upset by the remark. She set down the plate, itched at her nude-colored nylon, and went off to refill somebody's coffee. The truckers on either side of Rick—both independent operators—chuckled a little, though not too loudly, as they were regular customers, the little truck stop near the Arkansas–Tennessee border being the only one around here with clean showers. Rick looked down at the plate of food once more, then over at the waitress, and began to dig in, shoveling forkfuls into his gaping mouth, exaggerating his pleasure with a low, vulgar moan. He made sure to keep his narrow, well-trimmed black mustache clean, dabbing at his upper lip with the corner of the paper napkin so as not to appear uncouth. When he let out another moan, the waitress—a big girl somewhere in her forties, a single mother, definitely divorced—

shot him a dirty look, then immediately smiled a little, shaking her head at the man's coarseness. Rick was handsome-looking in a black Western shirt and black jeans, hair slicked with pomade, silver bolo tied about his sturdy neck. Beside him, on the counter, sat a white Stetson hat, the band having recently been replaced. Rick groaned with pleasure again and the waitress rolled her eyes, her smile widening even more. It was the smile, in response to his offensive antics— her eyes half-lidded, partly amused, partly embarrassed—that told Rick West all he would ever need to know.

"You're wasting your time on that one," the large trucker beside Rick whispered. "She got two kids. And a husband in and out of stir."

Rick grinned, turning to see the trucker's face. It was wide and red with uneven blotches. "I appreciate the information," he said, dabbing at the corner of his mouth with the edge of the paper napkin again. "But she ain't my kind," he called out a little too loudly, the words rising above the clatter and din of the other dishes being served. The waitress grimaced, shaking her head, jotting down someone else's order, hurrying back to pick up a hot plate from the line.

When he had eaten as much of the eggs and biscuits as he could—the taste of it piling up like vomit in the back of his throat— he peered down at the check, calculated a generous tip, pulled the bills from his wallet, and offered both the check and the cash to the dark-eyed woman as she floated past. She sped behind the front counter, handed the money and check to the hostess near the door, went and got some elderly couple's drink order, sped back to the hostess who had made her change, then bustled around to where Rick was sitting. She placed the odd dollar bills and change in front of where his two large hairy hands were folded. She began to speed off again when Rick lifted a finger and motioned in her direction. "Can I get a receipt, please? Hate to bother you but I'm on business." The woman sighed, still with a smile, hurried back to the hostess's station, grabbed Rick's receipt, and plunked it down in front of him. He nodded, thanked the woman, finished his coffee, and slid the receipt into his front pocket. Then he stood and approached the end of the counter, where the waitress was now taking a quick break, sucking orange juice through a straw. Rick reached into the front pocket of his dark jeans and then held his hand up to the glittery-eyed waitress. He slowly opened his fingers, revealing a motel room key with a forest-green plastic key chain resting in the center of his palm.

"How about you and I go watch some dirty movies?"

After the breakfast shift was over, Rick knelt above the woman, her hands and feet bound behind her back with nylon—the string having been cut from the motel room's gaudy flowered curtains—a pillow sheet pulled over her head, knotted along the side. He raised his hand back and smacked the woman's posterior playfully, then less so, again and again until it was red, welted, the woman screaming out, the sound muffled by the pillowsack, the flickering light of the cable television casting lurid shadows on the woman's bare skin; there was the sound of some other woman, an actress moaning in pleasure, jerking her head back and forth in nearly the same motion as this woman's own, though the waitress' screams rang out dully with anger and then pain; behind her, somewhere floating above the bed, there was the expressionless glare of Rick West's face, the hardness in his dark brown eyes, a slight sneer on his lips, the flat, enormous hand rising up and down, up and down, over and over again, until it became a fist.

The grandfather lay prostrate on the cement floor of the chicken coop, the birds upset by his presence at this late hour and making their discomfort known, cackling, scratching, fluttering about, though even in his debility he did not once take the flung feathers to be those of angels or any other supernatural power. The two Percocet the boy had brought him were now working to great effect. What ached were his bones, all of them, and the back of his head—which was lying on his balled-up shirt, the firmness of the concrete floor pressing up hard against the base of his skull. The boy was somewhere inside the house again. The grandfather glanced around to be sure he was alone before he tried to turn on his side, letting out a low moan. He placed the first two fingers of his right hand up against the wound on his shoulder. It seemed the bullet had passed clean through the bone and gristle. What he could feel when he felt anything was a dull soreness, as if he had fallen from some great height and landed on his back. When he heard his grandson charging out the back of the house, the broken hinge causing the screen door to slam with its ugly rattle, he tried to steel himself, closing his eyes, breathing slowly and deeply, so as not to frighten the boy again.

"Gramps?" the grandson murmured anxiously, crossing the gravel back lot, then kneeling beside him. "You doing okay?"

The grandfather nodded. The boy checked the wound once more, switching out a bloody dish towel for a clean one. "Dr. Milborne's on his way over," the boy said. "He told me he'd be here before you got thoughtful."

"Huh?"

"I dunno. I asked him what I should do and he just said he'd be here before you got thoughtful."

The grandfather blinked, then turned his head, watching a black-and-white-speckled Silver Sussex, a hen, its red combs angrily engorged, red eyes aglow. As he started to drift off, he began to consider the animal was his own vanity mocking him with its cawing; then he thought perhaps it was his overwhelming sense of defeat; and then finally, as his eyelids went to fluttering, he realized it was the simple, contemptible voice of outrage.

By the time the sun broke, they were one hour south and east of Louisville, on the outer edges of Lexington. They had gotten lost once, then talked to a fellow at a gas station and decided to turn around. There was supposed to be a road sign somewhere marking their exit but they could not find it. They drove on, around the circumference of the small Southern city, the older brother still behind the wheel, his pallid, sweating face growing more and more tense, brown eyebrows pointing down over his glaring red eyes.

"Fuck. This is astounding. This is why these people lost the Civil War. It's in the way they think. Look at it. I mean, they have the psychological predisposition of tragedy. There are no proper fucking road signs anywhere. Why would you need road signs if you already knew you were going to be lost before you got anywhere?"

The younger brother did not respond. He had said very little in the last few hours, his face growing increasingly severe. "This is how they pinch you," he finally had the courage to blurt out.

The older brother's eyes twitched, the corner of his lip too. "You don't ever mention that word again while I'm in your vicinity, do you understand? Do you? I've beaten the shit out of guys for less."

"What?"

"Do you have any understanding about the power of the mind? What you're able to summon in high-stress situations? Example: a hundred-pound woman who lifts her car off the body of her child. Example: an infantryman who saves an entire platoon through a sudden surge of strength."

"That's the same example."

"Example: Mind control. Hypnotism. Telepathy. Certain individuals who are able to communicate with each other through the power of their thoughts, and through these same thoughts they are able to ascertain their own future. I once met a Muslim, inside, who did everybody's fortunes, even the warden's."

"Bullshit."

"What do you know? All you've seen are the same four walls you've looked at since you were a little shit. I've been to the coast, man. I've looked out at the ocean and seen the face of God. The Devil. What I learned is it's the same face, whether you want to believe that or not."

"Whatever."

"Your problem, little brother, is that your whole personality is based on fear of success. You thrive on failure."

"How do I thrive on failure?"

"Example: you're a grown man who works at a pet store. Example: you live at your mother's. Example: you screw teenage girls."

"So? None of that stuff is bad."

"It's all bad, brother. I'd be surprised if there wasn't something more pathological with you. Like a blood virus. Like the failure's infected your brain. The sense of being defeated, I mean. I tell you: I am glad to find I don't share it."

"I just don't want to keep driving around. We got out-of-state plates and all. And you haven't gone under the speed limit since we left town."

"Only criminals do the speed limit. That is a well-known and timeworn fact."

"Ha."

And then, as if they had been summoned directly by the younger brother's worst fears, a pair of cherry-colored lights flashed in the rearview mirror dangling on the side of the truck; a police cruiser galloped to chase speed directly behind them.

"This is a perfect example of the power of pessimism," the older brother hissed, pounding the steering wheel. "I want you to remember this moment for as long as you live. Because it is completely possible to telepathically control your own destiny. Most people only use it in the negative. Like you. So I want you to remember this. Because this, this is why you are who you are," he growled.

"What do we do?"

The older brother engaged the right blinker and began to pull over, the gravel kicking up against the underside of the silver trailer. The pickup ached to a halt.

"I want you to imagine you are already a ghost. Because if you speak, you say anything, even once, I will fucking kill you first."

Gilby slid down in the seat, averting his eyes from the police officer's approach.

"I think you need to behold the power of the enlightened mind," the older brother whispered. Reaching down into his boot, he slowly retrieved a short-handled knife.

The state trooper, a bulky guy with a blond mustache, wearing the familiar mirrored glasses and tan uniform, slowly walked toward the cab, pausing beside the trailer, turning to glance inside, whistling a few bars of some old-time melody. And then he was at the driver's-side window, leaning in with his weight on husky forearms, a charming smile pleating his face.

"Morning, gentlemen."

"Morning."

"Come down from Indiana?"

"We did," the older brother answered, almost too quickly.

"Whereabouts?"

"Indianapolis. Its local environs."

"I was just up there last weekend with the wife."

"You don't say."

"Visiting her family."

"Hm."

"Reason I stopped you all this morning—you're supposed to have brake lights on that trailer."

"Why, Gilby, did you hear? The good man here says that we've seemed to have forgotten to connect the taillights."

Gilby just nodded, afraid to turn his head, certain his brother was going to stab the poor trooper in his neck if he so much as breathed too loudly. There was something wrong, something deeply wrong with him. Ever since California. It was like he was a villain out of some old black-and-white horror film. Vincent Price. Or the other one. Karloff. Whoever played Frankenstein.

"We'll be sure to make the appropriate connections at the next rest stop, officer."

"Don't give it another thought. I'll do it for you right now."

"You needn't put yourself through the trouble."

"Don't be silly. Only doing my job. You mind watching for traffic though?"

The older brother slowly nodded once, slipped the silver weapon into his palm, and leaned over to open the door.

Do not stab him. Do not stab him. Please, Lord. Do not stab him.

The trooper, porcine, was soon on his hands and knees, crawling beneath the rear of the truck, his fat-wrinkled neck pink with sweat, huffing a little as he worked. Cars flashed past every few minutes, their shadows darkening the police officer's face. Gilby decided he, too, would climb out of the truck, for as he watched from the rearview mirror, it was becoming clear that Edward was now making a number of final calculations, trying to decide how to best murder the patrolman.

The trooper was on his back, the fleshy gap of his neck plainly visible, ghost-white, pocked with stubble and some sort of shaving rash, as he whistled to himself, connecting the two sets of wires beneath the rear bumper of the pickup. The older brother was crouching beside the cop, sweating profusely, lost in an argument with himself, chewing his lips. His right hand was clenched at his side, holding the short-handled knife, turning white. A few tears ran from the corner of the older brother's eyes, the pupils darting back and forth, as if he was at the height of some serious prayer. Gilby stood there, hovering beside him, trying to silently arouse his attention, but the older brother was gone, lost in his mind now, the knife twisting at his side, neck muscles straining, nose having begun to run.

"Just one more," the cop muttered, starting on his whistling again.

Gilby began to shake his head violently back and forth, *No, no, no, no,* but either his older brother could not or did not want to see. He observed a single nerve, some vein that had begun to throb at the side of his brother's forehead, turn bright blue, the eyes still tearing up, the teeth busy picking at his own skin.

"No," Gilby finally whispered, but with his soft, helpless tone of voice, he was easily ignored. "Edward . . . don't."

For a split second, the older brother glanced up at him, his face seized by terror, strained by something otherworldly, something possibly demonic, the tears running down his cheeks, the knife now flashing out in the open, bright silver, then dull again, as it wavered in the morning sunlight.

"Almost there," the trooper chirped, his fat neck bulging beneath his formless chin.

The older brother, having settled whatever awful dispute had consumed his thoughts, began to raise the short, curved knife. Gilby, panicked, seeing the vicious intent in his older brother's eyes, trembled there momentarily before finally gathering the spit and words to blurt out, "It's not our horse . . ."

The trooper, with a smudge of grease on his wide, white cheek, squinted, pulling his face into the sunlight. "How's that?"

"The horse. It's not ours."

The blank, outraged glare of the older brother's face, contorted, tortured by confusion, turned on him then, the knife still twisting at his side.

"It's our grandfather's," Gilby murmured, itching at his nose. "We're selling it for him. In Lexington."

"Well, that's awful nice of you. Too bad he couldn't come along. That's one town that loves horses."

"Yeah. It's too bad," Gilby said with a half smile.

The older one was still silent, the knife shaking in his hand, the anxious, alarmed eyes now undecided.

"All done," the trooper announced, clapping the big paws of his hands together.

"We hardly know how to thank you," the older brother muttered, his eyes wet with dirty teardrops.

"Don't mention it. Glad to be of service. It's usually pretty quiet this time of the morning. And if I can find a reason to get out of that squad car, I'll take it. My cholesterol ain't what it should be."

"We will thank you in our prayers," the older brother whispered, knife resting in his hand, quivering at his side.

"No need to do that."

The trooper found his hat—which was kind of like the one Tom Mix used to wear—on the gravel beside him, fitted it over his balding head, and wiped his hands on his pants. He marched back toward his own vehicle, humming the same melody again.

When they got back inside the cab, Gilby cowered up against the passenger-side door, waiting for the hideous rage, the unthinking, instinctive horror to lash out upon him; it was like entering some wild den. But his older brother was strangely calm. He sat there behind the steering wheel, hands at ten and two, his face composed, his movements no longer sinister, the police cruiser honking once as it pulled back onto the highway, both Gilby and his older brother slowly raising their right hands to wave, the police car then disappearing over the sunlit horizon of the southern Kentucky hills. The

younger brother waited, his chest pounding, waiting for the terrible
eruption, the blood-swelled snarl of fist and tooth and fingernail. But
it did not come. The older brother only sat there, shivering as if he
was cold, his shoulders shaking a little, right hand reaching up to
brush away the tears which had slowly reappeared.

"I'm afraid," he whispered. "I am. Something ain't right with
me."

"What is it?" Gilby asked.

"I think I'm turning into a wolf or some such thing."

"You do?"

"Something's in my blood. Something's wrong with me. Nothing makes me happy but seeing things in pain."

"It was being locked up that did it to you."

"No. It wasn't that."

"You done too many drugs."

"No. It's not that either. It's me. It was in me all along and now
I'm finally seeing it. It's part of my nature. Who I am. I wasn't made
for no nine-to-five. I'm what people used to be. Before windows and
refrigerators. I belong in the woods. I've had dreams about running
naked. Running up on animals and killing them. Deer. And rabbits.
It ain't the drugs. It's how I am. It's how I'm supposed to be."

Gilby thought about reaching out a hand across the gray divide
of the bench seat, but seeing his older brother caught up in something tragic, immortal, torn between forces he neither had the sense
nor knowledge to understand, he simply waited, waited for the older
one to regain his composure, the eyes going dry, the hands becoming
steady again, the sound of the engine starting then idling, followed
by the left-turn signal, the wheels making their revolutions against
the gravel once again.

When the grandfather came to, he was coughing. The taste of both
blood and vomit was in his mouth, though he did not remember why
at first. He was on the sofa in the front parlor. There was a crocheted
blanket, blue and white and pink, one of the last things Deedee ever

knitted, laid over him. A girl, no older than twenty, in a white blouse, a nurse, was taking his pulse. He coughed again and then pulled his wrist free from the girl's fingers.

"How are you feeling, Mr. Falls?" she asked, but he didn't bother to answer. With some work, he got himself upright. When he did, his entire head began to throb. The left side of his face—his lip, his ear, his cheek, his jaw, his neck—all of it was stiff. He could feel his left eye watering, the tears dappling his wrinkled chin. Someone had taken his boots off. He noticed that right away. He was in his stocking feet. His pants were off too, revealing the faded white boxers, stained with urine along the left side of his lap. The girl tried to take his pulse again but he shook his head and said, "No need to grab at me like that, missy. I'm still here, ain't I?"

The girl frowned, finding a silver thermometer in the pocket of her blouse. She shook it and then placed it under Jim's tongue. He sat there patiently for a moment. The girl glanced at her tiny silver watch and removed the thermometer.

"One hundred even. You got yourself a little fever. Do you feel feverish?"

The old man coughed once more and remembered his shoulder, placing his right hand against the wound: the whole wing of his deltoid muscle had been bandaged and taped over. "No. I feel like I been shot."

The girl smiled, the old man still poking at the bullet hole. There was absolutely no feeling there, only a kind of hollowness, an echo of some distant, dulled pain. He looked over and saw his jeans had been set on the coffee table. Next to them, on the center of the table, was a porcelain horse-shaped ashtray, a birthday gift from his father some fifty years ago, bought at a Mishawaka flea market. The ashtray—a white statue of a horse rearing up on its hind legs, rising over a concave bowl, having never once been used, not even by the boy's mother—was a close likeness to the missing mare. The old man saw the figurine, saw the shape of the animal being led up the ramp, heard the shot, and felt his heart begin to palpitate with anger.

"Hand me my pants," he said to the girl.

The nurse smiled, shaking her head kindly. "Dr. Milborne was very specific about you getting some rest."

"Hand me my pants, missy, before I get cross. Whoever sent you here was mistaken. I've been taking care of myself my whole life. Go on now and mind your elders."

The girl obeyed, brown eyes wide with trepidation.

The old man hobbled into his pants, pulling them up around his narrow waist.

"You're dismissed or whatever you call it when someone sends you away."

"Dr. Milborne made it very clear that he intended for me to stay with you until he returns this afternoon."

"He drive you out here?"

"No."

"No?"

"I have my own car. It's parked right outside."

"Good. You got a way home then."

"Yes. But I don't think—"

"Thanks for your help. We'll be seeing you."

"But Mr. Falls . . . I think I should call the doctor first."

"You can do whatever you like once you're gone."

"I see. Well, the doctor's going to hear about this."

"I'm sure he will."

"Yes, well, good day, Mr. Falls." The girl packed her tiny black bag, jerked it over her shoulder, and hurried out through the front door.

The boy was eating cereal at the kitchen table when his grandfather stumbled in. Rodrigo was beside him, hands folded on the table; he stood when he saw the old man swaying there. "Mister Jim!" he said, gripping the grandfather under the shoulder. But already Jim was moving around a little steadier now. He was having trouble buckling his pants, but then he did, the silver belt buckle in the shape of an American flag finally finding the leather hole, snapping into place. The grandfather was shirtless and the sight of his own body—pale, blue-veined, a whitish-yellow crop of hair spread across the middle of his chest, the wiry-looking ribs, the wrinkled neck—all of it was the same color as some recently expired animal.

The boy set his spoon down, his mouthful of sugary starch going to mush. He did not swallow. He spat it back in the bowl and jumped to his feet, helping Rodrigo get his grandfather into a chair.

"Bottle," is what his grandfather first stuttered. He pointed to a wooden cabinet above the refrigerator that had been locked for some time.

"But you said never to open it no matter what."

"Go fetch me that bottle, son."

"But you told me not to, no matter what you said."

"This is not one of those times, this is the other kind."

"But you said—"

"Quentin, tote those keys from wherever you hid them and then hand me down that bottle."

The boy slipped out of the kitchen to the parlor, where he opened the front panel of the grandfather clock, found the liquor cabinet keys; he walked back across the kitchen, slid a chair into place, climbed up, paused before putting the key into the lock. He turned to face his grandfather again.

"You really . . ."

"Yes," the old man said gruffly.

The boy slid the key into the lock, opened the white doors, and found a dusty-looking bottle of sour mash sitting there, the seal not yet broken.

"You said this was for when you—"

"I know what I said. You two are gonna have to find some other way to miss me."

The boy climbed down from the chair, tore off the seal, unscrewed the top, and placed it before his grandfather. The old man stared at it for a second, at the amber-colored hue sparkling in the morning sunlight, and pressed the glass ridge to his lips, tilting the bottle back, slowly beginning to swallow. When he finished, the bottle looked a quarter empty, though the boy knew that wasn't right. The old man wiped his mouth with the back of his hand, his eyes stricken—gasping a little for air, the liquor constricting the muscles of his throat—and nodded at his grandson again. Rodrigo only looked down.

"Shirt."

The boy sighed, hurried up the carpeted stairs, grabbed the first shirt he could find in his grandfather's closet—a blue, gray, and black summer flannel—and hustled back down, handing it to his grandfather by its wire hanger. Jim struggled for a moment, trying to get it on, and realized he couldn't, as his left shoulder and left arm were now useless. He had to glance back over at the boy, who read the sorry expression on the old man's face before silently helping.

"Doc Milborne said he'd be back this afternoon. He said you weren't supposed to leave the sofa. He said he was gonna come back with a state trooper."

"Mister Jim, how about we go back to the couch?"

The grandfather shook his head, then winced as he fought to button up the shirt.

"Upstairs. My closet. On the top shelf. The gun. Bring it down."

The boy stared at his grandfather for a moment, heard the curtness, the unfriendly words, and tromped up the stairs again. Jim finished buttoning the shirt with a snarl, fitting the last one through just below his neck, his right hand shaking. By then the boy had returned with the gray-green metal box clanging before him. Jim nodded at the kitchen table and said, "Set it down."

The boy did. Jim leaned in close to study the rolling numeric lock placed just beside the front latch. He sniffed once or twice, then remembered, and thumbed the appropriate numbers into place. The metal box opened with a sharp click. The boy and his grandfather stared inside at the glossy M1911. When Jim began to fieldstrip the weapon, the boy watched his shaking hands working over the tiny pieces, until, only a few moments later, the gun had been reassembled. Once more, Jim ejected the clip, began thumbing in round after round, and snapped the cartridge back inside the pistol's handle. He cocked the hammer back, sighted on a bowl of fruit on the counter, and fired. There was an eerie silence, as the safety latch prevented the gun from suddenly exploding, though Rodrigo's eyebrows still jerked upward.

"That boy," his grandfather said, looking at his grandson now.

"Sir?"

"From last night. That one."

"Yes sir."

"You know him, don't you?"

Quentin nodded, ashamed.

"You know where he stays?"

Quentin nodded again.

"Okay."

The grandfather forced himself to his feet, both of his arms shaking, and carefully slid the pistol into the front of his jeans. Fumbling around through his pockets, he found his truck keys were missing. He spotted them on the kitchen table—the familiar red state-shaped key ring—and clumsily snatched them up. He stared absently for a moment, thinking something over, weighing something in his mind, and then he slowly placed the keys in the boy's soft hand.

"Go get some shotgun shells from the shed. As many that can fit in your pocket. And then go start up the truck. You're driving. Okay?"

"Okay."

They made their way awkwardly outside, the sun resembling a falling comet. Rodrigo, still holding the grandfather under the arm, helped him to the passenger side.

"Mister Jim," Rodrigo protested.

The grandfather steadied himself against the side-view mirror of the truck. "Rodrigo. You're a fine fella. But you're an illegal and the state police might come out this way if they find out what happened. You should go on home now and I'll call you when we get back.

Don't make sense for you to get in trouble on account of us."

Rodrigo frowned, accepting the grandfather's decision, then helped the old man into the truck. He closed the passenger door and said, "Vaya con Dios."

The grandfather nodded to himself as the boy struggled to get the engine to start.

The child was holed up in a cut-rate motel outside of Marked Tree, Arkansas. It was a dingy sea foam–green affair, not part of any national chain, the electric sign out front announcing its drabness in squalid blue light with the single word *Motel*, and beneath it in filthy, red lettering, *Vacancies*. He had tracked the girl here through the Western Union, the child—nineteen, a former beauty-pageant winner, a sometime runway model, the green apple of old Jacob Bolan's withering eye, and sole heiress to the family's sawmill and lumber fortune—had telephoned from an out-of-state area code, asking to be wired a sum of money in excess of two thousand dollars. The grandfather—heart-worn, dyspeptic, himself the survivor of two separate triple bypasses, waiting in bed with the gold antique telephone on his nightstand, a white satin handkerchief in his hand to dab at the drool on his chin—immediately agreed to send the money. An hour later, he nodded to where Rick West stood at the foot of the ornate four-poster, Stetson hat in hand.

From there, seven hours by truck, his a black Dodge pickup, stopping once at the Western Union in Little Rock, discovering the girl had already come and gone, catching a lucky break when the clerk remembered the rail-thin girl, the nervous blue eyes, the fringe halter top, and mentioned they'd asked for directions to Marked Tree, where apparently the girl and her escort—a dupe a few years older, a doorman at a Dallas nightclub, name of Brian—were going to meet their connection. The clerk—an old fellow in a vest, visor, and spectacles, like a telegraph operator out of the Old West—went so far as to show Rick the pad of paper he had written the directions down on. Rick stared at the now-blank page, took a stub of a lead pencil, and slowly began to rub, the hand-drawn atlas slowly appearing on the finger-smudged sheet. A few hours on, finding dawn breaking over the tiny town—at one time a railroad camp, at another time the hunting grounds of the Osage and the Cherokee, bordered by two rivers, the St. Francis and the Mississippi, each flowing in opposite directions—then the dreary work of driving up and down the main drags, the tiny residential homes, the cul-de-sacs, until he spotted the flame-red convertible parked at an odd angle in the begrimed motel lot. It was just past five a.m.

He left the truck in the side lot of a family restaurant which had not yet opened, and doubled back to do recon. Of the twelve or so rooms, only half were occupied. At this hour of the morning, there were only two rooms that were still lit; the bluish-white glow of a television set cast shadows on the green curtains in the first, a laugh track reverberating behind the window with some old comedy show. The other room had all of its lights turned on, a stereo blasting teenage pop music, as if the girl herself was doing all she could to send out the message: *I'm right here. Help me. Please bring me back home.*

Holding his left ear beside the window, he heard what sounded like two or three different voices. He peeked through the split between the curtains and saw the girl's pointy elbows leaning over an atrocious flowered bedspread, her lips curled around a bulbous glass pipe, white smoke escaping her lips. Rick reached beneath the black wool jacket, found his sidearm, switched the safety off, and tapped twice on the faded red door. He could hear everything in the room go still, the absence of breath, and then movement, things being quickly rearranged, items being shoved into drawers, a frightened male voice, a little high-pitched—Brian's—calling out, "Who is it?" and then Rick knocking again, saying, "Room service," or some such ludicrous thing, a befuddled argument then taking place, the girl—Rylee—the purposeful misspelling of the girl's name indicative of what Rick always assumed were deeper family problems, the misspelling somehow responsible for the girl's current sordid situation, or so Rick believed—the girl Rylee saying, "Don't be an absolute dumbshit, they don't have room service here," and yet there was the rattle of the door chain, the lock unwinding. Brian's husky face filled the sudden portal, white, slightly illuminated like a wet half-moon, and then seeing Rick's own long, smiling face—the oblong chin, the scar above the left eye, the thin mustache—recognizing who it was standing at the motel room door, all this way from home, the young man muttered, "Oh, fuck," and stepped back without trying to argue, as the big ones—Rick was forever certain—hardly ever put up a fight.

"Hello, shithead," he grinned at Brian, and then gestured toward the girl. "Get your clothes on and grab whatever you have," seeing she was only in a starchy white towel. There were three gentlemen in the room, including Brian, who was trying to apologize to a dark-skinned fellow—Mexican, or maybe an Italian—and a clod with a red beard, older than the rest of them, with jailhouse tattoos and a leather vest. Rick seized on him immediately, seeing he was the only one in the room worth worrying about, and quickly took aim with the pistol on his skinny chest. It looked like they had only been sampling the merchandise after all.

"Is this shit paid for?" Rick asked, looking down at the large bundle of white, unsure if it was meth or coke.

The biker shook his head, confused by the whole situation but clearly anxious about the gun. "No, we didn't get that far yet."

Rick turned to the girl, who was struggling to put on a pink pair of underpants. "Where's your geegaw's money?"

The girl shrugged, itching her neck. "In my purse."

"Did you spend any of it?"

"Some."

"Get your purse and start walking."

The girl groaned, grabbed her purse, waved goodbye to Brian, and slowly made her way out the door.

Turning back to the biker, Rick smiled broadly and announced, "We're bringing this with us. If you have a problem with that, I suggest you take it up with this genius," and nodded at the shame-faced stooge, Brian. He snatched the bag of product, shoved it under his coat, and began to back out, pausing just long enough to whisper, "See you later, shithead," to the hulking, pasty figure near the door.

The girl was waiting for him, standing in the parking lot, itching her rashy-looking neck. "Where's your piece of shit?" she asked.

"Parked down the street."

"Well, you can come back over and pick me up. I'm through being pushed around."

She tossed her shoes on the ground and crossed her stringy arms in front of her flat chest.

Rick stared at her then, at the daring cheekbones, the high forehead, the glassy eyes, now shot red, the long, elegant neck, the narrow shoulders, the pert breasts. There was a glimmer of powder ringing her left nostril, which Rick quickly wiped away, and in doing so he secretly felt like a parent.

"Pick those shoes up before I kick you in the goddamn belly," he whispered, and began to walk on.

The girl stood there, her arms still folded for a few seconds, then sighing, she reached over, grabbed the vinyl high heels, and began to follow on bare foot.

They were on their way back to Plano, it going on one p.m., the girl sleeping on the bench seat beside him, when the portable telephone—a bulky black instrument, attached to the truck's cigarette lighter—began to ring.

They came to the A-frame house and the grandfather struggled to get out of the pickup. Then he was pulling himself up the whitewashed porch, his left eyelid twitching from exertion. The boy walked behind him, watching his grandfather's advance until he had made it to the top step and was scuttling toward the screen door, which hung crooked on a pair of rusty hinges. The pistol, its black handle rising from the front of the old man's pants, looked comical, completely out of place. *There's no way he'll be able to reach down there if he ever needs to draw it*, the boy thought to himself.

There was a doorbell which had sprung from its socket, a pair of white and green wires trailing from beneath the illuminated button. The old man regarded the switch for a moment before pressing the doorbell, both of them hearing a faint chime, and then quickly, or as quickly as the old man could manage, he took a distrustful step back. There was silence for a few seconds more before the clumsy stomping of bare feet on wood stairs, the noise getting closer, the old man reaching slyly down, placing his right hand on the pistol's handle, the form of some human—a man—filling the doorframe, obscured by the dirty metal screen.

Quentin recognized him immediately—it was Walt, the youngest of the brothers, the one still in high school, the basketball player, taller than the rest of them, but gawky, skinny, wearing an Indiana Pacers jersey and a silver necklace. He stood there behind the screen door eating an enormous bowl of cereal, the silver spoon clanging there against the rim; as he approached the door his jaws worked over a mouthful of Cocoa Krispies. His hair was blond, cut short, and was ruffled flat on one side, which gave him the appearance of having just woken up from an afternoon nap. The cereal and the tussled hair made it seem as if he was younger, or maybe less deceitful than he actually was.

"We come looking for that boy," the grandfather said, his hand still on the pistol at the front of his jeans. "I heard he lives here."

The boy—who was eighteen at most—did not look particularly concerned. It seemed as if he was accustomed to various strangers appearing on the peeling porch, asking after one of his brothers.

"Which one you looking for?" he asked, shoving another spoonful of cereal into his mouth.

The grandfather did not ease; his posture, rigid as an elm, actually seemed to become more tense the longer he was forced to speak. "We come looking for the one who works at the pet store in town. Does he live here or not?"

"Oh, he lives here," the brother said with a chuckle. "Who's looking for him?"

The grandfather sniffed at the air a little, leaning closer still. "I'm looking for him. Is he home now?"

The brother shrugged, dribbling some milk down his chin. "Nah, I don't think so. Neither one of them is."

The old man glanced out of the corner of his eye at his grandson, then quickly returned his gaze to the young man's face in front of him, sizing him up, studying the shape of his mouth, his eyes, his ears; the mouth a little damaged-looking; the eyes squinty, a dullish blue, darting back and forth; the ears oblong, covered in small blond hairs, a little pointed at the top. The grandfather did not like what he saw. He loomed closer against the screen, nearly pressing his face there, and whispered, "We come to look for that boy."

"Well, like I said, he ain't here."

"What's your name?" the grandfather asked.

"What?"

"I asked you how you are called."

"What business of yours is it?"

"I'm asking."

"Well, I don't have to tell you shit," he smiled ruefully.

"It's Walt," the grandson whispered from the steps behind him. "His name is Walt. He's a senior. He plays basketball. He got scouted last year."

The old man nodded. "Now, I'm going to ask you one more time, son, 'cause the next time I'm not going to give you a chance to talk . . . You tell me: is that boy here or not?"

Walt seemed a little worried now. He licked his lips, stood

straighter, glanced over the old man's shoulder at the boy standing there on his porch. "I already told you. He ain't here."

The grandson, leaning against the porch railing, saw the old man's fingers tighten and jerk the pistol free. Without grace, his grandfather shoved the screen door open and held the pistol out. The youngest brother stumbled backward, dropping the bowl of cereal on the floor, the brownish milk spilling across the hardwood, the bowl itself splitting into several shards. He slid as he turned, tripping over his bare feet, hurrying off in the direction of the kitchen, where a plastic telephone hung on the farthest wall, glowing there like an instrument of salvation. The old man marched over the threshold, kicking the porcelain shards out of his way as he approached, his heavy boots striking the floor, his drawn-out shadow hanging above the young man's terror-stricken face. The kid was on his knees, and then with athletic quickness he hurtled toward the phone, overturning a kitchen chair, throwing it in the old man's way; the old man steady, silent, marching past the chair, the pistol still solemnly raised. The kid pulled the receiver off the hook as the grandfather took a final step closer, the muzzle of the gun arcing up against the side of the young man's face. Then the grandfather took the phone and set it back on its cradle. Quentin had now entered the house too, timidly, an observer only, watching from the front parlor.

The old man stared into Walt's eyes for a moment, seeing the shock there, the surprise. "On your feet. Go sit in that chair."

Walt quickly dropped himself into one of the wooden kitchen chairs, tears running from the corner of his eyes, snot gathering along his left cheek.

"What's the name of the one we're looking for?" he asked his grandson.

"Gilby," came the boy's answer.

Jim lowered the gun to his side. "You know where Gilby went?"

The younger brother shook his head.

"You got some idea, though, don't you?"

Walt nodded a little, his face flushing red.

"Who was the other fella with him? You can say that much."

Walt looked away, covering his face with his hands. "Fuck you."

"Now, son," Jim said, taking a step closer, "you seem like a nice enough boy. We only come to find what's ours. Who was that other one with him?"

"Fuck you."

"You got some idea but you don't want to tell us."

"I'm not saying another fucking word."

"Well, I respect that. I know he's your brother. But the other one . . ."

"I ain't saying shit."

"You know him and that other fella, they took something from me. They took something of mine and I intend to get it back."

"Fuck you."

"Fuck you, huh?" The grandfather seemed to pause then, taking a moment to cast his pale-blue eyes over the angles of the kid's face, over the tiny yellow room, glancing from counter to counter, table to refrigerator, back and again, searching for something, some sign, some clue, but finding nothing, the little kitchen grim-looking and untended, dishes piled up in the sink, pots piled up on the stove, a houseplant wilted along the counter. The kid looked unrepentant in the wooden chair, a deep, resentful, prideful gleam in his eyes. It was the same expression of ignorance Jim had seen in young men back in Korea, the same glare, the same arrogance. The pride, the belief in a future that, no doubt, would not, did not exist; it was something Jim knew he would not be able to argue with.

With the pistol still held out before him, but no longer taking aim at anything, the grandfather whispered, "You're a good boy not to go back on your brother. But he did wrong and so he's going to have to pay the bill for it. You don't want to lend to his troubles, I appreciate that. So you tell him, when you see him—if he's got any sense, he'll bring that horse back. You got that?"

The younger brother nodded, the fear gone from his eyes; now there was only the shocked arrogance, the assailed pride. The old man took notice of it again and backed out of the kitchen. From across the parlor, the boy Quentin turned toward the front door, peering down the street to be sure no one had been watching, and noticed a girl across the way, on the other side of the block—in the picture window of another blue A-frame—who was holding the drapes back, eyes wide with interest. The boy did not recognize the dark-haired girl at first but immediately felt worried. He helped his grandfather down the steps, his hand under the old man's arm, escorting him toward the curb, where they both stood silent, defeat filling the air.

The girl, the same dark-haired one, was out on her front porch then, crossing the street, still dressed in pajamas at this hour, a T-shirt and pink bottoms, wrapping a white robe about her shoulders. It was Belinda Clarke. The boy had passed her in the halls the last two years and had placed the yearbook photo of her playing clarinet among his most valuable treasures. She was not fainthearted, nor the least bit shy. She walked right up to the old man, standing barefoot before him and his grandson, and asked, "What did you want with him?"

"Pardon me?"

"Gilby? That's why you're here, ain't it? What did he do this time?"

"Miss?"

"He went off to Lexington. I told him if he did it, I didn't ever want to see him again."

"Did what?" the grandfather asked.

"Took that horse and went off to Lexington."

The grandfather turned toward the boy and smiled for the first time that day.

On and on, the horse bucking its head, nervous in the humid silver trailer, stirring as the highway fled past, stamping its hooves, waiting to be fed. The brothers had not thought to bring water for it and Gilby had spilled its food. They had also locked the gate at the rear of the trailer the night before, and then the next day, around noon, discovered they did not have the key. In the parking lot of a hardware store, somewhere among the outlying suburbs of Lexington, they argued over what course of action to take. The younger said that they should just leave it to its fate. That if they cut the lock off, the horse might somehow get out. He was afraid it would rush toward them and rear up, gauging their weakness with its dark, soulless eyes, and then tromp them both to death. The older, exercising a brief courtship with purpose and rationality, disagreed. If the animal was to die from want of food or water, it would be of no use to them at all. They pooled their resources and bought a twelve-dollar bolt cutter, snapped off the tiny lock, and flung the silver door open wide. The horse huffed a little, stamping in place, the heavy, ripe-smelling fumes of its manure rising sharply in the air. Gilby quickly backed away in fear. Although there was no room for the horse to turn inside the trailer, he thought its rear flanks looked more than capable of destroying both him and his idiot brother.

"What do we feed it?" Gilby asked, now a good ten paces away.

"You go across the street and get it a jug of water. And a pot or bowl or bucket of some kind to drink from. And some oats."

"Oats?"

"Hurry up now."

Gilby dashed across the main street to a small grocery with a faded wood facade, returning some minutes later with the jug of water, a large plastic bucket, and a box of oat cereal.

"How much do we feed him?"

"You finished high school, didn't you? You figure it out."

"I'm not going anywhere near that thing."

Disappointed, shaking his head, the older brother grabbed the box of oats from his younger sibling and made his way up the metal ramp. The horse flicked its gray-white tail a few times and whinnied. Hearing the high womanish sound, Edward panicked, leaping off the back end of the trailer, covering his head with his hands. Gilby began to laugh, slapping his thigh, but then saw his brother's face, which was once more strained with an unquantifiable rage. He quickly shut up, seeing Edward gather himself before once again, with as much coolness as he could muster, he climbed up the silver ramp step-by-step. He carefully extended his left hand, touching the animal's dusty flank, patting it gently, making soft kissy noises as he tried to sneak along its side. The horse stamped once or twice, and each time the older brother froze, closing his eyes, his long nose now dripping with sweat, and then, breathing irregularly, he gently patted the animal again on its back, then along its mane, finally making his way to the creature's snout.

The trailer was musty, hotter than he had expected, and staring eye-to-eye with the horse, he saw that what he had done—causing this thing of beauty to suffer—was damnable, would be the source of a great, lifelong doom. He did not consciously know that he now felt this, only became aware of it in the palpitations of his weak blood.

Tearing the box open, he held the unwashed oats before the animal, watching it begin to snuffle, its soft pink and black lips reaching like a hand into the box, disposing of its contents in a few mammoth gulps. "Tote that water up here!" he shouted, and Gilby, shaking his head, crept up the ramp, plastic bottle of water and metal bucket in hand. He passed both to his brother, who had set down the empty box. He watched as Edward spilled the water into the container. The horse drank avariciously, Edward refilling the makeshift trough again and again.

Together, the two brothers stood there for a few moments, pinned up against the steamy trailer walls, the horse searching around for more food, more water, its smell passing over them both, and also its quietude. The younger reached a hand up, touching its coarse mane, and smiled. "I always kinda wanted one. When I was a kid."

"Sure."

"For Christmas. That's what I'd ask for every year."

"I remember."

"One year she got me the cowboy boots," Gilby said. "That was good."

His brother nodded, staring into the animal's inky black eye.

"She tried anyway," Gilby whispered. "With us, I mean. She tried to do right by us. Just none of us turned out the way she would have liked."

They faced each other then, in the half-darkness of the horse trailer, the white-silver creature growing still as a shadow beside them.

The boy looked like a child behind the wheel of the pickup truck. The grandfather glanced over at him, trying to ignore his left shoulder as it throbbed. Almost immediately, he realized he had made a serious miscalculation, that this, this adventure, would turn out to be a mistake. There were spots of blood on his blue and gray shirt that had appeared from the taped-up wound; the stains made a red-leaf crocus shape that looked to have blossomed with the rising sun.

There was also the feeling in his belly, in his joints, his anus, all of it feeling knotted up, like he couldn't breathe. He glanced over at his grandson again; the boy was driving very cautiously, minding the speed limit, going a good five or ten below it, signaling whenever he was forced to change lanes, his husky shape never more straight than at this moment. The CB was on, and with it the static and infrequent gabbling of voices, this the only noise beside the engine's rhythmic knocking. There was an open AAA map on the bench between them, unfolded to I-65, the long blue line bisecting the state of Indiana. They approached the capital, with its grim, gray-toned skyline and traffic. At this rate, it did not matter how slow or fast the boy drove. There was almost no way they would get to Lexington in time.

"Sir?"

"Hm."

"There's a lot of traffic ahead. I wish you were driving."

"You just watch the speed limit and you'll be fine."

The boy, for the first time in the last two hours, broke his gaze from the road and quickly glanced over at his grandfather. "Gramps?"

"Hm."

"Why didn't you call the state troopers?"

"Because it's ours. And we know who we're looking for. We know who we're looking for and what we're looking for, and they don't. And they ain't got a reason to care about that horse in the first place. If we were to call them, they'd ask whose horse it was and we'd never be able to explain it. Not to their liking. Then it'd be gone either way. So we got to find her ourselves if we want her back. The ones who took her, they ain't smart. They already made a heap of mistakes. The ones they selling her to, they're probably a little smarter. But not much. I know their kind. All we got to do is be as smart as them, which isn't much."

"But you got shot."

The grandfather made a low sound that ended with a kind of whistle.

"Does it hurt?" the boy asked. "Now, I mean."

"Not much. Some."

"You ever been shot before?"

"No."

"Oh."

"I've been stabbed before but never shot."

"You been stabbed? By who?"

The old man shielded his eyes from the sun and glanced away, not bothering to answer the question at first, and then finally, drawing in a breath, he muttered, "It was back in Korea. But that's a long story."

"Oh."

"Watch your speed now," the grandfather said. "No reason to have a run-in with the law if we don't need it. And keep an eye on that fuel gauge. It likes to lie. I'm going to shut my eyes for a minute or two."

The boy allowed himself a second to glance over at his grandfather again; his courage flagged and his eyes shot back to the tarry road.

"Sir?"

"Yeah?"

"I thought you were . . . I thought you were dead."

"Huh?"

"Last night. I mean . . . this morning . . . I thought you were going to die."

The grandfather gathered his weakening voice, tugged down on the brim of his hat, and said softly, smiling now, "Ain't I though?"

The girl was watching him and pretending not to watch. She was going to go rabbit on him, he was sure of it. Rick West peeked at her out of the corner of his eye, then hung up the public telephone located in the parking lot of a rundown car wash. The portable phone in the truck was shit out of state, something with the frequencies or provider or what else Rick wasn't sure. He turned and saw the girl trying

to be coy, acting like she was busy, though the whole time he knew
she was waiting to make a break for it. She was sitting in the cab of
the truck, her feet up on the dash, retouching her toenails with bright
green polish, the color of which bespoke to Rick an unwell mind. It
looked like the color of the sky after a meteor had streaked through
it, fluorescent and otherworldly, and it made him consider that the
girl herself was like one of those satellites, doom-stricken though still
sort of brilliant. He opened the driver's-side door, climbed in, and
started up the truck.

"We're making a little detour," he announced.

The girl snapped her bubble gum and asked where.

"Kentucky. We got to go pick something up for your granddad."

"The hell I am."

"The hell you are."

"You're seriously kidding yourself if you think I'm going to butt-
fuck, dumbshit Kentucky. I'm taking off the first chance I get."

"That is your problem exactly, young lady," Rick said with a
smile, putting the truck into gear. "You try as hard as you can to get
caught. If you wanted to tear out of here so bad, you could've been
gone by now. I was just on the phone for ten minutes. I gave you
about as good a chance as you're gonna get."

"Just watch me."

"I don't intend to do that. You're a grown woman. You need to
attend to yourself."

"Fuck you, dipshit. You think you're so smart. All you do is clean
up after my stupid fucking granddad. You're just like one of his fucking nurses. I'm surprised he doesn't have you wiping his ass."

"You try and make a run for it now, I'll treat you the same way I'd
treat anyone dumb enough to cross me."

"Do you have any idea how ridiculous you sound?"

Rick ignored her, concentrating on finding his way back to the
highway. In truth, he did not care to judge how stupid his threats
now sounded.

As soon as they pulled up to the first stoplight, only a hundred yards or so from the entrance to the freeway, the girl made a run for it. She popped the lock, shoved the door open, and threw herself out. Rick tried to grab her, his foot on the brake, his hand grasping a few strands of hair, but then she was gone, her back a blurry conflagration in the corner of his eye. He had the sense to put the truck in park, hurrying out from his side, and chased her through the parking lot of a dumpy-looking gas station, the girl screaming something as she ran as hard as she could toward the glass doors of the Quik-E-Mart. He got one arm around her middle when she paused to grab hold of the door. Rick heaved the kicking, wailing thing over his right shoulder, the girl pounding furiously on his back and neck with her small bony hands. Then she was biting him, sawing at his ear with those diabolical teeth, the sharp pain of which caused him to tumble sideways, the two of them collapsing on the pavement. He did not think twice when he reached out to strike her. He caught her open-palmed across the jaw, shocking her with the unprecedented violence of the act, the tears welling up in her eyes, her expression not one of pain but incandescent fury.

She sat there like a child for a few moments, unwilling to believe he had struck her, holding her chin where she had been hit, staring up at him with those wild flame-blue eyes.

"My granddad is going to have your head," she hissed.

Rick pulled himself to his feet, dusted himself off, and muttered, "After this, your granddad can kiss my ass," equally surprised as she.

An old man, who had been filling up his camper and who had witnessed the scuffle, now edged near them. He seemed to be sizing Rick up; he slowly made his way between him and the girl, who was still seated on the pavement, pouting.

"I don't know if no one ever taught you the way to treat a lady," the old-timer said. "But this sure ain't it."

"I couldn't agree more," Rick replied with a wide grin. "You find me a lady anywhere near here and I'll be sure to inform her."

The old man took one more step forward, having no interest in backing down. Rick could see the faded blue-black ink of an anchor tattoo on his forearm. He nodded at the tattoo and asked, "How long were you in for?"

It took a few moments for the old man to understand, and then glancing down at his arm, he seemed to remember what the dark outline signified. "Four years. In the Pacific."

For no good reason, Rick pointed at the center of his chest. "I was in for four too. US Marine Corps. Got booted for choking some Filipino half to death. They gave me an honorable discharge though. I got fond memories."

"That's all I got," the old man muttered, his remaining teeth like the jawline of some exotic deep-sea fish. "That girl belong to you?"

"I'm minding her for her granddad. I came up from Texas to bring her back. She fell in with some Mexicans."

The old man turned and regarded the girl for a while. "If I'd known this is how it would turn out, I don't know if I woulda fought so hard. I seem to remember those Jap and German kids seemed awful well-behaved. These ones here . . . well, they don't got the faintest notion."

Rick gave a short laugh and reached out to shake the old man's hand. Then the old sailor trotted off, glancing over his shoulder once more to see Rick heave the girl to her feet. Holding her beneath her left armpit, Rick marched her back to where the black truck was parked in the middle of traffic, pushed her onto the bench, and fumbled underneath the seat for something. When he found what he was looking for, he grabbed the wrist of the girl's right hand, snapped the cold bracelet in place, and clamped the other end of the handcuff to the door handle. He shoved the door closed as the girl began to fuss and curse. Rick climbed back inside the vehicle and started it up once again. The girl went eerily quiet, staring out through the glassy windshield. When she spoke, the flame-blue eyes had become two specks of coal.

"You ever put a hand on me again, I'll kill you," she whispered, and there was no fear now, no equivocation in the tension of her voice. "I seriously will."

Rick aimed the truck onto the expressway, both hands on the steering wheel, tired eyes watching the traffic to the left and right and then directly ahead. His face felt a little flushed. He gazed at her briefly, certain then that the girl meant what she said.

After another hour they decided to park at a state-run rest stop. The drainage from the gunshot wound—which had been begun to ache sharply these last few miles—had soaked completely through the bandages.

"I oughta go change this dressing," the grandfather said, looking serious.

The boy had no idea what kind of pain the old man felt. He climbed down from the vehicle, walked around the front of the truck, and helped his grandfather hobble across the slate-gray parking lot. The old man shuffled lamely into the flat-roofed brick building, and together they sought out the men's room. Inside, the boy got the old man set up in stall.

"It might be a little while," the grandfather said. "Don't wander too far."

The grandson stumbled out of the restroom, into the lobby, and then over to a white-lit vending machine. It looked like all the candy was seventy-five cents. He checked his pockets and found he only had two quarters. He sighed, turned, and saw a number of arcade game consoles—*Tetris*, at which he was an unacknowledged master, Mount Holly having no machine anywhere in town, and the childish, repetitive, meathead-favorite *Mortal Kombat*. He decided at once he would add his name to the high-score roll on the *Tetris* machine, slipping both quarters inside the narrow slot, cracking his knuckles as the screen booted up. A few moments later, already onto the fourth level, he saw—in the brightly colored reflection of the glass before him—someone observing him from over his shoulder. Feeling self-conscious, he craned his neck and saw it was a girl, a fair-looking one, standing behind him. There was nothing remarkable in her face or appearance and yet, simply knowing she was there, his hands became paralyzed. One, then two, then a third block descended from the top of the screen, before he regained his senses, maneuvering them into their proper place, his score immediately doubling.

"My parents told me to come talk to you," the girl whispered, not moving any closer.

Quentin was so shocked by the funny lilt of her voice, as it rung there in the air—the sound containing all the secrets of a girlhood spent in the safety of the suburbs of some Southern city, an entire clandestine world Quentin would never, could never understand, not even amongst the most peculiar distances of his own imagination. Hearing that particular soft, mannered voice, he lifted his eyes from the video machine and turned, the colored blocks onscreen now piling up, the boy immediately forfeiting the game.

"They said I had to talk to you," she repeated.

He faced the girl. No girl had ever said more to him than she already had. In a white shirt and jeans, she was frowning, eyes as bright blue as a bird's egg, hair long and light blond, her skin white and scrubbed. She was taller than he was.

"They asked if you wanted to come pray with us," the girl said.

He glanced over and noticed the girl's parents standing in front of their station wagon, both of them smiling, the father peering over the rim of his glasses, the mother in a plain blue dress, left hand raised in a polite wave. Quentin, having been raised mostly by his grandparents, knew to wave back.

"Do you want to or not?" she asked.

The boy, glancing over at the arcade screen, seeing his game was over, felt cheated but mumbled, "Okay," intrigued by the girl standing there, by the idea of praying with strangers. He followed her over to where her parents were standing.

"These are my parents," the girl said.

The boy nodded at both of them, afraid to look either in the eye. The father spoke in a pleasant voice, like a radio announcer. "I'm David. And this is Jan. We're pleased to meet you."

"Hi."

"You met Denise, of course."

Quentin nodded again.

"And you are?" Jan asked.

"Quentin."

"Quentin," the father said, approving. The boy stared at the man's thin face for a moment and had a flash of what, all these years, he had secretly dreamt his own father might have looked like. "We're glad you've decided to join us, Quentin."

In a small, impromptu circle, the father leaned over and took his daughter's hand, grasping his wife's in his other, Jan, the mom, taking Quentin's hand, the girl, with an expression of minor disdain, taking his left. Each of them save Quentin closed their eyes. The boy now stared at them, at their lack of fear, at their stunning blandness, and felt chastened.

"Heavenly Father, we thank you for bringing our friend Quentin into our lives, and hope he has a chance to experience the wonder and glory each of us have in the service of Your mission, dear Lord. Grant all of us peace and safety on our journeys today. Through Christ our Lord, amen."

The girl let go of Quentin's left hand, the mother still holding his right.

From where he stood, he looked past the father and mother and saw a girl, a year or two younger than the one standing beside him, sitting in the backseat of the station wagon; the girl had long blond hair and skin that was too white, the white slowly fading to pink, the eyelashes white also, the shape of the girl's forehead a little too wide, too prominent, the rest of her body looking small, doll-like in comparison. He gawked there for a moment, seeing the other girl struggling in the backseat. The girl was huffing, grunting, moaning to herself, with an animal ferocity. She was bound up in some kind of special seat with dark blue and black seatbelts holding her in. It seemed like she was having a fit of some kind: her eyes kept flashing open and closed, her head jerking back and forth, her small, clawlike hands twitching before her.

"What's wrong with her?" Quentin asked without thinking.

The mother smiled numbly, still holding Quentin's hand. "That's Clarissa. She's handicapped."

"She looks like she's screaming."

"She has seizures. There's nothing we can do to about it."

The boy nodded, the noise of the girl screaming, twisting there, fighting against her restraints, her clenched fingers scraping uselessly before her, the sound now culling the soft words of their prayer back from the air. Somehow this encounter seemed to describe all the questions the boy had about God.

It was with obvious dread that the younger brother saw the older was no longer fit to drive, or do much of anything. The wheel was loose in Edward's hands, his eyes glazed and rheumy, so that wherever they were headed—an address on New Circle Road—no longer mattered; if Edward was driving they would never find the place, only circle around over and over again in infinite condemnation. It was because Edward had been ruined by the drugs he wanted to sell and was no longer even paying attention. He had been busy the last hour itching his neck until a red welt appeared, glowing there like a second, reptilian mouth. Finally, he announced that he had to find somewhere to piss. Gilby took it as no small relief, deciding he would either convince Edward to give him the keys or not get back in the truck with him.

They pulled into the parking lot of a tiny gas station with a sign that featured no prices for the gasoline it was selling. The older brother hurried from the truck, holding his hands over his crotch, limping toward the bathroom door which was located around the back of the squat, concrete building. It turned out the john's only urinal was already occupied, a slim-looking fellow with longish blond hair pissing silently, Edward hissing, springing from foot to foot, mumbling curse words even he didn't recognize. The man at the urinal did not seem to notice, only stood there, relaxed, head hung forward, one arm resting against the cold brick wall before him. There was something about the man's posture—about the red and blue tendons in his neck, something about his greasy hair and exposed genitalia—which Edward could not bear. Unthinking, nostrils flaring, he reached down into his heavy boot and gripped the small knife in his hand. The man seemed to take notice, glancing over his shoulder to where Edward was crouched. But it was too late, or so the older brother thought, knowing that as soon as he had opened the bathroom door and caught a glimpse of the man standing there vulnerable before him, he had no choice but to physically violate him. It was not even his own fault. The older brother lunged forward, forcing the tip of the knife deep into the man's side, slipping his left hand over the man's mouth, pressing the weapon through the clothing into the flesh deeply, the man's body going tense, arms flailing, Edward holding his left hand against the heat and moisture of the man's panicked mouth, and then forcing him to the floor, kneeling over him, seeing the pattern of red slowly forming there along the dirty tile, he finally felt calm, he finally felt like he could think again. He squatted there, marking the sign of the cross on the tip of his own forehead, on his sternum, his left shoulder, his right.

The man on the ground was alive, mouthing faint words no one could hear.

Gilby knocked once, opened the door—not hearing any answer—and saw the odd shape lying there, eyes wide open, mouth still working. His older brother was kneeling above the wounded man, the knife still in hand, and looked to be just as horrified. Gilby knew he should run away, should make for the truck and hope the keys were still there, but he did not. He felt trying to run from his brother now would be as dumb as trying to run from a storm cloud, the moon, the night. He took the knife from his brother's hand, made sure to lock the door behind them, and hurried off, leading Edward back to the truck, a conformation of fine red dots showing on his brother's neck, hands, and face, the daylight calling into question what had just occurred.

Both of them got out at a roadside Arby's, built beside the exit ramp of the highway; the boy was near starving, or so he claimed, and the grandfather needed to change the bandages again. The latrine was a dismal fluorescent crypt. Jim tossed the bloodied bandage in the garbage and replaced it with harsh brown paper towels.

When he returned from the washroom, the grandfather took a seat across from the boy, who was busy wolfing down his sandwich. Jim stared at the greasy potato cakes like they were some puzzle to behold, flicking at them with his thumb and forefinger, before fixing his glare over the edge of the plastic booth, through the bug-specked windows at the traffic flying past. They were getting close now; in less than an hour they'd be in Lexington. All he wanted was to see the horse again and get back home; to rest, standing beside his grandson along the snake-rail fence.

The boy finished his sandwich quickly and then spoke up, interrupting the old man's thoughts. "Grandpa?"

"Hm."

"Shouldn't we keep driving? I mean, if we want to get there in time?"

"That girl said the bus is supposed to pull in at six. We'll be there in an hour. Besides, we got to rest awhile so we keep our wits. That's one thing the army taught me. Something old Stan Mutter used to say. Anybody can go about waving a gun or pulling a knife. If you keep your smarts about you, you can be in charge of any situation.

You remember that now. You're smart enough as it is. You just got to learn to keep your wits."

"Did you like the army? When you were in it?"

The grandfather smiled tightly. "I don't know. When I was in it, no one ever bothered to ask me."

"Do you think I should join? When I'm old enough?"

"Well, I don't know if you'd like it but I think you should do something. Be good to get out of town. No place for young folks anymore."

"They've got computer specialists now. Doing radar and missiles and things. And they pay for college."

"Well sure."

"I was going to join last year. When I ran away."

"What?" The grandfather stared at the boy sitting before him. "When was this?"

"Last year. I ran away. I was going to go join the hunt for Sasquatch. Or enlist in the army. Either one, I guess."

"When did you run off?"

"When all those chickens had blackhead."

"Last October?"

"I left you a note but nobody saw it."

"Where'd you go?" the grandfather asked.

"At first, I was going to head up to Canada. Remember? We saw that show about the Sasquatch up there. So I just took some things and left. I borrowed one of your knives. The fishing one. The silver one. In case I had to stab something. I ended up just staying in the Kellers' barn."

"Whose barn?"

"The Kellers. Across the way."

"Well, that's not running off. They're right down the road there."

"But I didn't tell anyone where I was."

"Did they know you were there? The Kellers, I mean."

"After the first day, I guess. Mrs. Keller brought me some food and told me I oughta call you."

"Did you?"

"No."

"Hm. Did you thank her when you got back?"

"No."

"Well, I'll tell you—we didn't have running away when I sixteen. We called it becoming a man. You should think about it sometime."

"Yeah."

"It's the truth. I was your age, I couldn't wait to buck free."

"When I get back, I'm gonna see about the army."

"Well, you do what you think is best for you. There's plenty of other things besides the army. The army ain't for everyone."

"I'd like to see the world."

"Oh, you would?"

"I'd like to see different sorts of girls. British ones. And German ones. I'd like to go to Germany. See famous things. I'm not gonna live here the rest of my life."

"Where? Mount Holly?"

"No. America."

"Hm."

It suddenly saddened Jim to think that the boy would one day be somewhere he was not, somewhere he could not call or shout and expect to see the boy's face appearing in the near distance. He flicked at the larded ends of his potato cakes and said, "We can go talk to the fella together. From the army, I mean, if that's what you decide. All right?"

The boy nodded, slurping on his soda, and in seeing him do so, it was hard not to imagine he was still just a kid. The grandfather glanced at the other customers in the restaurant, resuming his solemnity. A little boy dressed as an Indian chief—with freckled skin, eyes a fair shade of green, wearing a feathered headdress and fringed buckskin—entered the restaurant, holding his mother's hand. Together they walked right past the booth where Jim and his grandson were sitting, Quentin fiddling with the remains of his fast food. The child—the Indian chief—seemed to study Quentin's face for a moment; the little boy tugged on his mother's wrist—the mother leaning over, the boy asking a rude question out loud before they ambled on toward the front of the establishment. In that moment, Jim had no reason to feel anger or shame, as he had asked that same question often enough—daily, sometimes in front of his own grandchild—and yet now he felt both. The boy did not even seem to notice he had been insulted, and if he had, he looked like he was accustomed to it—the vague finger-pointing, the dropped, muffled voice—as there was nothing in his face that betrayed any kind of resentment. This willingness to silently suffer—the boy's calm, gray-toned complexion in the light of ignorance—caused, in the grandfather's heart, an inexorable anger. He turned to his grandson and said, louder than he expected: "Quentin."

"Hm?"

"You need to learn to say something."

"Huh?"

"You need to learn to speak up for yourself."

The grandson looked down, guilt-faced.

Jim shook his head and snatched his hat from the adjoining tabletop, wincing a little as he got to his feet. He strode across the tile floor to where the woman and her young boy were now sharing a meal. Hovering there, hamstrung by a feeling of unpronounceable rage, the grandfather swept the feathered headdress off the child's head with the back of his hand, then muttered something indecipherable before he headed out the door in an angry blur. The mother put an arm around the child, who soon began to cry out. Quentin, still at the table, watched it all in shock, pausing in his mastication of a curly fry, setting it back down on the plastic tray before him, then started to his feet, still stunned, eyes open wide.

After they found their way to New Circle Road in Lexington, both the younger and older brother ignored the question of assault, of who or what may now be following them, and decided they had to find somewhere to eat. They pulled into the drive-through of the local Burger King, ordered a few Whoppers, and sat in the pickup's cab, the engine still running. A song by Shania Twain was playing. At the end of the song, the older brother, uncomfortable in the passenger seat, lowered his head and began to moan a deep-bellied howl, the sound of which caused Gilby's hair to stand on end.

"What is it? What is it?" Gilby asked, glancing out the window at the rearview mirror, sure they had just been pinched.

"It's over. I'm finished," the older brother moaned, folding his chin against his chest. "Whatever it is has got me. I'm going through some kind of motherfucking metamorphosis."

"What are you talking about? What's happening?" Gilby asked, still panicked.

"Look. Look at this shit . . ." Edward held out his dirty hand then, and in his palm Gilby saw a single, bloody tooth.

The grandfather told a story, trying to keep the boy awake at the wheel: "We were in the vice squad in Chuncheon. I told you before, it was a city in the north. Right by the thirty-eighth parallel. We were in charge of keeping the infantrymen in line. There were these two brothers, they were from Mobile, Alabama, and they were trouble. Their name was Mooney. They happened to get sent over in the same company. A thing like that almost never happens. But there they were. The two of them. The older one was . . ." and here the old man paused, searching his memories, remembering the face, the cold eyes, pale skin, blond eyebrows, the expression altogether impossible to discharge from his recollections, but still having a hard time with the actual name. "It was either Beau or Billy. Bart. No, it was Billy. He was the older one. He was the brains of the operation. The younger one, he was the one . . . gosh, what was his name? Pig. Pug. Peg. Something like that. He was maybe two or three years younger. They were both privates. They worked for the Fifty-Fifth Trucking Company. Those kinds of fellas, they were always selling things off the back of their trucks. They had all kinds of side businesses going. They were in the black market. You know what that means?"

"Yeah," the boy whispered, though it did not look like he understood, his eyes squinting at the road ahead, mouth slightly agape.

"They stole stuff from their truck and sold it to the Koreans. Or other soldiers. Anything they could get their hands on. Clothes, food, supplies. Anything. The older one, Bill, he was the scary one. He didn't care who you were. The first time I seen him he was kicking in some local's head. They were having some argument about something, money as far as I could guess, and Bill Mooney was beating the hell out of him for it. We ended up arresting him and he got court-martialed and told the judge that the Korean was trying to rob his truck. Nobody believed him but we didn't have any evidence. So they just fined him for the price of a new pair of dungarees."

"How come they did that?"

"Because we didn't have anything else to charge him with. And he got that poor fella's blood all over his pants. So that's all they could do. Charge him for ruining a pair of army-issue pants. This Mooney fella, well, there was a lot of guys like him. Criminals. That's what they were. He had already been over in Korea once before; he tried to murder his first sergeant, tried to cut his throat. So they sent him back home to Leavenworth, and then a few years later, they gave him the choice to volunteer for a year in a rifle company back in Korea, and if he did it, then his slate would be wiped clean. They gave that choice to a lot of those guys. This Bill Mooney, he took it. He was a bad fella. One of the worst I ever met."

"He's the one who stabbed you?" the boy asked.

"He was the one."

"What happened?"

The grandfather paused for a moment, wiping his runny nose, and then continued: "Well, this Bill Mooney, him and his brother, they'd try to make whole trucks disappear. They'd get away with it sometimes. It was up to me and my partner, Stan, to try to hunt them down. The CO from the Fifty-Fifth would call us up and say, *I got two trucks missing this month,* and we'd go through the registers and try to find a pattern, see if it was the same driver, or maybe a particular kind of shipment that kept getting stolen. But we couldn't find nothing. Whoever was disappearing those trucks knew what they were doing. They were paying off the supply sergeant to change the logs, so we had no way of knowing what was missing or who it was.

"But then a few of the soldiers got real sick. The medical officers thought someone had tried to poison them, but it turned out they had got themselves drunk on Korean whiskey. The whiskey over there, it was part embalming fluid—we'd warn them not to drink it but they all did anyway. They were all far from home and scared of dying and there wasn't much other recreation. Plus, it was cold a lot of the time. So sometimes they'd get ahold of a bad batch. The Koreans, you had to respect them, they'd go hunting for empty American whiskey bottles, fill them up with all sorts of stuff. It made one boy I met go blind. We guessed they had maybe put paint thinner in there that time.

"A week or two after a few of them fellas got sick, a body turned up. These fellas, they were supposed to stay on the compound, but some of them would sneak out. AWOL, it was called. This one AWOL fella, he wound up dead. A convoy of transport trucks drove past him one morning. They brought his body back and one sniff and you could tell what happened. It was the Korean whiskey. The commanding officer up there got nervous. He had never had so many cases of drunk-and-disorderly before, and now he had this dead one. He was afraid he was going to get court-martialed himself. So we did some snooping around and got to figuring there was some American over there who had to be bringing it onto the base. There was just too much of it going around.

"What we did was sit out on this supply road for about a week straight, stopping any truck heading in or out of the base, but still we didn't turn up nothing. Finally, by dumb luck, we had set up a speed trap somewhere a few kilometers off—that was part of the job too, trying to catch these soldiers speeding—and we saw this truck flying down a little muddy road. It had to be going thirty, forty miles over what was posted. We tear off behind them with our blue light flashing and the truck gets stuck in some mud and the driver, he throws the door open and runs out. Stan is shouting, *Halt, halt!* and then the fella, he was a soldier, he's got his own rifle—they were carbines back then mostly—he takes a shot at us. Now, Stan said no American soldier had ever taken a shot at him before. Here we are a thousand miles from home and one of our own takes a shot at us. Stan just stood there, stunned, I guess. It was starting to get dark and we were only a mile or two from the compound and the fella, he runs off through the jungle and the rice paddies—they were like swamps—to try to make it back. We call out for him to halt and he takes another shot at us, and then we know we are in for it with him. I follow Stan up to the truck and we throw open the tarp and there are three or four girls back there—Korean, but dressed up like American girls, with jeans and T-shirts, makeup, the whole thing— and Stan starts yelling at them and he tells me to stay put and runs off after the driver. They were prostitutes. It turns out whoever was running the black market up there had his hand in a lot more than just Korean whiskey."

"What did you do?"

"Stan told the girls to stay where they were, then he went off after him."

"Into the jungle?"

"Right into the dark."

The brothers' meet-up was an ignominious place on New Circle Road by the name of Rebel Lounge, though this was a misnomer, as it paid no tribute to the sacrifice the secessionists had made or functioned as any sort of place to socialize either. It was a strip club and a low-grade one at that. The yellow sign on its roof featured a silhouette of a buxom woman, though the figure's proportions were slightly off, the head appearing insignificant in relationship to the tremendous hips and breasts. The overall effect was one of absolute grotesqueness. It was located a few hundred yards off Highway 75, in a strip mall, set between an all-night laundromat and an Asian "massage parlor," and had, at one time, been a buffet restaurant, and before that a bait-and-tackle shop.

The two brothers parked the truck and trailer in the side lot and entered the establishment. The loud dance music—its heavy, digitized drums and pulsating, distorted bass—caused them both to grimace in discomfort. At this time of day, just around two in the afternoon, the place was mostly empty, though there were still a few patrons—truckers and out-of-town types—gathered in single tables around the canted stage.

The one they were looking for was the deejay, who was busy announcing the next dancer from behind a plexiglass booth. "And now let's put your hands together for Misty," he said, glancing over the top of his sunglasses at the stage-bound girl in a pair of green pasties and a G-string, her stomach bifurcated by a recent cesarean scar. Music by the band White Zombie began to play, the noise of which did little to arouse the clientele. The deejay switched off his mic and took a drag from a hand-rolled cigarette. He had his long brown hair tied in a ponytail, wore a ghastly purple argyle shirt, and had round-rimmed sunglasses perched in the middle of his long nose. The sunglasses were meant to disguise his rather weak-looking face; he was a coward and a coke addict and hoped to conceal both by hiding his eyes. His left arm was wrapped in a plaster cast and his neck was supported by a foam brace.

The two brothers ignored a slim waitress and walked directly toward the plexiglass booth. The deejay looked up from his glittering stack of CDs and immediately frowned, eyes darting back and forth between the two men with nervy agitation.

"You Davey-boy?" the older brother asked.

"Fuck. What are you going to do to me now? You guys already wrecked my fucking arm. I mean, look at me. Look at this shit. I'm supposed to be a deejay, man. Do you see any other one-armed deejays around? I mean, well, Jesus. This is my place of business."

"Are you Davey-boy or should we be talking to someone else?"

"Yeah, I'm him, Kojak. You fucking found me. But listen, man, you're gonna have to tell Chandra I don't got anything right now."

"What?"

"If you're all here to kick my ass, you can tell her I don't get paid till next week."

"We're here about the horse!" Gilby shouted, since it was hard to hear above the synthesized music. Onstage, Misty, mother of three, had flung off her green G-string to a dearth of applause.

"Oh, yeah, good, good," Davey said, wiping a sheen of sweat from his sloped forehead. "I thought you guys were gonna be here like a couple hours ago."

"We got lost!" Gilby shouted.

"Well, shit, man, that's no problem. I'm just glad you made it. Let's go talk in my office." He cued up another song for Misty, this one by Ministry, and motioned for the two brothers to follow him; together they traveled down a short hallway, past a kitchen that also served as a dressing room, and out a side entrance. The office, it turned out, was an unlit space beside a dumpster, littered with empty beer bottles and lint-specked detritus from the laundromat next door. He leaned against a wall and quickly lit up another hand-rolled cigarette, exhaling forcefully from his nose.

"So where is it?" the deejay asked.

"On the side."

"It's here?"

"In that parking lot over there."

"Well, shit, let's go take a look."

The three of them marched quietly around the back of the building to the side parking lot and stood before the rear of the trailer. The deejay climbed onto the bumper and stared inside, catching sight of the animal's massive hindquarters.

"Fuck. That really is a horse."

The older brother looked over at Gilby and shook his head in disgust.

"I mean, well, shit. I don't know if Gary said anything but I don't usually traffic in this kind of stuff. I got this buyer but I don't know how reliable he is. I never, you know, sold shit to him before. He sounds like he's got money though. He said he was sending someone who'd be here tonight. So I figured we can all, you know, exchange money then. You guys got a motel room or somewhere you're staying?"

"No. We expect to be paid upon delivery. That's what Gary said."

"Well, I know, but I usually don't handle this kind of thing, and the guy won't be here till tonight. It looks like we're all just gonna have to wait."

Edward glanced over at his brother, who was already nervously pacing back and forth, shaking his head. Edward gave the deejay a hard look. "We wait around here with that thing, we're just asking for trouble."

"It's just for a few hours. You go grab a meal. Catch a movie maybe. By tonight, all of us will be sitting pretty."

"I want you to understand something about us," the older brother said, his eyebrows peaked, the tendons in his neck swelling. He took a step closer to Davey, placing his wiry body in close proximity to the faint-looking deejay. "We are not fucking amateurs. You need to know that right now. You want us to leave this animal with you, and then who knows what the fuck happens to it or our money. No. I don't think we're going to do it like that."

"Listen, I ain't going anywhere, friend," the deejay replied calmly. "Fact is, I got to work until midnight anyway. You leave the trailer over here and I promise nothing's gonna happen. I'll have the doorman keep an eye on it soon as he comes in."

Edward leaned in even closer to the deejay now and whispered, "I have been to the coast. I have seen what I have seen with my own eyes, and there is a tidal wave coming. It's all full of blood and guts and I aim to be on top of it, not under it."

Gilby turned, unsure of the words that were coming from his brother's mouth. Edward's face had gone a ghastly white, his eyes twitching in their sockets. He was spitting as he was speaking, a droplet of saliva running down his chin, though he seemed completely unaware of it.

"I got powers," the older brother was saying. "Of several kinds. I am turning into something, something different right now, and so I suggest you do not fuck me on this."

"Of course. We're in complete agreement," the deejay said with a gutless laugh, his weak chin lowered against his chest. "How about I buy you guys a couple of drinks?"

"Where is your latrine located?" Edward asked.

The deejay led them back down the hallway, the older brother stumbling into the grimy john while Gilby leaned against the purple-lit bar, watching a performer by the name of Jasmine twirl an obscenely long string of pearls about her bare neck, looking absolutely bored, absolutely sexless. *It's like all the girls here work at the Department of Motor Vehicles*, the young man thought, *like they don't know this is supposed to be fun.*

After twenty minutes or so, with two or three other girls gracing the stage—their drawn faces caked in makeup—Gilby strode back down the corridor to the bathroom and found his older brother leaning over its only toilet. He looked like he had vomited. Gilby squatted above him, asking if he was okay.

"I'm okay, little brother. It's everyone else I worry about. This world, this world . . ."

"I'm going to go unhook the trailer and drive around some. See about finding a motel maybe. Do you want to stay here and watch that guy?"

Edward shook his head, wiping some spittle from the corner of his lip. "No. Let's go find a room somewhere. This place is too full of cooze. It makes me feel emasculated."

Gilby helped his brother to his feet, and, holding him under the right armpit, marched him into the unforgiving spectacle of the midday sun.

They unhooked the trailer, lowering the support struts in place—Gilby peering through the metal slats at the animal, whispering vague sounds of kindness to the horse—then hopped back inside the truck. The two brothers circled around town, finally settling on a chain motel, Gilby helping his brother from the cab, across the sticky parking lot, over the threshold like a timid bride, arm in arm, and into one of the single beds. Gilby fetched him a glass of water and stood by the bed, unsure what to do.

"I'm going to go drive around some. Maybe go back to that place and keep an eye on that guy."

"I trust you," Edward whispered, as if somehow, even in his mental decay, he was able to detect his brother's anxiety.

"Okay. I'll be back."

"Gilby?"

"Yep?"

"I keep seeing my future." The older brother coughed. "I keep seeing all the pain I got left to cause, and it terrifies me. Truly."

"I'll see you in a couple of hours."

"Knock before you open that door. In case I turn into something that doesn't recognize you."

Gilby nodded and carefully closed the door behind him, hoping he would never have to see his brother again.

The grandfather went on with his story: "And so we looked in the back of the truck and saw the girls, and Stan told them to stay put, and told me to watch them, and then he hurried off after the fella who had been driving. We both figured the guy was going to try to make it back to the compound on foot. You could see the lights of the place from where we were on the road, but it was starting to get dark and here we were, about as close as you could get to the thirty-eighth, right alongside this rice paddy, and the thing of it was, the people up there were always kind of superstitious about that place. It always made me jumpy.

"Anyway, there we are in the woods, and there's the mountains, some of which look like dust piles, they'd been bombed down to craters, and then there's the line of wire you can't hope to see through.

All of it haunted. And Stan, he tells me to wait with the girls. He says to keep an eye on them, because even though they're women, they know they're in trouble, and they outnumbered me, and so I shouldn't turn my back on them, and I told him, *No problem,* and held my rifle in front of me like I might shoot any one of them if they decide to try to run. So Stan heads off into the woods by himself; all he's got is his carbine—his rifle—and his pistol. He doesn't even bother to take a flashlight. Off he goes into the woods and he does this funny thing then—he looks over his shoulder like he was going to say something else, and then he turned back, and that was the last I seen of him. Standing, I mean. The next time I seen him, he had been shot. I heard the shots and decided to go see what happened, which was against an order from a commanding officer, but I went off into the woods myself because I figured it was the right thing to do, given the situation. As soon as I started on my way, I seen the whores take off running, but by then there wasn't anything I could do.

"It was muddy and easy to spot where Stan had gone. I followed his bootprints for a while into the jungle, and after a couple minutes I found him lying there, gasping for air. He had been shot in the chest. He wasn't dead yet but he had been shot right through the lung, I think, and it takes awhile sometimes to go like that. I think what happens is . . . what happens is your lung, it fills up with blood. So it was like he was drowning or something. So I sat with him there. I held his hand and watched him gasping there like a fish, trying to breathe, and I knew there wasn't no one around who was going to be able to do anything, certainly not me. I didn't have any medical training—I mean, I unbuttoned his shirt and all, tried to put pressure on the wound, but he knew and I knew it wasn't going to do much good. So we just sat there for a bit, and I held his hand, and his eyes were wild and white and his mouth was flapping . . . he was trying to say something. I couldn't figure out what it was he wanted to say. And so I put my ear up next to his mouth, and I could feel his breath there, and he kept whispering it, over and over again. But I still didn't know what he was saying. And then I looked down at him and he had gone white as a ghost and he stopped trying to breathe, and I knew he was dead."

"Then what happened?" the boy asked, eyes still on the road.

"Well, I leaned over and slid Stan's eyes closed, and then I heard something behind me, but by the time I heard it I knew it was too late, and I felt a hand go over my mouth, and I could taste tree bark and mud on it, and something else too, something that had the funny smell of perfume, and then I felt the knife go in, right between my ribs, right in the back there, and then I was lying on my side, and everything felt kind of heavy and I was looking up at the trees, thinking how they looked the same as they did back home. And that thought made me feel okay, so I thought I might go to sleep and die. But I didn't. I guess you already know that much."

The boy nodded.

"Yeah. Well, that was it. Whoever had shot old Stan had crept up on me while I was tending to him. Only I seen him. I didn't know that I did, but I did. While I was lying there. It was that roughneck Mooney. And that's what old Stan was trying to tell me. He was saying that fella's name again and again. Only I didn't know it until I was lying there on the ground and I saw him standing over me. I can see his face even now. It was floating above me in the dark, only it wasn't like no face at all. It was like the moon. Sometimes when I look up at the moon, that's what I see. His face. It was the oddest thing."

The old man went silent then, the memories continuing on behind his heavy-lidded eyes as the grandson held his hands steady against the wheel. They drove along for a few more minutes before the grandfather spoke again.

"So that's how I got stabbed. It ain't much of a story. I mean, it's nothing to brag on, I guess. After that, I was out of commission for six weeks, in a hospital in Pusan. They gave me the choice to check out or stay on, and since I didn't have anything waiting for me at home, I decided to stay on. They sent me right back up to Chuncheon, gave me a new partner, a kid a few years younger than me, somewhere close to your age, and the first night we drove around, I seen it was utter lawlessness. They all knew Stan was dead and nobody thought they had any reason to fear me, so they were drinking and whoring and sneaking in and out of the fence with all kinds of things they had stolen."

The grandfather tugged at the collar of his flannel and asked the boy if he wouldn't mind turning the heat on. "I get a chill in my feet," he said. "Any time I talk about it. I get cold in my feet and see that fella's face and it feels like I been stabbed all over again." He peered out the passenger-side window. A sign for *Lexington, 68 miles* flashed by. "But that's a thing they don't ever tell you in Sunday school."

"What's that?"

The grandfather stared straight ahead. "That the Devil sometimes wins."

Beneath a procession of stubby hills, mountains, trees, several narrow, unnamed streams that give way to a river; a few skyscrapers upon a lone, precipitous skyline; the sun like a dove reeling from a red-tailed hawk; the afternoon light—fading.

By five o'clock, Gilby had realized what a profound mistake he'd made. He was certain now that his brother had lost his mind somewhere out in California and was probably never going to be the same. Not soon anyway. All he could count on now was Belinda. He tried to call her two or three times to be sure she was on her way, but her mother answered both times and so there was no way to know if she was coming. He circled the bus stop once, then again, finding a parking spot in the back of the squat redbrick building. He watched six go past, then six fifteen, then six thirty, and finally, when the chrome bumper and oversized wheels of the bus arriving from Indianapolis rolled up, he hopped out of the cab of the truck, scanning the door for her soft, wide-eyed face. He was going to tell her that he had messed up again. That they had not gotten the money, and that, in his opinion, the two of them—he and Belinda—ought to take the pickup and drive as far away from Indiana and his brother as they could get. He had other ideas about what he wanted to say too, about how he was going to get a job somewhere and take care of her, how he was going to marry her but did not want to propose, officially, until he could afford the ring, but she could call him her fiancé if it pleased her, because something had happened to him over the last day or so, and he was a different person; he was done getting in trouble.

When a dark-eyed girl about Belinda's height stepped down from the bus, he ran forward and then stopped himself, seeing that her jaw was too wide and her hair was the wrong length. He turned back toward the pickup, feeling something blunt-shaped shoved up hard against the back of his neck. He started to laugh, expecting Belinda to have snuck up on him somehow, but went sick when he saw the face hanging there instead: it looked like a Halloween mask—long, weathered, the white eyebrows bedraggled, the mouth as stern and straight as the horizon line. The nigger boy was with him too, standing behind, the old-timer shoving what had to be a Colt or some sort of .45 sharply into his spine. Before Gilby could get the words out, before he could begin to lament, before he could make the face before him understand that what had happened had not been his intention, the grandfather began to speak quietly.

"Were you the one who shot me?"

Gilby shook his head, croaking out a faint, "No."

"Go on and tell me where that horse is."

There were still folks coming off the bus, but none looking this way.

"Make a peep. Go on and see what happens, son. I got the law on my side. And I know you ain't carrying. We watched you parked there for the last half hour. The only chance you got now is to tell me where to find that horse."

Gilby glanced from the old man's face to the bus door, which had swung closed.

"She ain't coming," the old man said.

"What?"

"That girl. She's the one who told us where you'd be."

Gilby stumbled back a little, his heart dropping to his knees. "Belinda? She was the one who told you?"

The old man leaned in closer, his breath a mixture of sleep and orange juice and coffee. The lips curled cruelly over white teeth, the blue eyes limitless now, as open as the sky above an unfurrowed field, the old man's voice unhesitant, without fear, now whispering directly into Gilby's ear: "It's either me or the police. You think on that for a minute. Because it don't seem all that hard to me."

Gilby's stomach began to ache, rumbling all the way up and down his spine. It felt like he was going to die. It really did.

"Now you tell me: which one's it going to be?"

The horse, stamping in its silver prison, the trailer now resting alone at the side parking lot of the strip club, the sound of laughter, of motor vehicles arriving and departing, of industrial music echoing through the thin walls, of the tenor of the afternoon giving over to night, of four o'clock on a Friday, then five, then six, then seven, the hour interrupted by the sound of a fight between a man and woman, the man knocking the woman down, rifling through her purse, the man walking off, the woman—crying, on her side, her black nylons bunched up around her knees—crippled by love, looking up and realizing at once that she was staring at something unfamiliar, the horse whinnying a little, cramped in its quarters, rearing back but trapped, the woman thinking, *Is this a dream?* but knowing and then not knowing that what she was seeing was the unchangeable, irredeemable depiction of her own fate.

Between the grandfather and the grandson rode the dull-eyed kid from the pet store, sweating, eyes blinking out tears. Quentin was behind the wheel, minding the road, afraid to look the other young man in the eye. Only a mile or two from the bus stop, they pulled

up in front of the chain motel, the grandfather slowly, with great ef-
fort, climbing out first, dragging the miscreant after him. The trailer
was nowhere around. Immediately the old man got a premonition
that the kid had been lying. He had the look of a liar. The old man
paused for a moment and turned to his grandson, muttering a few
particulars: "You wait here. Mind me, don't you follow till I come
after you." Then he marched the greasy-faced kid up the concrete
stairs to the wooden motel room door, a golden 209 hanging along
its warped center.

"Open it," the old man said in a low voice, the pistol tapping a
sore spot into Gilby's back.

Gilby found the key in his pocket, secretly hoping his brother
would be gone. And if not gone, then something else—a wolf, a bat,
something so terrifying that its gruesome shape would be enough to
frighten the old man without either gunshot or bloodshed.

The lights were switched off, the TV turned on—a talk show
where the guests were throwing chairs at one another—and both
beds were empty. *Gone. He became something else and disappeared.*
Then the toilet flushed, the bathroom door opened, the addled,
rough-skinned face creeping out slowly, crossing into the blue light
from the television set, it becoming clear now he was naked, the
frayed-looking limbs and desiccated ribs, the blue-black tattoos and
scars erupting from the frame that looked like it belonged to some
unnamed predatory bird, the older brother too sick to notice the
stranger standing there, until the grandfather moved past, shoving
Gilby inside, taking aim on the skeleton before him, something out
of an old horror film, some sort of spook, a ghost made flesh, caught
in that limbo between night and day. It was bleeding, the ghost, from
its hands, looking like it had punched the bathroom mirror with both
of its fists.

The grandfather approached unsteadily, not sure of what he was
seeing, holding the gun before him at some distance, until he could
be sure it was a man in front of him and not something he was imagining. He asked the very same question again—"Were you the one

who shot me?"—and the creature, weepy-eyed, mouth flapping like a silvery amphibian, muttered, "Yes," and then it was staggering forward, saying, "Kill me. Please. Kill me."

The grandfather took a step back.

Then the animal lurched forward, a shard of broken mirror in its bare hand, eyes wild, still hissing, "Kill me. Kill me."

The sound of the gun, over the rumble of the television set, was muffled. The old man winced as it echoed in his ears, the creature falling, hissing before him, holding the bloody spot above the right kneecap where he had been shot. The grandfather turned the point of the muzzle against the younger one and said, "I aim to get that horse back. If you want to end up like him, go on and tell me another lie."

The kid, his face cramped, backed away, pushing himself up against the room's green wallpaper. The other one was flopping around, howling, gritting his teeth, mumbling something like a prayer in a language the old man did not know or recognize. The kid was crying now, worse than his older brother, for all he wanted in the world at this moment was to tell the truth, but the words, the actual sounds, seemed so unfamiliar, so faraway. He was struggling with something more frightening than the terror of the moment; what he was wrestling with was the feeling that if he did not speak, he would become something as wretched, as weak, as miserable as his older brother. Finally, some seconds later, the words came, the name of the strip club, the trailer by the side of the building, the physical appearance of the deejay. The old man, after hearing what was said, took a step toward the door. Wary of the sound of panicked movement making it out into the hallway, he carefully slipped out, as the creature went on howling.

Quentin had disobeyed him again, and was standing at the top of the stairs, looking alarmed, his face whiter than it had ever been. Together they made their way down the stairs, the howl growing fainter with their descent, people emerging from rooms, staring from their windows, standing in the frames of their open doors.

* * *

By the time the deejay figured out who was standing before him, in the purple and yellow lights of the strip club, it was too late. This particular sort of myopia had been the cause of most of Davey-boy's troubles. It was also the reason he believed he was the best strip-club deejay in the world: he could not be distracted, not by the half-naked girls nor flashing lights nor the songs themselves, though, as in this case, it also meant he was unable to reckon with any of life's more complicated treacheries. As with Chandra, his ex. As with her multiple batshit, dangerous friends. He got punched in the belly before he knew what was happening. Then someone smashed a hard elbow against his face. He felt blood running from his left nostril, beading down the back of his throat. When he looked up, he was not surprised by what he saw. One of the attackers, a tall one with a reddish-looking beard, garbed in the manner of a gray-coated Confederate soldier, pulled him by the neck. The other, a wider, squatter one, also dressed in Civil War military costume, grabbed him under the arm, the two of them spiriting him down the dank hallway, past the girls' dressing room, and out into the alley, where they visited several more blows upon his face.

"Davey, I thought you said we'd never have to see you again."

"Jesus Christ, this is my place of business! How am I supposed to pay that crazy bitch back if you're intruding upon my line of work?"

"You know how much you owe her. We know how much you owe her. Why don't you just pay her back?"

"Jesus, don't you think I would if I had it? I swear to God, by the end of the weekend—by the end of tonight even."

"You got a deal cooking?" the tall one asked.

"By midnight, I promise. Please. Stop hitting me. I'm working things out. I promise."

"What things?"

And then, by arrogance or stupidity, the deejay glanced over his shoulder to where the silver horse trailer happened to be parked.

The squat fellow smiled, stepped slowly across the parking lot, leaning up on his tiptoes, and stared into the oval-shaped window. "What do we have here?" he asked with a whistle.

Once again, Davey realized he had said what he had ought not to.

The girl was asleep, or again pretending to be. He switched off the truck, slipped his hat over his head, and ambled through the door of the men's club. A burly giant of a boy, no older then nineteen or twenty, but nearly as big as an airplane factory, was working the front. Rick eyed him with a soft smile, not bothering to reach for his wallet. He strode past, blinking as a strobe light on the tiny stage caused a slender-limbed girl to vanish and reappear. He made his way over to the bar, ordered a cold one, and asked the acne-scarred woman working the counter where Davey was. She shook her head and pointed. Rick tipped the beer bottle back while he walked, drawing down a few sips as he approached the plexiglass deejay booth.

"You Davey?"

The deejay nodded, jamming another wad of tissues up his left nostril. He wiped a smear of blood from the tips of the fingers along the edge of his shirt and continued to ponder the poor decisions that had led to this recurring state of disabuse.

"I'm here about the horse!" Rick shouted into the deejay's hairy left ear.

Davey nodded, held up one finger to motion that Rick was to wait a moment, then grabbed the microphone and said, "And now . . . the lovely Tanya." The deejay crept around from the interior of the booth and offered his good hand—the right—to shake.

"What happened to you?" Rick asked with a laugh.

"I don't know. I think I got too easy a disposition. But listen, I got some bad news for you."

"What?"

The deejay raised both hands in absolution, no longer certain of anything, his right hand unharmed, the left covered in the plaster cast. He motioned to Rick and together they meandered down the leaky hallway, out the side door, and past the dumpster, the deejay pausing at the border of the parking lot, staring at the spot where the horse trailer had, only an hour or two before, been parked.

"Okay . . . Well, where the fuck is it?"

"I don't know. These guys . . . these fucking asshole reenactors took it."

"What the fuck are you talking about?"

"They work with my wife at that casino. Ex-wife. I owe her a bunch of alimony and so she sent these fellas to come take it."

"They took the horse?"

"Yes sir."

"The horse I came here for? The horse we agreed to buy from you?"

"Yes sir, just the way I'm saying it."

In the fading light, in these last few moments of day, Rick glared at the rube, glancing down briefly at his plastered arm. "You said you know where these fellas work?"

"Yes sir. The casino. Just outside of town. It's the one looks like a plantation. It's called Belle Plaine."

"A casino."

"You got it."

Rick glanced down at the deejay's cast again. "What happened to your arm there?"

"Same group of fellas. About two weeks ago. They're messing with my livelihood. I ain't ever gonna be able to pay that woman back."

Rick snatched the pistol from the holster beneath his jacket and shoved the muzzle hard against Davey's forehead, glaring at the awful asymmetry of his raw-looking face.

"On your knees."

The deejay nodded, falling to his knees quickly, his hands outstretched before him. Rick loomed above him, his black mustache an unforgiving dark line.

"You got no business pretending to be something you're not. You got no business trafficking with the likes of people like me. You lose that number, you get it? Anything having to do with me or the party that called you. That information has been wiped clear from your memory, understand? That, or else I'll come back through here and wipe it clear myself."

"Yes sir."

"How many of them came for the horse?"

"Two. And a third one driving."

"If anybody asks, you tell them you did this to yourself."

Rick peered down at the rube's right hand—the good one—and raised his boot up high, the sound of gravel and bone being grinded together beneath the slate-colored heel.

Night falling upon a smudged face, red eyes ringed with mascara; upon a crowd of gawkers and perverts, diminished by years of lethargy; upon the entirety of an unsatisfied Southern town, masquerading as a city.

On and on, with little trouble, they found the strip club. It was past nine o'clock now. The summer light was gone. The grandfather sat in the passenger seat of the pickup for a moment, then turned to his grandson, studying the unevenness of the boy's fearful face.

"If I told you to wait here, you wouldn't, would you?"

The boy shook his head.

"All right then. We got nothing to be afraid of."

Together they marched beneath the glowing sign, the lights flickering erratically above them, the boy's face looking bright yellow, sickly, like a child with jaundice. A baby-faced giant working the door put out his large arm, barring Quentin from entering.

"You got ID?"

The boy shook his head. Jim doffed his hat and muttered, "He's with me."

"Well, sir, this here is a private establishment."

"He's my grandson."

The giant smiled a little to himself, lowering his arm. The grandfather paid the cover charge and then he and his grandson ambled on, Jim placing the white hat back on the top of his head. Immediately, the noise of the night was swallowed up by the din and throb of the music inside.

The boy paused near the entrance, unsure where to set his eyes. A girl, a woman, was crawling around onstage like an epileptic. She wore high heels and enormous gold hoop earrings. There were, altogether, five dollars in singles stuck in front of her gold lamé panties. The boy watched her move, feeling an enormous ache well up in the center of his chest; it was the shame of knowing he was seeing something he would have never seen on his own, something he had done nothing to deserve. The girl was almost completely naked, bucking around like a deer, a jackal, an antelope, her skin the color of the flashing lights—pink, then purple, then pink again—her bare breasts smaller than he would have expected but somehow still mesmerizing in their movement, their shape, his eyes trailing down to the soft ridges of her navel, and in the flashing commotion he was surprised for a brief few seconds, in between the switching of the colored lights, by the field of whitish hairs just below the girl's belly, like the flesh of a peach, having never before known or even considered such a thing existed, as the photos in the dirty magazines he had explored never detailed such a mystery.

For the grandfather, it was a little like death; not fulsome, not the least bit erotic, but scary, loud, lights buzzing this way and that, young girls—half the age of his daughter, almost the same age as the boy at his side—half-dressed, or less than that. Here was one walking around inviting patrons to the VIP room. Here was one performing a lap dance, her posterior posed directly in front of the customer's face. It was not how he remembered it—the laughter, a radio playing the Armed Forces Network in the background, the hot whisper of a girl's silky yellow blouse. His heart seized some and he staggered, holding his hand out against the side of a round table, the half-filled glasses rattling with his weight, then righted himself, stumbling forward, the lights and sounds whirling about his head, holding his hand out again but finding nothing to grab onto, the fingers grasping uselessly at the air, the bass-heavy thump of some song upsetting his sense of balance, the wound on his shoulder throbbing with pain. The old man's hand reached out for something to grasp, and felt the insistence of the boy's palm under his damp armpit, leading him over to an empty seat.

"You okay, Gramps?"

"You find the fella!" he shouted, teeth gumming at themselves, breath coming in fits and starts.

The boy lifted his eyes and began to make a tour of the long room. He discovered the deejay booth in the shadowy corner, before a girl—only a few years older than him—topless, breasts like seashells, white, pointed at their tips—leaned over and asked if he wanted a dance. The boy shook his head, glancing down at her breasts again, and, looking up into her heart-shaped face, he grinned, as if he had been made privy to one of the world's most exceptional secrets. Walking on, he stood before the plexiglass booth, staring at the deejay's odd shape, the mangled left arm wound up in a cast, the foam brace cushioning his short neck, a recent bruise blooming beneath his eye. His right hand was wrapped in a dirty bar towel full of ice. It looked like he was sobbing to himself. Quentin watched him, the guy lifting his right hand, inspecting the oddly bent thumb, unable to properly flex it. After a moment or two, the deejay looked up and asked, "What the fuck do you want?"

The boy turned back toward his grandfather. Slowly, like a weathered carnival tent being pulled to its full height, the old man crept to his feet, then made his way over, eyes locked on the deejay.

"What? What the fuck do you two want?"

Jim reached into the front of his jeans, thumbing the pistol that rested there. The deejay's eyes followed, catching sight of the muzzle of the black weapon, the pupils then going narrow, the record escaping his grasp.

"We come for our horse," the old man said.

"Fuck. You people . . . I mean, Jesus. What the fuck? Why can't you people leave me alone?"

"Our horse. Where is she?"

Out the back once more, stepping down the dim tile hallway, past the brown dumpster to the empty blackness of the side parking lot, the old man stumbled, the crooked-necked deejay walking slowly ahead of him.

The horse was gone. There was no trailer, no rubber marks, nothing but the blank expanse of where it might have been parked. The grandfather squatted there a moment, touching his fingers to the dirty black pavement, fiddling with a stick, a soda pop cap, a brittle leaf, until he was sure there was nothing, no sign, no clue, no measure that still might help them. He stood up stiffly and turned back to the weepy-faced deejay.

"They took it," the deejay said. "My ex-wife's people. From the casino. It was a couple hours ago. Then someone else came for it. I think he was from somewhere out of state. Cowboy type. That's all I know. I ain't got the constitution to get bound up in this kind of shit. It's not worth it to me. I can make twice as much moving coke."

The old man felt his breath leave him for a moment, and then, when he could speak again, he asked: "You knowed it was stolen when you turned it over to them, didn't you?"

The deejay, whose age was nearly impossible to judge, so absolute was his ugliness, looked away. He spoke again, not answering the question: "The other people . . . they were the ones who was supposed to buy it. I don't know what happened to it. Those assholes come from the casino and . . . honest. I got to get back to work. I'm sorry for all the trouble I caused."

The old man pulled the brim of his hat down over his eyes and marched slowly past, the boy following, the noise of the rumbling, heartless music, the glimmer of the dispiriting orange and yellow lights, once again playing upon their hearing and vision.

Then the pale-blue pickup throttled back down the highway toward the casino, its muffler sounding like it was about to fall off, the boy with his hands at ten and two on the wheel. It was nearing eleven o'clock at night or so the radio read, its rounded dials flaking gray. The grandfather sat in the passenger seat, drowsy, dozing, the signs and billboards flashing past becoming distant memories: his father and mother, him walking barefoot in the corn as a boy, his stretch in boot camp, his partner Stan Mutter dying, a girl in Korea named Lola Lola—her mother a fan of the movies of Marlene Dietrich—who had a way of unbuttoning his clothes and hers with a kind of religious formality, the solemn bus ride home through Indiana, his father's face again, Deedee in his arms, the chickens, the smell of their feathers in winter, his daughter—her laugh, her dimples, then her standing at the back door, the odd-colored boy beside her—the mare galloping along the fence line, these memories traced in the shapes and subtle outlines of roadside advertisements, one after another, a parade of all the things he had prized and then lost.

They got a red paper ticket from a valet for their truck but did not need to go very far before they saw two local police cars parked perpendicular to each other, an ambulance idling behind them, red lights flashing. They ambled toward it—the casino—an enormous white gabled building constructed to resemble an antebellum Civil War plantation. By now it had grown dark, and the red light from the ambulance made the whole world look like a dislocated nightmare. There, sitting on the curb, were two men, both dressed in Civil War regalia, one still wearing his gray cap, bruised about the eyes and mouth. A third one was lying on his back, a bullet hole in his thigh being tended to by an androgynous blonde paramedic.

Jim surveyed the wounded men, glancing up, scanning the crowd, the gawkers' faces, the parking lot. He stepped along the circumference of where the onlookers were gathered, walking off a few yards toward a detective who was lifting a spent casing with a pair of silver tweezers. On a few more feet, there was a woman, her face a mask of both anguish and runny purplish mascara, an employee of the casino, or so her Civil War–era ball gown suggested, crying off a confession to a female police officer, who jotted it all down with pencil and pad of paper.

"He was from Texas. He had a black truck. I seen his license plates. I didn't get the number but I saw the state. It was a man and a girl. The man, he was terrible."

A few feet away, there was the strong odor of horseflesh, the reek of both animal urine and manure. Jim squatted the way he did to eyeball his chickens each day, taking in the familiar smell. Satisfied with what he had found, he stood, turned back to the boy, and said, "We need to go. Someone else has got her."

The horse, stall-bound, unable to move, stamping at the sawdust-lined trailer floor, one front hoof falling like a hammer, over and over, beating out a rhythm, the sound of which went unheard, except for the girl, Rylee, handcuffed to the armrest in the pickup's front seat, glancing over her shoulder every few minutes to see the obfuscated shape, the helpless pounding clocking there in her brain. At once, she decided she would turn the animal loose the first chance she got.

A motel room near the interstate was forty dollars for two beds. They stepped from the cab of the pickup, then entered the darkened room suspiciously, the layout green and beige, the fixtures gold, the curtains, bedspreads, and wallpapers not having been replaced since sometime in the late seventies. The grandfather dragged the CB set inside with him, placing it on the nightstand, between the two narrow beds. He searched for an outlet, gave up, then asked for the boy's help. Quentin found the socket but was unable to plug the device in, then the grandfather fumbled with the plug, both of them leaning over the outlet, finally getting it plugged in, the low, static hum of transcontinental conversations coming and going. The old man, sitting on the bed, picked up the microphone, switching from channel 19 to 10, then back to 17, from north to south, east to west, trying once again.

"Break 17 for a radio check. This is Old Rooster, anyone got their ears on?"

"Ten-four. This is Bluebeard. Over."

"What's your twenty?"

"I-40, heading north, driving empty. What's yours?"

"I-75, near Lexington, over in Kentucky. Anyone get a line on that horse trailer heading south, pulled by a pickup with Texas plates? Still waiting to hear anything. Over."

"No sir. But keeping my eyes out. Over."

"Much obliged. Over and out."

The grandfather set the microphone down and stared at the device for a moment before slipping off his boots. He rolled on his side, the channel buzzing with unfamiliar chatter. The boy, not yet tired or more tired than he'd ever been in his life, paced back and forth about the room, peeking through the curtains, inspecting the gray tile bathroom, opening and closing the bureau drawers, paging through the miniature green-sleeved Gideon's Bible, searching out the part about the white horse, somehow finding it near the back of the hardbound volume, Revelation 19:11–14:

> *I saw heaven opened, and behold, a white horse, and He who sat on it is called Faithful and True, and in righteousness He judges and wages war. His eyes are a flame of fire, and on His head are many crowns; and he has a name written on Him which no one knows except Himself. He is clothed in a garment sprinkled with blood, and His name is called The Word of God.*

The boy closed the dusty book and slid it back in the drawer, glancing over to see if his grandfather was already asleep.

"Gramps?"

"—"

"Gramps? Sir?"

"Hm."

"Do you think we did something?"

"___"

"Do you think we did something wrong?"

"___"

"Did we do something wrong, Grandpa? Should we have not raced her?"

"___"

"Grandpa?"

"___"

"I think that's why the horse got taken. I think we're being punished for something. I just don't know what it is."

"___"

"Grandpa?"

"___"

"Are you asleep?"

"___"

"Jim?" Quentin turned over, held his breath, and heard the belabored, unsteady respiration of the old man across from him. Then the boy sighed, itched his nose, and climbed from the bed.

He sat down in front of the antique-looking television set and switched it on with the volume low. Like always, there was nothing on, even though there was cable; he lingered for a few moments over the adults-only channel, trying to gauge whether the fuzzed-out limbs on the snowy screen belonged to a man or woman. He flashed past that image, tried once more, decided on some cartoons, then changed his mind, landing on a news update about the O.J. Simpson trial. The LA police detective was once again on the witness stand, and the jury was listening to further excerpts from some audiotapes he had made. There was the smooth white face, blotchy on the old color set, listening to his own words echoing there in the courtroom.

"*. . . all these niggers in LA city government, and all of 'em should be lined up against a wall and fuckin' shot.*"

Though the word *fuckin'* had been bleeped out for the television audience, it was still fairly obvious what the detective had said. The grandfather was now snoring loudly. Quentin glanced back at him, the fuzzy green bedspread slowly rising and falling, rising and falling, his breaths like the creaking bellows of some ship adrift at sea.

The white face of the police detective floated there on the TV for a moment longer, like a prisoner who had been decapitated, before the boy switched the television off, the room going completely dark. In the shadows, the boy laid on top of the starchy sheets and wondered where the mare was now, what it was feeling, if it had been allowed to run today, or if, like him, it was more afraid of the day lying ahead than any of the others that had passed.

At midnight the stars assembled in the sky. Edging ever closer to the gleam of Nashville's skyline, its silver-blue bridges and stunted skyscrapers, these lone shapes twinned in the surface of the Cumberland River. Friday night becoming Saturday morning. Already past Somerset, already past Nancy, past Glasgow, past Bowling Green, past the Tennessee state line, then the town of White House, the horse in its metal stall, eyes blinking rapidly; the road flickering past, the muffled roar of speeding traffic, appearing and then disappearing. The driver of the black pickup, Rick West, marked the hours along I-65 by the infrequency of other towns ahead and behind, yawning, eyes failing, then having failed, jerking themselves open just in time, coming up on I-40 and the town of Goodlettsville, then the familiar northern border of Nashville, its blue-white lights like from a dream—the dream having ended abruptly a good four or five years before. Beside him, the girl snored, face flushed against the passenger-side window, hands folded before her like a cherub. Taking the next exit, the black pickup departed from the expressway, the lumbering trailer echoing loudly as they slowed to a stop in the loose gravel of a motel's parking lot. *Skylight*, the sign read, flashing with red and blue light.

Inside, the motel lobby was dark, as bleak as an all-night pawnshop, the overhead fluorescent lights flickering on and off, making
Rick squint his way to the counter. A young Pakistani clerk—seventeen or eighteen years old at most—was busy playing an arcade game
in the corner of the lobby. He seemed startled by Rick's appearance.
The clerk nodded without a word and then hurried through a wood-
paneled door marked *Employees Only*, reappearing behind a plane
of bulletproof plexiglass on the other side of the counter. Behind the
glass, he began to mime instructions to Rick. Yawning, Rick signed
the register, using the company credit card—which old man Bolan
always agreed to pay, though only after a lengthy interrogation. The
blue key fob was dropped through the slot in the plastic shield. Rick
tipped his hat to the clerk and marched back to the truck, unlocking the silver handcuffs, waking the girl, the girl rubbing her eyes
with the back of her hand, cursing him in her sleep. He walked behind her down the outdoor corridor to a wood-paneled room, the
girl collapsing onto one of the single beds, which was covered with a
wheat-colored floral bedspread. Rick stood there for a moment, eyeing the layout, then ambled into the bathroom to be sure there were
no windows, no ways to sneak out, then gestured to the girl, who
wordlessly cursed him again, yawned, and then stumbled into the
john. The sound of water running, rushing, the girl gargling, the fau-
cet screaming like a murder victim. The girl stumbled back out, face
clean, eyes closed, collapsing onto the bed once more. Rick eyed the
bed frame, striding over, and slipped the jaw of the cuff through the
metal frame, attaching the other end as gently as he could to the girl's
left wrist. The girl did not even struggle, did not even make a sound,
just pulled the white pillow over her head, kicking off her shoes, each
one landing on the beige carpet with a thump. Rick stood there, feeling as if he was still in the cab of the pickup, the road flying before
him, the world still moving. He suffered an alarming sense of vertigo
as he leaned over to slip off his boots, fighting against the cowhide,
losing one sock in the process, falling forward onto his own bed, too
tired to move.

The girl was soon snoring, the snore also a kind of condemnation. Lying there, removing his shirt, the cracks in the ceiling branched above him like the blue and red highways he had traveled over the last two days. It was hard not to think of old man Bolan lying in bed, surrounded by nurses, nightstand lined with orange vials and trays of pills, not sleeping, never sleeping, lying in his magnanimous four-poster, perched up by half a dozen pillows, call button in hand, imploring Rick to sneak him a glass of scotch or a piece of "that black girl's chocolate cake," summoning him to sit at the bedside simply to avoid having to face those creeping, timeless hours past midnight on his own. Rick stared up at those endless lines and cracks and saw in them the indefatigable features of his bedsick employer and also the fractures of his own future, for when the old man finally did die—turning back to East Texas dust—Rick was certain he'd be cut loose. He was just a glorified ranch hand, and he knew that Bolan's son Dwight, a fancy entertainment lawyer and Rylee's father, had no love for him. As soon as the old man kicked and the land went to the heirs, Rick would be set to drifting once again. He closed his eyes but the sound of the highway rumbling nearby rang loud in his ears; suddenly he found he was too restless to sleep.

He pulled on his shirt, stood in the dark to be sure the girl was asleep—leaning over to check the silver handcuffs—then slipped open the motel room door and stumbled outside. He put on his boots in the corridor, straightening his bushy brown hair with his fingers, and brushed his teeth with his finger. He found a payphone at the end of the corridor and deposited a quarter and a dime, punching in a local number he was certain would no longer be in service. When it began to ring, his heart snagged in his chest. The voice answering after five or six rings was softer than it once was, groggy with sleep.

"Yes?" she asked, and even hearing her voice, knowing it was really her, still in the same place, was enough for him. He hung up the phone, stared at it as if it might rear up like a rattlesnake and strike, and then shuffled off. He discovered a crumpled pack of smokes in the back pocket of his jeans, fingered one out, and started down the road, whistling a made-up ditty to himself. He was feeling reckless now; angry; lost.

About a mile and a half from the motel he found a bar, and a girl of age who was willing. The girl was young, no older than twenty-one, and although her chestnut hair and gray eyes were winning, her yellow teeth and dirty fingernails made him loathe her a little. There was a white and pink tattoo on her neck—a unicorn—and beneath its front paws was a pink swastika. She saw him staring at it and said she used to run with a white-power guy who got a job at a plating plant here in town. She looked like a cokehead or crackhead or junkie or some such thing. They did it in an alley, standing up, him turning her away, pants around their ankles. She did not stop talking. The whole time she was telling him about her hometown, Memphis; her caterwauling mother; the concerned stepdad; a job she used to have at a tool and dye plant; her voice bright, unending, a star growing fiercer and fiercer as Rick was trying to concentrate— "So my mom said if I didn't like it I could leave, and after that I came up here . . . Wow, do you mind . . . my knees kind of hurt that way okay, thanks, and then I . . ."—but he was trying like hell to ignore her, glaring at the back of her shoulder, at the back of her head, the back of her left ear; he was saying something, some woman's name, then he was slowing down, his thighs tightening against the back of the girl's legs; then he came, and let go, and she fell on her side, looking up at him. He was digging into his wallet, unfolding bill after bill, and tossing them at her.

"You don't have to do that," she said, slowly picking up the bills. "I'm a person, you know. I'm a somebody."

"What's your name?"

"Wanda."

"Wanda," he said seriously, as if he had never heard the name before. "Wanda, do you know anyone around here who moves crystal? I've been out of town for a while and I've got a package I'd like to get rid of. You know anyone who can help me out with that?"

The girl nodded, shoving the rolled-up dollar bills into the front of her brassiere.

"You got their number?" he asked.

The girl nodded again, reached into her purse, found an un-capped black pen, and wrote the digits on the back of some religious tract. The faded, mimeographed cover was titled *The Beast*, the font grimly situated over a panel of red and yellow flames.

"Thanks," Rick said, slipping it into the back of his jeans. "And Wanda?"

"Yeah?" The girl looked up at him, eyes glazed red.

"You oughta call your folks," he said. "Because this town ain't no place for a somebody."

When he got back to the motel room, it was almost two a.m. He stood there smoking a cigarette outside the door, crushed it against the flat of his boot, and snuck back inside, climbing into bed. He lay there for a while, observing the cracks in the ceiling once again, thinking of old man Bolan, of the girl sleeping in the bed across from his, and slipped off to sleep, wondering what the old man could want with another horse.

Like a thunderhead, the shot rang out, creasing the air with a metal-lic crack, once again ringing in his ears, the old man startling awake, eyes penetrating the hoary shadows of the motel room, the smell of burned cloth and flesh, of copper, of antimony, of lead, the feeling of the projectile once again riveting his shoulder, knocking him back to the clotted ground, the crack of the bullet lodging itself somewhere along the back porch, metal striking wood, forever burying itself in the hand-painted grain of a colonial post. His heart was pounding so loud that he was sure it must have wakened the boy. He glanced over and saw that he was wrong; his grandson was fast asleep. The old man pushed himself on his side and stared at the clock, a blur of red dots and lines, tilting his head this way and that until he could read its digital face: *3:13*.

He held his hand over the spot on his shoulder and was again

startled, this time by the shape of the horse standing there, its great
and tensed quarters confined by the smallness of the room. He sat up
in bed, holding a hand out, the horse's long eyelashes flickering before him, understanding at once that the horse had been sent here by
Deedee, that if he could only put a hand to its mane, if he could only
lay his palm against its milky throat, then somehow the horse would
carry him to wherever his long-departed wife had been hidden. The
bedclothes slid to the floor as he got up on weak, spindly legs, his
breath as uncertain as his approach. When he saw the animal shudder, when he realized he was smelling its muddy, intestinal scent,
he knew it was no figment, that it had come here to bring Jim Falls
beyond the woods and green-capped hills to where his wife's voice
was a chiming wind, a solitary sound, where she was not just a ghost.
But he hesitated, pausing there, bare feet on the green carpeted floor,
seeing the boy lying there in bed, still asleep—like all sleeping children, looking younger than he really was. The old man worried what
would happen to the boy, what kind of life he would live. When,
finally, he made up his mind, turning to place his hand on the nape
of the mare's neck, he found it had disappeared.

Rick pulled himself from the bed, glancing down at his watch, unable to discern which way the two hands were pointing. Something
was trying to kill him, something was trotting upon his head. He
could hear the loud clang somewhere, echoing within the useless
cavity that ran from his left ear to his right; a low, metallic thumping;
and just then he was sure the girl had escaped. Shirtless, he crossed
the carpet, throwing open the motel room door, certain he was going to see the dark blond hair disappearing in front of him, but the
parking lot was lifeless: there was his truck and the trailer, three semi
cabs, and a compact car parked at the other end, but there was no
shadow of any kind of movement, no echo of a falling footstep. He
glanced over his shoulder, saw the lithe form of the girl still in her
bed, coughed a little, checked his watch once more. It was 3:20 a.m.
He stumbled back to the uncomfortable bed.

A moment or two later, he heard the wallop once more, the sound ringing out with a distinct clang. This time he sat up in bed, calmly surveying the room, trying to trace the cause of the noise. After hearing it again, Rick stepped out of the motel room altogether, standing shirtless in the doorway, gawking at the invisible shapes of stray clouds hanging on the horizon, the whump coming once more, then again. Rick strode off barefoot across the parking lot, wincing at the sharpness of the gravel, following the sound to the rectangular trailer, standing beside it now, trying to get a glimpse inside, the horse striking its cleats against the floor. What he felt was an embarrassment then, the horse snuffling there, whinnying a little, eye to eye with the stranger gazing at him through the foggy window and ventilation slits, Rick buckling his pants and sliding the trailer bolt open, the bolt missing its lock, the door folding down into a ramp, the horse growing frantic in its movements, tail swinging this way and that, cleating the metal floor over and over, Rick stumbling up the ramp, the ripe putridity of horseshit and piss causing him to gag a little, searching around for a lead, a simple rope for the animal's neck, bare feet squishing in manure and straw, whistling to the animal a little, placing a steady hand along its shoulder, talking to it, "Come on, now, come on," the horse edgy at first, its anxiety as palpable as its smell, Rick finding the reins, the horse trying to turn but unable, clumsily knocking its head and forelegs on the side of the trailer. Rick, patient, tugged on the line again, the horse following now, steady, steady, steady, down the ramp, the parking lot reverberating with each step, then down, rearing a little, huffing, taking in the night air, the borderless gravel, the grandeur of the sky.

Whistling softly, cooing like a dove, around the side of the oblong building to a half-filled swimming pool—lounge chairs floating haphazardly in its deep end—the horse trailed behind Rick, ambling gaily, Rick stroking its neck, its muzzle, finding a green hose with a red spigot. He twisted it open and let the horse drink greedily from its spray, then, its thirst slaked, it sniffed at a row of mums and pansies that had been planted as border around the pool area. There, in the blue-green light of the half-full pool, stars reflecting in the frothy murk, the horse grazing on scrub, its gray-silver-white form ancient, unasking, Rick watched it like he had been made privy to someone else's dream.

The boy stood beside his grandfather's bed trying to wake him, but found he was unable. The old man was lying prone on his stomach, his face buried in a pair of pillows, floral comforter wrapped about his narrow body like a shroud. The boy began to panic, leaning over, listening closely for the old man's breath, squatting there, staring at the stiff white locks of hair, the narrow ears covered in the same bristly fuzz, the neck long, badly wrinkled eyelids looking like they had been sewn up.

"Sir," he muttered, clearing his throat. "Gramps?"

On the nightstand, in between the two single beds, the CB crackled and chirped. Some trucker from Arkansas by the name of Thunderbolt was spinning a loose one about a speed trap in West Memphis and a female cop—a *mama bear* in his own parlance— whose big brown eyes and wide hips were well worth the ticket and the lost time.

"Gramps?" Quentin shook the bed gently, watching the old man's face. It did not move, did not tighten or twitch in the slightest. "Sir?" The boy sighed, panicking, his palms going moist with sweat. He put his hand on his grandfather's ribs and gave them a harder shove. "Gramps?"

It was nearing eight a.m. and the boy had not eaten since sometime the day before. He put his ear close to the old man's mouth, holding his own breath, listening hard, and there, clicking faintly against the still-glorious white teeth, was the sound of his grandfather's respiration: insignificant, wheezy, the noise rattling softly there in the back of his throat. Angrily now, the boy shoved his grandfather's chest, then again, the old, haggard-looking face still drawn up in ghoulish repose.

"Fuck this," the boy whispered, and grabbed the old man's wallet.

There was a vending machine at the end of the motel hallway with Stick-E-Buns and Pop-Tarts. The boy chose one of each, gobbling them up quick, standing beside the humming ice machine. He paused and thought of his grandfather, deciding to get him a stale-looking package of soda crackers. He leaned over and retrieved the crackers and then walked down the carpeted hallway, trying to listen to the sounds of other guests in their rooms. It was quiet. He thought he heard an electric razor, somewhere else a maid vacuuming. At the end of the motel corridor, a door on the right was ajar, and creeping along slower now, the boy paused, trying to glimpse inside. There was the sharp, snippy bark of a toy-sized dog, then another. Quentin peered around the doorframe to see an elderly woman in a pink Stetson and pink leather vest, white skirt ballooning above her knees, holding a pink Hula-Hoop, and through it—the hoop—one, then two, then three tiny white poodles were leaping. The boy stood there gawking, an unfamiliar smile breaching along his sturdy face, the woman whistling commands to the dogs, each of them yipping and leaping in reply. One, two, three, they leapt through the pink hoop, pink bows tied about their white furry necks.

Back in the room, the grandfather had not moved, a graying skeleton in a purple flower–patterned grave. The boy sat down on his bed, tearing open the Pop-Tarts, staring at the flickering images on the television set. A game show played on-screen. The boy watched for a few moments before the CB began to buzz again with garbled static.

"*Old Rooster, you got your ears on? Over.*"

The boy turned toward the CB, eyeing it suspiciously.

"*Old Rooster, this is Happy-Happy. You on 17? Over.*"

The old man did not move; the boy sat there, wondering what he ought to do.

"*Old Rooster, got a line on that Texas trailer you were hunting. Over.*"

The boy carefully set down the remains of his pink Pop-Tart and took the mic in his hand, awkwardly holding in the call button. "Hello?"

"Old Rooster, you the one looking for a pickup with Texas plates, hauling a horse trailer? Over."

"Where is it? Over."

"Got a twenty on that. Parked in a motel lot. Over."

"Where?"

"Right off 65th Street. Name of the place is the Skyline."

"Um. Okay. But . . . um . . . what's 65th Street? Over."

"That's I-65. Across the state line in Nashville. Still carrying its load. Over."

The boy stood, shoving his grandfather hard, forgetting the CB. The old man did not stir, though his breathing was louder now. The boy pulled the comforter back and saw there was a wide splotch on his blue-black shirt, the blood from his wound seeping onto the gray bedsheets and pillows.

"Gramps? You're bleeding."

He took the old man's right hand and shook it hard, squeezing the brittle palm, feeling the unfamiliar rigidity of the hand against the soft flesh of his own fingers.

"Sir."

"____"

"Jim."

"____"

"Jim Falls." The boy dropped the hand and muttered, "Don't be dead. Please, Lord Jesus, if you are not just a children's book, please don't let him be dead."

Slowly the boy reached out a hand and placed it over the old man's mouth. It was warm. He could feel his grandfather's breath faint against his palm. The boy pressed his hand down until the grandfather began to shudder.

One eye, bird-egg blue, finally parted open, the eyelashes like thorns stiffened by sleep.

"Come on, Grandpa. We got to go. They found her," the boy murmured, the words as tremulous as the sun pausing there behind the dust-flecked curtains. "Grandpa."

"—"

"They found her."

"Hmm?"

"They found her."

In the cold, midmorning light—the sunbeams tumbling in dazzling waves across the gravel parking lot, the light itself still shaded by the gathering clouds—he could see that the horse's left eye was pink and partly swollen. It did not look well, the animal. It had been cooped up in that metal box for far too long and had gotten both dehydrated and antsy, its tail flicking back and forth with a vicious commotion. He gave water to the horse once more and searched for something to feed it from the trash bins along the rear of the building, but found nothing. So he loaded the animal back into the trailer, filled its feeder with more water, swung the door closed, and fastened the bolt. He strode back inside the room, gathering his boots at the door. The girl was smoking, lying on her stomach, one hand chained to the bed, one foot raised up in the air, the toes curled back, the other leg stretched out, watching the television, biting her fingernails distractedly. She looked kittenish, like she was planning something, as she slowly glanced from the soap opera playing on the TV to where Rick was standing, setting sloe eyes on him.

"I'd like to ask you a question," she said.

"All right."

MARVEL AND A WONDER

"How much is my geegaw paying you?"

"For what?"

"For driving me back."

"Not nearly enough."

"Come on. How much is it?"

"He ain't paying me anything. I work for him. It's part of my job."

"Your job? Like those drugs you took off those guys in Arkansas? When they find you, they're gonna fuck you up."

"Do I look worried?"

"I swear to God, you are one of the stupidest people I know."

"Considering some of the folks you know, that takes some doing. I appreciate it. I do."

"How much to let me go?"

"Huh?"

"How much to turn me loose?"

"I don't know. What are you offering?"

"A thousand."

"A thousand? Shucks. I know you got more than that on you."

"Fine. Two thousand. All you have to say is I ran off."

"Then I'd be the fool, wouldn't I?"

"You know that as soon as I get to my grandpa's house, I'm running away again."

"Well, that's between you and him."

"This is totally fucking pointless."

"Maybe to you it is. It gives me something to do. I manage to get off the ranch this way."

"Why do you have to be a dumbass? Just take the money."

"Nah. For one thing, I wouldn't know what to do with it."

The girl huffed, throwing her head forward into her cuffed hands. "I guess you want me to suck your dick then."

Rick felt his face go flush. He looked away and then back at her again. "You oughta stop acting like you're stupid. People are liable to start believing it."

"Fuck you."

"Come on. Get dressed. We got some errands to run."

"What errands? I'm not running any fucking errands with you."

"That horse out there needs to eat. It looks like she hasn't been fed in a few days. I got that and a couple other things I need to do. Go on now and put some clothes on."

"Fuck you. I'm not going anywhere."

Rick closed his eyes for a moment, silently fuming. He grit his teeth, bracing himself, then strode over to where she had piled her trashy-looking clothes. "Put these on. I ain't got time to waste with you. It's eight a.m. and it's still another ten hours back, and I don't plan on spending another night away from home. Here. Now try and act like you were raised right."

"Fuck off," she said, taking a bite of her fingernail.

Rick closed his eyes again, then opened them just as quick, looking around for something to smash. There was a gray-green lamp near his knee that he seized, snarling, raising it up over his head, bringing it down hard, slamming it near his feet. The girl screamed, folding her legs up, as the fragments of porcelain and glass shattered across the carpeted floor. He stood there, hulking, shoulders tensed, searching for something else to demolish.

The girl laughed. "Wow, that was smart. I mean, that was, like, really intelligent."

"Put on those clothes before I ring your neck."

He slipped the key into the handcuffs and pulled her off the bed. The girl snatched her clothes from the corner of the bedspread and stood, pausing in front of the bathroom door.

"All you got is muscle," she said, glaring at him. "Which is why you don't scare me. Because you ain't smart. If you were, you'd turn me loose. But all you are is big and dumb."

The girl closed the door behind her. Sitting on the corner of the bed, Rick was forced to admit she was probably right. It had always been his trouble—no smarts. He sat there on the bed, waiting a few minutes, then paced around the room a little before knocking on the

door. There was no answer. He tried the doorknob and found she
had locked it.

"Goddamnit. I ain't waiting anymore. Get out here now."

"Fuck you. I want my father."

"What?"

"I said I want my father. I ain't going anywhere with you."

He could tell she was crying but he didn't care. He took a step
back, lined his boot up with the doorknob, and gave the silver appa-
ratus a solid kick. The door swung open; the girl was sitting there on
the toilet, half-dressed, face folded into her hands, eyes rimmed red.
Without a word, he grabbed her by her shoulder, shoved her toward
the bed, grabbed the unlocked end of the handcuffs, and slipped the
teeth back through the bed frame, snapping them in place. The girl
was now weeping loudly, but Rick only turned, grabbed his hat from
the bureau, and quickly slammed the motel room door.

Over the hood of the pale-blue pickup, the boy watched the road as
the buttes and craggy hills rose on either side, the highway dipping
up and down along the treacherous topography, short mountains and
rocky caverns nothing like the flat horizon he was accustomed to. He
began to worry about landslides. Or stray boulders. Or a puma running out in front of the truck. His grandfather, softly snoring on the
bench beside him, looked like a scarecrow. The boy began to fear
that if his grandfather continued to sleep much longer he might die
right there; that if he gave his grandfather the chance, the worn-out
heart and weary lungs would themselves stop working.

"Sir?"

"—"

"Gramps."

"Hm."

"Are you asleep?"

"Hm."

"I think we're getting closer now. Only another hour maybe."

"—"

"Does your shoulder feel all right?"

"—"

"Does it hurt?"

"—"

"Gramps?"

"Hm."

"I think you should try and stay awake."

"Shhh."

"You should try."

"—"

"Do you want some more soda crackers?" The package lay half-eaten in the corner of the window, silently vibrating. "Do you want some?"

"No," the old man whispered, tilting his hat farther over his face.

"Are you sure?"

The old man turned one blue eye on the boy. "Do you mean to pester me to death this morning?"

"No sir."

"Well, I'd like to close my eyes if you don't mind."

"I don't mind. I only thought . . ." The boy glanced over and saw his grandfather had shifted his weight against the passenger-side door, his white cattleman hat now pulled completely over his eyes. "Gramps?"

"—"

"Gramps?"

"Hm."

"Do you ever think about God?"

"—"

"Gramps?"

"—"

"Do you?"

"—"

"Did you ever think maybe God isn't real?"

"—"

"Gramps?"

"—"

"Do you ever think about if God's real or not? That maybe it's all made up?"

"—"

"I do. I think about it all the time. I don't know. I'd like to know but I don't. Gramps?"

"—"

"I don't know if He watches over us. Why would He? Wouldn't He have other things to watch over? Birds and other things?"

"—"

"Gramps?"

"—"

"Do you ever think like that? Like maybe He's real but isn't even watching? Like maybe He forgot about us. Or maybe He's angry?"

"—"

"Because how else . . . ?"

"—"

"Because how. How else could things be the way they are?"

The old man did not answer at first, only lifted his face and stared at the boy for a moment before he tilted his hat back over his eyes. He turned toward the passenger-side window and said in a weak tone: "I'm going to rest some, for a while. Keep an eye on that gas gauge. Remember: it likes to lie."

"Yes sir." The boy glanced down at the fuel needle that ticked back and forth, eyes darting back to the uneven road.

The girl had gotten most of her wrist through the teeth of the hand-cuff, but the metal bracelet was now caught on the wide ball of her thumb. She leaned over and licked the spot, slipping the ridge of the metal arm back and forth, back and forth, pulling with all of her weight until the joint and knuckle nearly separated, the cartilage and bone and muscle slipping apart, nearly sliding beneath the constricted metal, but it was not enough. She was trying not to cry but then she did. The cable TV was blaring some Technicolor horse opera: Jimmy Stewart was raising a pistol and firing at someone. She bared her teeth and tried once more, yanking as hard as she could, wishing the thumb would just break, but it would not, the metal cuff cutting into the back of her hand, blood raising to the surface in perfect pink dots. She sniffled a little, giving up, as this was her usual way.

She collapsed back on the bed, thinking of her granddad and what he was going to say when he saw her tonight, or tomorrow at the latest, the scandal in his eyes as he took in the gaunt frame, the bruised arms, the ruthless, desiccated eyes. Hissing, throwing her whole weight into it, she tugged once more, stretching the tendons in her neck until the thumb popped beneath the silver bracelet. Her arm, freed, nearly smacked her own nose as she flew backward onto the bed, breathing hard.

The first thing to do was run. Then think. No. No. She ought to call somebody first. She needed money and a way out of town. She was too tired to run. She rushed toward the phone, sweeping the receiver up from the desk, and began to dial Brian's number, then thinking better on it, she hung up and tried her friend Rinna. The line rang and rang, Rinna's answering machine picking up, the familiar bouncy voice, Rylee screaming into it, but there was no reply. She tried Brian's number, but there was no answer there either as it was still before noon and she didn't know if he had made it back to Dallas and hadn't even expected he would pick up the phone at this time anyway. She tried a guy she used to know named Sal, whom she had slept with twice, for coke, but some scag answered and kept hassling her about who she was, so she hung up.

She was in deep shit now, seriously deep shit. She thought about calling her granddad but stopped after dialing the first few digits, knowing he would just send that asshole Rick after her wherever she went. So she stood for a while just trying to decide, wondering if maybe she had burned out some important part of her brain with all the different drugs, had soldered shut whatever it is you're supposed to have up there that helps you make all the right decisions. All she could do was hover with the phone in her ear, listening to the dial tone humming like some mechanical whip-poor-will, the TV erupting with gunfire from the other side of the room. She sat down on the floor, phone in hand, eyes glassy with tears. She thought maybe she should call the bus station and find out how much a ticket to Memphis would cost. She had friends in Memphis, people she could stay with for a while, at least a couple of days.

She found the phone book next to the Bible in the bottom drawer of the motel's dresser and flipped to the right page. She dialed slowly and talked to the operator at the bus stop who told her it would be thirty dollars for a ticket to Memphis; there was a bus that left every three or four hours. The girl hung up and grabbed her purse, searching through her vinyl pink wallet, quickly discovering it was empty. Somehow she had blown through all of her geegaw's money. Or that asshole Rick had taken it. She stared down at the purse like it was an open wound and whispered, "Shit, shit, shit, shit, shit, shit, shit," wondering where she was going to get the money. This had been her problem her whole life: she wasn't good at figuring things out quick. She was like her dad, or her grandpa. She needed to think on things awhile before she could decide what to do. She then realized that asshole Rick would be back any second. The tears, coming so easily, made her wish she could call her grandpa. But he would only tell her to come home. But home was no good. So she sat there feeling sorrier than ever for herself. To which Lee Marvin laughed.

Searching through town, Rick West found a Tractor Supply Company—part of the national chain—and went up and down its aisles with a shopping cart, dropping in a bag of oats, a bundle of hay, some eyewash, and a salt block. In the parking lot, he slid open the trailer door, carefully climbed inside, and dumped the bag of oats into the feeder, the horse pushing the bag out of the way, rushing the clump of cereal. In the dank humidity and dusky scent of the trailer, Rick placed his hand on the animal's neck, listening to it chew softly, feeling the skin to be sure the horse was no longer dehydrated.

At a corner phone booth a block away, he stopped, parked the truck, picked up the receiver, slid in a handful of dimes and nickels, and dialed the same Nashville exchange he had tried the night before. The phone rang and rang and finally some child answered. The voice was high-pitched, the uncertainty in it sounding like an indictment, and so he hung up. He fingered another few dimes into the coin slot, found the number on the back of the religious tract, and spoke quickly, in hushed tones, to the other party on the line, and in less than three minutes arrived at an agreement. He would bring the package by in an hour and receive three thousand dollars for it.

If Wanda said he was straight, the voice reasoned, then he must be, because that chick did not think highly of anyone.

Back in the cab of the black pickup, he pulled out of the gravel parking lot and drove up and down the adjacent side streets, looking for something, circling once, then again, and then finding it— pulling the truck and trailer up in front of a grass-lined park. The children—it being a Saturday—stood at a cautious distance at first, then leaving their posts at the swings, the slide, the merry-go-round, they came over to where Rick held the lead rope, walking the animal, then giving it some slack, the kids gawking, sitting there in the grass or leaning up against a boxwood tree, the horse rearing up a little, Rick shortening the line, watching it trot smartly in a wide figure eight. Seeing it move, it was clear the horse was a racer, and a high-bred one at that, the animal switching to a steady canter in perfect effortless motion; Rick could not help but whistle, certain old man Bolan had no idea what he'd bought.

A thought sprung like a loose coil directly into the center of his mind, a thought he was partly ashamed to admit because of its stupidity, its grandeur, and its simplicity: what if he sold it himself? He smiled a little, shaking the thought off, and turned to watch the animal canter again. What if? What if he drove on to Memphis instead and sold it there? Or back up to Kentucky? It was worth forty, fifty grand easy. Maybe not. Maybe only ten or twenty. But think of the things he could do with twenty grand. He could start over. Move out to Wyoming. Buy a small spread of land. Rick made a few soft noises, the horse's white ears perking up, as he extended his calloused palm toward the animal's muzzle.

Stopping at a rest area, the grandfather glanced down and saw the bloody spot on his shirt had grown in size. He sought out the restroom, stumbled inside, and stood before a row of dirty mirrors. His left shoulder was throbbing, the pain reaching out across his arm and chest like japonica vine. Slowly, he unbuttoned the shirt, slipped it off, and set it down on the grimy sink. The paper tissue was pink now, smeared with blood. He lifted the reused medical tape and winced a little upon seeing it—the wound white and raw, pus-filled. It was oozing something, and what it was, Jim did not know. He tried to sop it up with toilet paper, then slowly he reaffixed the bandage, but the pain was too great, reaching all the way up to the side of his head. It was infected, and the infection had already begun to spread. Hands shaking, he fumbled through his jean pockets and found the last of the Percocet, slipping the two pills on his tongue, buttoning the shirt up, ambling out of the rest facility, pausing once near a pair of pop machines before his legs began to quit on him.

The boy was waiting near the truck, whistling. He saw his grandfather stalling, eyes looking foggy, mouth slipping open, and rushed toward him. He got one arm under the old man's right shoulder and shifted his grandfather's weight against his own, walking together like somnambulists, step by step, back to the caustic, human odor of the truck.

"I ain't got much," the grandfather said as the boy helped to buckle him in. "I ain't got much. Lord, let us have this one thing. Just this one thing."

Back at the motel room, Rick was surprised to find that the girl had slipped off the handcuffs and was now sitting on the floor, sobbing, the telephone receiver lying in her lap. She was inconsolable. When she peered up at him, she let out a howl, her narrow shoulders trembling. Rick stood, hat in hand, unsure if he should shout at her or offer to help her to her feet. He did neither, just simply stood there, wondering how in the world a nearly grown woman could cry so much. Where did they come from, all these goddamn tears? He tapped the brim of his hat against his thigh, clearing his throat. She was kicking at the floor, having a regular tantrum, when he finally leaned over and put an awkward hand on her shoulder. She brushed it off, slurred some invectives, and kept up her crybaby antics.

"We got to hit the road. I guess you can cry just as good in the truck," he muttered, trying to make a joke of it, but she only snarled some other curse his way.

Once more inside the black pickup, he locked her right hand to the passenger-side door, tightening it more than he knew he ought to. The girl fussed, complaining right away, "My hand's turning fucking purple," to which Rick replied: "That's your fault now, ain't it?"

Out along the expressway, passing the few skyscrapers, the bridge, the river, peeling out south and east, finding the exit, slowing the vehicle down, the girl glancing out the window suspiciously, watching as the modern-looking highway quickly spun out into a series of small houses, some A-framed, some squared off, the paint looking worn, dull in the afternoon light, broken windows like black eyes. Rick circled around the neighborhood, the girl sitting up now, asking, "Where are we?" Rick silent for some time before answering, "East Nashville."

The neighborhood was blighted; squat-looking shotgun houses, sinking front porches, yards full of scrub, cardboard boxes, automotive parts, raw, rotting garbage. Birds—crows, a gang of them—surveyed the streets from the telephone wires, huddled like vultures. Corner boys, only ten or eleven years old, called out the names of the dope they were peddling. The Nashville sun—hot, cutting through the air like a saw blade—gave the general impression that life here was not so very bad, only savage.

"What the fuck are we doing?" the girl asked, and Rick refused to answer. He slowed the pickup in front of one of the dilapidated shotgun houses. The structure appeared to be made out of old paper, not one of the corners straight.

"What the fuck?" she asked again as he switched off the vehicle.

"We're doing some business," he said distractedly, eyes appraising the empty streets, the boarded-up houses. "Wait here and don't make a fucking peep." He grabbed her wrist again, checked to make sure she was locked there tight, then climbed out, slamming the door behind him.

Almost immediately, a corner boy, this one a little older than the others, somewhere around twelve years of age, caught sight of him and hurried his way, calling out some name or number Rick did not recognize. He tried to brush the kid off, but the guy was a natural-born entrepreneur, and seeing that Rick was not interested in narcotics, he quickly changed his tactics.

"I got tires."

"Tires?"

"Tires. For your car."

"I got all the tires I need."

"Not if someone shoots them out."

Rick smiled. "Is that a threat? Are you threatening me?"

"No. I just got good tires is all."

"Well, I'm not interested, kid."

"What about a gun?"

"A gun? What kind of gun?"

"I don't know. A pistol. I don't know the name of it."

"No thanks."

"You can't afford it?"

"I can afford it."

"You don't look like it."

"Thanks, but I'm gonna pass. I appreciate your spirit, though. You know these folks who live here?"

"Them people there are crazy. They the only white people on this street," the boy said before strutting off to join his crew back on the corner.

From the passenger seat, the girl watched Rick climb the three cement steps, knock on the door, and disappear inside. Already, she was struggling against the metal cuff, forcing her weight against the door, but the handle was too strong and that asshole had made the cuff too tight. She kicked the dashboard, screaming to herself, pounding her fists against her lap. She tried to force the gearshift into neutral—why, she did not know—but it would not budge. She thought of honking the horn, then glanced around and decided that, from the looks of the place, no one here was going to help her. So she waited, cursing herself for her own stupidity, for having run off with Brian, for calling her grandpa and asking for cash, for not departing from the motel room when she had had the chance.

She reached down into her purse, fumbled around inside it, searching for anything at this moment that would help, and then paused, staring at her set of keys. There were three of them on a ring. She held them in her palm, feeling the dull edges, the sharp points, imagining how she might use them as a weapon, how, if the opportunity arose, she might poke him in the eye or try to jab him in the face. She folded the keys in her hand, deciding the best thing she could do now was to wait, to wait and be ready; for whatever she did, she would have to do it quick and without thinking. She held the keys for a few moments before realizing she did not have the courage to try anything like that. She shoved them back in her purse and started searching around the dashboard for something else that could save her. And then, almost as quickly, she realized there was nothing. She did not even bother to cry. She felt, for the first time in her life, that she had been given what she deserved.

About three minutes later, something strange happened. A weird light flashed from inside the dirty-looking house, then it flashed again, just a muffled pop, then a third one, erupting in the blank afternoon. The boys on the corner glanced up, with the trepidation of prey animals, then sprang off, disappearing from their stoops. Almost as quickly, Rick was making his way out of the house, the door behind him hanging open. He was cradling an armful of cash against his chest, holding his pistol in the other, walking rapidly up to the vehicle. He tore the driver's-side door open, pulled himself inside, and started up the truck, the wheels spinning as he threw it into gear.

"Shit. Shit, shit, shit, shit," was all he could mutter, glancing in the rearview mirror, seeing the horse trailer flashing there, then turning to peer into the driver's-side mirror. "Shit."

The girl knew better than to ask.

Rick took a quick peek in the side mirror once again, shoved the grimy-looking money in the various pockets his jacket offered, and spun the truck through the East Nashville streets. He looked over at the girl, as if he had only now realized she was there, and said, "Shut the fuck up. Not a word. Not a single fucking sound from you."

"Your ear is bleeding," she responded, staring at the right side of his face.

He held his hand to his ear, grasping at it with his unsteady fingers, shaking his head. "That's not me," he said, eyes on the road.

The boy said, sitting behind the steering wheel: "Do you remember that time when I got lost? When I was five?"

"—"

"The time we all went to the state fair?"

"—"

"I was just thinking about it."

"—"

"I was scared because I thought you left me. We were all in the 4-H tent and I walked off and when I looked up I didn't know anyone. Do you remember that, Gramps?"

"—"

"We were all there. Mom and Grandma and me and you. We all went together. That was right after Mom came back. The second time she came back."

"—"

"She came back with black hair. She'd been in San Francisco. When she came back, you didn't say anything for an hour. Me and Grandma thought you were gonna start hollering and we were all sitting there in the kitchen waiting for you to say something. Do you remember that? My mom brought me back a necklace with a shark tooth and I put it on. And then you looked at her and said, *What did you do to your hair?* And then Mom leaned over and put your hand on her head and you touched it, like you had never seen black hair before."

"___"

"I think she'd been gone for a long time but I don't remember how long it was. She'd call sometimes. I remember talking to her on the phone. I'd stand by the kitchen window and stretch the cord all out and ask her if she had gotten the sun yet. And she'd say, *Yes sir, thanks for sending it to me,* and then she'd ask me about my day."

"___"

"So she came home and a few days later we all went to the fair, and we went inside the 4-H tent and then I got lost. I went off by myself and when I looked up I saw I didn't know anybody and there was all the animals, the calves and ponies and rabbits, and they were all in their cages and for some reason they looked scary to me, and then I walked out of the tent and the fair was really big and there was a ton of people and I didn't know what to do, so I tried to find you, and I knew you had on your white hat so I tried to find somebody with a hat like yours. And I walked up to this man and he had a white hat but he turned and he had a brown mustache, and that was when I was scared of people with mustaches, so I ran off again."

"___"

"I don't know why but I was always getting lost."

"___"

"Even when I'd go to the grocery store with Grandma. She had that piece of blue yarn she'd tie on my belt loop. Do you remember that, Gramps?"

"___"

"And she'd tie it to her hand. Right around her wrist. So I couldn't wander off. But there was too many people at the fair to do that. Do you remember all that?"

"___"

"I don't know why I did it. Why I was always wandering off."

"___"

"I don't know why."

"___"

"I guess I thought I might be able to find my dad watching me.

That's what I used to think. That he was following me around all the time. And that one time at the mall, in Indianapolis when I got lost, I thought I saw him. I thought he was following us around, watching us. But he was just some stranger. I guess I was weird back then, wasn't I?"

"—"

"That day at the fair I was scared. They had that ride there, the Zipper, the one that spins you up and down, and it was all painted silver and blue and it was so high and I thought it looked like a crucifix, and I remember asking you about it and you said it was just a ride, and then you bought us all funnel cake and I didn't finish mine but Mom did and you said how I wasn't anything like my mother because she had the worst sweet tooth out of anyone you knew, and we were sitting there and I looked at Mom and she was so young and pretty, and once at Sunday school the teacher asked if she was my sister, and when I got older I figured out how old she must have been when she had me, and we were all sitting in front of the Zipper, and it was so tall and loud that it made me sick, and Grandma walked me over to a garbage can and there were flies all around it and inside were a bunch of paper plates and food and I vomited, and you said, *No more junk food for you*, and that's when we all walked toward the 4-H tent. My mom was holding my hand, and there were all these faces, old-people faces with cowboy hats and glasses and everybody dressed nice, and there were all these white faces everywhere, and then we were walking to the 4-H tent and Mom was holding my hand and we were looking at the rabbits, because she said she used to raise them in grade school and had once won a blue ribbon, and that's when I looked up and thought I saw my dad. He wasn't my dad but he looked the way I thought he would look and so I walked off after him."

"—"

"He was tall, like you, and he was wearing a cowboy hat. He was dark. His face was dark and he had dark hair. And he was walking like he was in a hurry. And then he turned and smiled at me and then

I knew it was my dad so I kept following, and he went to the bath-room so I stood in line and watched him go, and then when he was finished and went to wash his hands, I stood next to him at the sink. He was washing his hands and then he asked me if I had a problem and I shook my head no and then he asked me why I was staring at him, and I didn't know what to say, and then he asked me what did I think I was doing bothering strangers. Then I got upset and ran off, and that's when I ended up hiding behind the 4-H tent because it was dark there, and I sat down and didn't answer even when I heard them call my name on the loudspeaker, and I knew I should have come out, but I didn't want to, not until I had it all figured out, and then you and that man from town, the one from the bowling alley, you moved some sacks aside, and I was sitting there saying the Our Father and Hail Marys and you—you were the one who found me."

At a rundown shrimp house, Rick parked the truck so he could wash the blood from his neck and hands. He was in a panic as he barreled into the restroom. He shouted at his reflection in the tilted mirror, slipping off his undershirt, using it to wipe his face, his hands, his ear, then cleaning the gun, someone knocking on the restroom door, Rick barking, "Hold on a fucking minute," shoving the dirtied undershirt into the bottom of the trash bin, buttoning up his shirt, sliding the pistol in the back of his pants, taking a few deep breaths, staring at the lopsided image within the mirror. Then he shoved the door latch open and rushed out. By the time he was back at the vehicle his hands were shaking again. He climbed inside the black truck, ignoring the girl, and began to pound on the steering wheel with his fists, one blow after another, shouting the same word again and again, "Fuck! Fuck, fuck, fuck, fuck, fuck!"

The girl curled up away from him, hiding herself against the passenger-side door.

And then, as if she was meant to understand the terrible disagreement of his thoughts, he hissed, "Anyway, it's your fucking fault bringing my ass up here."

The girl did not think it made any sense to argue. In fact, she did not say much of anything.

"Okay. We're gonna sit here a minute and take stock."

The girl stayed silent.

"Let's just set here and try to think."

"I want to go home," she whispered.

"That's where we're going. I just need to think this through and make sure we don't screw ourselves by doing anything stupid."

"Fuck you! Let me go!" she hissed, shaking her braceleted wrist.

"You need to shut your mouth right now," he barked, grabbing her by the chin. "You need to shut the fuck up so I can think this through."

The girl pulled her chin free and spat in his face; the words she spoke then were as ferocious as the look in her yellowed eyes: "Fuck you! As soon as we're back in Plano, I'm telling my grandfather what happened, and then I'm calling the fucking cops!"

Once she had spoken the words out loud, she realized the dreadful, stupid mistake, the latest mistake in a series of dreadful, stupid mistakes, though maybe this one was going to cost the most. The expression on Rick West's face now, the eyes going blank, the mouth forming a serious line, a quick series of questions, answers, thoughts, proceedings, actions, all coursing through his brain, before he nodded at her blankly, realizing exactly what he had to do.

"Really?" he muttered softly. "You're really gonna call the cops on me?"

The girl did not reply, only looked down, feeling as if something dear had just been thrown away.

"Well, missy, you and I are going to have a talk," he announced, a smile appearing on his thin lips. "You and I are. What we're going to do is, we're going to go somewhere private, where we can be alone and talk. We're going to go somewhere and have a talk and see if we can't come to an understanding about things. All right, how's that sound?"

A flood of terror seized the girl's body. She did not notice her knees shaking, not until she placed her hand on them. Rick started the truck, sure of himself once again, sure of the course of action he needed to take.

Along highway I-55, ten, fifteen minutes outside of town, he pulled over to the side of the road, switching off the vehicle, the woods standing witness to what was about to occur. He walked around the front of the truck, opened the passenger-side door, unlocked the handcuffs, and then marched behind her, shoving her into the shadows of the staggered trees, the forest ahead growing darker with each step. As they walked, the girl stumbled ahead of him, glancing back every few feet, Rick prodding her, trying to think how this would all play out, wondering if he ought to wait a few minutes and think this through, but already knowing the answer, already sure of the consequences either way. He stared at the back of her head as she limped along, thinking of how like a foal, how like a nestling deer she had once been, darting among the fence posts on the ranch until she was old enough to ride, and then old man Bolan had her outfitted in the funny tan jodhpurs and red jacket like she was some young aristocrat going foxhunting, which in a way she was, for she'd had her pick of her grandfather's stable and chose a roan-colored pony about as reckless and lissome as she was. But that girl was somewhere else, and the person walking before him—with the wan red face, sallow eyes, nose running, hair looking like it had forgotten what it was to be washed—was only a job he had been told to do, and now, because of the circumstances, he was going to have to make some tough choices. The girl tripped then, falling to her knees.

Without a word, though with a tenderness he now felt he could afford, he reached down and lifted her up by her armpit. He marched her deeper into the forest, him taking a quick glance behind to make sure they were alone—no houses or places of business for miles. She fell once again, legs shaking, her body collapsing onto the leaves and twigs and dingy pine needles, him standing above her, frowning, the girl now crawling on her hands and knees, not fighting it but unable to get control of herself, the sound of her snuffling reminding him of the time she had been thrown from a pony and had the wind knocked out of her—more scared than hurt probably. A fog of sympathy clouded his mind just then—him remembering the sight of her in those funny tan breeches, holding her own rear, her tiny face wound up in inconsolable anger, glaring at the animal out of the corner of those wide blue eyes—and drifting in this reverie for a moment too long, he gave her an opening. For when he leaned over to get her to her feet, she turned with a sharp-edged stone in hand and swung it firm against the side of his face, catching him against the corner of his left eye, his boots flying out from under him, the dead leaves and stony earth coming up hard against the back of his head. Before the pain crept all the way across his jaw, he almost laughed, thinking of what a dolt he had been, what a greenhorn, knowing at once that she was and had always been much smarter, much more conniving than anyone ever wanted to admit. He saw the flash of the dirty-blond hair blaze above him, framed by the light breaking through the tops of the trees, and tasted blood in his mouth. She was running. He lay on his side and watched her dart through the woods, her hair like a long blond flame, his eyes still unable to focus on anything. It was almost like falling in love.

Near eleven a.m., the pale-blue pickup headed southbound, the boy's foot against the gas pedal, his leg growing sore, his grandfather snoring beside him, side mirrors rattling along I-65, fuel gauge ticking treasonously back and forth, the vehicle's engine screeching like some mythical cornet signaling the end of the world.

The girl hurried up a culvert along the western edge of the highway toward the pickup truck but then paused, skidding in the gravel, realizing she had not bothered to take the keys. Instead, she was still holding the stone. She cursed, a sound that was not even a word, and glanced over her shoulder to see if he was after her yet. He was not. What now? What the fuck was she supposed to do now? And then, in a rare moment of decisive judgment, she ran toward the back of the silver trailer, found the bolt, slid it away from her body, and gave the door a shove. The silver ramp slid down, the door flying open. The swart odor of the trailer struck her as she began shouting, the horse unconcerned, its gray-white tail flapping back and forth. She stomped on the ramp, then slapped its muscular buttocks, but the horse would not move. Finally, remembering the stone, she picked it up and pounded it against the side of the trailer, screaming at the top of her lungs, and watched the horse as it gave a start, scrambling out of the silver pen, tramping down the ramp, both of them dashing off along the highway in opposite directions: one going south, one going north.

Without hurry—as the grandfather was no longer capable of moving faster than a shifting, lopsided amble—they made their way into the motel lobby, the old man lurching forward, pulling the brim of the white hat down over the top of his eyes, the boy opening the glass door before him, holding it for his granddad, the two of them crossing the gray thatched carpet, treading beneath the fluorescent lamps to the front counter which was shielded in bulletproof glass. It was empty behind the Formica ledge, no clerk on hand. The old man surveyed the lobby, finding a young Pakistani fellow busy at the arcade machine in the corner of the room. The machine whistled and chimed as the young man tapped the red buttons frantically. The grandson squinted behind his glasses and smiled, immediately recognizing the sound effects and melody of the game's music before he had a chance to see the machine itself. It was *Donkey Kong*. The original. He was sure as soon as he heard the digitized character jump. The youthful clerk glanced over his shoulder, then turned back to the screen, reprimanding himself, "Jesus. Watch out." As a flaming digital barrel crushed the clerk's tiny pixilated hero, he cursed, slapping the joystick. "I can't ever get past this level." The game was now over, a sad tune playing, as the clerk turned to face Jim and his grandson, greeting them politely, hurrying through the employee door, then reappearing behind the plane of plexiglass.

"Sorry about that. Single or double?" the clerk asked, his voice muffled behind the plastic partition.

"Neither one. We're looking for someone," Jim rasped, leaning close to the glass. "They were toting a horse."

The clerk stared at the old man and frowned. "You don't want a room?"

Jim itched his nose with the back of his hand. The boy stood by his side, quietly watching. "No sir. Like I said, we're here looking for somebody. They had a horse trailer with them. It was a man and a girl. I believe their license plates were from Texas. I was hoping to get some information about them," and here Jim slid a folded twenty-dollar bill through the opening in the partition. The clerk stared down at it and shook his head.

"I don't think I can do that."

"We just want to know if they're staying here."

"I'm not supposed to give out that information."

Jim frowned, tapping his fingers against the cold metal counter. "What if you just nodded? Could you do that and let me know if they checked out or not?"

"My mom and dad, they own this place. They put their whole life savings into it . . . and I . . . I don't think I oughta. We don't want any kind of trouble."

The grandfather sighed, pulling the white cattleman hat down over his eyes once again. He knocked his fist against the counter and struck on a thought. "How about we buy a room? Can you put us in the same room they were in?"

The boy behind the counter smiled, his dark face widening in complicity. "Yes sir. Will that be cash or charge?"

Lying on his back, Rick realized he had been watching the sky through the shapes of the trees for a long while. He was dazed by the black and gold and green of the sunlight on the leaves and the figures they made. He blinked and found his left eye sticky with blood. He sat up, or tried to, and then felt the swell of his jaw, his head throbbing. He pressed two fingers to his brow and the tips came back wet. He must have had a good-sized gash up there. When he finally managed to sit up, his head swam with spotted light. He grabbed a corner of his shirt, held it over his left eye, and stumbled back toward the highway. All around, and from the trees above, the birds were chirping, telling him to lay back down. He nearly did, his legs buckling a little, him grabbing the side of a tree for balance.

The truck was parked exactly where he had left it. He trudged toward it, immediately noticing one of the silver doors of the horse trailer had been flung open. Then his ears began to ring with heat. He limped over, holding his hand out against the trailer—the surface of which was hot and dusty—and made his way around to the rear where he saw the depth of the girl's duplicity: in her escape, she had turned the fucking horse loose, here, right on the outskirts of this worthless goddamn city. The sight of the empty trailer, its floor littered with hay and manure, a pool of urine standing near the back corner, its ramp down, the smell of the horse itself still betraying the air, almost made him vomit. He bent over, holding the shirt to the side of his head, and staggered against the truck. He had been outsmarted. Twice. He had been outsmarted twice by this spoiled, unremarkable girl.

The highway traffic rumbled past, the sound of which caused his brain to vibrate unpleasantly. He wavered there, trying to think of what to do next. There was the horse. And the girl. And the cut above his eye. He felt himself going faint. First, the horse. Then the cut. Because he was going to bleed to death driving around if he didn't get it fixed. After that, if he got the horse, and if he got his eye fixed, then there would be the girl. One at a time. First things first. He thought of a sergeant named Ron Poland whom he had buddied around with in the navy. A nice enough fellow who always repeated the same damn thing when he was drunk: "First things first. First things first: we get liquor. Then we meet some girls. First, we eat. Then we fight. Okay? First things first."

His knees felt like he was on shore leave. He was happy remi-
niscing like this. He was getting pleasantly light-headed thinking
about all those times. Bells rang in his head, the traffic roaring past
like the engine of his old ship: the USS *Abraham Lincoln*. No. No,
that wasn't the name of the first one. What was the name of it? Jesus.
He had to get his head together. Shoot. Take a deep breath. Good.
He moved the shirt away from his forehead and saw it was stained a
motley red. Shit.

   He climbed inside the vehicle, searching for the keys in his
pocket; upon finding them he realized his eyelashes were stuck together with blood. He breathed for a moment and saw the driver's-
side door was hung wide open; he was sitting there in a fog, staring at
nothing, and bleeding. What had that girl done to him? He glimpsed
the digital clock on the dashboard, even though his left eye was now
closed with blood. It occurred to him that it was now one o'clock in
the afternoon, though for the life of him, he could not remember why
this even mattered.

The black man glanced up from the battered blade of the riding mower—the machine lying on its side, its metallic undercarriage gleaming, greased, exposed—running the whetstone against the edge, trying to get it sharpened once again, hoping to get one more run from it before he was forced to order its replacement from Dallas. Beyond the green hummocks of Spring Hills, the cemetery was peaceful at this time of the day, the headstones placed at solemn intervals, extending in all directions as far as the eye could see. Peering over the top of his glasses—the glasses which were all but useless, as the prescription was a good ten or twenty years out of date; his daughter, who would take care of such things, had finally gotten married to a man from her church and had moved away to New Orleans sometime back—the man felt a tremor run through him, right down to his toes. He placed a hand over his chest, directly beside his name tag, which was stitched with the name *Roy* in blue cursive.

A white woman—in a white veil—was walking through the woods. He set the whetstone down, crouching behind the overturned lawn mower, the apparition slowly moving among the graves, searching for its final resting place, moving only as a ghost could, in a languorous, drifting motion, rising and falling, rising and falling with the wind through the loblolly pine. And then, just as it was making its way toward him, his hand searching for a screwdriver or folding knife—anything with which to defend himself—it disappeared. The old man pushed the glasses flush again his face, seeing it was not the ghost of a woman but the ghost of a horse, some Confederate charger searching for its long-dead rider, as many of those gray soldiers of old had loved their horses more than their wives or children, stealing rations for them, blankets for them, sleeping right beside them at the edges of the battlefield. In some of these cemeteries were colonels and generals buried right alongside their famous steeds, and there were two or three plots only a half-mile off where a handful of racehorses had been buried. The groundskeeper was no longer startled by the white horse tromping there, as it was only one of a dozen ghosts he had seen over the course of his years working that particular job; and so, resuming his work, he eyed the blade, taking the whetstone in his hand again, and set it against the dulled edge.

Inside the motel room, the grandfather glanced around at the rumpled twin beds and blotchy carpet like it was a crime scene. He took a seat on one of the beds, pulled the telephone into his lap, and hit *Redial* on the glossy receiver. Soon someone on the other end answered, announcing that it was the bus depot in a twangy drawl. The grandfather smiled and asked for a street address. They immediately headed back to the pickup as it was now past two o'clock and there was no telling how much time they had lost already.

The girl ran. The first thing she came upon was a long concrete embankment leading up to an overpass. She followed the sound of traffic until she made it to a thoroughfare where she thought it would be safer to try to walk like a normal person. She decided the most important thing was to keep moving; anywhere, as long as she was moving. She could think about the rest later. Because that asshole would be after her, and when he did find her, he was going to seriously fuck her world up. Just keep moving. She peered both ways down the drag, saw a strip mall, a Bob Evans restaurant, some sort of factory where they made frozen chicken, and a wax museum. What she needed was a telephone right now. And somewhere she could hide out for a while so she could have a chance to think. All right. She decided on the wax museum, limping there, her soles sore from running in stupid fucking heels.

The museum looked like an old-time general store, and when she stumbled inside, she found she was in the middle of a chintzy-looking gift shop. She asked the elderly lady behind the counter if there was a public phone anywhere. The woman pointed to a pay phone, down a short hall, outside a pair of restrooms. The girl smiled, rummaging through her purse for some change, knowing there were only a few nickels and dimes. She would call her father this time, collect. She was through fucking around. If she sounded desperate enough, he would have to help her. She picked up the phone, dialed the operator, told her it was collect, and waited for it to ring. Her father, a Dallas entertainment lawyer, would never answer it himself. It would either be her mother or Marta the maid. After the third ring, Marta's heavy accent offered a greeting and Rylee immediately started shouting for her father. A few moments later, her daddy picked up.

Apparently he was working out on the treadmill, the sound of its whirring gears, his shoes slapping the belt, and Lynyrd Skynyrd blaring in the background.

"Daddy?"

"Hello?" came the deep voice—a basso profundo—the tone of which made her feel bad for everything she had done.

"Daddy?"

"Kaylie?"

"No, it's Rylee, Daddy. Dad, I'm in trouble. Real trouble. I need some help."

She could hear him slowing down, switching off the machine, the Southern rock still rising from the speakers.

"Rylee, Jesus, honey—where are you?"

"Daddy, I need help. I'm in Nashville. I want to come home."

She could imagine his expression now, him pinching the space between his eyes.

"Rylee, you know the deal. Your mother and I . . . we said we're not sending you any more money. If you want to come back home, the door's always open. But I . . . we've been down that road too many times with you."

"Daddy, I'm scared. I really need your help."

"I don't know how to help you, sugarplum. What can I do to help?"

"You can send me money for a ticket. I'll fly home today."

There was an odd pause, and some sniffling, and suddenly she realized her father was crying.

"Rylee . . . I don't know what to do," he whispered. "Jesus, why do you keep doing this to us?"

"Daddy, please. Please. I just want to come home."

He blew his nose and seemed to regain his composure.

"That last place, that one, Sunnyvale, they said we were enabling you. They said this was our problem too. I'm not going to send you any money. I want to, I do . . . but your mother . . . We just can't."

"Let me talk to her."

"She won't talk to you, Rylee. If you want to talk to her, you got to come back home."

"Daddy."

"We will always be here. If you need to talk. If you need to come home. But we can't . . . You did this to yourself. We loved you, we trusted you, we sent you whatever you asked for, and all of it . . . you took this family . . . you took this family and turned it into something . . . It's all bullshit, Rylee, it's all bullshit. Nobody's happy now. If you want to come home, we'll be here. I promise we will. But if you want to stay out there, then you got to be on your own."

The girl slammed down the phone, her eyes glossy with tears. She wiped her face with the corner of her sleeve, the old lady behind the counter asking if everything was okay. She nodded and saw the sign on the top of the counter. It was a dollar to visit the museum and she paid it with the handful of dimes, nickels, and pennies still in her purse. She walked down a hallway demarcated by velvet ropes and came upon the first exhibit which featured Hank Williams, his lean face emaciated, the flesh the same color and texture as a corpse. The figure's fingers were overly long, as gravity and time had both done a number on them, the digits looking more like melting candles. There was a layer of dust over everything, his guitar and blue suit looking like they had been stolen from a tomb. It made her think of her geegaw for some reason, and she realized if he died it would be her fault. She had broken his heart and the heart of everyone who had ever bothered to love her one too many times. She had taken his money once again, and now, now there was no way she could ever go back home.

She stared at the figure awhile longer, leaning against the red velvet rope, passing Johnny Cash—her daddy's favorite—then George Jones, Charlie Rich, Minnie Pearl and her unassailable price tag, the whole cast of *Hee Haw* done up in wax, and around a corner, Barbara Mandrell and her two sisters. Then she came to Ernest Tubb, who was decapitated, the sign on the exhibit reading, *Under Repairs*. There was something about the shape of the figure standing there, missing its head, the sight of it strangely unnerving, the lapels of his suit and shoulders forming an empty plane above which was only darkness, only black. The room was silent except for a distant hiss—the sound of traffic passing by on the interstate outside—and as she leaned forward, she felt a tremor run through her. The girl suddenly knew what she was staring at, though she could not name it at first: she finally realized it was the permanently occluded face of death, whose death she did not know—hers, her grandfather's, someone she loved, she wasn't sure—only that it was death before her now, and death behind too, death all around. If that man Rick West found her, he would kill her. She was sure of it. All she could do was think to run, as running was all she had ever known or done.

* * *

As they drove, the grandfather rested his head against the passenger-side window, daydreaming. He saw himself walking in the dark, aged twenty-seven, stiff in civilian clothes, looking up at Deedee Calbert standing on her front gallery, at her bare white neck; then he turned and saw the pickup, his father's pickup, shipyard blue. He took one step toward it and saw himself inside. He was inside the truck now and there was a girl before him and the girl was in his arms and he was reaching behind her, his hands searching beneath the tight yellow sweater for the clasp of her brassiere. For the life of him he could not get it undone. Overseas, the Korean girls did everything. Here, in the front seat of the pickup, he was all thumbs. He realized he had never in his life tried to unsnap a bra on his own. The girl was being patient, which he took as a kindness. He could feel her heated mouth against his neck, her arms draped stiffly around his shoulders, as if she were holding her breath, waiting for him to get the brassiere off, but he was having no luck.

The girl smiled, a smudge of pink lipstick along the corner of her mouth. She folded her right arm back, and it was this moment—with her thin right arm turned behind her like a bird wing, and a partly amused grin on her lips, her forehead pressed up against his, rolling her eyes and saying, "You can't tell me you never done this before," unhitching the pale, rigid garment with one deft movement, laughing, the laugh a shape against his lips—the one moment where he fell crashing into love. The film played before them on the gigantic screen, the other cars and trucks parked in close vicinity, rows and rows of steamed windshields, couples in similar moments of candor, the Western *Silver Lode* going mostly unseen, Jim fighting to remember he was not overseas, knowing the girl would not want to see him again if he did what he wanted to do, his hand creeping up the girl's goose-bitten thigh, brushing the fringe of her skirt, making its way upon her stockings, struggling at the garter there, the girl not pushing his hand away but not making any kind of sound either, him struggling to get his pants unbuckled, the oily, perfumed smell of her hair reminding him of the girls over there, what had they done to him, how they made him uncouth, unchristian—and then something went wrong, the feel of her breasts too much or the fuzzy fabric of her sweater, him not getting his pants off in time, something which had happened a few times with the girls over in Korea, him going slack now, burying his face in her hair, and then, for no good reason, absolutely no reason at all, him seeing Stan's face—lying there in the mud, eyes searching the leaves for a familiar color, a familiar shape, dead, dead, dead—Jim feeling like a child then, muffling tears into the girl's hair, squeezing her harder than he knew he ought to—knowing no girl worth her salt would bother to see him ever again—and here he was, with a girl from church, a girl his mother had called up for him, an American girl, and he was moaning, the white flash of Stan's face still rising before his eyes, Deedee's cheek against his cheek, and then the faint words that ricocheted in his ears, "It's okay. It's okay," she said. "Shush, shush. It's okay."

To see her like that again. What I would give.

The boy asked him a question. The grandfather turned, unsure of what had been asked.

"Which is why I don't know if there's a heaven," the boy said, serious, small hands gripping the steering wheel.

The grandfather nodded once and thought, *Not a place,* and then, *but a person, a fragment of an hour.*

Rick's left eye was tacky with blood, his head echoing, thrumming like a jukebox that had been dropped down a mine shaft, as he drove along the breakdown lane of the highway, searching the leafy woods along the side of the road for any sign, any flash of gray or white. Before him was a thick forest, and far beyond the rearview, more of the same. Behind the steering wheel, his fingers gummed up with blood; he realized it might be easier to just drive off now, to forget the horse, the girl, old man Bolan and his job, to get as much distance between him and anything else that might happen. Then he remembered that old son of a bitch's rage, the look in Bolan's dyspeptic face, how—

propped up by a legion of pillows and afghans—he would receive
the news of the missing horse and the missing girl and Rick himself,
and would, in his inestimable rancor, assume he had been cheated.
It would be this assumption, this old Texan and his unvanquished
sense of honor and valor, that would cost Rick West his freedom or
his life, for as far as everybody in East Texas knew, the old man was
not one to be cheated—not in business nor horse deals nor any other
quarter. He would call the Texas Rangers himself, or hire someone,
someone with the ferocity of the local Mexican drug cabal, a group
originally from Mexico City whom the old man had gotten friendly
with—renting out his lumber trucks to the traffickers for their state-to-
state distribution—no, if he burned the old man, the old man would
issue his revenge, even with his final, foggy breath, and that, that
was no way to live, on the run, as he once had, leaving Fannie in this
wasting little town five or six years back. No. What he had to do was
to find the horse and get his eye to quit bleeding. He took the next
exit off the highway and cruised slowly past the muted colors and
overcrowded structures of nameless motels, of failing auto dealer-
ships, of row houses too worn for welcome mats, each of these re-
iterations of the same dreary dream, taking shape outside the bleary
windshield. It would be nothing to spot a fine horse in a shithole
such as this.

In the front of the age-old Winn-Dixie, its white facade withered
and peeling, there were two children riding the mechanical carousel,
a boy and girl, brother and sister, the boy on a green frog, the girl on a
silver pony. "Again," the little girl kept saying. The mother, wanting
to avoid another blowout with her husband—who was busy spending Saturday afternoon in bed trying to get sober—decided to take
as much time with the grocery shopping as possible. She searched
through her purse, found another fifty cents, and slipped the coins
into the machine, the two children galloping on with joy, their faces
pink with excitement. The mother lit a menthol cigarette and wondered if she ought to call her sister. Deb always had an extra room.

She held up a tentative finger to her sore face, thinking on it. Her left eye was turning blue-black, and no matter how much makeup she used, it was obvious what it was. She sighed, took a long drag on her menthol, and saw something moving fast between the rows and rows of parked cars, something fearsome and unequivocal, like a vision, insistent in its own opulence. She turned and stared at it full-on, a white horse, unsaddled, unbridled, clambering directly across the Winn-Dixie parking lot at a steady bolt, its hooves striking the pavement with a metallic ring. The children gaped, all three of them, this small forlorn family, for a moment at least, feeling blessed.

It did not matter if she was lost: the important thing was to keep moving. Anyway, it was better than just standing around waiting to get killed. The girl Rylee had thrown her gold high heels into a gutter a few miles back, finding it easier to go barefoot. Then she found a phone booth, searching for the bus station's address, tearing the soft yellow page from its binding. The bus stop was on Charlotte Avenue, somewhere on the other side of town. Already the sky had started to go dark. She walked on, sure she could feel the black pickup pulling beside her.

About seven miles from the bus stop, the girl stopped tumbling forward on her bare feet and remembered she was broke. She had no money and nothing on her worth anything. She had pawned whatever jewelry she had back in Arkansas and that asshole Brian had pocketed the small roll of bills they had gotten for it. She did not think she could do what she knew she might have to for the bus fare, though she had done all sorts of things in the past, as recently as a few days ago with the dealer they had met in Marked Tree, the old biker with prison tattoos and sun-spotted hands, who, at once, decided Rylee would be part of the transaction. He had been in two different federal institutions, or so he claimed, not bothering to take off his pants. When he placed his pockmarked hands on her bare shoulders, the age showing around his wrinkled eyes and mouth, it occurred to her that what was happening was kind of like incest.

Moments later, when he ejaculated, it was quick and violent, though what was lasting was not the sensation of his bristly flesh, but the oddly grateful look Brian gave her when he returned to the motel room. He was a fucking coward and did not care for her, which she realized as soon as she met his face.

It seemed she had been surrounded by men her whole life who were weaker than her and she felt she would never get out from under them. So there, in the middle of River Hills Drive, her left foot stiff and scraped pink, she rifled through her purse, then her wallet, then purse again, searching for a rolled-up bill, a flattened twenty. But there was nothing, nothing but a silver dime and two dull pennies, which she had known was all there was before she had even bothered to look. She stared down at the coins, feeling betrayed. The bus ticket was thirty dollars, which was twenty-nine dollars and eighty-eight cents more than she had. She spat at the ground and slung the purse over her shoulder, trudging on.

At the next intersection some black children were playing ghost-in-the-graveyard in the middle of the street. It was a game she faintly remembered: a girl was standing with her eyes closed, hands folded over her face, while the other children ran in all directions, flinging themselves under porches, over railings, underneath parked cars. Rylee stood there smiling dumbly as the young girl counted out loud, "Ninety-five, ninety-six, ninety-seven, ninety-eight, ninety-nine, one hundred!" The girl dropped her hands from her eyes and was startled to see Rylee standing there, her face caked in dirt, smudged makeup across her eyes, a bruise appearing along her chin, barefoot, reaching out desperately from the half-shadows of fallen darkness. "Help me," Rylee hissed, her mouth cracked and dried, "help me," to which the young girl screamed, quickly disappearing behind the corner of a small house. Rylee paused there, feeling the exhaustion and emptiness of the last nineteen years of her life, and sat on the front steps of the nearest house, peering down at her dirty toes.

A few minutes later, two girls approached, both under the age of ten and wearing the same handmade outfits—blue dresses sewn from a grubby floral pattern. They walked up to Rylee without suspicion and asked her what was wrong and what had happened to her shoes and where did she live. Rylee stared at them and began to lie, knowing that in doing so they would never trust a white stranger again. She told them she was a country singer who was lost. She told them her tour bus had broken down. She told them back home, in Texas, she had two mansions, each with its own guitar-shaped swimming pool. She told them she had dozens of gold records on her bedroom wall and she could send each of them one if they wanted. She told them she only needed a few cents so she could call her bodyguards who were probably worried out of their minds about her. When the two sisters came back with their mother's vinyl pocketbook, searching through it for change, Rylee snatched the wallet from the eldest girl's hands and took off running faster than she ever had. She did not feel shame at that moment, only regret, regret that what she was now running toward was nowhere near as lovely nor welcoming as what she had said.

As they sped across the Southern city, the boy glancing out the window at the crumbling midcentury facades lined with decay—the square-shaped brick buildings, the once baroque electric signs advertising joints and jukes that no were longer open—he lost track of the one thing his grandfather had warned him of. The truck wound down, its engine having seized up, the vehicle coasting to a stop just past the intersection of Lufton and Gatewood. The boy stared at the wheel as if it had somehow failed him, the grandfather groaning awake with a snort.

"What is it?"

Quentin, unsure, knowing and not yet knowing—not wanting to know, as it would mean he had failed his grandfather—tried the key again and again, the ignition switching on and off, though the truck refused to start.

"I don't know. It just died on me."

"It did, did it? When was the last time we filled it?"

"I dunno. While we were on the highway."

"That was awhile back, wasn't it?" The grandfather looked the boy directly in the eye.

Quentin glanced down at the gas gauge with a cumbersome feeling of guilt. "It says there's still some in there, but I guess maybe we ran out."

The old man reset the white hat upon his head. "Well, son, I'd have to say you're probably right."

Embarrassed, the boy asked, "What do we do now?"

"We got to find some gas."

"There was a gas station a couple blocks back."

"You grab the gas can from the back. We'll have to walk that way and see if it's where you remember it."

"No," the boy said, feeling brave suddenly, hoping this show of courage would somehow make up for his mistake. "I'll go. You wait here. Just in case."

"In case of what?" the old man said with a short smile.

"In case someone tries to take the truck. In case someone tries to tow it or something."

The grandfather nodded, proud of the boy, of the shape he was trying to make of himself at that very moment. "You got money?"

The boy said he did, then turned to meet his grandfather's eyes once more, and hurried off. He snatched the metal gas can from the bed of the pickup and ran as fast as he could in the direction of where he thought he had seen a gas station a half-mile back.

Rick felt faint, his head swooping down, heavy lids folding over his eyes; he pulled to the side of the road, feeling sick to his stomach, the hood of the pickup before him seeming soft and fluttery. Good God, that girl had done a number on him. He looked up from his tingling hands, out the passenger-side window, to where a couple of black kids were playing cops and robbers. As the pickup slowly trailed past, they all froze, watching it go, suspicious of the man with the bleeding eye, a red oil rag held up against the left side of his face. A boy, no older than five or six, braver than the rest, raised a cap gun—a chrome-painted, six-chambered Colt—aimed at Rick, and fired three times, each shot echoing with a sharp, burnt-smelling ex-

plosion. Rick took it as a verdict that the boy—like all children and
some keen, undomesticated animals—had an innate sense about
these kinds of things: life and death, morality and immorality.

The boy had seen something in Rick West's face and had fired
three times to try to ward off the sudden appearance of evil. But it
could not be forestalled, not like that, not ever maybe. The pickup
coasted on, Rick turning away from the children, feeling unmoored,
feeling as he did when he was a young man in the navy, as he did
the day he awoke to find himself in the brig with the dried flakes of
some dumb Filipino's blood in the webbed crevices of his hands.
He decided in that moment, clutching the steering wheel firmly in
his hands, that if he found the horse, he would take it and run. He
would find it, get his eye fixed, see if he couldn't chase the girl down,
drop her into a ditch somewhere, and sell the horse for whatever he
could get.

Among the Mexicans awaiting work that Saturday in the Home Depot's parking lot was Reynaldo, who tried to look unconcerned. He
leaned up against a parked car and ate a green apple, the last remains
of his lunch. Out of the corner of his eye, he watched the borders of
the parking lot for the white man from the suburbs—a kind, older
stranger who had hired him three times this week already—but it
was now past four o'clock.

"*A donde su güero?*" his compatriot Luis asked.

Reynaldo shrugged his shoulders and glanced around, still hoping to see the silver station wagon once again loaded up with land-
scaping supplies—shovels, dirt, black plastic trays overburdened
with mums, sweet potato vine filling the backseat. The white man
told Reynaldo he was selling his house—the man was a professor
and was getting a divorce; he had been cheating on his wife with a
student and his wife had found out—and so he was now trying to
clean the place up before he put it on the market. The white man
talked all day, incessantly, some of which Reynaldo understood,
most of which he did not. But he paid Rey incredibly well and even

fed him, pork one day, flank steak another. He had even given Reynaldo a book, a cloth-bound hardcover edition of *Don Juan*, the book written entirely in English. Though the words themselves were mostly indecipherable, Reynaldo still found the gesture profound. In the little room he kept in his sister-in-law's house, the book had been prominently placed beside a photo of his wife Luisa and their two children.

"*A donde su güero?*" Luis asked again, this time elbowing Reynaldo roughly in his ribs.

"*No se,*" Reynaldo whispered, holding the side of his hand up against his eyes. "*Es tarde.*" Just then he saw something silver cross his line of sight. His mood lightened, thinking it was the white man's car, the small globes of sunlight obscuring the actual shape of the thing, before Luis and some of the others began to whistle, "*Caballo! Caballo!*"

It was a horse.

The others started to clap their hands and stomp their feet, the horse speeding past them in a quick, wide circle, then starting back again, its hooves hitting the pavement with an irregular metal clang. It passed in front of him once and looped around, Reynaldo making himself very still, shushing the others around him, the horse sniffing the air with its great pink nostrils. A shiny, silver-embellished bridle was set upon its long snout. Rey blinked and slowly held out the half-eaten apple. The horse paused, turning its head wide, then circled back, sniffing at the air once more. Rey took a cautious step forward, the horse snorting a little, the apple still held aloft, Rey pausing to take in the animal's smell, its nervous, spasmodic quickness. The horse moved forward cautiously, snuffling the stranger's palm, taking the apple into its jaws with its yellowed teeth. Reynaldo slowly extended his other hand, placing it along the side of the horse's head.

The rest of them waited in the parking lot, watching. Reynaldo kept his hand placed against the animal's throat, gently stroking it, whispering what sounded like a song. Soon he was walking slowly, step by step at first, the animal following him, snuffling his hand again. Then he took hold of the bridle. He was now leading the horse from the parking lot, thinking if he could only keep it from getting excited and walk it the five or six blocks to his sister-in-law's yard, then all of the waiting, all of the fear—the long walk into San Diego, lying there on the beach, robbed by a group of fellow illegals he had traveled with, leaving his mother and wife, his children, his town, all of it—all of it would have been worth something.

On the other side of an abandoned lot was the gas station, bordered by the shadow of the highway. The boy saw there was no way to reach it except by climbing over a wire fence which was ringed at odd, haphazard intervals with heavily banded barbed wire. The street he had been walking along had become a dead end, an empty block of rectangular, tomblike warehouses and deserted factories, windows punched out. Posted along the wire fence were three different signs that warned against trespassing. The boy studied them, looked around, saw he was alone, then tossed the empty metal gas can over the ridge of the fence. It landed on the other side with a pitiful clang. He unbuttoned his jacket, struggled to the top of the fence, placed his jacket over the rusty-looking barbs, and heaved himself over, already sweaty, already out of breath. He fell on his knees in the dust on the other side and wheezed a little, wiping his forehead with the back of his hand. He stood upright and noticed a strange-looking shack pieced together by slats of discarded boards, unwanted scraps of wood paneling, drywall, and warped two-by-fours. He waited a moment to be sure no one was around and then leaned over, grabbing the gas can, and unhooked his jacket from the fence. He walked quickly, scraping his shoes in the dirt, feeling proud, lips pursed, loudly whistling the theme from *Donkey Kong* to himself.

All of this before the appearance of the dog.

The dog was no breed the boy could recognize, just a grimy mongrel. Beyond that, it appeared to be only teeth and jaws, with a patch of ruddy brown fur along its abdomen, more hyena than dog. The animal did not bark at first, poking its nose out of the tiny shack, sniffing the dry air. It took a few paces and grew tense, lowering its head, a line of drool springing from its pink lips. Upon seeing it, the boy froze, capsized by fear, at once realizing the shack was its house and this patch of fenced-off dirt its yard. The dog was more rangy-looking than any animal the boy had seen, lean though heavy-shouldered. Glancing to his left, Quentin saw that the opposite end of the fence was too far to try to run to. He realized that he was going to die. He was going to die, he was going to die, he was certain of it. All he could do was try to hit the dog in the head with the gas can. But it was light metal and wouldn't do much. Squinting over his glasses, seeing the dog's broad flat skull, almost like a copperhead in its wide appearance, the boy did not think any number of blows would stop the animal from ripping out his throat.

The dog began to growl, baring its fangs, squatting low to the ground, preparing to lunge. Quentin braced himself, covering his genitals with the gas can, his bowels ready to loosen themselves. He then realized he ought to try to talk to it, to explain his situation, and so he began to whisper, lowering himself as well, "I come in peace," extending his left hand cautiously. The dog snarled, treading backward.

"I know that I am in your yard. This is your yard and I know that I am in it."

The dog snapped its jaws, reeling to the left, circling now, its paws padding along the dirt.

"I am in your yard. It is your yard. I am just walking through. I am walking through to the other side. It is your yard. I am only walking through."

The boy stood up slowly, his left hand still out in front of him, the gas can above his privates. He took one decisive step forward, placing his foot down slowly. The dog barked but did not move, its ears perking up.

"I am only walking through." He took another step, the dog going quiet now, watching him. "I am walking. I am walking. I am going to walk over to the fence and climb it."

He heaved the gas can over the top of the fence, wincing as it hit the pavement and rattled dumbly. Hearing the ruckus, the dog began to bark again. Quentin raised his hand to calm it, speaking in a low, soft voice, "I am climbing the fence now. Now I am climbing the fence and then you will have your yard to yourself."

He hefted himself up the fence, fingers gripping the wire braids, slipping his jacket over the top once more, getting one leg over, then the other, sliding down, catching his right foot on a crooked wire, swearing a little, the dog watching him the whole time, no longer barking but with a look of interest, regarding the stranger with an affectionate concern, eyes bright, tongue loose, tail wagging.

"I'm okay," the boy whispered to the dog, examining his ankle. His sock had been caught on the fence somewhere and had ripped a little. "Thank you for allowing me passage through your yard. You are a benevolent creature and I salute you." The boy bowed now, grabbed the can, and hurried off down the street, the enormous electric sign in front of the gas station coming on with a dull blue light.

Rick sat in the cab of the pickup, his left eye swollen shut, his forehead and cheek dusty with flakes of dried blood, tendrils of gray fog rising above his head like various succubae, angrily exhaling cigarette smoke through his nose. Only halfway through the square, he flicked the remainder of the cigarette out the window, the sun now setting, its rays cutting across the dirty parking lot; a faded black tattoo of a spider on the back of his hand momentarily regained its former shape.

It was not the bloodied eye that caused him so much anger now. It was the girl. It was the thought of that stupid rich-bitch princess tricking someone into giving her a ride all the way back to Plano, to her father—or worse, her grandfather—and all the lies and bullshit she would spout. No, that would not do, not one bit. He shuddered a little, imagining what the crazy old coot would do, knowing how brutal, how relentless he could be—certainly the law would be involved, and if not, then so much the worse for Rick.

He circled past a fried-chicken stand, past a dilapidated hardware store, past a jewelry store that looked like it had folded decades before, riding up and down, back and forth across the twilit streets. He touched the back of his hand to the ridge above his left eye and saw it was still bleeding. It needed stitches probably, which would be more fucking time he did not have. It was going on six thirty p.m. and the fucking horse was nowhere in sight. The sun had nearly set and the arrival of night for Rick meant that he was coming to an end—not just with his search for the horse, but his job, his association with the rich old man, whatever meager sense of direction his life had previously had.

He began to daydream about running off to Cancún—or Costa Rica, where he had heard there was no law. He could get a job at a fruit plant and marry a brown-skinned girl who would want a half-dozen babies. As his mind reeled through these pleasant, far-flung thoughts, he remembered old man Bolan, the sight of him in bed—sickly though indomitable—weak hands curled around the telephone, speaking his awful half-Spanish. It made Rick seize a little, thinking of his employer. If the girl got back to Plano before him, if he did not find the horse and figure out a way to keep her quiet, there would be no end to his troubles.

So on he drove, the dusk appearing like a curtain, which the hood of the pickup slowly parted.

About a half mile or so down the road, two kids darted out in front of the truck; Rick slammed on the brakes, his head jerking forward. He was too startled to even bother swearing at them. He gripped the steering wheel, watching the two kids—brothers maybe, dark-haired, brown-skinned Mexicans—running down the street, the older boy tugging the younger by his sleeve. There was a look in the older boy's eyes, one of fierce excitement, of some sort of unforeseeable exhilaration, the older one forcing his brother to accompany him on some adventure, the two of them fleeing down the block. Rick watched their shapes for a moment and then softly swiped at the left turn signal, creeping along the curb, trailing beside the brothers for another block or so. Glancing out the passenger-side window, he saw a group of them, maybe seven or eight kids—all Mexicans—gathered in the side yard of a grubby white house that looked like it had been built with matchsticks. It was a party of some kind, the kids standing around, clapping. They even had a pony in the backyard. A man was leading it in a short circle. There were children piled up on the animal's back, two and three at a time, the man smiling in a straw cowboy hat, the horse bobbing its head up and down, its elegant-looking neck stretched out sinuously as it moved. The horse was a muscular-looking one, wide-shouldered, stark white.

"Fuck," Rick said, his bruised face erupting in a wide smile. "Fuck."

He threw the pickup in park, left the driver's-side door open, checked to be sure his pistol was beneath the flap of his jacket, then pulled it wildly from its holster. He slipped a little as he tried to remember how to walk, head still foggy, knees weak, gravity reeling all about him like the ground had gone soft. The kids who had gathered there did not notice him at first, and then panic starting on their faces, the boys glancing at the gun, going quiet, stepping in front of their younger sisters, the girls seeing the bloody, cauliflowered eye, turning to each other and gasping, the man in the straw hat with the horse, still unaware, leading the animal into a turn, two tiny girls, no older than four or five, perched like exotic birds on the creature's back. Rick did not need to speak, seeing the whiteness of the animal, its formidable shoulders, its haunches, the unashamed, untroubled glare in its eyes, recognizing it as the one he had been sent to retrieve only yesterday, placing the gun calmly at the back of the fellow's head, some of the kids yelling something in Spanish, other kids running off, the two girls atop the horse still smiling, then looking as passive as saints, the horse no longer stalking, the man turning, eyes wide with hope, Rick no longer in favor of thinking, only action, only momentum, only motion now, pulling the trigger, hearing the shot, the noise rippling through the air, straw hat drifting like a slow, wide leaf, the horse rearing up a little, Rick grabbing the reins with his free hand, calming it down, whispering softly, his palm against its muzzle, the man on the ground, eyes staring up with a questioning look, as if there were answers scrawled somewhere up in the darkening clouds, the rest of the kids disappearing now, Rick slipping the gun back into its holster, turning, seeing the two girls still sitting there on the horse's back, carefully, as if they were made of the finest porcelain, lifting them off, and placing them back on the ground.

The girl found that there were only thirteen cents in the wallet she had stolen. She knew the number was bad luck but decided to pocket the money anyway. She slipped the empty wallet inside a mailbox, hoping it would get sent back to its rightful owner, and struggled on, bare feet grayed with grit. She was still more than twenty-nine dollars short and had no idea where she was going to get the rest of it. So she wandered around for a while, wondering if she ought to try to call her geegaw directly.

A few blocks on, the girl turned down an alley, picking her way among a few garbage cans, hoping to find a place to pee. She glanced over the back fence of a small white house and saw a yard that was filled with worn-looking toys—nude dolls with faces that been rubbed off, a castaway pogo stick, a rocking horse that had faded—before spotting, there, on the back porch, a half-dozen pairs of shoes piled near the kitchen door, most of them kid-size. She ended up stealing some pink cowboy boots that must have belonged to a child but still fit her small feet, and then ran off back down the alley, smiling a little, proud of herself, all out of breath. A few blocks on, she hunched over, gasping at the air. She had never walked around this much in her life. She had never been on her own for this long before.

By and by, she was ambling along the street in the direction where she hoped the bus station lay, south by southwest, when she realized she had not eaten. She stopped walking and saw a rundown grocery store up ahead on the left and then strode listlessly inside, the electric eye reading her with condemnation. She snuck an orange and apple inside her purse and was hidden behind an ice-cold door in the frozen-food aisle—biting the orange, drinking greedily from a glass bottle of milk. A moment later, a towering, slope-shouldered security guard, face dark as night, appeared. Before she could begin to explain, he pulled open the door and placed a large hand upon her wrist.

Already the boy had filled the gas can, some of it sloshing at his feet. He hunched over, replaced the cap, and dragged the heavy can inside the fatal-looking gas station. The shelves had not been stocked in some time—there were two aisles with nothing for sale, the freezers also strangely absent of merchandise. A black girl with a blue baseball cap, her black, straightened hair pulled through the back in a ponytail, looked up from a glossy hair magazine. She frowned at the boy instead of smiling.

The girl's face was the smoothest Quentin had ever seen. She was chewing gum and he could see two dimples appear and disappear along her cheeks. He lowered the can beside him on the fog-colored tile and reached into his pants for the roll of cash.

The girl said a number out loud with disinterest, glancing back down at her magazine.

Quentin counted out the money and handed over three bills. As she recounted them and shoved them into the open drawer of the cash register, he noticed in her face a level of boredom, yes, but something more—a kind of loneliness—this girl only seventeen or eighteen, chewing her gum, leafing through magazines. Holding the gas can at his side, he saw for the first time in his life someone who seemed as lonely as him. His eyes dropped to the plastic name tag pinned above the soft slope of her breast. It said *Shanya*, which made the boy smile, the sound of the name like some far-off African princess. He realized she was trapped; there was nowhere for her to go. He decided for once he would say something; he would do something he had never done before and try to be someone else, an older, braver version of himself; he would stare at her a moment longer and then look her right in the eyes and say something like: *I can talk to animals.*

The girl glanced up from her magazine, the pink wad of gum indistinguishable from the contours of her soft tongue. "What?"

"That's why I'm interested in herpetology."

"What's that?"

"Herpetology. It's the study of reptiles. I'm planning on maybe becoming a biologist. Or a veterinarian. I like working with small vertebrates."

The girl's eyes were a little wide, puzzled, the gum still motionless in her mouth.

The boy continued: "I'm not gonna see you again so it doesn't really matter. But I thought maybe you'd like to know."

Then the boy heaved the gas can up against his hip and turned, slightly beaming, proud of himself, feeling that today was one of the better days, one of the best days, the glass door to the gas station slamming shut behind him, the familiar *Donkey Kong* theme now on his lips. *Da-da-da, da-da-da-da, da-da-DA, da-da-da-da.*

The fence rose in front of him once again, the gargantuan dog silent beside its shack, tongue flapping, the boy eyeing the wire enclosure for a moment, for a moment panicking, having forgotten that the gas can would be full on his way back. Then, smiling once again, he tied his shirt through the handle of the metal can, climbed halfway up the fence, and, using the shirt, lowered the can gently over, then pulled himself between the rolls of wire. He whistled louder, bopping his head back and forth, *Da-da-da, da-da-da-da, da-da-DA, da-da-da-da*, awkwardly landing on his knees on the other side of the fence, the dog still sitting there, its ears pitched, snout slightly raised, tongue no longer lapping at the air, the boy nodding to it, lowering his shoulders to the ground so as not to appear threatening, speaking to it slowly, respectfully, "I once again appreciate your generosity. I will make my way through your kingdom as fast as I can."

The dog was on its feet now, wary of the boy's swift motion before him.

"I am every bit your inferior, oh kind and wonderful dog."

The dog made a sound, its teeth bared tightly together. It began growling, head lowered, massive shoulders going tense.

"I only wish to pass through your domain safely."

The boy was at least a good ten yards from the opposite side of the fence. The dog began barking louder, inching forward slowly, head still lowered.

"I bow to your greatness, oh dreadful and benevolent beast. You are ruler of all you see. I am only a speck in your glorious kingdom."

Then the dog was in motion, a cruel flash of black and brown, the boy seeing the shape hurtling toward him, moving as fast as his legs would let him, feeling the animal gaining, the sound of it pouncing behind him, its paws padding quickly over the dirt, the scrape of its nails as Quentin darted left, lifting the gas can high, liquid spilling recklessly from its yellow rubber nozzle. *Now what?* he thought. *Now what?* He could smell the animal's stink, the ruinous decay of its yellow teeth, breath like hot garbage; he felt the dog nip at his calf, missing, then leaping and missing again. He made the mistake of turning to glimpse the animal, and in doing so slowed down and stumbled over his own shoes, only a foot away from the fence, the dog taking the moment to strike again, burying its fangs into the soft meat of the boy's right leg, snarling, snapping its head right then left, the boy screaming, howling girlishly, then remembering the metal gas can in his hand, swinging it back boldly, bringing it down hard upon the crown of the animal's wide head.

Boy and dog were both a little dazed, lying a few paces apart, the boy whimpering, pulling himself to his feet, mumbling as he made his way up the fence, lowering the gas can to the other side, blood darkening the right leg of his pants.

Back in the truck and down Covington to Catalpa, then a few more left turns, then a right, Rick pulled up beside the Pentecostal church, which at this hour on a Saturday evening, somewhere past seven p.m., had its doors propped open, an organ playing a lament, a grayish voice crooning out a prayer at the height of evening service. Beside the storefront church was the old house, which was the exact same color it had been when he'd left—sneaking off in the middle of an argument. He did not know why he expected the house to be a different color. It still had its white and blue trim, the gray roof still missing a few shingles, though now there was a worn-looking plastic Big Wheel out front, overturned, and a pair of metal roller skates lying near the front steps. He placed his hand against his left eye, which was a dried mess of blood and pus. He would need to drain it if he was going to see out of it anytime soon. And there was no way he could drive the ten or so hours back to Plano in the dark night, with only one good eye. And so here he was.

He parked in front of the old house, Fannie's house, and stared from the driver's-side window, taking it all in, wondering if she would still be there, knowing that she would be, as the phone number had not changed, and he had recognized her voice the night before. He wondered what color her hair was, how she looked, what she would say when she saw him. He did not think on it too long, as the more he considered the possible expressions her face might make, the more uncertain he began to feel, remembering the time when—on her birthday—he had offered her a pawnshop ring and said the words he had thought would appease her but hadn't. She had just thrown her head back and laughed, laughed, laughed, right in his face.

He was gathering his thoughts now, or attempting to. He tried the radio for some encouragement but got only got a religious program. Someone was shouting about penance. He switched the radio off and lit another cigarette. When he was ready—not ready, but afraid that if he didn't move now, he might not ever—he threw open the driver's-side door, cleared his throat, fixed his hat atop his head, fixed it again, and then strode up the cracked pavement leading to the front steps.

He climbed over the roller skates, the Big Wheel, pausing once more on the porch, his knees knocking a little, midsection cramped like he had some stomach rot from south of the border. He pressed the doorbell and stepped back, blinking his good eye over and over again—a nervous habit. She came to the door in a yellow robe, bleach-blond hair—nearly white—piled up atop her luminous, almond-shaped head, face appearing just-washed, cigarette burning in the corner of her mouth, fighting with her left flip-flop which must have come off on her way to the front door.

In that moment, Rick wished he had never stepped out of that truck, had never pulled off the highway, had never answered the ringing phone Friday morning when old man Bolan called with the location of his granddaughter's whereabouts. Because Fannie was, and had always been, the one thing that could undo him. There was just something about the way her head happened to sit upon her neck, crooked at an angle now, poring over him—or what she could do with a disapproving expression, because that was the face she was making now—lips downturned but still smirking, eyelashes flashing over the blue eyes which weren't actually blue but gray, taking a long drag on the cigarette, ashing it right on the carpet, the moment awkward and yet sort of sweet, her squinting at him, taking in the sight of his rounder face, sloping shoulders, hair which had begun to thin. The two of them stood silent for a good while before, looking disappointed now, she said, "I oughta spit in your face."

He readjusted the hat on his head and said her name, the sound of it on his lips intimate, pleasurable, as luscious as a kiss: "Fannie."

He touched a finger to his bad eye, stepping into the light, the eye itself appearing a little greenish, Fannie making a sound, clicking her tongue, saying, "What did you do to yourself this time?"

The boy limped along the street toward the pickup, finding his grandfather asleep inside. He leaned up against the passenger-side window; the old man's hat covered his face, his long legs stretched out into the space in front of the driver's seat. The boy stood there catching his breath, watching the old man to see if he was still breathing. He was, his blue flannel rising slightly, his nostrils fluttering with each breath. The boy sighed and crept around the side of the truck where he forced open the tiny metal door, unscrewed the gas cap, slipped the yellow nozzle in, and poured the gasoline inside, the fluid dripping along his bare hands and down the side of the vehicle. When it was empty, he put the gas can back in the bed of the truck and sat down on the curb, sucking in his teeth as he inspected his bloody leg. He rolled up his pants and saw his sock was pink and red, and there were two whitish wounds along the side of his calf. The fact that the wounds were white, that they were deeper than he had thought, made bile rise up into his mouth. He started to whimper, poking his finger at the wound, once again feeling as if he might vomit. The pain was now creeping up his entire leg, past his groin, his hands growing clammy. He looked up and noticed his granddad standing over him now, the shape of his narrow shoulders and wide hat, still as a ghost. Then the grandfather helped the boy up from the curb and into the passenger seat of the pickup truck. Both of them were soon installed back inside the cab. The boy handed the grandfather the truck keys, frowning once the grandfather had started the stricken-sounding engine. Quentin held the sore spot on his leg, sweaty forehead pressed up against the passenger-side window, making angels on the glass.

The girl sat outside the manager's office, hands folded in her lap, her fate as yet undetermined. The security guard sat silent on her left, mopping his bald head with his uniformed wrist. On the other side sat an elderly black woman with enormous tinted glasses, overstuffed bags of groceries sprawled near her feet. The old woman smelled strongly of rosewater and ointment, the odor of which reminded the girl of her grandfather. Propped between her legs was a long, metal red-and-white cane, which had been marked with several dark indentations.

The manager, a harried-looking fellow with a beard and bifocals, finished arguing with a supplier on the telephone and approached the old woman first. "Miss Parkson, we don't have anyone to take you home right now. If you want to wait an hour or so, Billie'll be in."

The old woman clamped her jaw and muttered, "I don't like her too much. Too nosy. But it don't look like I have much of a choice. How long did you say?"

"About an hour." The manager turned and surveyed Rylee. "What about her?"

The security guard sat upright. "I caught her drinking from a bottle of milk."

"And?"

"And she don't have the money to pay for it."

The manager lifted his glasses from his face as if this particular intrusion into the private workings of his professional life was more than he could bear. The girl took notice and quietly spoke up.

"My purse. I was robbed. Someone took the money from where I was staying at. You can search me. It was an accident. I thought I had money when I came in."

The manager replaced his glasses. "Are you from around here?"

"That's Angel's girl," the old black woman said. "The younger one. She's from down my way."

"Do you know Miss Parkson?" the manager asked.

The girl did not know how she should answer. She nodded her head slowly, just once.

The manager groaned. "Seeing as this is the first time this kind of thing has happened, I'd be willing to let you go with a warning. Call it bad circumstances. But don't let me catch you in this store without money again."

The girl nodded in relief.

"And if you'd be nice enough to see Miss Parkson home, I'd appreciate it. But I want you to remember: we're not running a charity ward."

The girl stood and shook the manager's hand. The old woman also climbed to her feet and gently put a palm on the girl's shoulder.

"Hold on a second and let Reggie get your picture," the manager added, then disappeared back into his office.

The security guard pulled an old Polaroid from his desk and raised it to his eye. "Say cheese." There was a sharp flash and the photograph shot out. He shook it, wrote down the date, and taped it on a wall of other offenders outside the manager's office.

Before they had made their way back through the electric eye, tottering together, the old woman remarked, "Never much cared for this place myself."

In the silent arrangement of the Nashville night, as the sky turned the color of faded steel, of gunpowder, of dolomite, the horse stood patient in its silver prison, snorting at the muggy air. A cloud of mosquitoes had settled in the stall, buzzing around the horse's head with a grim, primeval viciousness, the horse flicking its ears, stamping a little, tail snapping about, turning its head this way and that to get clear of them. The sharp drone of their paths—darting in the near darkness—made the mare edgy, but finding no room to turn, it once again settled down, its eyes patient, resigned, the mosquitoes landing upon its skin, proboscises sinking in, beads of blood rising like red moons along the animal's white flesh.

The grandfather staggered into the brightly lit pharmacy, boots shuffling loosely across the tile, taking in the smell of antiseptics and adhesives, of toothpaste and bandages, the steady whisper of the pharmacists and the soft monotony of an instrumental song congregating in the air like a chorus. He did not know what he was looking for exactly, only that he would know it when he came upon it, his shoulder feeling as stiff as it ever had, the left arm dangling there like a broken branch, stopping a little to lean against a box of disposable diapers, then forcing himself to walk on. He was in the wrong aisle, and then, limping on, he found the bandages, all sorts and sizes, cotton balls, rubbing alcohol, Mercurochrome, iodine. He placed his hand upon a bottle of iodine and felt a shudder of pain, dropping the plastic bottle to his feet. He knelt there, shaken, ears ringing. When he finally got his hearing back, he tried to stand and felt a hand upon his shoulder. He looked up, unnerved, face still tightened into a frown, and saw a woman in a white coat standing there with thick round glasses, the frames of which were purple. There was a name tag on the woman's coat, though Jim could not focus to read it. He did not need to look much closer than her mouth to know it was Deedee.

"Did you need some help, sir?" the woman asked, and Jim smiled, stunned by the shape of her face all over again.

He gathered his wits, adjusted his hat, and motioned at the bottle of iodine in his hand. "My grandson got bit by dog. Which one of these is for dog bites?"

The pharmacist turned to face the shelves of antiseptics. "A dog bite's pretty serious. Maybe you oughta bring the boy to the doctor."

The old man peered down again at the brown bottle in his hand. "We're not from around here."

"Well, there's a hospital with an emergency room not two blocks down the street."

"I guess I'll just take this," he said, afraid to meet her eyes, and held up the brown bottle of iodine. He reached for a box of white bandages and some medical tape, then held them against his chest before walking away, feeling her still standing there, slender, all in white, the color of her eyes soft blue, like hyacinth; he knew that if he turned to look back again, she would be gone; or worse, he would fall apart right there, which is how it always happened in the Bible.

By the time he made it back to the pickup, the boy had rolled up the leg of his pants and was poking curiously at the twin red indentations along the calf of his right leg.

"It might be rabies," said the boy.

"Did the dog have a tag on it?"

"Huh?"

"Did it have a collar? Did it have tags on it?"

"I don't remember."

"We'll have to take you in soon as we get home and get a distemper. We'll clean it up and put a bandage on it for now. Does it hurt any?"

"No," the boy said, hoping the answer would make his grandfather proud. "It's just sore is all."

"Here," the old man said, leaning over, the driver's-side door open, the boy's leg outstretched across the bench seat. He uncapped the small brown bottle of iodine, dabbed at the two small holes, the red dots brighter than blood, and hunched over, blowing at his grandson's wound. The boy was surprised, watching his grandfather do something like that, the gesture seeming somehow beneath him, matronly. The grandfather saw the curiosity in the boy's eyes and smiled a little, screwing the stopper back in place. "Don't know why you're supposed to do that. It's what my mother always did."

The old man tore at a piece of bandaging, trying unsuccessfully to pull it free from its wrapper. After the third attempt, he got it open and laid it across the two dark holes, and then, feeling around inside the white paper bag once more, he unwound a length of medical tape, fixing the bandage in place. "Okay," he said, rolling up the paper bag. "That does it."

"I can drive," the boy blurted out. "It feels okay."

"Why don't you rest it some?"

The boy shook his head, holding his hands out for the keys. The old man examined him then, seeing and not seeing him—a face, the face of a child, of a baby—still hanging in the air and then fading away. *Where was the small one? The gray-faced one? The one who toddled about the kitchen on chubby legs?* There was hair on the boy's upper lip which he had noticed but never considered before. The grandfather looked down at the keys and slowly placed them back in the boy's soft hand.

* * *

The old woman, though she was blind, managed to live on the third floor of a worn-looking walk-up, right above a bait store and a boarded-up church. The girl helped her all the way up, eyeing the old woman's purse as she searched through her sweater for her keys. It would be nothing to grab it from her hands. But before the girl could act, the old woman had put the key in the lock and thrown open the door.

Even at this hour, the apartment was filled with stray fragments of light. Children's drawings had been taped everywhere and there were several birdcages placed on stands throughout the cramped room. A goldfinch was swinging on a piece of wire. The old woman set her purse down on a counter crowded with junk mail, walked over to its cage, and began whistling.

"Used to give piano lessons," the old woman said, nodding to where an upright piano was buried beneath a mountain of newspapers. "Now the birds are my music."

The girl studied the children's drawings on the wall, saw an angel and devil singing to each other, then turned and inched closer to the woman's purse.

The old woman lifted her head and said, "Come on over where I can talk to you."

When the girl took a seat beside her on the cluttered couch, the old woman leaned over and opened the cage, then carefully placed her hands around the bird, cupping it in her palms.

"I'd like to give you something for your time. For helping me. But first I want to know who it is I'm talking to." She sat down and gently handed the bird to the girl.

Rylee tensed, feeling the living thing trembling between her fingers.

"You're lost, aren't you?"

The girl felt like she might begin to sob. "Yes," she said, swallowing it down.

"You're lost and far from home."

"Yes."

"Everybody gets lost sometimes. Everybody gets tested. You're being tested right now, aren't you?"

The girl nodded silently.

The old woman placed her hands upon Rylee's and took the bird back. She stood and carried the animal back to its cage, shoving the wire door in place. "Now hand me my purse."

"Sir."

"—"

"Gramps?"

"Hm."

"Did you ever think about that horse? Where it came from?"

"—"

"Gramps?"

The old man glanced at the boy behind the steering wheel and muttered a curt, mendacious, "No."

"I have. I thought about it."

"You have?"

"I have."

"I'm not surprised."

"How come?"

"I'm finding out you got all kinds of thoughts."

The boy smiled, proud of himself.

"Well?" the grandfather asked.

"At first I thought it was just a mistake like Mr. Northfield said."

"—"

"But now I don't know."

"—"

"I don't know."

"—"

"I think maybe God is that horse. That He sent it Himself."

The grandfather squirmed in his seat.

"I think maybe God is that horse and He sent Himself and now we're being tested. Like Jonah. Or Jesus. How He likes to test all kinds of people. Those sort of things."

"—"

"Gramps?"

"—"

"Gramps?"

"Hm."

"What do you think?"

"I thought . . ." the grandfather started. "It feels stupid to talk about."

"No," the boy said, encouraging.

"I guess. Well, I guess I thought your grandmother had sent it."

The boy was silent.

Then the grandfather added: "I still do, I guess."

Rick sneered as the needle pierced the loose flesh above his left eye, Fannie's fingers working the black thread through, crisscrossing the rancorous white wound. He could see right down the front of her dress, the bony bridge of her clavicle sloping toward her teardrop-shaped breasts. She smelled like dish soap and sweat. She leaned over him, fingers pressed against his face, and as she slipped the needle through again, he felt an ache somewhere in his stomach. He thought of saying something, of maybe winking at her and whispering a few of the old, soft words, but then thought better of it, for just then, Jerry lumbered into the kitchen. Jerry was a pale, gargantuan mountain of human flesh, bigger than any other person Rick had ever seen. In fact, it seemed like the room shrank as soon as Jerry had entered, the corners and ceiling all bending around him. It wasn't just his shoulders or chest, or even his mammoth-sized head—really closer to that of an elephant than a man—it was him, everything about him—moles, wrinkles, scars—everything twice, maybe even three times the size of a normal person's. He had long blond hair that was stringy, thinning out along the top and downright bare in spots. He took a seat beside Rick, nodded with a dumb, happy grin, and mumbled, "They're both asleep. The baby was a little fussy. I think maybe she has a tooth coming in."

"Thanks, hon," Fannie said with a smile, black thread hanging from her tightened teeth.

"So, Rick, you ain't back to stay?" Jerry asked.

Rick blinked, wincing a little as the needle pierced his skin again. "Nope. Just passing through. Got in a jam. I got to be heading on as soon as I'm able."

Jerry nodded, looking a little relieved, staring down at his immense hands. "You didn't say what kind of trouble you're in."

"I didn't."

Jerry tapped his fingers twice, cleared his throat, and then stood, once again filling the span of the tiny kitchen with his unfathomable bulk. "Guess I'll see what's on TV." He waddled through the kitchen door, collapsed on the dingy sofa, and flicked on the television set, the sofa rattling with each reverberation of Jerry's oil-drum laugh.

"He's been depressed," Fannie whispered from the corner of her mouth, the black thread slipping from her soft lips.

Rick peered through the kitchen door to where Jerry was sitting and noticed an oversize glossy poster on the far wall which featured a photo of Jerry from more than a decade ago, when his blond hair had been long and full, when he had worn a brownish beard, his arms impossibly large, red tights straining at his gigantic thighs, an opulent golden championship belt fitted around his waist. Beside him, on the poster, was Fannie—in a lacy white dress—his ring girl, though at the time of the photo she had been in love with Rick. Those had been the days, although Rick had been too dull to notice.

He stared at the poster, seeing her long, long legs like two scissor blades, and winced a little as Fannie tightened the thread again.

"They asked him to retire about a year ago and now all he does is mope around. They got him doing commentary, you know, at the matches, but he's not his old self. He's great with the kids but they kind of broke his heart when they said he was getting too old."

Rick blinked, knowing better than to say a word.

"It was the best thing in the world marrying him," Fannie whispered with a smile. "He needs me almost as much as I need him."

And here the needle slipped a little, poking at the open cut, Rick sucking in his teeth.

"Sorry 'bout that. You want another drink?" she asked, motioning to the half-glass of bourbon sitting before him.

"I'm good."

Fannie, squinting, more careful this time, threaded the needle through the skin yet again, drawing the wound closed.

"How come you stopped by?" she asked, her voice slightly muffled, glancing across the kitchen at the shape of Jerry on the sofa.

"I didn't have anywhere else to go."

"You and I know that ain't the truth."

"Well then, guess I wanted to see you."

"Hmmm."

"I'm coming into some money," he said abruptly. "In a few days or so. I can stop back this way."

Fannie, having finished, bit the thread, snapping it in half with her small, sharp teeth. "All done."

"You hear what I say?"

"I did," she said, a flush creeping into her cheeks. She set the needle and thread down on the kitchen table, turning away from him. "We're done."

"Fannie . . ." His hands reached out for her but she was already across the kitchen somehow.

It was now near eight p.m. The pale-blue pickup was parked before the bus station, the old man—his legs stretched out before him in the passenger seat—watching the double glass doors for any suggestion, any sign of the horse, of the trailer, of the thing they had come all this way for. The driver's-side door opened and Quentin climbed back inside, favoring his right leg as he slid behind the wheel.

"It's not anywhere around here," he said flatly, turning to his grandfather. "I looked all over the parking lot."

"We'll just have to be still."

"Sir?"

"We'll just have to sit here and wait until something happens."

"Shouldn't we be doing something?"

"We are. We're waiting for those other folks to make a mistake. They already made a few. We just need one more and then we'll be in the catbird seat."

"And then what?"

"I don't know. Anyways, we're better off getting that horse back when there isn't anyone else around. We'll wait for them to show up and then follow 'em to where we can take her back, trailer and all."

The boy's eyes darted back to his grandfather. The old man's breath seemed irregular and shallow. "Are you okay, Gramps?"

"I'm okay. I just need to rest my eyes. You seeing anything funny, you wake me, all right?"

"Okay."

Silence once again seized the pickup.

Rick limped back out into the night, stepping over the pair of metal roller skates, shuffling down the front steps, and turned back in the middle of the street to face the shabby house. It was not as if he had expected her to say yes; he was not fool enough to think that. It was how she had treated him like a child, like he posed no threat, sewing up his eye, her husband sitting in the other room laughing at the television, like they had never been young, like they had never been wild. He crept into the cab of the black pickup and lit a cigarette,

holding the smoke deep in his lungs. Before he slid the key into the
ignition, he thought how there was now no kindness, no reason, no
obstacle to keep him from finding that girl and putting the hurt on
her, putting an end to all the anguish she had caused. He reloaded
the pistol, slid it back under his unbuttoned coat, and drove off, feeling wrathful.

Like a polecat, the girl slunk through the parking lot of the bus station, glancing back over her shoulder once, then again, dodging from
shadow to shadow until she could lay her fingers on the cold steel
door. She flung it open in a hurry, darted inside, and spread out the
wrinkled dollar bills on the beige counter only to discover the next
bus wasn't until four in the morning. She bought her ticket, scraped
the remainder of her change into her jeans pocket, and strode over to
a bank of faded plastic seats. She had more than six hours to kill and
not enough in her pocket for something to eat. She peered up at a TV
in the corner of the room. The screen was fuzzy with snow, the picture kept rolling, the image unclear, and then it gradually sharpened
into a pale, eyeless face. It was her face and it was on TV because
she was dead. Rylee stood, stepping toward the screen, and watched
the image vanish, electronic snow buzzing before her with brilliant
ferocity. She fell back into her seat, stared down at her hands which
were pink and blistered. She put her feet up on the seat next to her,
admiring the pink cowboy boots, and feigned sleep, watching the
clock across from her. It was almost nine p.m.

The horse, sleeping now in its silver stall, paid no notice to the harried lights flashing outside. The dark pickup wound down the street,
past the motels, the hotels, past an adult movie theater. At each location the truck stopped, its driver slowly, angrily climbing out, treading across whatever grime-specked parking lot laid before him, the
driver disappearing indoors for a moment, and then returning, once
again slipping the color photo of the girl into his front shirt pocket,
the engine starting up, the clutch engaged, truck and trailer once

again carrying on, the forward movement and its cessation matching the animal's steady sway, undisturbed in its sleep.

Nine o'clock. The sound of nine o'clock, a shade being pulled down in a dark room. Nine, the faltering, final dismissal of daylight. Then ten. Ten, a fragile wick of a white candle being worn down. Ten. Then eleven, an old phonograph quietly announcing a song of regret, melody of old memories, the tune of another useless day spent. Eleven, then midnight. Midnight, the voice of a stationmaster, with a locomotive approaching, midnight set to arrive like a stranger aboard a westbound train, the engine surrounded by clouds of steam, the stranger faceless, unassuming, the cold certainty of one more day advancing. One o'clock, a barn owl perched in a high tree, branches bare, leaves blown clean. Two, a fog-covered lake, the haze of wanting, of waiting, of wishing to sleep. Three o'clock, the hour of neon, of fading colored lights, of aqua and pink flashing, electric signs reminding *JESUS DIED FOR OUR SINS* and *ALL-NITE JACUZZI SUITES AVAILABLE*. Three, religious in its quietude. Three, the hour of confession, of supplication, of forgiveness before the Holy Trinity, terrified prayers whispered in the dark, in between breaths, in between kisses, upon the muted colors of drawn motel sheets.

At three a.m. the girl was asleep, the child-size pink boots which had been stolen placed on the floor before her, bare feet curled beneath her posterior, the toes covered in grime, a wadded-up newspaper serving as a blanket, slightly covering her lower half. She looked like a refugee: her left nostril gummy with snot, her hair a tangled bramble, cheeks and chin waxy in day-old makeup. Rick stood above her, staring at her sad shape for a second, before he squatted, placing his hand beneath her chin, softly whispering, "Rylee."

The girl blinked, the look in her eyes one of confusion before rapidly turning into horror. She tried to scramble to her feet but he put his hand out, grabbing her by the shoulder, sure to keep her from running again. She fought him, shucking her arm loose, eyes wild, searching for the nearest exit, seeking out a security guard, a well-meaning stranger, anyone. But at this hour of the night, this hour of the morning, the waiting room was empty. There were two derelicts nodding off in the opposite corner of the room. The TV set, which was affixed to a metal arm, its volume muted, was a field of scattered electronic snow. He got her back down in the plastic seat and tried to sound reasonable.

"Calm down," he muttered. "Calm down, just try and calm down."

"Fuck you," she hissed, trying to dart off again.

He grabbed her by the back of the neck, still squatting, staring at her solemnly. "Come on, we ain't got time for this."

"Fuck you."

"Listen, little girl—"

"Get the fuck off me."

He let go of her neck and blurted out the words as soon as she was on her feet again: "Your geegaw—he's dead."

She turned, her yellow eyes wild-looking again, an animal caught in the headlights of a fast-moving vehicle. "Fuck you. I know you're lying."

"Rylee."

"Get the fuck away from me."

"Why do you think they sent me all this way?"

"You're so full of shit, you stupid fucking—"

"Rylee."

"It was the day before yesterday. Why do you think they sent me?"

"You think I'm some stupid fucking kid? Well, I ain't. You're fucking nuts if you think I'm getting into that fucking truck with you."

"Have it your way. We're already a day late as it is. Tomorrow, they're having the service. You want to miss it? After all that old man did for you?"

"Fuck you," she said again, though this time it ended with a sob, her shoulders shaking, folding her face into her dirty hands. "Fuck you," she repeated, a narrow slip of a girl trembling beneath the awkward fluorescent lights of the waiting room.

"You can either get in the truck with me or stay here, I really don't give a shit. You want to run, keep running. But I'm leaving now. I aim to get back in time to pay my respects."

The girl looked away.

"You got enough for the bus?"

The girl nodded her head, eyes wide and opalescent.

"Come on, I won't bother you," he said in a voice just like her father, or her granddad, or Brian, or any number of them, showing her a little affection.

The girl sniffled again before she lowered her head, grabbed the stolen boots, and slowly limped toward the glass doors. They headed from the waiting room out to the paved parking lot where his black truck had been parked in a handicapped spot.

Two forms emerged from the double doors of the bus stop as the boy finished sipping from the glass bottle of Coke. He watched them without interest at first: a man with a lean build, dark eyes, and mustache; the second, a girl, a young woman, it was hard to tell, whom the fellow was leading by the shoulder. They paused in front of a dark pickup—and there, attached to a hitch, was the silver trailer, their trailer. The boy rubbed his eyes, watching the girl whisper something to the man, the man, helping her up and inside the cab. Once she was situated, the man crossed in front of the vehicle and climbed behind the steering wheel.

"Sir?"

"—"

"Gramps?"

"—"

"Jim?"

The old man snorted awake.

"Gramps. That's them. That's them," the boy whispered loudly.

The grandfather nodded, wiping at the sleep which had gathered in the corner of his eyes.

"What do we do now?"

"Hold on. Hold on," the grandfather said.

"What do we do?"

"We watch."

"Watch for what?"

"The right moment. They're gonna drive off, and then we're gonna get that horse back when the time comes."

The boy nodded once more, though not in agreement.

The girl—it was maybe the man's daughter or girlfriend, Jim did not know—shouted something, shoving the passenger-side door open, trying to make a break for it. The man reached across the seat and, without so much as a frown, offered the girl the back of his hand—a wide, arcing blow that caused the girl's head to snap to the side. Then the man leaned over and pulled the passenger-side door closed, quickly starting up the truck.

"We're not gonna do nothing?" the boy asked.

"We are—just wait."

"But they're gonna drive away."

"Just wait."

"He's starting it up."

"Hush now. Keep your eyes out."

They watched as the dark pickup slowly crept from its parking spot.

"Go on," the old man said. "Start her up. Follow two or three cars back. Take your time. We ain't in a hurry now."

Once again the black pickup made its way along the highway, advancing with a reckless velocity north along I-40; only now it was being followed, the pale-blue truck rumbling along in the distance, the old man's eyes fixed on the road ahead, the silver trailer—its square shape—the vanishing point of his line of sight.

An unblinking eye, the moon peering pale over the tips of white dogwoods, the red crumbling brick edges of industrial buildings, black voluminous smokestacks angling skyward—their vapors ringing the skyline, the moon glancing down at a green glass bottle left like an offering, broken at the neck, at the gold and silver necklaces lining an all-night pawnshop window, all of them see-through with moonlight. Darkness falls, darkness falling, the city of Nashville fading behind.

Along the side of the road was an unfathomable order of trees: the girl held the sore spot on her cheek and watched them whip past with their lifeless fury.

"We're going north. We're going north, I know it," the girl whispered bravely.

Rick, his left eye unblinking, remained silent behind the steering wheel. He looked straight ahead, the wooded highway hurtling past with a violence all its own.

The taillights of the pickup and the silver trailer flashed brightly before the boy's eyes, constant, undeniable, quietly dividing the borders of the night. Beside him, his grandfather had gone white. He looked shaky. The boy steered the vehicle and kept watch on the red lights ahead. He whispered his grandfather's name several times, "Gramps? Gramps? Gramps?" but heard no reply, and so, after about ten minutes, he finally said his name directly once again: "Jim?"

"___"

"Jim."

"___"

The boy slowed the vehicle down, taking his eyes from the road. He reached over and touched his grandfather's blue-veined hand. It felt brittle, cold. The old man was murmuring to himself—the boy could see his lips moving—and his eyes were trembling beneath his wrinkled eyelids, the eyelashes also shuddering. The boy turned back to the road and saw the other truck drifting off in the distance, the silver trailer flashing beneath the occasional billboard or highway light, and sped up, the engine slow to respond, the hood rattling before his eyes.

* * *

The woods were a blur of black edges and dull lines: all of a sudden, seeing their shadows, the skeletal, gloomy outlines, the impenetrable black figures, shapes from a bad dream, the girl realized she did not want to die. Not anymore. She did not know when she had figured this out, but she was suddenly aware of how important it was that she stay alive. The pickup was moving faster and faster now, the entire city of Nashville lost somewhere behind, one town, then another appearing before vanishing along the side of the highway; billboards, advertisements, attractions faded into view, then departed from sight, the road ahead lit only by the truck's headlamps; and beyond the twin globes of yellow light, there was nothing, the night having shifted to the epic, uninterrupted land of blackness. The girl realized she would have to do something quickly if she was going to escape. It was obvious now that he had driven her all the way out here to kill her—she was as sure of this as she had been of anything in her life. So she watched him, studied his stony face. She saw the line of his thin gray lips, the unforgiving glare in his squinting eye, saw him crouched over the steering wheel like some kind of gargoyle, saw a hand on the wheel, the other floating above the clutch, then saw the unfastened seat belt. She almost smiled to herself, feeling her own belt buckled across her chest. Then, without another thought, before the doubt and wordless terror could settle back in, she grabbed hold of the steering wheel and pulled it with all her might, baring her teeth as Rick shouted and tried to fight it free.

The black pickup spun wildly from the right-hand lane, plowing into a plastic mile marker, roaring directly into a ditch, the front end flying up from the ground and burying itself into a culvert overgrown with cattails and brambles. The silver trailer came crashing from behind, slamming into the truck's rear bumper, tearing loose from its hitch, landing on its right side. The sound of the collision was fearsome—glass spiderwebbing in brilliant shrieks, plastic exploding outward with concussive groans and snaps, metal sheering metal.

* * *

When things had stopped moving, when the dirt had settled itself earthward once more, there was a low hum, the engine running down, and a fierce wailing from the upended trailer. Then there was a thump, and another, then a third; hearing it, Rick knew it was his pulse pounding, reminding him that he was alive, and what a damnable fool he had been.

He held one hand to his forehead, the blood hurrying down his face, the thump coming from somewhere inside his head again. He pulled himself free from the wreckage, jaw sore, left shoulder popped from its joint. He limped away through the crushed door, afraid something might catch fire, knees buckling as he fought his way up the incline, falling on his side, his breath coming in sudden, uneven gasps. He heard the thump once more, realizing then it was the horse, before it began to whinny—the sound of its pleas unlike anything he had ever heard, guttural though high-pitched. Cursing, he made his way back down the culvert, sliding through the upturned mud to the trailer, placing his hands on the lopsided handles. The trailer door was bent, forced shut, and it took all of his strength to pull it open. The horse came galloping out of the warped, silver prison like a cloud, like a cannonball, leaping free, though as it moved, Rick could see its rear flank was seeping blood and its foreleg was split, broken below the knee. It cantered a few paces on, then stopped, huffing at the cool night air, flicking its head, ears erect, turning to glance back at where Rick was squatting in the mud.

He did not think of the girl; not until he was breathing properly again. Shifting his weight to his left side, he limped back to the driver's-side door, folded upon itself, and peered inside. The passenger seat was empty, the door hanging wide open, no shadow nor trace of her shape visible anywhere in the night. He began to laugh, as he had once again underestimated her, thinking how much she was like her old, sickly grandfather, how vicious, how fearless. He pulled himself up out of the ditch, keeping his eye on the horse, seeing the animal stumbling slowly toward the highway.

"Ho! Ho!" he called to it, holding out a hand, taking a wobbly step forward, spooking it. And then, once again, it was gone, taking off wildly down the hillside—broken leg or not—disappearing in a white-and-red-specked flash, the sound of its hooves striking the dirt, marking time with the thrum of blood in Rick West's head. He stood there numbly, blood-soaked, staring off as if he were born mute or dumb, watching it go.

The pale-blue pickup halted a good fifty yards from the crash, slowing down along the shoulder of the road, the pernicious rattle of loose gravel beneath the vehicle's tires startling the grandfather awake. He grunted a little, lifting the white cattleman hat from his eyes, peering out into the darkness at the abstract, rectangular shapes rising from the edge of the highway, just beyond the yellow circles cast by the flickering headlights. Before bothering to even ask, he had the door open and was limping out, staring at the upturned trailer flung on its side, its door torn open, the horse gone. There was the man, the one who had been driving the other truck, squatting along the side of road, shaking his head, laughing a little to himself, out of his wits maybe, whistling at some far-off point in the distance. Jim followed the man's gaze and saw a white streak passing across a wide-open field—saw, at once, that it was the mare, running off-kilter, one of its forelegs hitting the ground awkwardly, as if it did not trust its own step, though, somehow, the animal still appeared to be flying. The grandfather turned back and hurried toward the open door of the pale-blue pickup, seeing that the night in the distance had just begun to blossom with color—a smear of orange, then blue, then

red—and the eastern sky, where he was now staring, already showing light.

Back in the truck, the grandfather slammed the door behind
him. "She's off the other way."

The boy quickly threw the truck into gear. The vehicle jerked
forward, its headlamps momentarily lighting the raw-looking face of
the man sitting alone on the side of the road, laughing at the balled-up
truck and trailer, before passing on.

"That was her?" the boy asked.

"That was her," the grandfather said, looking back over his
shoulder.

"How do we get her?"

"Turn around. And then we'll hop on that exit over there."

The pale-blue pickup rattled off, its engine clattering, returning
to the road. The grandfather glanced in the side-view mirror as the
man on the side of the culvert stood, pulled a weapon from beneath
his coat, and began to stalk off through the weeds toward the barren
field where the horse was now standing frightfully still.

The boy piloted the truck across the center of the road, the vehicle fighting through the unmowed grass, and then sped in the opposite direction, back toward an off-ramp they had just passed. The
grandfather was quiet, trying to catch sight of the horse, but it was
already moving again, trotting from the field toward a small town
that sprung like a gash among the heavy acreage of trees.

Soon the animal was rushing along a narrow main street, past a
liquor store, then a motel, then an abandoned movie theater. From
there, the horse disappeared down a side street, the pickup truck
speeding in pursuit. Stopping at a street corner, the boy stared
through the early-morning light for any sign of white. In a wide lot,
there were several pieces of laundry hanging along two lines, and
for a moment the boy thought it was the mare, and then blinking,
leaning forward, he thought they might also be ghosts. On the third
blink, he saw them for what they were, and asked, his voice a whisper, "Where did she go?"

"You drive down that way," the grandfather murmured. "I'll walk from here."

"But what about—"

"Go on now. We don't got time to argue."

The old man pulled himself out of the cab, fixed his hat straight on his head, and marched with an awkward limp down the main street, whistling a little, clucking softly with his tongue. The pale-blue pickup pulled away from the curb, its red taillights tracing the arc of its path down a narrow side street.

The girl huddled in the underbrush, hidden by the high sweep of brambles, arms folded across her chest, lips chattering, entire body trembling, not from fear or shock but the shape of the shadow crossing before her, pistol in hand. It was him. She could smell him, the dank odor: like a rat's den, oily, nervous. She could hear him groaning a little to himself, snarling as he pushed his way through the weeds, passing only a few feet from where she was now crouching, her eyes closed tight, hands folded fiercely in prayer against her left cheek, Rick West's figure pausing there for a second before it strode on, disappearing into the lightening shadows, traveling down the declination of meadow, heaving itself over a low barbed-wire fence. When she was sure he was gone, when she had crouched there for as long as she could, daring to think she was safe, she darted out from the thicket and made her way toward a pair of headlights as they approached down the highway, arms raised before her in a plea. It was an elderly couple, an old man and an old woman, in an ancient Ford station wagon. The car stopped, and the girl—fleeing from the night and whatever she'd been—climbed inside.

The grandfather loped on a little farther and was surprised when he saw the horse standing there, grazing in front of a small white church. It had its muzzle buried in an azalea bush and was nipping at its leaves, ears flattened along its narrow skull, teeth working over the fibrous twigs, breath pluming from its nostrils in twin puffs. Jim slowed his gait, striding with his hand upraised, still clucking, kissing the air slightly, stopping about ten feet from where the horse was feeding. Suddenly, it lifted its great neck, blinked its long, feminine eyelashes, then turned quickly from where it was standing and galloped off once more.

"Son of a bitch." The old man watched the animal dazzle away into the dark, a flash of lightning curving along the horizon, shooting west down an ever-widening street.

The shape hurried on, pistol in hand, left leg dragging a little, as the ribs and thighbone on his left side felt desperately sore. His forehead had stopped bleeding and so he folded his handkerchief back into his jeans, pausing to look up at the small unlit town, shades and curtains drawn, inhabitants still asleep. Rick spat something from his mouth, trying to get rid of the taste of blood, and then moved on, finding no sign of the horse, nor any other semblance of life. And then, like another lost soul gleaming before him, the horse came around the corner and made a wild dash through an abandoned lot, clods of dirt rising. Rick fired blindly, shooting at wherever it had just passed.

The boy pulled the pickup to a halt at the end of a brick-paved alley, glimpsing the horse with its head in a dented silver garbage can standing in a long row of other silver garbage cans. It snuffled at some trash and then raised its eyes, hearing the squeak of the pickup's brakes. Quentin hurried from the vehicle, leaving the door open and the engine running. The horse lifted its small ears, looking alarmed.

"It's me," the boy said, no longer moving.

The horse shifted backward when the boy slowly held his hand out.

"Don't you remember? It's me." He took another step forward, thinking if only he were to touch it, if only he were able to get close enough, if only he could place his hand along the side of its neck, then there'd be no reason left to doubt.

One more step, he smiled and put the flat of his palm against the animal's soft throat. Feeling it tremble, feeling its pulse, he thought, *It's going to be all right. There's nothing to be afraid of.* Then there was a gunshot and the horse fled again.

The grandfather huffed a little as he limped his way over the sidewalk, past a gray slate parking lot belonging to a rundown funeral home. Directly behind him, the steeple of the church clanged to life; he could hear the bell in the tower begin to toll, the sun's brightness now visible in the easternmost edge of the sky, parked cars, windowpanes, leaves of trees all suddenly beginning to glow with light. The bells behind him chimed one, two, three, four, then five, though in their reverberations what the grandfather heard was unfamiliar, distant, frightening. Instead of the clangor of the blue-bronze clapper against the blue-bronze bell, it was an exhortation, an appeal for the old man to stop his clumsy advance across the parking lot; one, two, three, four, then five, the echo of the Sunday-morning chimes no longer a far-off sound but now altogether an immutable sort of voice. The old man trudged on regardless, marching past the funeral parlor—multicolored caskets displayed indiscreetly in its window—here was a gold one, a bright blue one, trimmed in bronze, one all white—the pearly handles, the silk cushions, the filigree shapes like harps and angels. He trotted past their mute, rectangular shapes and spied the horse at the end of the street, drinking softly from a yellow fire hydrant that had sprung a leak. He held his hand out against a blue mailbox a moment, observing the horse leaning there in the early light, its rear flank bloodied, its foreleg badly bent, a silver lather having gathered along its muscular shoulders and neck. He held out one hand toward the animal, trying to call to it, but it did not heed him, only lapped at the trickling water before galloping on.

It was standing in the center of a used-car lot by the time the grandfather caught up with it again, the animal resting gallantly between several rows of rusty vehicles. Jim could see its sides heaving, its nostrils trembling. There were colored plastic flags flying in the air overhead, red and orange and yellow and green, and behind him an enormous banner of the stars and stripes. He could hear the flags whipping above his head, the horse standing there, huffing at the air, whiter than white, the skin around its muzzle gray and pink, like some imaginary creature, breathing hard among the columns of Toyotas and Fords, former competitors parked side by side. The grandfather limped forward, raising his hand, reaching out toward the horse, pausing, afraid to spook it, afraid to find it no longer standing there. He placed a hand upon the horse's nape, feeling the lather gathered there, the heat of the animal's skin, its blood coursing beneath his own, palm against neck, flesh against flesh. It was like meeting an old friend; and so he smiled a little, seeing that it did not startle, only stood there, foreleg split, blood sparkling along its shin.

Then there was a hot feeling along the back of the old man's neck, as if someone was standing behind him, and when he glanced over, he saw that he was not alone; it was the same yellow-eyed man from the wrecked pickup, the one who had been on the side of the road. He looked like he had been lashed; his black hair was plastered up against his sweaty forehead with a swipe of blood. He was standing gingerly, leaning against one of the used cars, balancing himself with the fingers of his left hand, the right holding a pistol. The grandfather's eyes did not shift, locked upon the other man's, the horse motionless now.

The two of them—the grandfather and horse—stood like an old-time photograph or pulp illustration, white hat tipped back upon the old man's head, a grim expression on his face. The stranger pushed off the hood of a car, then inched forward. He stumbled from the front end of one vehicle to the front end of another, the gun still upraised. The grandfather studied the stranger's eyes, seeing the pain in the man's wrenched-up features, noticing the desperate glare in the mark of his lip, and watched as the intruder slipped some, catching himself on a weather-beaten Chevrolet. The stranger steadied himself, moaning; and it was then that the grandfather went for his own sidearm, clumsily lifting it from the back of his pants, the gun wavering before him like a flag, some indistinct warning, though the stranger kept on coming.

The grandfather could see the fearlessness, the nerve in the other man's face, and held his own weapon out, tightening his grip, knowing it would do no good, seeing the inevitability of what was coming like night and day; the other's shadow inched closer, now only a couple of feet away, the horse standing beside the grandfather with an air of exhaustion, quivering, both of them struggling to remain upright. Grimacing, the stranger pointed the gun at the grandfather's stomach, the old man finding himself too tired to fight, his arm feeling heavy, the pistol now dangling uselessly before him.

The stranger said something Jim did not hear but understood the import of. The grandfather shook his head. The stranger said whatever he had to say again, taking a final step forward. The old man ignored this and looked over at the animal. He put a weak hand out, touching its shivering white flesh. *If it is God; if it is only a test; if it is a message; if.* Then the old man thought, *To give in; to come so far; to just let go;* and lowering his hand to his side, he thought, *Go.* Then again, *Go.*

Unspeaking, the grandfather pointed the gun toward the sky and jerked the trigger, the gunshot an eruption of both sound and light, the mare rearing up, tossing back its great neck, front hooves rising upward then crashing against the pavement, flying off once more, a blur of steaming silver-white, the grandfather having done all he could, all there was to do, seeing the animal vanish as it rounded a corner down the street, the stranger holding the gun out before him, infuriated, mouth slightly agape, discharging the pistol directly at the old man's middle, a flash of muzzle fire, the grandfather there for a moment, swaying, legs going weak, collapsing to his back along the uneven blacktop, the stranger pausing, glaring down into the old man's face with a look not of remorse nor guilt but one of pity, then disappearing, the stranger moving off in an clumsy hurry, away from where the horse had just fled, having given up now too, creeping back between the parked cars, his shadow replaced by the shadow of some other shapeless moving thing. The old man lay there as drapes quickly unparted, shades pulled open, the sound of gunfire traveling through the town's sleep and dreams, the horse's advancement along the town's street reporting like the bell tolling once again, then growing fainter, beautiful, indistinct. He peered up into the sky and tried to catch his breath, placing his hand upon the thudding cavity of his chest. Now he could sleep and there would be no horse nor highway nor town nor trees. He smiled and saluted with his eyes the colored flags snapping in the breeze.

The boy heard both gunshots and ran off in their direction. Before him, kneeling in an open lot of mottled grass and broken pavement, was the horse, its ribs appearing and disappearing between short breaths; then it was falling onto its side, head impassive, heavily lidded eye opening and closing with difficulty. The boy knelt beside it, careful of its bloody foreleg. There was also blood from somewhere near its front quarters and somewhere else along its back. He placed a hand on its throat and looked down, watching the eyelid blink, the sun streaming across the horse's skin with an unjust light.

Forty yards away he saw his grandfather's legs jutting out from beside a row of used automobiles. The boy ran toward the worn-looking boots just as a state trooper's vehicle and a local squad car pulled up behind him. Ten minutes passed before an ambulance from the neighboring town of Coldwater arrived. The two paramedics got his grandfather on a stretcher and loaded him headfirst into the back of the ambulance, the old man's eyes closed, mouth agape behind a plastic oxygen mask, pulse failing. Everything then—the sun, the stars, his grandfather's face—had gone white.

Over the muddy fields, the meadow grass bowing beneath the platinum hooves—horseshoes flashing like gunfire, like silver in a mine, one after another, brief points in a distant sky—thrashing over the sodden earth, on and on, the horse moving so fast it looked like it had climbed directly into the firmament, the grandfather and boy standing against the snake-rail fence, their twin shadows reaching away from the sun, the two of them silent, their mouths drawn, their hands too far to touch, the sun beginning its descent, the two shadows at the fence shifting toward one another, becoming a single figure of blackness, the horse a third shadow racing against itself with a violent, unassailable abandon, the two of them, grandfather and grandson, together against the fence rail, dreaming of other things.

By the time Jim came to, he found he was flying, a silver gurney stretched out beneath him, feet pointed skyward, the two paramedics lifting him headfirst onto the emergency room bed. The boy was beside him then, face appearing like a globe in the corner of the old man's eyes. The grandfather blinked as a sign of recognition, of appreciation. The boy stood in silence near the open curtain as the doctors and nurses worked, seeing the old man's chest rise then fall, rise then fall, rise then fall. His grandfather's eyes looked softer than anything the boy had ever seen before. The boy took a step forward and held the old man's hand, the fingers callused, the palms full of blisters, and saw his grandfather's face staring back obscured by the oxygen mask, eyes full of fear and something else unfamiliar. Beneath the plastic mask, there was a weak smile. The boy tried to smile back. The electronic monitor began to drone, the old man's heart failing, the doctor placing his white-gloved palms on the old man's bare chest, pushing anxiously, counting out the compressions, the monitor repetitive in its static lull, then there was a cough, then a gasp, the electronic alarm wailing, the boy looking down at the darkened, yellowed half-moons of the grandfather's fingernails, the old man's hand in his own hand becoming the most important thing in the world, the contours of the grandfather's uneven lips, the map of his wrinkled neck, all of it too important to shut your eyes to.

In the emergency room, three hours later, the boy sat watching the nurse take his grandfather's pulse behind the pale-blue curtain. She held his wrist like it was a child's, then set it down and tucked it beneath the blue blanket. She wrote something on the chart, checked the IV, and wrote something else before exiting.

Then they were alone. The boy stood there still for some time before putting a hand on the old man's blanketed foot. "I didn't know who to call so I called Mr. Northfield. He said he's gonna drive down tonight. He wanted to let you know he was gonna bill you for every mile."

The grandfather blinked slowly.

"There's a policeman and a state trooper out there. They said they want to talk to you. But the doctor said they have to wait. So all you got to do now is rest."

The grandfather blinked again.

The boy coughed, then adjusted his glasses and peered down again. "You have to get better soon." Then, lowering his head, speaking softer now, "You're all I got left."

The grandfather blinked once more. The boy lifted his hand

from the old man's foot and turned to face the curtain. He couldn't decide if he should stay or go out in the waiting room.

"I better let you rest," he finally said.

The grandfather squinted sharply.

The boy saw his pained expression and frowned. "Unless you'd like me to stay."

The grandfather answered with his eyes and the boy sat down. The grandfather seemed to smile before slowly shutting his eyelids. Tomorrow, when he awoke, he would tell the boy what he thought, he would tell him everything. Tomorrow.

For A.L.

Thank you to Koren, Lucia, Nicolas. Thanks to Johnny Temple, Johanna Ingalls, Ibrahim Ahmad, Aaron Petrovich, and everyone at Akashic for their unending courage and unflagging support. Thank you to James Vickery for his insights as an early reader, Todd Baxter for his conversation and encouragement, Jon Resh for his enduring friendship and design acumen. Thanks to my family. Thanks to the Department of Creative Writing at Columbia College Chicago, its faculty, staff, and students. Thanks to Maria Massie, Sylvie Rabineau, Gil Netter, and Arthur Spector.